CUNNINGHAM SECURITY

OBSESSED

A.K. EVANS

Editing & Proofreading
Ellie McLove, My Brother's Editor
www.mybrotherseditor.net

Cover Artist
cover artwork © Sarah Hansen, Okay Creations
www.okaycreations.com

Formatting
Stacey Blake at Champagne Book Design
www.champagnebookdesign.com

DEDICATION

The start of any new series goes to the loves of my life: Jeff, Jaden, & Jensen.

CHAPTER 1

Elle

BREATHE.

Breathe and run.

Those were my only thoughts.

Well, those were my thoughts until I made it to my car. Then they shifted to breathe and drive.

And I knew exactly where I was going.

There was no choice.

The only place that made sense: Cunningham Security.

Never, not once had I ever expected what I just walked into in my own apartment. Maybe I should have. I was Elizabeth Blackman, twenty-five-year-old musician. It wasn't out of the realm of possibilities that I could have ended up in this situation.

But I never thought it would happen to me.

This was the kind of thing that happened in the movies. This was the kind of stuff I read about in books. Not real life. Not *my* life.

Only a few minutes ago, I'd gotten home from an afternoon out. I'd just had a two-hour lunch with my new sister-in-law, Charley. She got married to my brother, Wes, only three weeks ago, and they had just gotten back from their honeymoon. It was the first I'd seen her since the wedding, so she took a long lunch at work to meet up with me.

Charley worked as the lead graphic designer at Blackman Boards, my brother's company that manufactures snowboards and winter sports accessories.

Between my brother's business and my music career, it was safe to say that we'd made the Blackman name a household name here in Rising Sun, Wyoming. Of course, Wes was on a much larger scale than I was. Yes, I was a musician, but I mostly performed at local establishments, only occasionally traveling to perform a few gigs at smaller venues. I liked my life that way, and I loved the feel of the small hometown.

And living in a small-town, I couldn't believe that what had just happened to me actually happened. Wasn't this the kind of thing that happened in the big cities to the famous celebrities?

Following my lunch with Charley, I made a quick stop at the drug store to pick up some things. Then I went home. I was going to be performing at Big Lou's Restaurant and Saloon tomorrow night, and I wanted a quiet night in tonight. Big Lou's Restaurant and Saloon was the spot I performed at the most, and with so much love and support from my hometown fans, it was hard to not want to perform there weekly.

But when I entered my bedroom, I immediately froze.

Given my chosen profession, I had done several meet and greets locally over the years where I'd signed headshots to give to my fans. One of them was sitting on my bed propped up against the pillows, and something had been written on it.

I picked it up, read it, and bolted out of there as fast as I could, clutching the photo in my hands.

Someone had one of my headshots, knew where I lived, and had entered my apartment. I wasn't sticking around. That's how people died in the movies. For whatever reason, they are courageous and daring and try to investigate on their own.

I was no fool.

I was no investigator.

But I knew one.

And that's why, early on a Friday evening, I pulled in to the lot at the Cunningham Security in Windsor, Wyoming.

Panic was still running through me. I was still trying to breathe, still attempting to control the shaking of my body.

I didn't know if someone had followed me or if they were watching me, but I knew what I needed to do. I pulled the keys from the ignition, left everything in the car, got out, and ran to the building.

When I got to the door, I pulled to open it and found that it was locked.

Fuck.

I tried again.

Nothing.

Shit.

I turned around, looking behind me to make sure nobody had followed me.

I banged on the door.

Then I noticed a call button off to the side of the door. I pressed the button and continued pressing while I kept checking behind me until finally a man appeared at the door.

It wasn't him.

Damn it.

After he noted the panic and terror in my face, the guy opened the door to let me in.

"Are you okay?" he asked, reaching out to grab my arm and pull me inside.

"Levi," I spat desperately. "Is Levi here?"

He wrapped his hands around my biceps before he explained, "No, he just left, but I can get him back here. Are you okay?"

I shook my head as my eyes welled with tears, and I could still feel the burning in my lungs. "I…I can just come back tomorrow," I rasped.

"Looking as terrified as you do right now, I'm sorry, but that's not happening," the man said. "Are you hurt?"

I shook my head.

"You were looking behind you when you were outside," he noted. "Is someone following you?"

My bottom lip began to tremble before I whispered, "I don't know."

"What's your name?" he asked.

"Elle. Elle Blackman."

The guy jerked his head back and repeated, "Blackman? Any relation to Wes Blackman."

"I'm his sister," I shared.

Then it hit me.

"Please don't call him and tell him I'm here," I begged.

He nodded and assured me softly, "Okay, I'll get you Levi. Have a seat."

I sat on one of the couches in the waiting room area and watched as the guy who let me in pulled a phone out of his pocket and walked away from where I was sitting. He was out of earshot, but kept me in sight as he put the phone up to his ear. Not even two minutes later he walked back over to me and said, "Levi's three minutes out."

I nodded.

"Thank you…" I trailed off realizing I didn't know his name.

"Pierce."

"Thank you, Pierce."

Pierce sat next to me but remained quiet. I appreciated the fact that he knew enough to know that I wasn't real fond of being alone at the moment and, at the same time, respected that I asked specifically to speak with Levi.

I noted the large clock on the wall behind the reception desk and followed the second hand. It made its way around two and a half times before the front door opened. My eyes shot to the door to see Levi walking in.

His eyes came to mine, and I could see the worry in his.

Levi's gaze shifted to Pierce's and jerked his head to the side. Pierce got up and walked down the hall out of the reception area.

Levi came to me and sat down.

He was close.

Super close.

Close enough that his thigh was pressed up against mine.

"I'm sorry to make you come back here, but—" I managed to get out in a shaky voice before I was cut off.

"No apology needed, Elle. Tell me why you're here," he instructed, his voice firm and confident.

I swallowed and explained, "I'm here because I believe you are in the business of keeping people safe."

His body went alert before he asked, "Are you unsafe right now?"

I shrugged my shoulders.

Levi stayed silent and relaxed only slightly.

"Somebody was in my apartment," I finally blurted.

I felt him go solid again. "When? Did they hurt you?" he questioned me.

I shook my head and answered, "No. I don't know who it was because I never saw them."

His brows drew together.

"Wes and Charley just got back a few days ago from their honeymoon. I made plans to go out to lunch with Charley today to catch up. I was out for a couple of hours and when I got back home I realized someone had been there."

"Did they trash the place?"

"No. I didn't stick around long enough to really assess anything. I saw what they left on my bed and got out of there."

"What was it?" he asked.

The creepiness of it swept over me. It freaked me out. My insides began shivering again. Levi noticed and wrapped his hand around the back of my neck. His touch instantly settled me.

"Elle, what was it?" he pressed gently.

"A photo of me."

Levi's fingertips tightened ever so slightly on my neck.

"What kind of photo?"

"It was a signed photo from a meet and greet event I had done a couple months back," I explained. "The only difference is that the person wrote their own note on it."

"What did they write?"

I couldn't say it. Just thinking about it made my body begin to tremble again. Levi's hand moved from my neck to my shoulder so that his arm was now wrapped around my back and he pulled me just a bit toward his body.

It felt nice.

Safe.

"Elle?"

"I will always be watching," I whispered just before the reality of the situation hit me full force and tears started to fall down my cheeks.

I dropped my head and buried my face in my hands.

"Oh my God," I mumbled. "Someone knows where I live, got into my apartment, and was in my bedroom. What do I do?"

Levi's voice was soft when he answered with a question of his own, "Is the picture still at your place?"

I tried to pull myself together and croaked, "In my car."

"Okay. I'm going to need you to give me your keys so I can get it," he started. "Then, I'll need you to give me the address of your place. I will take care of everything else."

I brought my eyes to his. He searched my face and I wondered if he could see just how terrified I was.

I got my answer when he spoke again. "You were right," he began again. "One of the things I do in my business is keep people safe. Right now, I need you to know that I'm going to keep you safe."

Hearing those words from him made me relax a bit. I believed he would do just as he said and keep me unharmed. At least, physically speaking.

"Thank you, Levi."

He nodded at me and asked, "Are you okay?"

"Not really, but I feel a bit better now than I did when I first got here. Can I ask you one small favor?"

"Sure."

"Please don't tell Wes," I begged him.

"I thought you two were close."

"We are," I assured him.

"So why are you keeping this from him?" he wondered.

I sighed. "He just got married and returned from his honeymoon only a few days ago. He and Charley are getting settled in their new lives together. I don't want to mess that up for him."

Levi gave me a look.

"I think you should tell him," he suggested. "He's going to find out eventually, and he won't be happy to learn that his sister kept this from him."

"Please," I whispered. "I will tell him, but not right now."

He held my eyes a beat before he begrudgingly let out a sigh and nodded. He stood, offered me his hand, and requested, "Come here."

I pulled my brows together, but put my hand in his and stood.

Heat spread through my body the second my skin touched his.

Caught off guard by the feeling, my eyes shot to Levi's. He had a look that told me he felt what I did.

Levi quickly recovered and offered an explanation, "Here's what's going to happen. You're going to give me your keys so I can run out to your car and grab the photo. Then, I'm going to get one of the guys working on figuring out anything they can about that photo and possibly who put it there. You are also going to give me your address so I can get that to Trent. He's going to look into any security footage from your apartment building. Once I get that in motion, I'm going to take you to your place. You'll sit in my truck with the doors locked until I do a sweep of your space. When I confirm that all is good, I'll come out and get you. You can pack up some stuff that you'll need for the next few days. After, I'm going to take you back to my place where you are going to stay until I know what I'm dealing with."

My eyes nearly popped out of my head.

"I'm sorry…what?"

Levi didn't answer me. He held out his hand and said, "Keys, sunshine."

Sunshine?

I had no immediate response so I gave him my keys.

"Wait here, I'll be right back."

Levi walked outside and I watched as he approached my car. Once he made it there, I turned around and began to think about everything he just said to me. Mostly, I was focusing on the fact that he said I was going to be staying at his place until further notice.

That was going to be a problem for me because up to this point, Levi really wanted nothing to do with me.

And, sadly, I'm overly attracted to him.

In a very serious way.

I met him a couple months ago when he was providing security detail for Charley's best friend, Emme. Back then, Emme's abusive ex-boyfriend was stalking her, and Zane, her fiancée and Levi's younger brother, insisted on her having around the clock, one-on-one coverage whenever he was unable to be with her. The day I met Levi was the day he was providing coverage to Emme when we were at Wes and Charley's house. The minute I saw him, I felt my knees get weak.

He was beautiful. Dark hair, dark blue eyes, a strong jaw, full lips and, from what I could see, an impeccable body.

Everyone around us felt the sparks between us, too. I denied it at the time, but they could all see right through me.

I talked with Levi later in the day, but before there was even an opportunity for something to develop between us, my brother put a stop to it. I had just met Levi that day and Wes was already taking his role as big brother way too seriously. His protectiveness was appreciated to a certain degree, but thinking he could tell me who to date wasn't something I was prepared to tolerate. Unfortunately, even though I refused to allow Wes to stand between us, Levi wouldn't budge.

I saw him again not long after that one night at Lou's and, while he was friendly enough, he wasn't acting very interested. I knew he felt attracted to me, but he noted his respect for my brother as the reason to not pursue anything. What frustrated me was that I couldn't possibly come up with any good explanation as to why Wes was so against it.

As I let the disappointment filter through me, I heard the door open. I turned back around to find Levi carrying not only the photo, but also my purse and the bag from the drug store with my lip balm haul.

He walked over to stand about two feet in front of me and handed me my purse and the lip balm. As I took them from him his eyes dropped to my lips. He assessed them a minute before he brought his eyes back to mine. I couldn't miss the heat swirling in them. He held the picture up so the back of it was facing me and informed me, "I need your address so I can get that to Trent and this photo to Pierce. Then we'll leave."

Given the intense scrutiny my mouth had just been under I couldn't manage to speak, so I simply nodded, pulled my license out of my purse, and handed it to him.

Levi walked off.

I decided I needed lip moisturizer.

I walked over to sit on the couch, dug through my purse, and pulled out the strawberry tube. After applying it, I tossed it back in my purse, and tried to come up with a way to tell Levi what I thought of his plan.

A few minutes later, he reappeared.

"Ready?" he asked.

I stood and said, "Um, Levi?"

"Yeah?"

"I appreciate what you are willing to do here, but I can drive myself home and pack a bag. I can just check into a hotel for a few days until you have time to figure out what's going on."

"Elle?" he responded.

"Yeah?"

"That's not happening."

"Levi —" I got out before he cut me off by positioning himself inches in front of me.

"It's. Not. Happening. You can fight me, but you aren't going to win. You came here because you feared for your safety. I talked to Pierce. He just showed me the footage from outside the building when you got here. You were terrified, Elle. I'm not allowing you to go back to your place alone where someone managed to break in not more than a few hours ago and could then possibly follow you to a hotel where you'd also be alone. I'm taking you to your place so you can pack up some of your things. Then, as I already said, you're staying at my place until I figure out what's happening."

"It's a Friday night. You had already left for the day when I got here. I don't want to put you out or inconvenience you."

"Sunshine, I'd hardly consider *you* staying at my place an inconvenience. You aren't putting me out and if you want to fight me on this, then I'm going to be forced to call Wes to let him know what's going on. If you're with me right now, I can keep you safe. If you aren't and I don't know yet what I'm dealing with, I can't do my job properly."

I took in a deep breath and let it out.

"Okay," I agreed. "But just to say, if you think Wes wasn't happy before when nothing was going on between us, I can assure you he's not going to be happy to find out I've been staying at your place."

"I don't really give a shit."

I jerked my head back.

"Elle, your brother has an issue with us having a romantic relationship. I don't believe he has a reason to be against it, but I respect his position. Wes is not going to have a problem with me doing what I've got to do to keep you safe," he explained. "And if he does, like I said, I don't give a shit. I'm making it my job to see to it that you remain unharmed. Got it?"

I nodded.

With that, Levi and I walked out of the Cunningham Security offices and over to his truck. He stayed close to my side the entire walk there and made sure I was safe inside before he rounded the front and got in behind the wheel. Then he took me to my place so I could pack up some of my things.

Someone had it out for me. I didn't know who and I was certainly worried, but I decided to look on the bright side. I was sitting in Levi's truck after he had called me sunshine twice, breathing in the manly scent of him, while he did what he promised by taking me to his place.

CHAPTER 2

Levi

"**W**HY ARE YOU LOOKING AT ME LIKE THAT?"

That came from Elle. I was standing in the doorway to her kitchen watching her, completely astonished.

I narrowed my eyes and stated, "We're here so you can get the things you need to live for the next couple of days, Elle. I'm not sure potato chips are part of that equation."

"Maybe not for someone like you, but they are a necessity for me."

"Potato chips?" I asked, my brows shooting up. "A necessity?"

She let out a frustrated sigh.

"Not just any potato chips," she clarified. Holding one of the bags up in front of her, she went on, "These ones specifically. And yes, they are a necessity. I may have an unhealthy obsession with them and I realize they aren't good for me, but they do wonders for my voice. I'm performing at Lou's tomorrow so I need the chips."

"You eat three bags of chips before you sing?" I questioned her.

"No, but I'm not really keen on coming back here by myself any time soon and I don't want to inconvenience you further by making you do it, so I figure I should bring a couple bags."

I grinned at her.

She didn't want to come back here any time soon. I didn't like that she was essentially being forced out of her place, but I didn't mind that because of it she was going to be taking up residence at my place.

"Is that okay?" she pressed.

My voice was soft when I answered, "Yeah, sunshine. Bring whatever you need. And you aren't an inconvenience. I'm going to need you to stop referring to yourself as one."

She looked away.

I took a few steps closer to her and brought my hand up to cup her cheek. When she was looking at me again, I explained, "Elle, you're in trouble right now. I intend to help you and keep you safe. I don't want you thinking that you are bothering me. You came to me for a reason. I'm good at what I do. Let me do my job while you worry about eating potato chips for your job. Deal?"

She nodded and gave me a small smile before she requested, "Speaking of jobs, we need to discuss payment."

"Payment," I repeated because it was absurd that she thought she was going to pay me.

"Yeah," she started. "You just said this was your job. We have to discuss your fees and how you expect to be paid."

"Let's get you packed up and out of here right now," I suggested, hoping she'd forget all about it. "We'll talk about payment later."

"Okay."

As Elle went about the business of packing up her things, I let the events of the last hour and a half run through my mind.

Pierce called me not even five minutes after I had left the office for the day telling me that Elle Blackman was there, terrified out of her mind, and asking for me.

"Talk to me," I demanded as I maneuvered my truck and started making my way back to the office to get to her.

"Not sure what's up. She buzzed at the door incessantly. I opened, let her in, and all she managed to get out was asking if you were around. Her whole body was trembling, but I confirmed she wasn't hurt. I saw her checking her back before I opened the door, so I asked if someone was following her. She nearly broke down in tears and said she was unsure."

"Stay with her until I get there," I ordered. "I'm three minutes out."

"You've got it, boss."

I disconnected with Pierce and hauled my ass back to work.

Elle Blackman.

In trouble.

Scared.

And she came to me for help.

Fuck.

The girl had been on my mind since I met her a couple months ago. I'd only seen her once since our initial meeting, but that didn't mean I forgot a thing about her. Her older brother, Wes, and my younger brother, Zane, were the best of friends who started snowboarding together back when they were kids. Since then, Zane has become a professional rider and is now sponsored by Wes' snowboard company, Blackman Boards. Wes made it very clear to me that he respected me, but was not even remotely interested in entertaining the idea of Elle and me together. He did this the day that I met her. She was not happy about it; I can't say I was either. Even still, I didn't want to create tension between the two of them, and I respected Wes enough to not cross that line.

It hasn't been easy, though.

She's so fucking beautiful.

And her voice is something else entirely. I heard her sing

for the first time not long after I met her, and it was the most angelic thing I'd ever heard.

We had an instant connection. It wasn't something I could explain, but I knew she felt it, too. Elle refused to hide her attraction. On more than one occasion she voiced her unhappiness about the fact that I shot down the idea of us being anything more than just friends.

But when I arrived back at my office and saw her face as she sat scared on the couch, I wanted to walk over and wrap her up in my arms. I wanted to take her back to my place where I'd keep her until I knew she was no longer in any danger.

At least I'd be able to do that.

Once Elle managed to finish packing up her things, we got in my truck to head to my place.

The drive to my house was quiet. It wasn't awkward or tense. Just quiet. Every time I'd been around Elle prior to now she had always been forthcoming with conversation. I think the reality of her current situation was weighing on her mind, and while I didn't want her worried, I figured I'd give her the ride to the house to live inside her head.

By the time we got to the house and I unloaded her bags from the truck, it was approaching dinnertime.

"Are you okay with homemade pizza for dinner?" I asked as we walked into the house from the garage.

"What?"

"Dinner. Will you eat homemade pizza?"

"Oh, Levi. You don't have to feed me, too. This is too much already."

I was beginning to get pissed. If she insinuated one more time that she was putting me out, I was going to lose my shit.

"Elle?" I called, a bit of an edge to my tone.

"Yeah?" she replied.

"Do…you…eat…pizza?"

She stared at me in silence a moment before she whispered, "Yes."

I shook my head and turned toward the kitchen.

"I'll get it made and in the oven. While it cooks, I'll show you where you'll be staying."

"Can I help?" she asked softly.

Fuck.

That angelic voice.

I turned around, took in her beauty and the sweet look on her face, and responded, "Sure."

Elle and I spent the next fifteen minutes assembling pizzas on flatbread. Generally, I was strict about my diet. Given my line of work, I felt it was important that I not only made sure my mind was sharp but also that I took care of my body. Situations arose on occasion that required a degree of physical fitness that wouldn't be achieved by me eating crappy food. I allowed myself indulgences on occasion, but mostly never had the desire for the sweet stuff. Pizza was one of the things I wasn't prepared to give up, so I figured out how to make it work for me so that I could still have it and not see my physical performance suffer.

During our pizza-making extravaganza, I learned that Elle was the complete opposite of me when it came to food. Of course, I already knew about her obsession with potato chips. I was willing to accept the whole 'chips are good for my voice' excuse, but then she made a pizza and loaded it with cheese. It wasn't just extra cheese, either. It was insanity.

I didn't understand where she put it.

Elle was petite. She was around five feet five inches tall with long white-blonde hair that I had always seen her wear in loose waves and a set of sparkling rich, honey-colored eyes. She always wore loose-fitting clothing. At least, she had every time I was around her, but I could tell she was tiny under all of it. As I allowed my eyes to scan her from top to toe, I realized how much I wanted to see what was underneath all of the oversized sweaters I had always seen her in. We lived in Northwest Wyoming where it was usually chilly, but now that it was July, I was thinking I might get lucky enough to see a hint of her skin.

I popped the pizzas in the oven and moved to get Elle's bags. She followed behind me as I walked her through the house and up the stairs. When we got to the second floor, I took her bags and put them in the guest bedroom.

"Will this work for you?" I asked her as I set the bags down.

"Levi, your home is beautiful."

"Thanks. There's a bathroom just across the hall," I told her as I pointed in the direction of the bathroom.

Ignoring my comments, she said, "Thank you for doing this for me."

"No problem, sunshine," I insisted. "Make yourself at home. If you forgot anything at your apartment and need something, just ask."

She nodded.

"Come on," I urged. "I'll show you the rest of the house."

I took Elle on a tour of the house. I wanted her to know where everything was and that she was free to use it as if it were her own. It wasn't her fault she had to uproot herself out of her apartment, so I figured I'd do what I needed to do to make sure the change wasn't any more difficult than it already was on her.

We finished the tour just in time because the scent of pizza had filled the kitchen. After pulling it out of the oven, I grabbed a couple of plates, a large cutting board, and transferred the flatbread over to the board. I cut them and took them into the family room. Elle followed behind me with the plates and napkins.

"What do you like to drink?" I asked as I set the cutting board down on the coffee table.

She shrugged her shoulders and said, "Whatever you've got."

"I'm gonna be honest here. I'm a bit health conscious and I get the feeling based on your chip and cheese consumption that you don't down the water the way I do. That said, my mom drilled into my head that I should always be prepared for company. So, I've got beer, wine, and sweetened raspberry tea if water's not your thing."

"I'll have the tea," she answered.

I grinned.

I knew that's what she was going to choose.

"Have a seat. Start eating. I'll be right back."

I went back to the kitchen and grabbed drinks. When I returned to the family room, Elle was sitting, but hadn't started. I gave her a look. She must have noticed my concern because she spoke.

"I'm not going to be rude, Levi," she started. "I can wait until you get back to start eating so we can eat together."

I smiled at her and handed her the tea. She thanked me as she took it out of my hand.

After putting pizza on each of our plates, I handed hers to her and we both started eating.

Once we had both taken a few bites, I asked, "So what do I need to know about tomorrow?"

"I'm sorry?"

I took another bite of my food, chewed, swallowed, and explained, "You said that you were performing at Lou's tomorrow night. What time do you need to be there? When does the performance itself start?"

"Oh. I start at nine, but usually get there an hour ahead of time. Why?"

I continued to eat as I raised my eyebrows at her.

She stared back at me as she slowly chewed her food.

"Seriously, Elle?"

She nodded.

"I'm going to be there with you to make sure nothing happens to you. Depending on what my boys find between now and then, I may have an extra guy or two on hand tomorrow night as well. Lou's is usually packed just because of what it is. I've seen what it's like when you perform. There's hardly standing room."

She swallowed hard and fretted, "Levi, it's not snowboarding season."

My brows pulled together, confused at her statement.

"Unless there's a snowboarding contest, Wes, Charley, Zane, Emme, and the rest of their friends all come to watch me," she explained. "My brother is going to see you there and know something is up."

"You aren't going there alone, sunshine," I insisted. "I think you're going to need to figure out quickly how to break this news to him. I know you're worried that he just came back from his honeymoon, but I've got to be honest, I think he's going to be pissed you didn't tell him what was happening the minute you knew something was wrong."

"I won't be alone. They'll all be there," she retorted.

"Not saying they don't all love and care about you, but none of them has the training and experience that I do. If something bad went down, I'm liking your chances of survival more with me there."

"Survival?" she repeated nervously.

She set her plate down on the coffee table. She hadn't even finished eating.

Fuck.

"Sorry, Elle. I shouldn't have said that."

"Do you think they want me dead?" she began to fret.

Fear was written all over her face. Her eyes got wet and her breathing grew shallow.

I leaned forward and dropped my empty plate on the table.

After I leaned back on the couch, I held my hand out to her and demanded, "Come here."

She immediately crawled over to me and curled up into a ball next to my side. I wrapped my arm around her back and held her tight.

If I didn't already know she was terrified, the shaking in her body would have been a pretty good indication.

With her head on my chest I offered gently, "I don't know yet what we're dealing with, but no matter how bad it is I will protect you. I promise you I will keep you safe. Do you trust me to do that?"

She nodded and pressed her body deeper into mine.

"I promise."

Her body had so much tension coursing through it. I did what I could and held her close. I alternated between running my hand up and down her back or through her hair. Eventually, she began to relax.

"Are you okay?" I asked.

She pressed her hand into my chest and pushed off. When she pulled her face away, she looked at me and apologized, "I'm sorry. I'm okay now."

"There's no reason for you to apologize," I told her. "You didn't ask to be put in this situation and it's normal to feel scared. I just want you to know that I'm not going to let anything happen to you."

She nodded her understanding before she shared, "I

usually try to get a good night's sleep the night before a performance. It's been an exhausting day for me. I think, if you are alright with it, that I'd like to go up and unpack some of my things, take a shower, and get to bed early."

She needed time to herself. I'd give her that.

"Sure. I already told you to make yourself at home. I'm going to go change and then head down to the weight room to get a workout in."

"Yeah, I'm definitely *not* going to do that, but you have fun."

I gave her a grin, happy to see she was no longer looking frightened, and then moved to take the cutting board and plates to the kitchen. Elle followed behind me with the glasses.

The two of us climbed the stairs.

She went to the guest bedroom.

I went to my bedroom.

After changing my clothes, I walked out of my room and knocked on her door.

"Yeah?" she called.

I opened the door and saw her sorting through her bags. "I'll be working out, but if you need anything just yell."

"I will. Thanks again, Levi."

"No problem, Elle. Goodnight."

I walked out of the room and closed the door behind me. I needed to get a workout in immediately. The frustration was building, and I needed a release. Nothing a tough workout wouldn't cure.

I put in a brutal workout attempting to tamp down some of what I was feeling. I had been pissed off and angry that someone was targeting Elle. My job now was to protect her and make sure I didn't see that look of fear on her face again. But on top of her stalker issue, I now had her staying with me. I needed to keep myself focused and professional, but I couldn't stop thinking about how all I wanted to do was taste those lips of hers. She had all those damn lip products in her car earlier. When I first saw them, I thought she was crazy, but then I assessed her lips and realized that she clearly knew what she was doing.

But it wasn't just her lips. It was her sexy as fuck, honey-colored eyes that I wanted to look into while I brought her to the height of pleasure.

My workout was doing little to help with the mix of emotions I was dealing with, so I decided to call it quits just over an hour later when I was dripping with sweat. I grabbed my T-shirt that I'd removed in the middle of my workout and went to the kitchen. After downing two glasses of water, I went upstairs to shower.

When I made it to the top of the steps, I walked toward my bedroom. The bathroom door across from the guest room opened.

Fuck me.

Elle walked out and stopped dead in the middle of the hallway. Her eyes roamed my body and I watched as they turned to liquid honey. I was now fighting an internal battle with my brain and my dick because my little ray of sunshine was standing there looking at me with her sexy hooded eyes wearing nothing but a delicate satin, yellow nightie.

Yes, she most definitely was a ray of sunshine.

And any sexual frustration that I managed to unload during my workout was suddenly back again.

Seeing her now without the oversized, loose-fitting clothing confirmed what I already knew to be true. Shapely slim legs, a trim waist, a great ass, and a perfect set of tits were all that made up her gorgeous body.

And then there was her neck.

Slender and exposed.

I wanted to run my tongue along the skin of it, up her jaw, and to those lips. I wanted to do that while I was buried deep inside her. My dick was hard at the sight of her, and thinking about what I wanted to do to her sexy little body had me struggling to appear unaffected.

Neither of us moved.

I watched as her hardening nipples poked at the satin fabric covering them.

Fuck me again.

She was just as turned on as I was.

"You don't have an ounce of fat on you," she remarked, her voice husky.

"I eat well and I exercise," I explained. "Though, you do the exact opposite and, judging by what I'm seeing right now, that's not exactly been a bad thing for you."

Her face flushed and she looked away.

I started moving and closed the distance between us. When I stopped in front of her, she tipped her head back to look up at me.

Those fucking eyes.

I couldn't help myself. I pressed a kiss to the top of her head while my fingers wrapped around the hair at her neck.

I pulled back, looked at her eyes again, and with my throat tight, I rasped, "Goodnight, sunshine."

Her voice was just a touch over a whisper when she replied, "Goodnight, Levi."

My hand fell from her hair and I walked into my bedroom. I sat down on the edge of my bed just to try and catch my breath.

This was not a good idea.

Ten minutes later, I was still sitting on the edge of my bed trying to get my head together. I needed to figure this out and I needed to do it quick.

A nice cool shower was a great place to start.

I stood and was about to walk into my bathroom when I heard it.

Elle.

Her moans.

I was convinced that I must have done something bad in my life to deserve this kind of torture.

Elle Blackman was in the bed in my guest room touching herself.

She was in the room right next to my bedroom doing that while I did everything I could to stop myself from going in to watch her.

It wasn't even two minutes later when she climaxed.

Fuck me if it wasn't the most beautiful thing I had ever heard.

In that very moment, I made a decision.

Tomorrow, this was changing. I was going to do whatever I had to so that I could keep Elle safe. There wasn't a doubt about that. I was also going to do whatever Elle needed me to do to help her deliver the news to her brother, sister-in-law, her parents, and her friends about what was going on and the fact that she had someone who was actively stalking her to a level that was of great concern. And lastly, I was going to make sure that Wes knew that while I planned to do everything in my power to keep Elle safe and find out who was targeting her, I was also not going to hold back any longer and continue to fight the attraction between the two of us.

I didn't need Wes' permission and no matter how he responded I wouldn't back down from her any longer, but I respected him enough to not do it behind his back. I also didn't want Elle being in a position where she felt she needed to hide whatever would happen between us.

On these thoughts, knowing that Elle was likely fast asleep, I jumped in the cold shower.

My efforts to quell the heat and sexual tension I was feeling by taking a cold shower were futile because all I could do was think about her little body in that nightie, her honey eyes staring up at me, and the moans coming from the guest room only minutes prior.

CHAPTER 3

Elle

I WAS IN TROUBLE.

On the one hand, there was the frightening, scary trouble with some crazy psycho stalker, who may or may not want to kill me, with which I had to deal.

And then there was this issue with Levi.

The stalker issue was trouble. Big trouble, in fact.

The Levi issue, though? That trouble was so big I wasn't sure there was even a word for it.

I had just woken up and was currently cuddled up under the blankets in the guest room just outside of Levi's bedroom.

And I found myself a bit baffled at everything.

A few words written on a picture had changed the entire course of my day. Somehow, someone breaking into my apartment translated into me ending up in this very spot. The sad thing was, I wasn't sure which was worse.

It hadn't even been a full twenty-four hours since I went to his office and my attraction to Levi was already growing stronger. Throughout the day yesterday, his insistence that he would do whatever he had to do to protect me only served to deepen my attraction to him.

Then, last night happened.

I unpacked most of my things while Levi went downstairs

to get in a workout. After unpacking my clothing, I grabbed my bag with my toiletries and went to the bathroom. I also took a nightie with me.

While in the shower, my thoughts drifted to my stalker situation. I did a mental inventory of everyone I knew. Images of people I had encountered over the years as a performer went through my mind, but nothing stood out to me. I knew there was a very real possibility that I had an obsessed fan and it was likely that I hadn't ever met the person. The thought, despite the burning hot water from the shower, sent shivers through my body.

I finished my business in the shower and completed my nighttime routine. I was hoping for a good night's sleep free from worry over this horrific situation.

On that thought, I turned toward the door, opened it, and stepped out to walk to the guest bedroom.

That's when I saw him.

And all of the gloriousness that was him.

Well, not exactly *all* of him, but certainly more than I had ever seen before. And it was all that I had imagined it would be and then some.

Levi had apparently finished his workout. It resulted in a lot of sweat. So much so that he no longer had a shirt on. I stood there watching as the beads of sweat glistened on his impeccable body. I had just gotten out of the shower, but right then and there I was ready to press myself up against his sweaty body so I could lick every square inch of him.

After I spent an unreasonable amount of time checking him out, I let my eyes drift up to his face. He was checking me out as I stood in the hallway in a nightie and nothing else.

No bra.

No panties.

Just a nightie.

All I wanted to do was rip it off, jump into his arms, and wrap my legs around him. Unfortunately, while I knew that he found me attractive, he had already made it very clear that nothing would happen between us.

Even still, he made no apologies for the fact that he appreciated what he saw when he looked at me.

I felt heat spread through my body at the lust in his gaze. That was only amplified when he put his hand in my hair and kissed the top of my head before he wished me a good night and went into his bedroom.

I was so turned on and restless. How could he do that to me?

It had now been hours since all that happened and I could still feel his hand in my hair and his lips on the top of my head. And that's when I came to a conclusion.

This was not going to be a good long-term solution. There was no way I was going to be able to continue staying with him for the foreseeable future and not be *with* him. I was going to take the next few minutes to collect my thoughts on it and hopefully I'd be able to talk to him about it this morning.

I threw back the covers and got out of bed.

Bathroom, change, talk with Levi.

In that order.

Unfortunately, I must have lived in some crazy universe that wanted to relentlessly punish me because when I stepped out of the bedroom, Levi's door opened.

His eyes did a full body scan and when they came to meet mine he gave me a wicked smile and greeted, "Good morning, sunshine."

"Morning, Levi."

"We've got to stop meeting this way," he shared.

The perfect opening.

"I was just thinking the same thing. I need to talk to you," I told him.

"Okay. About what?" he asked.

I couldn't do this here when I was still under the intense scrutiny of his very appreciative gaze.

"Well, I was planning to use the bathroom, put on real clothes, and then talk to you."

The corners of his mouth twitched before he insisted, "I'm fine with what you've got on now."

No way. Not happening. I'd never get through it.

"Please?" I pleaded.

Disappointment washed over him. "Alright. I'll meet you downstairs for breakfast. Eggs and bacon?"

My eyes rounded and I nodded.

"The bacon is what did you in, isn't it?" he teased.

I bit my lip and looked away.

He groaned and ordered, "Do what you've got to do and come down when you're ready."

"Okay," I murmured and shimmied past him into the bathroom.

I did what I had to do in the bathroom, went back to the bedroom to change into a pair of cut-off jean shorts and a V-neck tee, and made my way downstairs. The scent of bacon was intoxicating. It would be the perfect way to start my day preparing for a performance tonight.

I stepped out into the kitchen and Levi's eyes did another body scan. His grin was back and he mumbled, "Definitely changing things today."

"I'm sorry?"

"You first," he insisted as he flipped the bacon in the frying pan. "How do you like your eggs?"

"Over easy."

He nodded and went about making the eggs. He already had a heaping pile of scrambled eggs set on a plate.

"I can eat scrambled if you've already made them."

"I'm willing to share with you if that's what you really want, but I normally eat that many every morning."

My eyes bulged out of my head.

"How many eggs are there?"

"Six."

"You eat a half dozen eggs every morning?"

"Many mornings I'll have a protein shake for breakfast. But when I do have eggs, this is how many I eat."

"With bacon?"

"I don't usually add the bacon," he assured me. "Only on special occasions."

I tried not to let the hidden meaning even penetrate my skull. I already had enough problems to manage.

"I'll just have two over easy then," I told him.

He grinned at me and gave me a wink.

He needed to stop doing that.

He was so hot as it was.

The wink and the grin didn't help me to stay strong in my decision so that I could focus on what I needed to discuss with him.

Levi finished cooking the food and set it in front of me at the kitchen island. He had water in a glass for himself.

"Coffee?" he asked.

I shook my head. "No, I don't drink coffee. Do you have hot tea?"

"Do I look like the kind of guy that sits around sipping hot tea?" he countered.

"Not exactly," I remarked.

"We'll stop and get some later today so you can have it here for tomorrow."

I swallowed. We wouldn't need it for tomorrow because I wasn't going to be staying here.

"Just water then."

He nodded, filled up a glass, and set it down next to my plate.

"Okay, shoot," he said as he sat down next to me on one of the barstools.

I was nervous and unsure of how to start the conversation, so I quickly picked up a piece of bacon and took a bite. I chewed, swallowed, and took another bite. I did this several more times as Levi watched and laughed.

He might have thought I was being funny, but I was a bundle of nerves.

We both ate in silence a while before I realized that I was beginning to feel sick. I needed to stop eating and start talking.

"Okay," I started, putting my fork down. "We need to talk."

"Yeah, I've been waiting for you to tell me whatever it is that you want to discuss."

"Right. Well, I wanted to let you know that I really appreciate what you've done for me for the last however many hours it's been and I can't thank you enough for being willing to look into this whole stalker situation for me. That said, I can't stay here another night."

Levi pushed his empty plate back, took a huge gulp of water, and turned to face me.

"And the reason for that would be?"

I didn't have a reason that I could tell him.

"Um, well, I just feel that it would be best if I stayed somewhere else. I won't go back to my apartment until we know more and you feel that it's safe to do so, but I don't think it's a good idea for me to stay here anymore."

"Where are you planning on staying?"

I shrugged my shoulders. "I'll figure it out."

"Sorry, that's not going to happen."

"Levi—" I got out before he cut me off.

"The only place I'd be okay with you staying is with your brother and his wife because my team put that security system in. It's top of the line and I know you'd be safe there. Considering you don't want to even tell him about what's happening, I'm guessing you really don't want to start living with the newlyweds," he said.

He had me there.

"I'm uncomfortable here," I blurted.

Damn. I hadn't meant for it to come out like that.

The look on Levi's face changed. He was worried.

Following a brief pause, his voice dipped low, and he asked, "Did I do something to make you uncomfortable, Elle?"

He was genuinely concerned.

I hated that I said it the way that I did.

I shook my head.

"Maybe I should share with you what I was referring to earlier when you walked down here. Then, we'll talk about where you are staying tonight."

I was curious to hear what he had to say, so I sat back and listened.

"You have to perform at Lou's tonight and your brother is going to be there," he began. "So, here is what I plan to have happen today. I'm going to be with you while you break the news to Wes about what happened yesterday. Then, I'm going to explain to him what the plan is moving forward regarding your safety. He's going to know that you stayed here last night and that I intend to have you here until we know there is no longer a threat. Finally, I'm going to make sure he knows that I have no intention of continuing to ignore what's going on between the two of us."

"What? There is nothing going on between the two of us."

"Not yet. I plan to change that, though, Elle. In fact, I plan to change that tonight."

"You're joking. Levi, this is crazy," I declared because I was so shocked by what he'd just said.

"No, sunshine. What's crazy is me avoiding the electricity between us since the day I met you. What's even more crazy is the fact that I saw you last night in that nightie and didn't act on it. And finally, I think I'd need to have my head examined if I continued to ignore the fact that you want me just as bad as I want you."

"I do not," I scoffed, shifting restlessly on the stool.

Levi moved on his stool and brought his face close to mine when he shared, "You moaning in my guest bedroom last night minutes after you fucked me with your eyes in the hallway says otherwise."

My lips parted in shock.

He heard me last night.

The heat hit my cheeks.

"That's right, sunshine. I heard you. Sexiest thing I've heard in all my life. The next time I hear that it's going to be with you lying underneath me."

Oh my God.

"Levi," I whispered.

"Do you still want to stay somewhere else tonight?" he asked.

I bit my lip and shook my head.

"Are you uncomfortable with anything I've just said?"

"No," I murmured.

"Do you want to tell me why you said you were uncomfortable staying here?"

No, I absolutely did not.

"Not so much," I croaked.

"Elle, if there is something that's making you feel like

being here is not a safe place for you to be, I need you to tell me that."

"I feel safe here. That's not it," I insisted.

"I know you feel physically safe. I'm talking about in your head. If you feel uncomfortable about anything, you've got to tell me. And you've got to know that you are safe to do that. No matter what, you can say whatever you need to say without worry of judgment from me."

"You're so hot."

I gasped. Apparently, my mouth had a mind of its own this morning.

Levi gave me his wicked grin.

I looked away from him.

His hand came up to cup my jaw as he turned my face back toward his. Then, he stroked his thumb across my bottom lip.

I felt the wetness immediately pool between my legs. My heart was beating so hard, I thought it was going to beat right out of my chest.

"I think it's adorable that you're feeling embarrassed, but the feeling is mutual."

I shook my head.

"Why are you shaking your head like you don't believe what I just said?" he questioned.

"You're you. You've got to have the world's best body," I announced. "Are you kidding me? I can't compete with that."

"Lucky for you I'm not looking for someone who looks like me. I'm looking for someone who looks just like you. What I saw last night was a pretty good indication of what you're working with, and I'm more than okay with what you've got."

I threw my hands up in the air and cautioned him, "Alright, I'm just saying. Don't say I didn't warn you when you learn that I don't have a matching six pack."

"Elle," Levi started. "You've got a great body. I'm not looking for a woman with a matching six pack. I want a woman that's going to feel soft underneath me, a woman whose skin will feel silky and smooth under my fingers."

"Oh," I murmured.

"So, will me being hot still make you uncomfortable?" he teased with a grin.

"If you tease me about it, yes."

"Noted," he responded as he dropped his hand from my jaw. "You need to call your brother. Tell him you need to talk to him and that you'd like to stop by to do it."

"He's going to lose his mind," I warned.

"I know, which means we better hope Charley is there."

I dropped my head to the side, confused at his statement. "Why?"

"It doesn't matter how angry or frustrated a man gets. If he's got a good woman there to talk him down and help him through it, that's the only thing that'll help in a situation like this."

I thought on this a minute and suggested, "Maybe I'll call Wes and set it up, but then I'll send Charley a text to make sure she knows that Wes is going to need her to be there."

"Sounds like a good idea. Go do that while I clean this up. If he's free now, we'll go right away," he said.

I thanked Levi for breakfast, hopped down off the stool, and went upstairs in search of my phone.

I called Wes and he started panicking as soon as I told him I needed to talk with him. I didn't want to do it over the phone, so he insisted I come to his house right away. When I hung up with him, I tapped out a quick text to Charley.

Hey, love. I'm leaving soon to stop over there. I need to tell you and Wes something. He's probably going to lose his mind. Please tell me you'll be there.

A few minutes later, Charley responded.

He just told me you were coming by and he's already freaking out. I'm here, honey. See you soon!

Just wonderful.

At that, I got my things together and went back in search of Levi. As much as I wanted to think about and try to process everything he said to me at breakfast, I needed to focus on figuring out how I was going to break the news to my brother and sister-in-law. Charley would take it in stride. All of it. She'd worry for me over the stalker situation, but I had a feeling she'd be happy about the Levi situation. Wes wouldn't like either.

Twenty minutes later, Levi and I were in his truck on the way to deliver the news. I couldn't remember ever feeling so anxious before. Not even before a performance.

As we pulled into the driveway, Levi tried to calm me.

"Relax, sunshine," he urged. "It's going to be fine. I've seen you around Wes before. You know how to handle yourself."

"Of course, I do. That doesn't mean that I don't respect his opinion. I want him to be on my side and I'm pretty convinced that he's not going to be thrilled to hear that you have plans for the two of us that don't involve you strictly being there to keep me safe."

Wes had the garage door open, so after we parked, Levi and I walked through the garage to go into the house. I tapped lightly on the door before I opened it. When I walked in, I saw Charley and Wes immediately. Their faces were both warm.

At least, they were warm until Levi stepped in behind me. Wes' gaze turned murderous. Charley's face broke out into a huge smile.

Wes didn't hold back.

"This early on a Saturday morning, Levi is walking into my house behind my sister after she called me to say she needs to talk," he started. "I'm already not liking this conversation because everything I see is telling me that either she spent the night at his place or he spent the night at hers."

He was definitely going to lose his marbles. I hadn't even said anything and he was already at level ten. I didn't get a chance to respond because Levi did.

"She was at mine," he started. "And I mean no disrespect to you, but I'm going to ask that you calm down and let her explain why that is. Then, I have some things to say."

Wes' mouth tightened. He was not happy.

"Wes," I called attempting to direct his attention from Levi to me.

His eyes came to mine.

"I'm in trouble."

Instantly, the look on his face changed. I didn't take my eyes from him, but I noticed Charley shifted her body closer to his and wrapped an arm around his waist.

"I assume you know I met with Charley yesterday afternoon for lunch. After lunch, I ran an errand. Between the time I left my apartment and the time I got back there, several hours had passed. When I walked in, I went to my bedroom and saw something sitting on my bed. One of my signed photos from the meet and greet I did a while back was sitting on my bed propped up against my pillows."

Wes said nothing and his face remained impassive.

"Someone got into my apartment while I was out yesterday, Wes. They left me that picture, which they decided to write their own creepy message on," I shared.

Wes' face was no longer impassive.

"I was scared. I didn't know if anyone was still in the apartment. I ran out, got in my car, and drove right to Levi's security firm," I told him.

"Why am I just now finding out about this?"

"If I had my way, you wouldn't know at all," I mumbled.

"Excuse me?" he jerked his head back, genuinely concerned why that would be the case.

I could see the hurt written all over his face. That was the last thing I wanted to do. So, I explained, "You just got married and returned from your honeymoon. I didn't call you because I don't want to ruin the high of all that."

"Elle…" He trailed off.

I didn't know what to say.

Thankfully, Levi spoke up.

"Elle stayed at my place last night because I refused to allow her to be alone. The note on the picture was creepy enough that I have no intention of allowing her to be alone until I know what we're dealing with."

"What did it say?" Charley asked.

"I will always be watching," Levi shared.

My eyes immediately welled with tears and I felt the quivering inside my body. Not even two seconds later, Wes had his arms around me.

That's when I lost it.

I sobbed in his chest and cried, "Someone was in my apartment yesterday and they're watching me. I have a stalker."

My brother's arms tightened around me, and I felt his chin settle on the top of my head.

"What happens now?" Charley chimed in.

She must have realized that Wes needed a minute to get his head together.

Levi answered, "I already had my guys check the security footage from her apartment. When Elle called Wes this morning, I took the opportunity to check in with them. Trent said there was nothing on the footage to note. Nothing points directly to her door. To top it off, there were two cameras that weren't even functioning, so that's all a dead end at this point.

Now, we have to hope we can get something from that photo. I'm guessing it's been handled a lot, so it might not give us anything we can use. If the person has a record and is smart, they would have made sure their prints didn't end up on that photo. Unfortunately, this might mean we have to wait until he makes his next move."

Wes had pulled back slightly from me, put his hands to my shoulders, and insisted, "You're staying with us until this gets sorted."

"I can't," I argued.

"Why not?"

"You're newlyweds. I feel awful enough knowing that you'll be distracted mentally by this. I don't need to be getting in the way here."

"Elle. If something happens to you, it won't matter that I'm a newlywed. That'll destroy me and, considering you've become like a sister to her, Charley too."

"He's right, El. We'd rather know you're safe," Charley assured me.

"Guys?" Levi called.

Wes let go of my shoulders as we turned our attention to Levi.

"Elle said her bit. Now I need to say mine."

He took in a deep breath before he continued, "When she came to me yesterday, Elle was terrified. I asked why she was there and she told me she believed it was part of what I did for a living to keep people safe. As you already know, she isn't wrong. I'm going to do whatever it takes to make sure nothing harms her. That includes giving her a safe and secure place to stay. Up to this point, Wes, I've not done anything behind your back to make you not trust me. Now, I'm going to tell you something and I'm guessing you aren't going to like it. Elle stayed in my guest bedroom last night. She's welcome to stay there at least as long as it takes to make sure she's not in any danger. That said, I think you, Charley, and several of your friends, my brother and his woman included, know that Elle and I are attracted to each other. Nothing has happened between us to this point, but it's something we both are looking to explore."

Wes' eyes came to mine and he ordered, "You're staying with us."

"Wes..." I trailed off.

"Elle, I'm not going to even think about trying to find someone else to investigate this stalker situation. I respect the work Levi does and I know he's the best in this area, hell, probably the best in the state. I'm not going to sacrifice your safety, but he shouldn't either. His focus should be on keeping you safe and figuring out who is stalking you, not on trying to get in your pants."

"Wes," Levi warned. "I'm going to let that slide because I understand where you're coming from, but I'm not going to tolerate you being insulting. I will always have my head in the game when it comes to protecting her. Elle's a grown woman and can make her own decisions. You've known my family nearly your entire life; my brother is your best friend. I think you need to give me a little credit here. If I was just looking to get laid, I can easily find that anywhere. Bottom line, I wasn't telling you any of this to get your permission. I was doing it out of respect for you and her. If the two of us decide together that this is what we want, it'll be our decision. I don't want her to need to worry about hiding it from her family."

Wow. That was nice to hear.

"Can you be sure that your work isn't ever going to put her in danger?" Wes retorted. "Can you guarantee that she won't ever have to fear for her safety because of the work that you do?"

Is that what this was about? He was worried that something would happen to me. I didn't know all the ins and outs of Levi's work, but I imagined it could get dangerous from time to time.

"Wes, honey?" Charley piped up.

He turned to her.

"Levi's responsible for saving my best friend. His team worked hard after she was kidnapped and it's because of him that Emme wasn't raped. I don't think he'd ever let harm come Elle's way. I know how much she means to you, but try to keep in mind that she's in trouble right now and Levi didn't bring that on her."

I seriously *loved* Charley. Wes was my only sibling, but if I had been given the opportunity to pick a sister, I wouldn't have been able to find anyone better than Charley.

"Wes, please," I begged. "You know how much you mean to me. I don't want animosity between us because of this. If Levi was a jerk and hurt me, I could understand it. He's not and I think it's only fair you give him a chance. For me. As Levi said, we don't need your permission, but I'm asking you for your support. It would mean everything to me."

Wes took in my words. I think those coupled with Charley's words made him reconsider. His eyes went back to Levi's.

"If you hurt her…" Wes trailed off as his jaw clenched.

"I plan to see to it that that never happens. Even though this should go without saying, I'll say it anyway. If anything at all ever came her way, whether as a result of my line of work or something else, I'd do whatever I had to just to be sure she was unharmed and, if necessary, I'd lay down my life to do it."

My lips parted in shock at his declaration.

I stared at Levi a moment in the silence permeating the room. Finally, I turned my attention back to Wes. He brought his eyes to mine and his face went soft.

"Love you, Elle. I just want to see you safe and happy."

"Love you, big bro," I echoed the sentiment as I wrapped my arms around him and gave him a hug. "Thank you."

Wes hugged me back and kissed the top of my head.

We spent the next little while with Levi giving everyone a rundown on what to expect for that evening at Lou's. After going over his game plan in detail with Wes, Levi and I left. Before he took us back to his place, he made a quick stop and made good on his promise from earlier that day. Levi bought me some hot tea.

CHAPTER 4

Elle

IT WAS APPROACHING SEVEN-THIRTY AND I NEEDED TO BE OUT THE door in the next fifteen minutes if I was going to make it to Lou's on time to warm up and prepare for my performance. I was standing in the bathroom putting the finishing touches on my makeup. All I needed to do after this was throw on my jewelry, grab my guitar and my bag of chips, and I was ready.

Since we were now officially in the summertime, the weather was warm and I could rock a pair of shorts and a tank. For tonight, I threw on a pair of cut-off jean shorts, a loose-fitting, scoop neckline tank, and a pair of cowgirl boots. My hair, which fell to just below the middle of my back, was done up in loose, beachy waves. I kept my makeup natural, except for my eyes, which had a dramatic, smoky, rose gold look. Satisfied with my makeup, I ran out of the bathroom and into the guest bedroom to grab my jewelry. I didn't wear anything too fancy; I put a few dainty silver chains around my neck and a pair of dangly silver earrings in my ears.

Having completed my look, I grabbed my oversized purse, applied my peach flavored lip balm before tossing it in my handbag, and took off down the steps.

After leaving my brother's house earlier and getting my tea, Levi brought me back to his place. He wanted to go into the office to get an update from his guys to see if they had any updates on my stalker situation. At the same time, he told me he'd make sure that my car was brought back to his place by the end of the day. So, he left me at his house to do my own thing after he set the alarm and programmed his cell and office numbers into my phone.

Alone at his house this afternoon, I spent the time working out my setlist and strumming on my guitar for a bit. Eventually, I realized I needed to let the other important people in my life in on what was happening with me.

My parents and my best friend, Leah Price.

I figured talking to my best friend would be the easier of the two. And considering she also worked as my manager, assistant, and publicist, I thought it was wise to bring her up to speed. I've known Leah for eight years now. We met each other during our freshman year in college and were inseparable during our four years there. After college, I pursued my music career and she went on to become a veterinarian and work in her family's vet office.

During our call, I filled Leah in on what happened yesterday. I told her that I was currently staying at Levi's place, which required another explanation.

She went crazy.

That is, she went crazy over the stalker situation, not over me staying with Levi. I assured her, as best I could, that Levi had everything under control. She was still so worried and insisted on coming out to Lou's to see with her very own eyes that I was still okay. I understood her concern and appreciated it; I knew if the roles were reversed I'd be feeling the same way about her.

I needed to set aside some time to bring my parents up to speed on what was happening, but there was no way I was going to do it right before my performance. My parents would have completely lost their minds and I didn't need that on my conscience before I stepped onstage. Plus, after having to go through the whole story once with Leah, I realized I wasn't prepared to do it all over again right away.

Now, I descended the stairs and went in search of Levi. He promised me earlier that he'd be back from his office in plenty of time to make sure he could take me to Lou's early.

He made good on his promise once again and arrived back at his place a little more than an hour ago. I was in the middle of getting ready, but he knocked on the bathroom door as I was fixing my hair and yelled in that he had returned.

As I stepped out into the kitchen, I saw Levi standing with his back to me downing a glass of water. He pulled the glass from his lips, turned toward me, and did a full body scan. His eyes heated and a playful grin spread across his face.

I tried to remain focused.

"I just need to grab my chips and I'm ready to go," I announced.

Levi said nothing but walked over to me. He stopped in front of me, brought a hand to my hip, and the other to cup my jaw.

"You look beautiful, sunshine."

I squirmed under his gaze and muttered, "Thank you."

His eyes held mine and it seemed as though he was struggling with something.

"What's wrong?" I asked, slightly panicked. "Did you find anything out about the photo when you were at the office?"

His hand at my jaw moved to the side of my neck, where the fingers of that hand and the one at my hip squeezed my skin.

"No," he answered, his voice husky.

Confused, I pressed, "Okay, so what's wrong?"

"I'm just trying to figure out if you'd be pissed at me if I kissed you right now. I know there's a whole makeup thing I'd probably get in trouble for messing with, and I'm not looking to start this off with you slapping me across the face for not being mindful of that."

My body quivered at the mention of him wanting to kiss me.

"Lip balm is easily reapplied," I rasped.

I was beginning to tremble at the excitement I felt.

"What?"

"I don't typically wear lipstick, just lip balm. What I'm trying to say is that you won't mess up my makeup if what you're looking to do is put your lips on mine."

A sexy grin spread across his face and his thumb began to graze back and forth along the skin at my throat. Slowly, he lowered his head and closed the distance between the two of us. Before I had time to think, my eyes closed and I felt the gentle pressure of Levi's lips against mine. My hands were at his sides, balling his shirt in my fists as I held on for what I knew was coming.

The pressure against my mouth increased. Then, Levi's tongue came out to tease my lips. I wasted no time parting them and allowing him to taste me. His hand at my hip wrapped around my waist and pulled me closer to him allowing me to feel his arousal between us. I don't know what came over me, but one of my hands traveled down from his sides and went to his ass.

He groaned.

My tongue slipped into his mouth.

His hand at my neck went to the hair at the back of my head while the other hand at my waist traveled down to cup my ass. He squeezed me there and pulled me tighter to his body.

I moaned.

Levi tore his mouth from my lips and rested his forehead against mine.

He didn't say anything.

"Levi?" I called softly.

He pulled his head back to look at me. "Yeah, Elle?"

"I never would have slapped you," I confessed before I smiled at him.

He chuckled, "Good to know. Are you planning on performing tonight?"

I nodded, though I wondered why he was asking.

"Right. Then, I'm going to need you to get your hands off my ass," he teased.

Disappointed, I dropped my hands and tried to take a step back. Levi didn't let go of me.

"Just to note," he started. "When we get back here later tonight, I expect your hands to go right back to where they were."

That was good news, so I wiped the look of disappointment off my face and gave him a coy smile.

He still didn't let me go.

"I need my chips," I reminded him.

Levi grinned, shook his head, and dropped his arms from around me.

We were out the door two minutes later. This was only after I reapplied my lip balm and grabbed my guitar and some chips.

Just over an hour later, I had finished my final warm up for the evening. Levi gave me my privacy in what had been officially dubbed my dressing room at Lou's but waited just outside for me. I had a couple minutes to spare before I was set to start, so I made my way out of my dressing room to the saloon.

As I had expected, and as was always the case, my loyal

group of supporters were there. Not quite a year ago, that group consisted of Wes, Zane, and their two best friends, Stone and Luke. Recently, that group had grown. Wes is now married to Charley; Zane is engaged to Charley's best friend, Emme. To everyone's shock, Stone had settled down and was very newly engaged to Charley and Emme's best friend, Monroe. Lastly, there was Luke who had some kind of a relationship with Nikki, who was also best friends with the girls, but nobody knew the extent of their relationship. Nothing had been made official that I was aware of other than the girls talking and knowing that Luke was giving it to Nikki regularly.

Levi and I made our way over to them and greeted everyone. I got a round of hugs from the entire group. When Zane pulled me into his hug he whispered in my ear, "Happy to hear that you and Levi have decided to stop ignoring what's between you. You should know that you both have my full support."

My belly flipped hearing those words from Zane. Levi was his older brother and I was glad to know that he wouldn't be an obstacle for us the way that Wes had been. Though, I was surprised at how quickly Wes caved. To top it off, it was nice to know that Wes' initial disapproval of it was only due to his worry over my safety given Levi's line of work and that it didn't have anything to do with how he felt about Levi as a person.

I pulled back from Zane, gave him a smile, and thanked him.

The girls surrounded me and pulled me out of earshot of the men. I could tell they were just about to launch in with their questions when I felt a hand on my shoulder and a sweet voice declare, "My bestie has lots of details to fill me in on, the first of which is that fine piece of man over there."

I turned to the side to see a mass of red hair in my line of vision. Leah had arrived. She immediately wrapped her arms around my body and squeezed me tight.

Leah was tiny. She was just under five feet tall with red hair that fell right to the middle of her shoulder blades. She had fair skin, so when we hit the summer time her freckles were out in full force, which is precisely what I was noticing now.

"Hey, love. Looks like you've been out in the sun. I'm so happy you're here," I started as I hugged her back. When I pulled away, I gestured to Charley and continued, "You remember my sister-in-law, Charley, right?"

"Of course, I do. It's good to see you again. Congratulations on the wedding," Leah said, looking to Charley.

"And this is Emme, Nikki, and Monroe," I added, pointing to each of the girls.

They all exchanged pleasantries, but Nikki was quick to dive back into the issue at hand.

"Charley gave us what I'm guessing is the shortened version of your troubles, babe. Sorry to hear about what's happening, but how lucky for you that you're now staying with Levi?"

"I know," I agreed. "I was so panicked yesterday when I got that photo, but within minutes of being around Levi, I felt safe. I ultimately tried to tell him that he didn't need to take me in; however, at the mere mention of me staying in a hotel for a few days, he got all tough guy on me. I realized I wouldn't win the battle and figured I'd take advantage of being able to be around him on a very consistent basis."

Emme chimed in. "Charley told us that Levi pretty much told Wes that you were no longer going to be staying in his guest bedroom. I can't believe Wes didn't go crazy, but I'm happy to hear that Levi is pursuing you."

I was, too. I was about to respond to Emme when Leah interrupted, "What?! You didn't tell me that when I talked to you earlier today."

I tilted my head to the side, feigned innocence, and shrugged my shoulders. "I didn't want to make a big deal about it. Nothing had happened between us at that point, so I figured it was best not to jinx myself."

"Has something happened since I spoke with you earlier?" she pressed.

I bit my lip and nodded slowly at my friends. "Before we left his place to come here, he kissed me. It was hot and I really, really want to do it again. The good thing is, he made it clear he really wants to do it again, too."

"Oh, this makes me so happy," Charley beamed.

"Me, too," Emme added. "I can't wait to share the good news with Zane. He wants to see each of his brothers settle down with a good woman. I hope you're it for Levi."

"They're not married yet," Leah chimed in. "Elle's got all her quirks that Levi's going to have to look past."

I rolled my eyes. "He already knows about my chip obsession and he doesn't seem to be the least bit bothered by it. And he has seen my lip balm collection… well, that is, he saw the purchase I made yesterday before I went home. But he hasn't said anything about it, though. Either he thinks I'm a freak or he doesn't care."

"You've got to keep us in the loop, babe. Once he's given you the goods, we need the juicy details," Monroe added.

My body shuddered at the thought of him giving me the goods.

"Oh my goodness," Leah began. "She's practically salivating now and she needs to perform in less than five minutes. As your acting publicist, I'm going to be honest and tell you I'm not sure I have a way to spin it if we end up canceling your show tonight because you were too busy drooling and couldn't find your voice. Enough with the sex talk until after you perform."

"Alright," I lamented. "I'm going to go find my voice and get ready. See you girls afterward."

They all wished me luck and I took off. I didn't go to Levi to tell him, but the minute I started walking away, he followed behind me. When he caught up to me, he put his hand to the small of my back and leaned in.

"I'm going to be standing off to the side of the stage throughout your performance," he started. "I'll be scanning the crowd throughout looking for anything or, more precisely, anyone that's out of the ordinary. Lou's guys do a decent job at the door spotting oddball individuals, but I'm not relying on that."

I nodded as I listened, but this wasn't helping to calm me.

"I don't want you feeling nervous, but I need you to know where I'll be and what's happening. You do what you've got to do here tonight and trust that I'll do what I've got to do. Okay?"

Having reached the side of the stage, I stopped walking, looked to Levi, and admitted, "I trust you, Levi. That's the reason I came to you yesterday."

His eyes warmed and his face softened.

Not even a minute later, Lou announced me and I took the stage. My hometown crowd always made me feel special, cheering the moment Lou said my name. I loved them all.

I had to be honest, though. As much love as I was feeling from them and even though I trusted Levi implicitly to keep me safe, I was nervous. It was unnerving looking out into the crowd and not knowing if one of the people there was the person that had been in my apartment.

I looked back to Levi, who was hidden offstage, got a wink

from him, and decided to do what I came to do. After turning back to the crowd, I took a deep breath and started my set. Once I got through the first song, the anxiety was gone. I was lost in the music and didn't have the space in my mind to think about anything but that.

Just over an hour later, I finished my last song. I received my usual round of applause from the crowd, thanked them, and walked off the stage toward Levi.

"Everything was all good, I assume?" I asked as I stopped in front of him.

He nodded.

I gave him a coy smile and shared, "Normally, I'd stay for a bit and hang with everyone, but I'm not really feeling up to that tonight. Are you cool with heading out now?"

"Do you really need to ask that question?"

"I figure it's good to be sure."

He laughed, put his arm around my shoulders, and confirmed, "Yeah, I'm cool with it."

"Alright. I just need to grab my bag out of the dressing room," I told him.

With that, Levi walked me back to the dressing room. When I opened the door and walked in, I looked to my purse and saw a bouquet of flowers lying next to it. My lips tipped up into a smile. Occasionally, I'd come back here after performing to find a fan had sent flowers to me. I loved it.

"Yay," I began as I walked over to them. "Someone sent flowers."

Levi followed me.

I picked up the bouquet and brought them to my nose. I inhaled the scent with my eyes closed.

Fresh flowers.

There was a card attached so I set the bouquet down, opened the envelope, and pulled out the card.

I'll be watching you tonight. Don't choke, bitch!—B.B.

My blood ran cold.

My stomach roiling.

I was shaking immediately.

Levi noticed and took the card from my hand.

My eyes went to him.

His jaw was set. His knuckles were turning white.

He looked to me with worry on his face. That's when I lost it.

Levi pulled me into his chest. I cried and trembled in his arms. He held on to me as he pulled his phone from his pocket. A moment later, he ordered, "I need you in Elle's dressing room now. Bring Wes and the girls."

The door swung open not even a minute later. I pulled my tear-stained face from Levi's chest and watched as Wes, Charley, Zane, Emme, and Leah walked in.

"What's going on? Elle, are you okay?" Wes asked.

I shook my head, but couldn't find any words.

"I called Zane because I needed you guys to come back here with her," Levi started. "I'm here solo tonight and don't want her left alone. I also don't want to parade her around out there. We came back here so she could grab her things and these flowers were here. This is the card that was attached."

Levi handed Wes the card. He read it while Charley looked on. Wes looked pissed and angry. Charley was worried. The same was the case when Wes passed the card off to Zane and Emme looked on. Leah glanced at the card as Zane held it and turned her frightened face to me.

"I've got to talk to Lou and find out who brought these flowers. Can you stay here with her until I get back?" Levi asked.

"Of course," Emme vowed.

"She does not leave this room," Levi ordered.

"Levi," Wes started, his jaw clenched. "Go figure out who sent the flowers and is torturing my sister."

Levi gave me a quick squeeze on my shoulders before he walked to the door. "Lock the door. Nobody comes in, nobody goes out."

"We've got her, bro. We'll stay with her until you get back," Zane assured him.

At that, he gave Zane a nod and walked out. Zane locked the door behind him while Charley, Emme, and Leah came over to me.

"I'm so sorry, E. This is terrifying," Leah murmured as she took my hand in hers.

"Why is someone doing this to me?" I cried.

"We might not ever know that, babe. What I do know is that Levi will find out who is doing it and he'll keep you safe," Emme answered.

"I'm really starting to worry," I squeaked out.

Zane walked over and pulled me into his arms. His voice was low when he said, "I see the way my brother looks at you, darling. He's not going to let anything harm you. You've got to believe that he'll do whatever it takes to figure out who's doing this. Once he does, trust me when I say that he'll put a stop to it."

I was too upset to talk, so I simply nodded.

"Elle," Wes called softly.

My eyes went to him. Helplessness was written all over his face. Seeing him like that sent me over the edge. My body began shaking again. Zane held on to me until Wes moved to where we were standing. He put me in Wes' arms where I cried my eyes out. Wes held on tight, offering me the comfort and security I needed for a long while. Unfortunately, it wasn't enough, and I couldn't settle.

It didn't matter, though, because Wes refused to let me

go. His hold only changed when we heard a knock at the door. His arms tightened as my body went solid.

"It's me," Levi yelled.

Wes relaxed.

I was still tense.

I turned my head toward the door, my cheek pressed to Wes' chest, and looked to Levi as he gave us what he knew.

"I found Lou and talked to him about what's going on. From what we managed to find out, the flowers were delivered downstairs to the restaurant earlier this evening. One of the waitresses was going to bring them up then, but it got busy and she got sidetracked. By the time she got a free second, Elle was already onstage. The flowers were delivered by the floral company. I don't know yet how the order was placed, but I intend to find out. Trent's my IT guy, so I'll have him look at the details of the order if he can. With any luck, it was placed online and we'll be able to track an IP address."

"I want to get out of here," I pleaded.

"Sure. I just have one question," Levi responded. "Do you know anyone with the initials B.B.?"

I thought about it for a minute, but couldn't recall anyone with those initials.

"I can't think of anyone. Wes? Leah? Any ideas?" I asked.

They both shook their heads.

"Oh, I'm so sorry," I gasped. "I didn't introduce you. Levi, this is my best friend since my first year of college, Leah Price. Leah, this is Levi, also known as the guy who's risking his life right now to protect mine."

"Please tell me you're going to catch this guy," Leah begged. "When Elle told me what was going on, I didn't realize just how bad it was. Now I know how serious this whole situation is, and I'm petrified for her."

"I'm going to find him; there's not a doubt in my mind."

"Is there anything we can do to help, Levi?" Emme asked.

Before Levi could even respond, Zane answered, "You aren't getting involved, sweetheart. I know you love Elle. We all do, but you are not putting yourself in danger. Levi and his team will take care of her. You, of all people, know that's the truth."

She nodded and Levi offered, "There is one thing you can do."

Zane looked like he was about ready to murder his brother when Levi quickly explained, "Be there for Elle when she needs you. Call her regularly to check in on her. She's staying with me, but I'm working on this case until I figure out what I need to figure out. That means I'm out of the house a lot. You're all welcome to visit with her at my place. I'm okay with her being at Wes' and Charley's house or Zane's and Emme's house considering I know what security is at both spots. So when you can, please try to make yourself available to Elle and be a good friend to her. In doing that, I can work on this knowing she's not alone all the time."

"We can do that," Charley assured him.

"I want updates, Levi. Regularly," Wes demanded.

Levi gave him a chin lift in acknowledgment before he brought his gaze to mine, "Ready, sunshine?"

I dipped my chin in agreement, grabbed my purse, and walked to him.

"I talked to Lou and told him I'm taking you out the back door. If this person is still here, I don't want them watching you. Before I came back to your dressing room, I took your guitar and put it out in the truck," he explained

"Okay. Thank you," I answered.

He put his hand to the small of my back and ushered me out of the room. We made our way down the hall toward the back room offices, where Lou was waiting with anguish in his face.

"Elle, my darlin', this news shreds me. I don't know how anyone could want to see harm come to you. You stay safe and don't go anywhere alone until Levi and his guys find out who's doing this."

I nodded to him, having found it very hard to talk about what was happening.

"Promise me, darlin'," he demanded.

"I promise, Lou."

Lou's eyes went to Levi and he shared, "This girl is like a daughter to me. You keep her safe."

"I fully intend to."

Satisfied with Levi's determination, Lou stepped aside and allowed Levi and me to pass. We made our way outside, where he helped me into his truck before rounding it and getting in on the driver's side. He pulled out of Lou's lot and got on the road back to his place. It wasn't until Levi's hand reached over and wrapped around mine, giving it a gentle squeeze, that I finally felt some comfort and safety. Only then did I start to settle.

CHAPTER 5

Elle

I WAS STARING AT MY REFLECTION IN THE BATHROOM MIRROR.

Levi and I had just returned from Lou's and I immediately climbed the stairs, walked into the bedroom to grab a nightie, and came into the bathroom.

We hadn't spoken most of the ride home. I was lost in thought regarding the situation surrounding my stalker and needed time to get my head on straight. I didn't know for sure where Levi's mind was, but I had a feeling that he was feeling the same way. His mood had shifted from the time we were in Lou's to the time we ended up in his truck.

After stripping out of my clothes, I threw my hair up into a messy bun on the top of my head, and hopped in the shower.

Now, I was standing in front of the mirror. I had just gotten out of the shower and threw on my baby blue, lace-trimmed, satin nightie. If I was being honest, I was terrified. I knew Levi's home was secure and that I'd be safe here, but I couldn't help feeling scared. More than anything I wanted him to hold me.

I took a deep breath, gathered up the clothes I wore earlier, and walked back to the guest bedroom. After putting the clothing in my laundry bag, I climbed into the bed. My head dropped to the pillow, but I never went under the blankets. Not even a minute later, the tears leaked from my eyes.

I was dumbfounded.

I couldn't understand why someone was doing this. What was the obsession about? Was it an obsession? Why me?

Most of all, I was afraid.

There was a knock on the bedroom door before Levi opened it and stepped inside. He took one look at me and walked over to sit on the edge of the bed.

"Elle…" He trailed off as he brought his hand up to cup the side of my face.

I couldn't bring myself to look at him, but the tears continued to fall.

Levi's hand moved from my cheek to my shoulder, where he gave me a gentle squeeze. "Talk to me," he urged.

I tried to take a few calming breaths, but it didn't work.

He shifted his body and settled himself in the bed next to me, his front to mine. His arms wrapped around me and pulled me close.

"Why would someone do this to me?" I cried.

"I don't know. Not yet, anyway. I will find out, though, Elle. At least now I have something else to work with."

I pulled my face from his chest and looked up at him. Then I whispered, "I'm scared, Levi."

He looked down at me and with a soft voice he tried to reassure me, "I promise you, I'm going to do everything I can to make sure nothing hurts you."

Another tear fell from my eye.

Levi brought his hand that was wrapped around my upper back to the back of my head and pulled me tighter against his body. He held me like that a long time.

"Levi?" I eventually called.

"Yeah?"

"Will you stay with me just until I fall asleep?"

"No."

My body tensed and went cold. I hadn't expected that from him at all.

"I told you earlier today that things were changing tonight, Elle. So, no, I'm not going to stay with you just until you fall asleep. I'm going to pick you up and carry you into my room, where I'm going to put you in my bed and hold you not just until you fall asleep but for the rest of the night."

"Levi…" I whispered my relief.

"Are you okay with that?" he asked.

I nodded in his chest.

At that, Levi shifted in the bed so that he was sitting again. He pulled me into his lap and, with one hand under my legs and the other at my back, he stood and carried me into his bedroom. Somehow, Levi managed to pull the blankets back before he settled me in the bed. Then, he took to stripping out of his clothing.

While Levi did that, I pulled my nightie down making sure I wasn't exposing myself. I always wore pretty nighties to bed with nothing else underneath. Perhaps I should have thrown something on considering I was now in Levi's bed, but I hadn't originally intended on ending up here once everything went down at Lou's.

I didn't spend much time fussing with my sleepwear because Levi was stripping. His shirt was now off and he was currently stepping out of his jeans.

Holy. Smokes.

The man certainly knew how to make a girl forget all her troubles.

I had already seen his upper body yesterday, but now he was standing before me in just a pair of boxer briefs. It felt wrong to stare, but I couldn't help myself. Besides, it's not like I hadn't already told him that he was hot. He had to expect if he was going to strip to essentially nothing that I was going to look.

As soon as he got everything except for the boxer briefs removed, Levi climbed in the bed and pulled the blankets up to about our waistlines. He turned off the light on the bedside table and scooted his body closer to mine. Levi pressed a kiss to the top of my head and urged, "Try to relax and get some sleep, sunshine." Then he draped his arm over my waist and continued, "Goodnight, Elle."

I already felt the warmth emanating off his body, but I wanted to touch him. I shifted closer to him so that our legs were touching, pressed my hand to his chest, and echoed the same sentiment, "Goodnight, Levi."

Light was just barely filtering in through the wall of windows behind the seating area that was to the right of Levi's bed.

It was very early in the morning.

My back was to Levi and his arm was curled around my waist. It felt good. There was only one small problem.

I needed to pee.

I figured I could make quick work of it and not wake Levi if I lifted his arm while I slid out from underneath it. So, I wrapped my hand around his wrist, or as much of it as I could get my hand around. I took in a deep breath and lifted. Just as I was about to shift my body out of the bed, Levi's arm clamped back down around my waist.

His voice filtered into my ears. "Where are you trying to sneak off to?"

"The bathroom. I have to pee," I answered.

Levi lifted his arm from me and instructed lazily, "Use mine."

I scooted to the side of the bed opposite of him and made a beeline for the bathroom. I did my business and quickly washed my hands. I noticed the mouthwash sitting on the sink, figured it was a sign, and quickly rinsed out my mouth, too.

Levi kept his house cool, which I preferred, but I also didn't like feeling cold. This meant, the minute I finished in the bathroom I rushed back to the bed. Levi watched me as I climbed in the bed. He made a quick trip of his own there before he hopped back in bed and pulled me toward him so that I was against his body, my front to his.

"Feeling better this morning?" he asked gently.

I could smell the minty freshness of his breath and I had to stifle a laugh. We both had similar thoughts that morning.

"Yeah," I answered quietly. "Thank you for letting me stay in here with you. It helped to ease my mind."

His hand squeezed my hip. "Happy to hear it, but would have preferred the reason you were in my bed had nothing to do with what happened last night and more to do with what happened before we went to Lou's."

"Sorry," I responded. "I didn't mean to ruin the night you had planned."

"It's not your fault, Elle. What happened at Lou's last night meant that you needed something else from me. I was happy to give you what I thought you needed and am relieved to know that it helped you relax."

I brought my face closer to his chest, where my hand was resting, and continued to look at him.

"Well, if it makes you feel any better, I would say that I'm a bit disappointed your plans were ruined."

"Is that right?" he teased with a smirk on his face. His hand was now wrapped around the back of my leg just above my knee.

I looked away and moved my face closer to his chest because the feel of his hand on my leg was so overwhelming that I found it difficult to speak.

"Look at me," he encouraged me.

I pulled my head back to look up at him.

"I'm not a man who likes to disappoint," he started. "Especially not you. Can I make it up to you?"

Heat spread through my body as I gave him a coy smile.

"Normally I'd say that you went above and beyond last night," I replied. "But in this case, I won't turn you down if you decide you want to make it up to me."

Levi's fingers pressed into the skin on my leg as he brought his head down to meet mine. Seconds later, his mouth was on me. His lips were moving across my lips. His tongue came out to tease me, looking for a way inside my mouth, and I instantly opened for him.

While we kissed, Levi's hand slid up the side of my thigh. It continued its journey up my leg to the hem of my nightie. He didn't stop there. Instead of remaining on top of the nightie or making a blatant attempt to go under it, Levi moved his hand in a way that allowed him to push the nightie further up my thigh.

I didn't mind.

In fact, I didn't mind so much that I moaned against his mouth.

Levi's hand had made it just above my hip when he went solid. He pulled his mouth from mine and looked down at me.

He had an assessing look on his face.

Given his silence and body language, I was beginning to feel a bit anxious.

"Levi?" I croaked.

"Elle, where are your panties?" he questioned.

"I don't have any on," I shared, as though he was unaware of this fact.

"I own a PI firm, so you have to imagine I've figured that much out by now," he returned. "I'm curious as to why you don't have any on."

I bit my lip.

His eyes dropped to my mouth.

When they came back to my eyes, I explained, "I wear a nightie to sleep. That's it."

"You're telling me that you slept next to me in my bed all night last night with nothing on under this?"

I nodded.

"And the night before?" he pressed. "Outside the bathroom with the yellow one... there was nothing underneath that?"

I shook my head.

"Let me get this straight. You went into the guest bedroom two nights ago and touched yourself and all you were wearing was that yellow nightie?"

"Yes," I whispered.

There was a moment of hesitation before he declared, "I guess I'm lucky I didn't figure this out last night. I struggled to keep my shit together a good portion of the night just feeling the warmth and softness of your body against mine. Had I known you had nothing underneath, I'm not sure I would have been successful."

"This isn't a deal breaker, is it?"

"Fuck no."

"Then, um, would you mind if we went back to what we were doing before you made this discovery?"

Levi rolled me to my back and settled his body over mine. His face disappeared in my neck, where I felt his mouth against me.

My legs were wrapped around his waist and, as he trailed kisses along the skin of my neck, I squeezed my thighs. The ache between my legs grew stronger and I needed to find a release. Levi's hands traveled to my waist and began pushing the satin fabric up my body. Seconds later, he pulled it over my head.

Levi wasted no time. His hands went to my breasts and his mouth went over one of my nipples. As he licked, sucked, and nibbled, I put my feet to the mattress and used them to roll my hips. While I sought the friction against my core and he lavished my breasts with attention, I moaned.

"Levi."

My voice was throaty.

His mouth came back up to mine. With his lips just barely touching mine, he pleaded, "Tell me what you want, sunshine."

"You. I want you inside me," I rasped.

He smiled against my lips.

"Please," I begged.

Levi pushed up off me onto his knees and leaned over to the nightstand. While he grabbed a condom and opened it, I sat up and brought my hands to the waistband of his boxer briefs. I pushed them down his legs and he shifted so I could get them past his knees and off his legs. Before he had the chance to sheath himself, I brought my hand to his erection. I looked up at him through hooded eyes and wrapped my mouth around the tip of him.

He groaned as he watched me, the condom in one hand while the other came to the side of my head and clutched my hair.

I took more of him in my mouth.

My eyes remained focused on Levi's.

"Damn, Elle," he bit out as I ran my tongue along his shaft and teased the tip before I sucked him back into my mouth.

He allowed me to work him a little longer before he pulled himself from my mouth. After he rolled the condom on, Levi brought his mouth down to mine and guided me to my back again. Once my head hit the pillow, he trailed kisses along my jaw, down my neck, and to my breasts.

Levi pulled his head back and watched as his fingers went straight to the spot between my legs.

"Dripping."

One finger slid inside me. Levi almost completely withdrew the finger and added a second one before he pushed back inside. He continued his torturously slow assault on me, building me up.

"Fuck me, Levi. Please."

My voice was filled with desperation, need, and lust.

And it was enough that he didn't make me wait. Within seconds, Levi filled me to the root of his cock. My hips were in his hands as he drove into my body.

Pure bliss.

"Oh," I moaned.

Levi gave it to me. It wasn't slow, but it wasn't fast. It was steady. More than that, it was gratifying.

Sexy.

All Levi.

"Such sweetness," he whispered.

He had already built me up using his hand and now, as he continued to deliver exquisite movements with his hips, I knew it was coming. I struggled with whether to fight against the mounting pleasure to prolong this or whether to give in to everything he was giving me.

Levi knew I was close. He dropped my hips and brought his hands up to frame my face. I wrapped my legs around his waist. My fingers were holding on tight to his arms, and with each thrust into me, my grip on him tightened.

"Liquid honey," Levi rasped.

I couldn't begin to decipher the meaning behind what he said because my body was on the verge of something extraordinary. With each stroke, he took me higher. I closed my eyes, bracing for it.

"Eyes, Elle."

I couldn't open them.

"Give me your eyes," he demanded.

"I can't," I panted.

He stopped moving.

My eyes shot open and I whimpered.

"I want your eyes, sunshine."

I nodded my understanding.

Satisfied, Levi began moving again. It took seconds to get me back to where I was and, this time, he didn't stop.

"Oh, Levi. I'm gonna come," I managed to get out through my ragged breathing.

He increased his pace and I shattered, exploding around him.

His eyes never left mine.

Levi worked me through my orgasm and just as I started to come down, he found his. He called out my name just before he brought his mouth to mine. I kissed him and swallowed his groans while his thrusts began to slow until, eventually, they stopped.

He collapsed on top of me briefly before rolling to his back and taking me with him. Our bodies covered with a sheen of sweat, we took the next several minutes to catch our breath.

"I hope you're no longer disappointed with me," Levi teased.

"That's not possible, my hero."

His body vibrated with laughter underneath me.

"I'm a hero now?"

"You're my hero," I answered honestly.

His arms tightened around me.

I gave him a moment to absorb what I said before I continued, "I don't just mean here in the bed, Levi. What you're doing for me by keeping me safe, I could never repay you. We need to talk about that, by the way."

"Sunshine, look at me."

I lifted my head from his chest to look at him.

"Is my cock inside you right now?" he asked.

I blinked and jerked my head back.

"Yeah."

"Right. I thought it'd be self-explanatory, especially now, but I guess not. First, don't ever talk to me about paying me anything to keep you safe while I'm still inside you. Second, don't talk to me about paying me anything to keep you safe... ever."

"Levi—" I got out before he cut me off and started moving.

"Need to get this condom off," he explained as he slid out of me and shifted me over in the bed.

He walked to the bathroom to dispose of the condom and left me there wondering what his deal was. Of course, I did this while I admired his flawless backside. By the time he strolled back into the bedroom a minute later, I had pulled the sheet up to my underarms. Levi climbed into the bed and settled on his side, facing me. He propped his head up in his hand and looked down at me.

"We've got to talk about this," I insisted.

"There's nothing to talk about."

"Is this case going to require some of your time, effort, and resources?" I pressed.

He nodded.

"That stuff doesn't come free, Levi."

"It does for you," he said, softly.

I pulled my brows together and asked, "Why?"

"Elle, a couple months ago my brother's girlfriend was being targeted by her ex. I didn't charge her nor Zane a dime for doing what we needed to do to make sure they stayed safe."

"Zane's your brother, though. He's family."

"Yeah, and do you really think I'm going to let the woman who's sharing my bed pay me to keep her safe?"

I rolled my eyes.

"I haven't even been sharing your bed for a full twenty-four hours yet."

"Are you going to be in my bed again tonight?"

"Yes."

"There you have it. And, just to say, now having had a taste of what you in my bed is like, I can tell you it's something I would have loved to have had since the day I met you."

"It was your choice to not be with me," I noted.

"And it would seem that I changed my mind yesterday. Given that, and the fact that you seem to be on the same page with me as far as the two of us go, I'm going to settle this whole payment thing now. I'm not accepting payment from you, Elle. Even if you get to a place where you don't want to be in my bed anymore, I'm still not accepting payment. If you decide you're not okay with this and want to fire me and my firm as your security and private investigation team, I'm not going to accept that. You can hire someone else, but I'll still be covering you until I know that there is no longer anyone threatening you. Bottom line, sunshine, I'm not going to not do this for you," he exclaimed.

"Why?" I asked quietly.

"Because I'm not okay with the possibility of never hearing this voice or seeing these fucking eyes again, particularly when you're on the verge of coming. To add to that, I liked the peaches yesterday, but I saw what you had in that bag in your car the day you came to my office. I'm very much looking forward to tasting all the flavors on your lips."

He liked my eyes.

He also didn't mind that I was obsessed with lip balm.

My belly flipped and my insides grew warm.

I turned myself toward him and pressed a kiss to the middle of his chest.

"Okay, superhero. You win."

CHAPTER 6

Elle

"**W**HY DID WE NOT DO THIS MONTHS AGO?"
I lifted my head from Levi's chest and looked at him, waiting for an answer to my question. We had just finished round two of sex and, after disposing of the condom, Levi came back to the bed where he curled me into his body.

Round two was incredible and was precisely the reason I was beginning to regret the time we wasted in not allowing ourselves to enjoy this sooner.

"I was trying to do the right thing," Levi answered.

"The right thing for who?" I asked.

He shot me an incredulous look. "It wasn't exactly a walk in the park, Elle. Emme's birthday celebration at Lou's was probably one of the most difficult times for me. Zane and Emme showed up late because, well, everyone knows why they were late. I'll never forget when you stood up from the table to wish Emme a happy birthday and you said you wished you had a reason to be late. I wanted to pick you up, carry you out of there, and make your wish come true."

"Really?" I pressed.

"Absolutely. I've got to be honest; I'm not happy about this situation you are in right now, but I'm over the fucking moon that it has led to this," he shared.

"What's the plan for my situation?"

"I would love nothing more than to spend the day with you today, but with the flower delivery you received last night, I need to get into the office and get to work now," he replied.

"It's alright," I assured him. "I have some last-minute planning and details to get squared away for my upcoming tour, so I'll be able to keep myself busy."

"Upcoming tour?" he repeated.

I nodded. "Yeah. Nothing crazy. I'm not some international superstar, but I'm doing a small tour here on the west coast."

"How small?"

"Eight stops."

"Fuck," he clipped. "When and where?"

I grew tense and a bit upset. "Are you angry about this?"

"I'm not angry," he insisted. "I just need to know when and where."

I took in a deep breath before I answered, "The first stop on the tour is next Friday. I'll be in Denver. Then I'm heading to Arizona. I'll be doing a stop in Phoenix and one in Tucson before heading to Los Angeles. After LA, I'll do a stop in San Francisco followed by two nights in Las Vegas. Finally, I'll end the tour at Lou's in Rising Sun."

"Alright. I need to get up, get ready, and get to the office because you just added a bunch of work to my caseload," he declared.

I wasn't sure what that meant and decided it might not be a great idea to ask. Levi seemed a bit distracted. I didn't want to add any additional concern or worry to what he was already dealing with, so I simply suggested, "How about I go downstairs now and make breakfast while you get ready?"

"You don't have to do that, Elle."

"I know, but I want to." He held my eyes a minute before I continued, "A half dozen eggs, right?"

Levi nodded and smiled at me.

I flattened the palm of my hand to his chest so I could get up, but he held on to me. When my eyes came to his, he challenged, "Are you forgetting something?"

My brows pulled together and my eyes darted back and forth.

Was I?

I felt his body shake before he spoke through his laughter, "Kiss me, sunshine."

Oh.

Right.

That.

I leaned in and pressed a kiss to his lips.

After, Levi let me go so I could make breakfast for us.

No sooner had we finished eating when Levi gave me the rundown on the security system at his house. He wanted me to arm it after he left. Essentially, if something happened all I needed to do was push a button that would send a signal to the Cunningham Security offices. He had hidden cameras in the house—though he didn't say where—and said that they'd immediately be able to see what was wrong and get help to the house.

If I was being honest, I was a bit freaked out by this.

"Someone is stalking me, Levi. They might know where I live and where I perform, but what are the chances they know I'm staying here?" I worried.

Levi put his hand to my neck. His thumb brushed back and forth against the skin just below my jawline as he answered, "I don't know yet. Until I know more and can possibly get a handle on who this is, I can't give you that answer. I'd like to think he doesn't know you're here, but I'm also alright with him knowing that. If he's got any brains at all, he'll know my house is not the place to target you."

"Okay," I responded meekly.

"Would you prefer to go with me into the office?"

I shook my head.

He needed to work and didn't need the distraction. I had to get these last-minute details regarding my tour ironed out and I needed to call my parents.

After pressing a closed mouth kiss to my lips and giving my neck a gentle squeeze he went on, "Okay, sunshine. I've got to get going. I'll get back here as soon as I can. If you need anything, just call me."

"Thanks, Levi."

With that, he left and I set the alarm before I went about cleaning up the breakfast dishes. After I finished them, my phone rang.

I picked up the phone, checked the display, and answered, "Hey, LP."

"Well, I'm thrilled to hear you sounding like that," Leah started. "I wanted to check in on you after last night."

I loved Leah. She was the sweetest person I'd ever met. Most everyone who met her felt the same way. Initially, this was usually because she was a very quiet and shy person. As she got to know someone better she opened up and was a bit more vocal. That's when you couldn't help but love her even more.

"It wasn't a good night," I admitted. "Thankfully, Levi was with me."

"Did he figure anything out yet?" she asked.

"No, not yet," I sighed. "He spent the night comforting me and holding me, but he left just a little bit ago to head into the office this morning so he could work on my case."

"He left you alone in his house?" she worried.

"Yeah, but he's got a state-of-the-art security system," I explained. "I'll be fine."

"I'm surprised he was willing to leave you. Though, considering you sound like you're in a better place mentally, I'm guessing that's the reason why."

"He's the reason for my mood shift," I shared.

"What exactly does that mean?" Leah asked, her tone accusatory.

She knew what I was hinting at and she was not going to allow me to not share details with her.

"Nothing," I began, a small smile spreading across my face. "Levi held me and comforted me last night, but then this morning he made good on our original plans for last night."

"You slept with him."

It wasn't a question. She already knew that I had, so I admitted, "It was amazing, Leah. He's got this incredible body. Seriously...it's to die for and he knows how to use it. He was really good to me in bed and I like how he makes the effort to take care of me out of bed, too. He's got such a genuine heart."

"Wow, E. I mean, I get the hotness thing, but you barely know him. You mentioned him to me once before back when you met him, but I didn't realize you had gotten to this point with him. I hope he continues to treat you right."

I felt my insides warm thinking about Levi. After the conversation we had about me paying him or, more accurately, me not paying him, I knew he would treat me well.

"So," she announced, breaking me out of my daydream. "Since you are there alone and I'm stuck at my parent's house for one more night because they're out and people are here working on the roof, you should definitely come over."

"People work on roofs on the weekend?" I asked.

"Apparently the people my parents hire do," she mumbled. "Please tell me you'll come and keep me company. Bring your swimsuit. It's so hot and humid today, so we can use the pool. Besides, I want more details on your morning with Levi."

"I've got the tour starting next Friday," I reminded her. "I planned on working out the last-minute details of that this afternoon."

"We can do all of that here. You know what, bring your laptop with you. I really need to get you set up and using your own social media accounts anyway."

"You already know that I have no interest in that," I retorted, rolling my eyes.

Leah had set up accounts for me on nearly every social media outlet a very long time ago. I told her I didn't mind so long as I didn't have to deal with using them. She agreed at the time, but for the last six months she's been trying to get me to take over the accounts. According to her, there were things I could do that would grow my following immensely. I explained several times that I didn't necessarily care about growing my following. Since she took her many roles in my career seriously, she insisted that not having social media was not an option.

"Yeah, yeah. I know. We'll talk about it when you get here. You are coming over, right?" she asked.

"I'm coming. Let me get my stuff together and call my parents. I need to fill them in on this whole situation. After, I'll head over. See you soon."

"Love you, E."

"You too, L.P."

I got myself ready to go. But before I armed Levi's house and got in my car, which had been delivered from Cunningham Security sometime the day before, I made a call to my parents.

"Hello," my mother answered after two rings.

"Hey, Mom."

"I was actually going to call you today, Elle. I wanted to

make sure you were planning to stop by to see us before you head out on tour next week," she said.

"Well," I started, a bit nervous. "I'm not exactly sure. I would like to, but I'm in a bit of a situation right now."

"What's wrong?"

I took in a deep breath. "I don't want to worry you or Dad, but I think you need to know what's going on. I'm not currently staying at my apartment," I revealed.

"Why not?" my mother asked. "Where are you?"

This was more difficult than I thought it was going to be. "I'm staying at Levi Cunningham's place," I admitted.

"Levi?" she repeated. "Zane's brother? Why are you there?"

I went on to tell my mother everything that happened after Charley and I went out for lunch on Friday. To say she took the news hard was an understatement. She went crazy.

Eventually, my dad got on the phone because my mom was so worked up. I explained to him what was happening and what we knew to that point, which wasn't much. He was upset, but managed to keep it together much better than my mother.

"I promise I'll try to check in as much as I can while I'm on tour. Wes knows and he's insisted that Levi give him regular updates, so he'll be able to fill you in as well."

"Is Levi going to be going on tour with you?"

I didn't know.

"I'm not sure," I answered honestly. "He asked me about the dates for the tour today and told me I just added a lot to his caseload, but he didn't confirm that he was going. I would feel horrible if he did go."

"Why?"

"Because he refuses to let me pay for his services as it is. Going on tour with me would be ridiculous."

"He's not charging you?" my father asked, clearly shocked.

"No. And I've tried talking to him about it. He won't listen," I complained.

My dad chuckled. "My guess? He's going to go with you. If he's not, I want to know. I'm not real keen on you traveling all over the place with a crazy person after you."

"Okay, Dad. I'll keep you posted. I'm heading over to Leah's now, so I've got to get going. Tell Mom I'll call her before I head out on tour."

"I love you, Elle."

"Love you, too, Dad."

I disconnected the call and left.

An hour after I'd gotten off the phone with Leah, I was glistening.

I had packed a bag that included, among other things, my laptop, my notebook and pen that I always carried in case inspiration for a song came to me, and my bikini.

The minute I entered the Price residence, Leah was giving orders for me to get my swimsuit on.

"I can't stand to sit in this house listening to the banging on the roof any longer!" she shouted.

As quickly as possible, I put on my suit and we made our way out to the pool. We lathered on the sunscreen and settled in two of the loungers. I, of course, had to also apply a generous coat of lip balm. Today's flavor was candy apple. I secretly wondered if Levi would enjoy this flavor.

"I'm not sure I understand your hardship," I told Leah as I looked through my shades back at the house where several tanned, half naked men were working on the roof. "There might be some noise, but you've got all that to look at in exchange. Doesn't seem like a bad trade-off to me."

"Yeah, that'd be great if I could do more than just look at them," she muttered. "I stayed here last night because my parents left so early this morning. When I answered the door, the guy asked me if my parents were home. When I told him they left two hours earlier, he asked who was home with me."

"Oh my God. I would have died."

"Well that would never happen to you because… well, look at you. He was gorgeous, I wanted to lick his entire body, and he thought I was a tween!"

I burst out laughing.

"I'm sorry," I got out through fits of laughter. "It's not funny."

"It's so infuriating and frustrating," she sighed. "Anyway, what do you still have left to figure out for the tour?"

"Everything is squared away for Denver. I've been in touch with the venue and the hotel is booked. I've not confirmed anything beyond that."

"I'll take care of it for you between today and tomorrow," she offered.

"It's okay, Leah. I've got the time on my hands now anyway, so I can do it," I insisted.

"Listen, I'm stuck here until my parents get back tomorrow, so I might as well give myself something to do. Besides, I have other ways for you to spend your time now."

"I'm not tweeting," I huffed.

Leah laughed. "Elle, you've got to get with the times. Social media is the key to expanding your career here. If you are trying out this mini-tour to see if you want to take it to the big stage, it'll be good to already have a loyal fan base."

"I like the fan base I have now, though," I argued. "I don't have high expectations for this tour to lead me to a place where I suddenly decide that I don't like the feel of a small town. I'm trying this mini-tour out, but I really love my life as it is now."

"Okay, but you never know what could happen. You

might feel differently after the tour," she reasoned. "All I'm saying is that you should try it out."

She leaned toward my lounger and snagged my phone from the table beside me.

"Let me at least put the apps on your phone and show you how they work," she started. "Give it two weeks. If after that you decide it's too much or you really don't want to do it, I'll take over the role again."

I let out a frustrated sigh.

Leah was not going to let up on this.

Two weeks. I guess I could manage that. I'd put in the time, make a valiant effort to use the apps, and then I'd tell her that it wasn't my thing.

Perfect.

"Okay, fine. Two weeks. But if I hate it, I'm done."

She shot me a huge grin and agreed, "Deal."

Half an hour later, I had learned all about tweeting, stories, and statuses. Leah made me post my first story on Instagram before I had to send out a tweet on Twitter with a link to the details of my upcoming tour. Finally, she had me go live on Facebook. It seemed as though she had already done an amazing job of building up my followers because I had no less than forty thousand people following me on each platform but much more on some. When I went live on Facebook, I was bombarded with questions from fans. I had to admit that it was a bit fun being able to interact with my fans that way. I hadn't realized I had these options available to me.

"See?" Leah pressed. "Wasn't that worth it?"

"Alright, I'll give it to you. I had fun."

"So, you're going to keep it up for the next two weeks, right?" she confirmed.

"I promise I'm going to do my best," I answered honestly.

And I would. It wasn't as terrible as I thought it would be, so I figured it was worth a shot.

"Now, considering my love life is nonexistent, I'm going to need you to share some details on what's happening with you and Levi," she ordered.

I didn't get a chance to answer before I was suddenly no longer being warmed by the sun. I looked up to see one of the roofers was standing off to the side of my lounger, staring down at me. He wasn't even trying to hide the fact that he was checking me out.

Feeling a bit uncomfortable under his gaze, I shifted in the seat.

"Um," I started. "Is something wrong?"

The roofer's eyes drifted from my body up to my face. He broke out into a beautiful grin, which I had to admit was breathtaking. It only slightly detracted from the fact that he felt like a total creep standing there gawking at me.

"Nothing at all," he replied.

He answered in such a way that I knew there was far more meaning behind his words.

"Okay…" I trailed off.

"I saw you when you arrived earlier. I've been trying to focus on my work on the roof and finally decided I needed to just come over and talk to you."

"Me?" I asked. "About what?"

"I'd like to take you out if you're free anytime soon," he said, cutting to the chase.

"Of course," Leah scoffed. "How does this always happen?"

I hoped this wasn't the same guy she had met at the front door this morning. If so, then I was really going to feel horrible for her.

"I appreciate the offer, but I'm currently seeing someone."

"Lucky guy," he mumbled as he pulled a card out of his back pocket and handed it to me. "If that ever changes or if you ever need roofing work done, call me."

I nodded as I took the card from him.

He turned on his boot and walked back toward the house.

I looked to Leah. Tears were in her eyes.

"He's the guy from the front door this morning, isn't he?" I asked.

She nodded.

"I'm sorry."

"It's not your fault, E. It's not like you wished all my faults on me," she replied.

"What are you talking about? What faults?" I questioned her.

"The fact that I look like I still belong in grade school, the fact that I hate what I'm doing for a living, or the fact that I have no knight in shining armor coming after me."

My heart hurt for her.

"LP, those aren't faults," I insisted. "At least, not all of them. You might look young now, but imagine how that'll be when you're sixty and you only look like you're thirty-five. There is a knight in shining armor out there for you. He just hasn't found you yet."

"Yeah, I'm beginning to believe that my knight fell off his horse and broke his neck."

I laughed before I continued, "What you're doing for a living is another story. If you want that to change, love, only you can do that. I've told you this how many times now?"

Not long after getting her DVM, which was less than a year ago, Leah realized she wasted the previous four years in school just to get a degree that would allow her to do something that was expected of her instead of something she could be passionate about. We've had so many discussions about it and I've tried to tell her to follow her heart, but she's too stuck on not wanting to disappoint her family. It's frustrating for me to see my friend so unhappy with who she is pretending to be instead of who she wants to be.

Of course, I don't know exactly who she wants to be since she hasn't really given herself the opportunity to be that person. So, she spends her days caring for animals, happy to provide that to them, but miserable all at the same time.

"I know, but I can't do that," she replied. "I'm worried about what people will think of me if I followed my heart and did something that I was truly passionate about. It's my family. Being anything other than a vet is something they'll frown upon. It's expected for me to have this career. According to them, anything else is beneath me. And in a way, I guess I agree. I mean, I get to call myself a doctor now."

I wanted to roll my eyes. "But if you're not happy, who cares that you get to put those three letters at the end of your name?"

Leah ignored that and sighed, "I miss our days at college. Hanging at The Grind was the most fun."

Now I was feeling nostalgic. The Grind was the coffee house on campus at college. They did karaoke nights and allowed students who were in bands to perform. Leah and I always got up on the stage for karaoke nights. I performed solo a few times throughout my years at school, but didn't get serious. I knew I wanted to be a singer, but I didn't want to overshadow my college experience by spending it focused on my career.

"You're right, Leah. We should do a karaoke night performance together at Lou's after the tour."

"What?" she asked astonished.

"It was a blast when we did them at The Grind. It would be fun to relive old times."

"No way. I couldn't, Elle. You are a superstar and I'm just me."

"You could be a superstar if you allowed yourself to follow your heart instead of worrying about impressing other people."

"Let's get off the subject of me and get back to the question you never answered. What's the deal with you and Levi?"

I rolled my eyes behind my sunglasses. She knew. We had had this conversation many times before and it always ended with her not answering my question or finding a way to skirt around the issue. I wasn't going to force her to talk about it, so I usually just moved along.

That's precisely what I did now.

I spent the next few hours with my best friend telling her all about my morning with Levi and where I hoped to see things go between us. As she always did, Leah sat there and listened before she offered me her thoughts. Through it all, I hoped that I'd one day be able to give her the same support she had always given me.

CHAPTER 7

Elle

I T WAS APPROACHING DINNERTIME WHEN I PULLED INTO THE driveway at Levi's place. I was happy to see that he had arrived back home because I didn't have a key and, quite frankly, I wasn't thrilled with the idea of waiting in the car until he returned. This was something about which I was going to need to have a chat with him.

I turned off my car and walked through the open garage door to the man door that led into the house. I twisted the door knob and walked in to find Levi at the kitchen island, leaning against the back of the barstool with his arms crossed over his chest. He did not look happy.

"Hey," I greeted him, caution resonating from my voice with just that one word.

"Hey?" he repeated.

Yep.

He was not happy.

"Is something wrong?" I asked.

He tilted his head to the side and assessed me. Other than the head tilt, he hadn't moved from his position on the stool.

"I don't know, Elle. Can you think of anything that might be wrong?"

I looked around the kitchen. I didn't believe I'd find the

answer there, but his angry gaze was beginning to make me uncomfortable. I came up with nothing.

"I can see you are upset about something," I started as my gaze drifted back to him. "I'm not sure what it is, though. Considering that it's nearly time for dinner and I'm feeling particularly famished, it'd really be nice if you'd tell me what's going on so we can discuss it because I would like to go up, strip out of this bikini, take a shower, and eat."

His expression changed as his eyes traveled the length of my body and his face softened. The warmth lasted not even ten seconds before he went on to explain his mood.

"I got back here about thirty minutes ago," he began. "Imagine my surprise or, more accurately, my worry when someone who has a psychopath actively stalking her isn't here. It didn't make me feel very good to get home expecting to see someone I'm beginning to care a great deal about and then have no clue if something bad happened to her because she was nowhere to be found."

Someone he was beginning to care a great deal about.

"Levi..." I started, but trailed off when I saw the look on his face.

"I tried calling you, but you didn't answer your phone. Thankfully, I've got cameras in this house. Slightly panicked that something could have happened to you, I immediately went to check the video feed. I saw that it was not long after I left when you took a call, had what seemed like a pleasant conversation, got on another call, and then you left the house on your own. To say I no longer felt sick to my stomach is an understatement. The longer I've sat here, the more confused I've grown trying to figure out why you wouldn't simply give me a call before you left to let me know."

"I didn't think I needed to ask permission to leave the house."

Levi sighed deeply. "Elle, I'm not some asshole who demands that a woman I'm dating asks me for permission to go somewhere, but considering the nature of your situation right now, I thought you'd at least give me the courtesy of a phone call and a heads-up."

He was right. There was still too much that was unknown with this whole stalker situation. I should have let him know I was stepping out of the house for a bit just so he didn't worry unnecessarily. My eyes welled with tears.

"I'm sorry," I whispered. "I didn't think, Levi, and I certainly didn't mean to worry you. Leah called to check in on me after what happened last night. She found out that I was here alone and asked me to come over to her parents' house since she is staying there while her parents are away. The roofers are there and she was bored to tears. And I didn't intentionally ignore your call. The battery on my phone died."

I looked down at the ground, trying to regain my composure. I hated feeling like Levi was disappointed with me, and I was surprised at how much it bothered me that he wasn't happy with me.

I managed to take in roughly two and a half settling breaths before I saw Levi's feet in front of mine and felt his finger under my chin and his thumb in front of it. He lifted my head and looked in my eyes. If I wasn't mistaken I could have sworn I saw a bit of remorse in his.

"Sunshine," he said, the single word instantly comforting me.

"I'm sorry, Levi," I rasped.

His face warmed and he pulled me into a hug.

"I don't need you to apologize, Elle," he told me. "I was worried. I know it wasn't your intention to take off without telling me simply to make me worry, but I am going to ask that until we have this situation dealt with that you check in with me. Can you do that for me?"

"Yeah."

He pressed a kiss to the top of my head.

"Didn't like it," he stated after a few minutes of silence.

"What?" I asked as I pulled my face back from his chest.

"The way I felt when I didn't know if you were safe or if someone had taken you."

I gave him a small smile before putting my cheek back to his chest and wrapping my arms tight around him.

"I'll reach out to you next time, but rest assured that I was only with Leah today and nobody took me. Other than one of the roofers who approached us when we were out by the pool and wanted to take me out on a date sometime, I was only with Leah," I shared.

Levi's body went solid. "May I ask what you said to this roofer that wanted to take you out on a date?"

I tilted my head back while Levi dropped his eyes to mine.

"After he expressed his interest in me vocally, which I was grateful for, I told him I was seeing someone."

"You were grateful he expressed interest in you?" he asked, an edge of annoyance in his tone.

"No. I was grateful that he spoke to express it instead of continuing to stand there and stare at me like a creep. It was uncomfortable."

"Let me guess—you were in the bikini you mentioned a few minutes ago?"

"You would be correct."

Levi's jaw clenched.

"He gave me his card and told me that if things ever changed I should call him. Then, he walked back to the house and started working again."

"Where's the card?" he asked.

"What?"

"His card. Where is it?" he pressed.

A grin spread across my face when I answered, "I threw it in the trash when Leah and I got back inside the house."

Now it was Levi's turn to grin.

"You said you wanted to take the suit off and take a shower before dinner. How do you feel about a little company?"

"In the shower?" I asked quietly.

Levi nodded.

"That could be fun," I admitted, my voice hoarse. "That is, as long as you are no longer angry with me."

"I'm sorry for that. I'm not angry," he assured me. "More than anything else, I was worried about you."

I let those words sink in before I responded, "Considering you explained that I'm someone you're beginning to care a great deal about, I'll let it slide."

His face moved closer to mine and he smiled at me.

With his lips inches from mine, I whispered, "Just so you know, I like that you are beginning to care a great deal about me."

Levi dropped his head and gently brushed his lips against mine. I was certain he could smell the scent of my candy apple lip balm I reapplied before leaving Leah's because he wasted no time in moving from gentle brushes of his lips against mine to full-fledged, open-mouthed, lip nibbling, tongue exploring kissing. His arm around my waist pulled me tighter to his body. He groaned into my mouth and I swallowed his sounds.

My hands went to the hem of his shirt, where I pushed it up his body. He separated his mouth from mine and helped me remove the shirt. My hands instantly went to his body, but couldn't explore for long because Levi bunched my sundress up on my sides before he lifted it over my head, forcing my arms in the air. He tossed the dress to the floor with his shirt and took in my bikini.

"Shower and dinner are on the agenda tonight, sunshine, but you'll be occupying my pool with me very soon."

Wanting to tease him a bit, I turned around, looked back at him over my shoulder, and asked, "So, you don't think this suit makes my butt look big?"

His eyes traveled to my ass and I watched as his jaw clenched. He brought one hand up to squeeze the cheek of it, and praised, "I think it makes it look fucking phenomenal."

Levi's hand that had been resting on my ass moved around my waist. He pulled me against his half naked body, my back pressing against his front, my ass settled nicely against his erection.

I tilted my head back, wrapping my arm around the back of his head. I brought my lips to his and kissed him. His free hand came to settle just at the base of my throat and slowly moved down to my breasts. As his finger flicked across the fabric of my swimsuit covering my hardened nipple I moaned and pressed my ass further into his lap.

Levi groaned, pulled his mouth from mine, and bent down to pick me up. He carried me upstairs, straight to his bedroom, and right through to his master bathroom. After setting me down on my feet, he ordered, "Suit off, Elle."

I did as he asked while he moved to the shower and turned it on. By the time he turned back to me, I was standing there with nothing on. He kept his eyes on mine as he brought his hands to his belt. Levi made quick work of the belt, opened the button and zipper on his jeans, and let them fall to the floor with his boxer briefs.

Not liking the distance between us, I walked toward him. My arms went around his neck while his hands came to my waist. Levi lifted me. My legs immediately went around his waist.

Just as I was about to kiss him, he pulled back.

"Wait. I need to put you down."

"Is something wrong?"

"These fucking eyes are going to get me in trouble, sunshine. I'm planning to fuck you in the shower. I need to grab a condom."

I bit my lip and nodded.

Thank goodness one of us was being responsible.

I was on birth control, so I wasn't concerned about that. I'd only had two other partners and I was never unprotected, but I didn't know Levi's situation. Discussing his sex life before I came along was something I was not interested in bringing up at the current moment, so I unhooked my legs as Levi set me back down.

Levi walked out of the bathroom and came back not even thirty seconds later. He wasted no time in stalking toward me, guiding me into the shower, and getting my back against the wall. His face was buried in my neck, one of his hands at my hip, the other at my breast. Levi's mouth worked its way from my neck down along my collarbone, and down my chest. He stopped at my breasts, where I fit perfectly into his hand. His thumb stroked back and forth across my nipple, the pink bud hardening under his deliberate touch. The ache between my legs grew more intense as Levi's mouth covered my breast and sucked. The pace of each swipe of his tongue across my nipple alternated between slow and savoring to quick and needy and was somehow synchronized with the pace of his thumb on the other side.

Someone I'm beginning to care a great deal about.

As the thought flittered into my brain, I dug my nails into his shoulders.

Levi growled.

He pulled his mouth from me, gripped my hips in his hands, and lifted me. The moment my legs wrapped around his back again, Levi used one arm to hold me up while one hand went between us. He positioned himself directly at my core, brought his eyes to mine, and pushed inside me.

I closed my eyes and dropped my head back as I moaned.

"Eyes, Elle," he demanded.

I brought my head forward again and just barely managed to open my eyes.

"Love the honey in your eyes," Levi rasped.

Levi thrust into me relentlessly. My thighs squeezed his sides while my arms wrapped around his shoulders.

His eyes bored into mine until he finally claimed my mouth.

It was frantic.

All of it.

The kissing.

The touching.

The sex.

His words from earlier were still swirling in my brain.

His hips were continuing to power his cock inside me.

It was building and I knew I was going to crash hard.

"Levi," I said, trying to catch my breath after pulling my mouth from his.

I was close.

It was coming.

My head went to the side. My eyes closed.

"Give them to me, sweetness."

He wanted my eyes.

I turned my head and gave them to him.

He smirked and declared, "That's my girl."

Sweetness. My girl. Someone I'm beginning to care a great deal about.

My breaths came quicker.

My muscles began tightening.

"Take it, sunshine."

I took it, crying out his name as the heels of my feet dug into his backside.

Since I knew it was what he wanted, I kept my eyes on

Levi throughout it. It was difficult, but the reward of seeing his heated gaze staring back at me added to the pleasure.

It was as I just barely started coming down from my orgasm when Levi found and groaned through his release. He pumped into me a few more times, his pace incredibly slow but still very strong.

When he stopped moving inside me, his eyes held mine a moment before his mouth captured mine. He kissed me hard.

After pulling his mouth from mine, he admitted, "Candy apple was a good flavor."

I ran my fingers through his wet hair and shared, "There are so many flavors left to try."

"Well, the peaches are still on top for me. I'm looking forward to seeing what's going to beat them."

I gave him a knowing smile and said, "I'm glad you joined me in the shower."

"Me too."

Levi pulled out of me as I unhooked my legs from around his waist. Once I was steady on my feet, he let me go and dealt with the condom. I went about my shower business. Levi did the same.

We finished, toweled off, and I walked back out through Levi's bedroom to the guest room. With the towel still wrapped around me, I rummaged through the drawers and found a pair of cotton shorts and a camisole. I snagged a pair of underwear, grabbed the clothes, and walked across the hall to the guest bathroom.

After slathering the moisturizer on my body, I put on my clothes and searched for some moisturizer for my lips. I figured it was best to go with a new flavor, so I settled on grape. As I was applying it, there was a knock on the door. I walked over and opened it to find Levi in a pair of loose-fitting sweats and a T-shirt.

His eyes immediately went to the tube in my hand that was being held at my lips. I stopped applying the lip balm and rubbed my lips together. Levi watched my mouth the entire time.

"What's up?" I asked.

He looked at me and responded with a question. "What flavor?"

"I think it's more fun when you taste test to find out," I teased.

"Are you okay with me doing that now?"

I nodded my head furiously.

Levi slid his hand in my hair, which was still wet from the shower. He lowered his head to mine and brought his nose close to my lips. After taking a deep inhale, he confessed, "I love grape. As a kid, whenever there was candy or popsicles that offered grape as a flavor choice, that's always what I picked. The best part about it is that so many people hate grape. Neither Zane nor Cruz liked it, so I always lucked out."

"I am partial to strawberry with stuff like that, but if grape were the only flavor left I wouldn't turn it down. That said, on the occasion that I'm buying chewing gum, I always pick grape gum."

Levi just stood there staring at me.

After several beats of silence, he spoke.

His voice was deep and gravelly when he asked, "Do you have your nighties in one of the drawers in the guest bedroom?"

"Yes," I answered.

"You're in my bed tonight and every night from here on out for as long as we're both happy with what's happening between us," he started. "I made room in one of my drawers for you. Move your nighties there before you come downstairs. I'll get dinner started."

I made room in one of my drawers for you.

"Levi," I started before he cut me off.

"Don't argue with me about it, Elle. Just move them," he huffed.

"I wasn't going to argue. I was just going to ask what you planned on making for dinner tonight."

"Are you hungry for something in particular?"

I looked away and tried to act indifferent when I responded, "No. Whatever you're planning will be fine."

"Look at me, sunshine."

I brought my eyes to him.

"What do you want to eat?"

"Earlier today while you were getting ready and I was making breakfast I made note of what you had in the kitchen. I saw the chicken breasts in the freezer. I moved them to the refrigerator this morning. I hope that was okay."

"You want chicken?" he asked, shock in his tone.

I smiled and answered, "Yeah."

"What am I missing here?" he continued.

"Well, obviously, we know you have the eggs. I also noticed this morning that you have flour and the seasonings needed to make really incredible fried chicken."

"Fried chicken?" he repeated.

Levi looked ready to run. I decided to compromise.

"It doesn't have to be fried. We could bake it in the oven instead. And we can have a salad with it."

"If you move your nighties to my drawer, we can do half of the chicken baked and the other half fried."

A grin spread across my face as I looked up at him through hooded eyes. "You don't mind? It'll make your house smell."

"Elle, I'm probably going to regret telling you this, but if you're ever looking to get your way with me, all you have to do is look at me with those rich, honey-colored, fuck me eyes. You do that and I'm never saying no."

I approved of him sharing this information. "That's good to know."

"Please don't exploit my weakness," he begged.

I pushed up on my toes and with my mouth inches from his I insisted, "I would never do such a thing."

Then, I pressed my grape flavored lips to his.

Levi groaned the second he tasted me.

After giving him what I felt was sufficient time to explore and taste this new flavor on my lips, I pulled my mouth from his and announced, "I'm going to go move my nighties. Then I'll come down and make the chicken."

He gave me a gentle squeeze and said, "Okay. I'll go down and get everything pulled out. While I'm waiting for you, I'll get the salad ready."

"That works."

With that, Levi gave me a quick kiss on the lips before moving to the steps to head downstairs. I went to the guest bedroom, loaded my arms full of my nighties, and moved them to Levi's drawer.

They fit perfectly.

Minutes later, I joined Levi downstairs where we made a batch of oven-baked chicken and a batch of fried chicken.

It was exactly what I had been craving.

CHAPTER 8

Elle

"**I**'M SERIOUSLY SHOCKED RIGHT NOW!"

That was me talking to Levi.

We just finished having dinner about thirty minutes ago and Levi surprised me. After eating a piece of the baked chicken, he stuck his fork into a piece of the fried chicken. He cut it in half and only ate that single half, but I was blown away.

"Because I ate half a piece of fried chicken?"

I gave him a disbelieving look and answered, "Um, yeah."

"I mean, I might not eat unhealthy foods, but that doesn't mean I don't know when something is going to taste good. You can fry pretty much anything and it's going to be great. The baked piece was so good that I knew it would be worth it to try it fried."

"So you enjoyed it?"

"It was great, Elle. All of it. Was this your own recipe?"

"No. I'm in love with Pinterest."

"You're in love with what?" he asked.

"It's an app that allows you to collect and pin images to boards. It's a great way to plan for future events or to get inspiration for your wardrobe. I love finding new recipes to try."

"Enough said. Sounds like social media stuff to me."

"I'm not a fan of social media either, but Pinterest is different," I argued. "Speaking of social media though, I did make a promise to Leah today that I'd make the effort for the next two weeks to manage my social media accounts. She showed me today how each of the apps works. I tried it out and had fun. I even did a live session and interacted with my fans. Of course, that's why the battery on my phone died so quickly today."

"You've got to be careful, sunshine."

My head dropped to my shoulder and I asked, "With what?"

"You want to post stuff to promote what you do, I get it. Please try to limit the live sessions."

I stared at him, waiting for further explanation.

"When you go live, people can see where you are and who you're with," he started. "It leaves you vulnerable. We don't need to add to the current stalker situation. It's bad enough someone knows when and where you are performing. I'm not keen on them knowing where you are day-to-day."

"I hadn't thought of that," I admitted. I paused for a moment to reflect on the sad state of affairs. "Well, this is frustrating."

"Sorry," he lamented.

"Any luck today at the office?"

Levi shook his head and explained, "This guy knows what he's doing. He didn't place the order online. The owner of the floral shop said it was a kid who, looking like he was just out of high school, came in to order the flowers. He paid cash."

"What about the card? Didn't she think what was written on the card was enough cause for concern?" I questioned him.

"She had no idea what was written on the card. They have the cards there and allow the buyer to write their own personal message if they wish. The kid filled out the card and sealed it in the envelope before handing it over to her."

"This is so infuriating," I complained. "Of all the things I want to say to this guy when you find him, my biggest question is why."

"Hate to burst your bubble, but depending on how this all plays out I'm not certain you're going to be given an opportunity to say anything to this guy."

"Why not?" I challenged. "He's attempting to destroy my life right now; I think that entitles me to have it out with him. I'm heading out on a mini-tour in a few days to see if I want to take my career to that level and I've got to be worried about some psycho who has nothing better to do with himself? How am I supposed to focus on my music?"

"I'll be there with you, sunshine."

I shook my head in disbelief and gasped, "Excuse me?"

"Not sure if you planned on going on this tour alone, but I'm coming with you."

Well, at least my father would be pleased.

"You can't do that. Levi, you have a business," I reminded him.

"Like hell I can't," he retorted. "I do have a business. I also have a highly-skilled, extremely qualified team that I employ. Cruz is more than capable of running the show until I'm back. My most important case right now is yours."

I dropped my head in defeat.

"I'm sorry I'm ruining your life right now," I lamented.

"Elle, look at me."

When I lifted my head, Levi insisted, "You are not ruining my life. I'm very serious about the work I do, and I fucking hate that someone is doing this to you. But there is an upside to all of this."

"And that would be?"

His face changed and he seemed slightly alarmed.

"I can sit here and name at least five things that have me

looking at the bright side of this situation. I've got to admit it stings a little that you can't think of one good thing that's come from all of this."

Oh no.

"Levi, I didn't mean it like that. I just think it would have been nice for us to get together under different circumstances," I reasoned.

He nodded, but said nothing.

I got up from my chair and walked toward him. He remained seated as I stepped between his legs. I took a chance and settled myself in his lap, bringing my hands up to frame his face. He wrapped his arms around my waist.

My voice was soft when I spoke. "Please believe me. I didn't mean to diminish the one very incredible thing that has happened because of this debacle. I'm beginning to really like you. I like the way you make me feel, especially when I'm scared. You bring me a comfort that nobody else does. The two of us together is the only thing that makes me happy about this whole situation."

Levi continued to stay silent, but something changed in his expression.

"It's good, Levi. You and me...it's so good," I whispered.

A hand wrapped around the back of my neck as Levi leaned forward and captured my mouth. He kissed me for a bit before bringing an arm under my knees and dropping the other from my neck to the middle of my back. Then he carried me to the family room.

After setting me down gently on the couch, his hands came to the hem of my shirt before lifting it over my head. Levi wasted no time in removing my shorts and panties next.

He looked down at my body, taking in my figure. His eyes heated.

Then his voice dipped low. "I need my mouth on you,

sunshine. I need to know if you taste as sweet as I think you will."

My body trembled in anticipation.

I wanted Levi's mouth on me.

He pulled his shirt over his head, tossed it aside, and sat on the couch next to my thighs. His fingers came up and caressed the skin at my throat.

"So soft," he said, his voice hoarse as his fingers slowly moved from my throat down my chest.

My hand gripped his thigh.

The lower his hand went, the more I wanted him. In any way that I could have him.

His fingers brushed over my breasts, my nipples hardening under his touch.

My breathing was shallow while I eagerly waited for what was ahead.

Levi lowered his head and took my breast in his mouth. His tongue teased me and his hand continued to travel down my body. When his hand reached the lowest part of my abdomen, he freed my breast from his mouth and looked down at the spot he planned to devour next.

The wetness had pooled between my legs and, attempting to relieve the ache there, I squeezed them together.

"Let me see you, sweetness," Levi urged.

I parted my thighs and allowed him to look at me.

His dark blue eyes were pure ink when they came up to meet mine. The intensity of it all was too much.

"Be my hero again and save me from this torture, Levi," I pleaded. "Put your mouth on me."

He moved quick and settled himself between my legs. With one hand wrapped around my leg, Levi's lips trailed kisses all along my inner thigh.

I moaned in agony.

This was cruel.

I needed his mouth on me and he thought teasing me was the way to go. I couldn't take it anymore.

"Please," I begged.

He didn't oblige me.

I desperately needed him to relieve this ache.

"Levi?" I called as I propped myself up on my elbows.

His eyes came to mine. I gave him the sexiest, bedroom eyes I could muster up and hoped that what he said to me earlier was true. Sure, I said I'd never exploit that weakness, but he was tormenting me. I figured it was only fair.

Thankfully, my plan worked because within seconds of delivering those eyes, Levi's mouth was on me.

I moaned loudly in relief before I heard the sounds coming from him. He was thoroughly enjoying himself, and I was thoroughly enjoying what he was doing.

"Oh, fuck," I groaned.

Levi's tongue licked and tasted me before he sucked on my clit.

Never.

Never in my life had I felt something so incredible.

So intense.

So phenomenal.

It was all Levi.

I moved my hips, looking for more.

He knew it and he gave it.

Levi's tongue pushed inside me and worked me while I reached down, wrapped my hand behind his head, and held his mouth against me. He continued working until I climaxed, my body shattering at the sensation.

I barely had time to think. Levi stood and removed the rest of his clothing. He sat back down on the couch, picked me up, and situated me so that I was straddling his lap.

"Are you on birth control?" he asked.

Nodding, I replied, "Yes."

"I'm clean, Elle. Promise you. Are you good with nothing between us?"

"I'm more than good with it," I answered.

"Ride me, sweetness."

Bringing my hand down between my legs, I lifted my hips and positioned him. I gave him my eyes before I lowered myself onto him. His fingers sunk into the flesh of my thighs.

"Fuck, sunshine," he started. "You taste like honey and feel like Heaven."

Considering he had done such a remarkable job with his mouth mere moments ago and was now saying all kinds of sweet stuff, I decided it would only be right if I gave him what he deserved. With that, I began riding him.

I moved my hips and worked myself over his length. He felt unbelievable and I loved that I was having this experience of nothing between us with him.

His couch had deep cushions, so while Levi was sitting, he was still leaning back quite a bit. I moved my hands from where they were resting on his shoulders and placed them on either side of his ribcage. Then, while shifting my weight into my hands, I moved my hips faster. He brought his mouth to mine and consumed me.

Levi's hands roamed my body.

First at my thighs.

Then at my ass.

Up my back and over my shoulders.

Down to my breasts.

It wasn't long before I was there again.

"Levi," I rasped as I tore my mouth from his and threw my head back.

It was coming.

I moved quicker, seeking my release.

When I was nearly there, Levi ordered, "Eyes, Elle."

I dropped my head and gave them to him.

Levi kept his hungry eyes on mine.

We never dropped our gazes as we came apart together, the heat of his release now inside me. I loved it. Even though I was always so caught up in how I was feeling when we were having sex, I loved that Levi always made me give him my eyes. The connection to him only grew stronger in those moments. I liked that he gave that to me.

I collapsed on top of him, my head falling to his shoulder. His arms wrapped around me and held my heated body tight against his.

After several minutes, I managed to regain control over my breathing. I lifted my head and looked at him.

"I'm sorry," I whispered.

Thoroughly confused, he asked, "For what?"

"For exploiting your weakness before. You were doing too much teasing and I was certain I'd die from the torture of not having your mouth on me."

Levi chuckled and reassured me, "I'll let it go this time considering I've never tasted something so damn sweet. Maybe you won that battle but, I've got to be honest, I think I'm the one who reaped the greater reward."

I gave him a soft kiss on the lips and let him believe he'd won. When I pulled back from him I wanted to make sure he knew how I felt about us.

"We got a bit sidetracked there, but I want to know that you know how I feel about the two of us together," I started. "It is everything good and special and wonderful. I just don't like how it came to be, that's all."

"I know, Elle," he assured me. "I need to assume some responsibility here. You expressed interest in me back when we first met and, even though the attraction was mutual, I didn't pursue you. That was my fault."

My body, already sated, loosened even more.

"I feel sleepy," I announced as I brought my head back down to his shoulder.

Levi laughed and pointed out, "That's because you've just had two orgasms."

"Hmmm."

A smile spread across my face as my eyes drifted shut.

That's when I felt movement.

"Wrap your legs around me," Levi instructed as he sat up on the edge of the cushion. "I'll carry you up to bed."

"I can walk," I replied with my head still resting on his shoulder.

"You can't even pick your head up, sunshine. I've got you."

He was right. I was spent.

I wrapped my legs around him and he carried me upstairs.

He stopped just outside of the bathroom and asked, "You want to get cleaned up?"

I nodded.

Levi set me down on my feet and once I was steady I walked into the bathroom to take care of business.

When I walked out a few minutes later, I found Levi in bed with the blanket pulled up to his waist. I walked over to the drawer newly cleaned out for my nighties in and pulled one out. After slipping it over my head, I walked to the bed and climbed in. Levi watched me the entire time.

I settled in next to him on my back. He was on his side with his head propped up in his hand looking down at me.

"What?" I asked.

His eyes lit up and he gave me a warm smile. It melted my heart.

"Just feeling happy," he admitted. "I loved being with you that way. Nothing between us."

I closed my eyes briefly trying to recall that feeling of him inside me for the first time with nothing between us and my body tingled at the thought.

"I loved it, too," I confessed when I opened my eyes. "I've never been with anyone like that before. I'm happy that I had that with you."

Levi lowered his head and pressed a gentle kiss to my lips.

After a bit, he asked, "What day are we leaving for Denver?"

"I'm planning to fly out on Thursday afternoon."

"Okay," he began. "Tomorrow, I'm going to need to go over the schedule with you. I'm going to need the details on the Denver flight. I need to be booked on it or you don't fly it. I'm also going to need to know what days we are traveling, what hotels you have booked, and at what venues you'll be performing. Depending on the size of the venue and how many people each one can hold, I might have one of my guys meet us for a few of the stops on your tour."

"Levi, are you sure about this? You already won't bill me for this and you are planning to drop everything to come with me. Now you are talking about flying one of your guys out, too? It's too much and I feel like I'm taking advantage."

"Elle, we've had this discussion already. You aren't paying me. I'm doing this whether you want me to or not. Let it go," he ordered.

I let out a frustrated sigh.

Then, I figured I'd try one last thing to get him to see reason.

I closed my eyes briefly, thought about something naughty, and opened my eyes to look at him.

Sexy eyes.

I was hoping I delivered just that and, thankfully, didn't have to wait too long for an answer. Unfortunately, it wasn't the one I wanted.

"Sweetness, I'd do anything for that look in your eyes. Full of honey and sexy as fuck, but it's not going to work this time."

I harrumphed.

"Care to enlighten me on what put that look in your eyes?"

"No," I pouted. "I'm angry with you right now."

Levi laughed.

"Okay, so you'll share with me later when you are no longer angry?"

I turned away from him in the bed.

"I'm going to sleep," I informed him.

"Like hell you are," he protested as he snaked an arm around my waist and hauled me back against his body. "You aren't going to bed angry at me, especially when what you're angry about is ridiculous."

"It's not ridiculous," I argued.

"Elle, listen to me," he said softly as his arm tightened around my waist. "I've already told you that you're someone I'm beginning to care a great deal about. Seeing this sassy little side of you is cute and something I'm hoping I'll see a bit more as the days go by because it's a huge turn on, but don't throw an attitude with me about your safety. Your life is nonnegotiable."

I tensed hearing those words.

Levi didn't stop. I barely had a moment to digest what he'd just said when he continued, "I know you don't want to hear me say that, but it's the truth. I'm busting my ass and I've got my team busting their asses to figure out who's after you. We're going to do it as quickly as we can so that you can feel safe again and your life can return to normal. By normal, I mean the new normal, which includes me in your life and you in my bed. Don't be bitter about this and don't fight me on it. You won't win."

I didn't respond.

My body was still tense.

Levi's arm stayed tight around my body.

"It feels like I'm trading my body for your protection."

Now it was his turn to go solid.

"Sunshine, that is not what's happening here. I thought you would know that considering there was clearly an attraction long before this. If that's how you really feel, then I'm not having sex with you again until your situation has been dealt with and your safety is no longer a concern," he asserted.

My eyes nearly popped out of my head and I turned to look back at him.

"You aren't serious."

"Absolutely. If you're truly uncomfortable with us being together like that because I'm not charging you, then this is how I rectify that. If I'm being honest—it's going to suck, but I am *not* okay with you thinking I'm viewing your body as some form of payment for me to make sure nobody harms you. That's not fucking what it is at all, Elle, and I'm pretty pissed that you believe I'm the kind of person that would use a woman like that."

My lips parted at the harsh reality he just delivered.

Suddenly, I wasn't so sure I had a problem with him not charging me. Unfortunately, I was not going to admit that just yet.

I swallowed hard as his hold on me loosened and his arm left my waist.

Levi fell to his back and stared up at the ceiling.

I was going to cry.

The wave of disappointment flooded through me and I knew I had to get out of there. I rolled away from Levi and sat up on the edge of the bed.

When I stood and walked to the door, he called, "Elle?"

I didn't answer. I stepped through the open door and walked into the guest room.

The second I crawled onto the bed and collapsed on the pillow, the tears flowed. This was going to be an ugly cry. I let the tears fall as I thought about how I made Levi feel. That's what this was about. I was crying because Levi was disappointed with me. He had been nothing but good to me from the moment he knew I was in trouble. And because he wouldn't let me pay him for the use of his firm's services, I shelled out payment in the form of insults.

I'm not sure how much time went by before I stopped crying, but I knew it had been quite a while. After, I just stayed there with my head buried in the pillow for a long time wishing I could fall asleep. Every time I closed my eyes all I could do was hear Levi telling me that I wasn't going to go to bed angry at him. Hearing those words replay in my mind I realized I also didn't want him going to bed angry with me.

Even though I knew he had probably already fallen asleep, I climbed out of the bed and walked back to his bedroom. I tapped lightly on the door and walked in to find I was wrong. The light on his nightstand was still on and he hadn't moved from his position lying on his back, looking up at the ceiling. Standing next to his side of the bed, I looked down at him and struggled to speak past the tightness in my throat.

"I don't want you to go to bed angry at me either."

He held my eyes a moment before he held his hand out to me.

I placed my hand in his palm and fought to keep the tears at bay.

Levi tugged gently on my hand, and I fell forward onto him. His arms wrapped around me as his body turned to the side.

"You okay?" he asked tenderly.

I was going to burst into tears again. I made him feel like shit and he was worried about how I was doing.

I shook my head and answered, "No. I said something horrible to you. I know you aren't that kind of person, Levi. I don't know what's wrong with me. My mind is all out of sorts over this whole thing, but that's not an excuse to treat you the way I did. I don't like feeling like I've disappointed you, and I'm sorry for what I said."

"Are you done telling me you need to pay me for this?" he asked.

I nodded into his chest.

He didn't say anything else, so I repeated, "I don't want you to be mad at me. I'm really sorry, Levi."

His hands sifted through my hair as I felt his lips touch the top of my head. He kissed me and said, "It's okay, sunshine. I'm not mad."

I let out a breath I hadn't realized I was holding and snuggled into him. His arms tightened around me in response.

We stayed like that a long time and I was still feeling tense, unable to find sleep.

"Levi?" I whispered, unsure if he had fallen asleep.

"Yeah, Elle?"

My voice was a hair over a whisper when I asked, "Can we still have sex?"

I felt his body vibrate with a bit of a laugh.

"Are we good on what us having sex means?"

"Yeah," I breathed. "It's not about what I insinuated a little bit ago. It's all about what happens when you make me give you my eyes just before we come together."

"Fuck. You were bitter not too long ago and I wasn't sure how it was going to go after that. But now I'm thinking if it's like this, I'm okay with it because when you get sweet, it's so fucking good."

"Is that a yes?" I pressed him for a definitive answer.

"Yeah, sweetness, that's a yes."

CHAPTER 9

Levi

I T WAS FINALLY THURSDAY MORNING.

Finally.

Yeah, right.

Saying it like that made it seem like I was relieved we had gotten to this point or that it was something I had been looking forward to.

Not in the least.

My reasoning had nothing to do with Elle singing or touring either. It had everything to do with her stalker. There hadn't been any activity since the flower delivery at Lou's, but I knew that a person like this would not just simply stop. I just hated to think that they'd act when we were out of town.

I was overly concerned and worried about her but did my best to hide it from Elle. I couldn't stand seeing the stress and anxiety in her face whenever she thought of or talked about the whole situation.

Currently, I was standing in the doorway to the guest bedroom watching her frantically pack her suitcases. One suitcase was already overflowing with clothing; the other was halfway there. She also had a large bag sitting on the bed that looked as though it was coming with us as well.

Elle turned her head and saw me standing in the doorway.

"I don't think I can do this," she fretted.

"What's the matter, sunshine?" I asked keeping my voice calm hoping to relax her a bit.

"I don't like this," she started. "I don't do well with deadlines and schedules. I'm certain that this is not going to be the lifestyle for me. Everything it requires is everything I hate: living out of a suitcase, packing my things, traveling by plane. It makes me feel overwhelmed and I don't like it. I like it here. In Wyoming. I love my life here. I love singing. That's all I want to do."

I had to admit that deep down it felt good to hear that. The more time I spent with Elle the more I was beginning to feel something for her. In the back of my mind I wondered what would happen if she went on this tour and decided it was something she wanted to continue to do. I knew I was the kind of person that wouldn't be able to let her go alone on tour unprotected, even after her current situation was resolved.

I pushed off the doorjamb I had been leaning against and walked to her. Wrapping both arms around her, I cradled her body against mine. She immediately melted into me.

"I'm cool with whatever you decide to do, Elle. I think if you have the slightest idea in the back of your mind that this is something that you want to do down the road on a larger scale, then you should not pass up this opportunity to test the waters. If you don't want to do it, though, you don't have to do it."

"I'm not sure what to do."

"Based on everything you've shared with me this week leading up to right now, I'm pretty certain you're going to have a lot of fans that are disappointed if you cancel this."

"Yeah, there's that. I'd never want to disappoint my fans, especially if this is the only time they'd get to see me perform in person."

"So, do it," I urged her. "Just try to go into it with a clear head and really make the effort to enjoy it. If you want to keep things as they've been, at least you can make that decision knowing that you've explored this avenue."

Elle pulled her face back from my chest, looked up at me, and wondered, "How do you do it, Levi? You know just what to say to me to make me feel better. Thank you for talking me through this; otherwise, I might have had a total meltdown."

"No problem," I responded. "If you're good now, I'm going to let you finish your packing while I go get my stuff loaded into the truck. I'll also get your car pulled into the garage since we'll be gone for a while."

"Okay."

I gave her a quick kiss on the top of her head and walked out of the room, where I grabbed my suitcase and went downstairs. Before walking out into the garage to load the suitcase into the truck, I snagged Elle's keys off the island. After tossing my bag into the truck, I opened the garage door and walked out to her car.

I had been telling her for days now to pull the car in the garage and she refused to do it. I wasn't necessarily worried because I had state-of-the-art security outside of my house, but since I had the space in the garage, I figured she should just use it.

I climbed in, started it up, and adjusted the seat. She was quite a bit shorter than me and my knees were practically hitting the dash. Then, I flipped up both visors since she had them down. When I pushed the driver's side visor up, a folded piece of paper fell from it. The paper floated down and landed in the center console with part of her collection of lip balm.

I had to laugh.

This girl.

I don't know why, but she had this crazy obsession with lip

balm. I thought it was adorable and I had a great time tasting every flavor she put on, so I didn't give her shit about it.

I'm not sure what I was thinking a few days ago when she brought up the fact that I wasn't billing her for my services again. When she told me that she felt like she was giving her body up as payment, I made a split second, emotional decision and told her we wouldn't have sex again until her stalker situation was no longer a situation.

The second I said the words, I instantly regretted them. Deep down, though, I knew it was the right thing because I was not even remotely okay with her thinking that I viewed her body as payment. It killed me to watch her walk out of my bedroom that night. It was even worse listening to her cry in the guest bedroom.

As much as I wanted to go in there, pick her up, and carry her back to my bed, I couldn't. She needed to come to me on her own terms.

And thankfully she did.

Since that night, she hasn't brought up paying me for keeping her safe and investigating this case. I think she's finally accepted that I genuinely care for her.

So now, as I looked down to pick up the piece of paper that had fallen in with her lip balm I simply smiled inwardly at the fact that I still had the opportunity to taste her lips.

I grabbed the paper and was about to put it back in the visor when something caught my eye.

Initials.

B.B.

My gut clenched as I opened the paper completely.

I read the words that had been maliciously typed and directed at my ray of sunshine and immediately pulled my phone out of my pocket.

It rang twice.

"Yeah?"

"Need you to come to my place. Call Pierce and Dom, too, and have them come as well. I just walked out to pull Elle's car into the garage and found a note stuck in her visor," I explained to Cruz. "We'll be leaving for the airport shortly and she's not finished packing yet, so making a trip into the office is not an option right now."

Cruz was my youngest brother who, shortly after I opened the firm, joined my team. I trusted him, as I did all my guys, implicitly. There was that added layer of confidence with him because he was family. That's why, when I found out that Elle was going to be going on tour I had no doubts about leaving my operation up and running in Cruz's hands.

"On it, Levi. See you in fifteen," he responded.

I pulled the car inside the garage and went back into the house to look at the camera feed. I already knew I wouldn't find anything on them because I would have known if someone had stepped foot on this property and put that note in her car while it was parked here. I also knew that this guy wasn't an idiot. It was likely he realized that he knew he'd be caught if he came here.

I checked the feed anyway.

Part of me was hoping that I was wrong. That part of me was the part that didn't want Elle to have to worry more than she already was about this tour.

As I suspected, the feed was clean. The only person that ever approached Elle's car was Elle.

I walked out of the room that had my security equipment in it and locked the door. I always kept it locked on the off chance that someone was ever stupid enough to come here. I didn't need the evidence of whatever they did or would attempt to do removed.

Elle was walking down the stairs trying to carry a bag and a suitcase.

"Seriously?" I called as I ran over to take the bags from her. "You could have left it all upstairs and I would have gotten them."

"Well, there's one suitcase still up there."

"I'll get it after," I said.

"After what?" she asked.

I didn't get a chance to answer her because Cruz knocked on the door and walked in. A look of confusion washed over her face before she shook it off and questioned him.

"Hi Cruz. Are you here to see us off?"

When his eyes immediately shot to mine, I gave Cruz a look that told him everything he needed to know, which was that Elle had no idea what he was doing there yet.

Not even thirty seconds later, there was another knock on the door and in walked Pierce and Dom. That's when Elle knew. She never met Dom, but she knew who Pierce was since he was the one there when she first got to Cunningham Security looking for me.

She instantly tensed.

"What's wrong?" she questioned, her terrified eyes coming to me.

I watched as she shifted nervously back and forth on her feet and her hands started fidgeting.

"Elle, you already know Pierce. This is Dominick, better known as Dom. Dom…Elle."

Dom gave her a chin lift and she acknowledged him with a nod of her head and a small smile. Then, her eyes came back to mine and pleaded with me.

"Come here," I urged her.

She shook her head. "Just tell me, Levi. What is it?"

I took a deep breath and explained, "I brought my suitcase out to the truck and walked out to your car to move it in the garage until we get back. I adjusted the seat so I could fit in there and put your visors up since you left them down. When I put the driver's side visor up, a piece of paper fell from it. I didn't think anything of it initially, but as I picked it up and lifted my hand to the visor to put it back, I noticed the initials on it."

She jerked back. "The same ones from the flower delivery?" she asked.

I nodded and then watched as her chest rose and fell rapidly. She was starting to panic.

"What did it say?"

"Elle, listen. I don't want you to worry," I got out before she cut me off.

"Levi, please."

I took in another deep breath and repeated the words on the note, "Best wishes on your upcoming tour. Remember, he can't always be with you."

"Oh my God," she whispered as she brought a hand up to cover her mouth.

I went to her and pulled her into my arms.

"Sunshine, I will be with you the entire time. I'm not letting you out of my sight," I tried to reassure her.

She held on tight to me, her fingernails digging into the skin at my sides. I looked up at Cruz, Dom, and Pierce and found them all looking concerned.

Cruz spoke.

"Any idea how the note got there?"

"I checked my security feed here already. Nothing… which is what I expected."

"Where else has the car been?"

Elle answered, "I went to Leah's yesterday to go over a few last-minute items for the tour. Levi knew I was there and I called him when Leah and I decided to take a trip to the Windsor Mall in the afternoon. I wanted to pick up a couple of things for the tour. Oh my God, this guy probably followed us there. Do you think he went to Leah's place, too? Do you think he'll go after her?"

I wished I had the answer for her, but the truth was I had no clue.

"Probably not," I answered. "It appears the obsession is with only you, but just to be safe we'll have you give us her address before you and I head out of town. Cruz will have the team check in on her regularly. We'll keep it quiet so she doesn't begin to worry unnecessarily. In addition, he's also going to have Trent look at the Windsor Mall parking lot footage."

"Thank you."

I nodded to her and looked up at Dom and Pierce. "Elle's performing in Denver tomorrow night. As you know, after Colorado, the rest of the tour has two stops each in Arizona and California followed by two performances in Vegas before coming home to perform at Lou's. I'm looking to have you two split the time. I'm prepared to cover Denver solo, since it's cutting it close, but I want a second person for the remainder of the tour. Pierce, I'll have you cover both Arizona performances and the first in California. Dom will get the second California performance and the two in Vegas."

"No problem," they answered in unison.

"Cruz, have Deb take care of booking their flights. The hotels we'll be at are in Elle's case file. Make sure Deb gets rooms booked for each of them as well. Same floor."

"You've got it, bro."

At that, Elle slid her hand in her back pocket and pulled out her phone. We all watched as she held it up and scanned it across the space where Cruz, Dom, and Pierce were standing. Then she moved it to me. She moved it back to the guys, held it steady, and moved back to me and held it steady briefly.

Then, she lowered the phone and began tapping away at the screen.

"Elle? What's going on?"

She continued tapping on the screen furiously. Her brows were furrowed as she remained focused on her task.

"El?" I called again.

Not looking up from her screen, she replied, "One sec. Almost done."

We waited and watched her.

Finally, she dropped her arms and looked up at us. I gave her a look that indicated she needed to explain what just happened.

"Social media," she stated, matter-of-factly. "I just took some quick shots of all four of you and posted to my social media accounts. I know Cruz isn't going to be there, but nobody needs to know that. My thought is that if this person is following me on any one of those platforms he should know what my security team looks like. Besides, that note said you can't always be with me. What it fails to assume is that maybe you can't always be with me, but there's a whole team looking out for me. A team that looks menacing. If I were stalking someone and they had a security team that looked like mine does, I'd probably find someone else to stalk."

I looked to the guys. The looks on their faces told me that they all had the same thoughts as I did.

"How many followers do you have on social media?" Cruz asked.

"Depends on the account, but no less than forty thousand on any one platform. Facebook has the highest number of followers."

"How many there?"

"Roughly a hundred and fifteen thousand."

"Jesus Christ," I muttered.

Elle's phone rang. She looked down at it and answered.

"Hey, LP."

I watched as a smile spread across her face.

"I know. The situation sucks, but at least I've got some good stuff to look at during the tour."

What?

"That's Dom. I just met him today. The one in the middle is Pierce. Cruz is on the right."

That quick? Someone saw that shit already? It hadn't even been a full two minutes.

Elle continued her conversation. "Right? I didn't believe Emme back a few months ago when she was telling us all about Levi's team. There was no way they could *all* be hot, but apparently, she wasn't lying."

I was going to lose my shit.

"Oh, right. Well, we think someone got into my car yesterday when you and I were at the mall. Levi found a note in my visor this morning. The initials B.B. signed the note again."

Silence again.

"Wished me well on the upcoming tour, but then reminded me that Levi can't always be with me. Levi rectified that by organizing a team to travel with me."

She listened to Leah's response.

"It's a sucky situation, but I figure I need to look on the bright side if I'm going to make the best of it. I'm thinking that the way my bodyguards look is part of the bright side."

I was losing my patience with this. A noise came from the back of my throat.

Elle's eyes came to mine and she gave me a questioning look.

She had no clue what was wrong.

Cruz, Dom, and Pierce were laughing.

"Hey, listen LP, Levi's looking at me a little funny right now. I've got to go, but I'll see you in California."

She waited while Leah, I'm assuming, said goodbye.

"Love you, too."

My stomach clenched hearing her angelic voice say those words. What the fuck?

Elle disconnected the call and began quizzing me. "What's wrong now?"

I didn't answer her. I looked to the guys and announced, "Thanks for stopping by. Get the details sorted with Deb for the trips. Cruz, I assume you are already planning on it, but have Trent look into the social media accounts. Maybe we can narrow it down to a handful of individuals with the same initials. Report any updates to me right away."

Dom and Pierce nodded their agreement. Then, because everybody in the room besides Elle knew where my head was, Dom walked over to Elle, gave her a hug, and said, "Nice to meet you Elle. See you in California." He finished with giving her a wink.

He looked at me and I warned, "You're lucky I need a crazy motherfucker like you on my team; otherwise, I'd fire your ass for that."

Dom laughed, put his hand on my shoulder, and retorted, "It would have been worth it. Catch ya later, Levi."

Pierce and Cruz laughed.

Cruz then walked over and pulled Elle into a hug. He kissed the top of her head and reassured her, "We'll find this guy and keep you safe, babe."

"Thanks, Cruz."

"And your ass is lucky you're related to me. Fuck, now I know what Zane felt like when you pulled that same shit with Emme."

Cruz jerked his head to me and informed Elle, "Don't let this guy give you a hard time after we leave."

Confusion marred Elle's features as Cruz turned around and walked out of the house behind Dom and Pierce.

When the door closed, I looked at Elle, who still looked as confused as ever.

"Did I miss something?" she asked.

"Nothing at all, Elle," I explained as I brought myself to within mere inches of her. "That is, nothing except for the fact that you stood here talking about how hot my team is with not only me here but some of them as well."

"Seriously?" she began. "Levi, there are few people in this world that could even come close to holding a candle to you. That said, you can't deny that your team is hot."

"I don't spend much time checking out my guys, Elle," I noted.

She closed the distance between us and with her luscious lips barely touching mine, she reasoned, "Then maybe you should just take my word for it."

I wrapped my arm around her waist and replied, "You think so?"

She simply nodded and pressed her lips to mine.

The kiss was soft and unhurried. Elle's arms wrapped around the back of my neck and she pulled her mouth from mine.

She looked up at me with her golden, bedroom eyes.

"They might all be hot, but you are the only one that's ever taken my breath away."

Fuck.

I couldn't say the feeling wasn't mutual.

Especially when I looked into those fucking eyes.

With that, my mood shifted. Talk of my team went out the window and my face softened.

"Are you finished packing all of your stuff?"

She nodded.

"One hundred percent ready to go?" I continued.

"Yeah," she replied softly.

"Good. We've got two hours before we need to head to the airport. I can think of a few ways I'd like to spend those two hours."

Elle's beautiful eyes turned liquid honey and I knew she was content to spend the next two hours doing exactly what I wanted.

A grin spread across my face before I bent down, pushed my shoulder into her belly, and picked her up. Then I carried her upstairs and thoroughly enjoyed the next two hours with my woman.

CHAPTER 10

Elle

"**A**RE YOU KIDDING ME?"

That was Levi.

He was on his phone and he was not happy.

We arrived in Denver late yesterday afternoon and all went smoothly on the way here. Before we checked into our hotel I told him I needed to make a stop at a grocery store so I could pick up some chips.

After we checked into the hotel, Levi asked what my plan was for the rest of the day. Oddly enough, I'd only ever been to Denver once before, but I didn't have much time at all to explore. I didn't want to do anything too crazy, so I asked him if he'd mind keeping it pretty low-key for the rest of the day. We decided to get dinner and stroll around downtown Denver afterward. I went into a couple of small shops and picked up a few of my favorite things, a coffee mug and a book. Some people might call them obsessions.

I collected coffee mugs, even though I don't drink coffee.

And books. I love to read. And while books in digital format are convenient, I have always preferred holding a book in my hand. I already started a collection of my favorite contemporary romance novels, which is my favorite genre, but I had no place in my apartment to display them. It was my dream that one day I'd end up living in a home that would have a gorgeous library where I'd load up the shelves with my most loved novels and could sit in a comfortable space just to read. Of course, it'd also have to have a place for me to be able to sit and write my music as well.

Levi asked me about my purchase yesterday. I told him about my dream and he returned a simple nod. He didn't seem to have an opinion on it one way or the other.

Now, it was early Friday morning and I was pressed up against Levi's side in bed. He had his phone to his ear and, as I said before, he was not happy.

"Check through them all. I know it's going to take time, but we can't overlook any of them," he demanded.

He waited silently as whoever was on the phone spoke.

"Keep me updated on what you find."

Silence again.

"Thanks, Michaels."

Levi disconnected the call and tossed his phone on to the bedside table. He rolled toward me and kissed my forehead. "Good morning, sunshine. Sorry if I woke you."

"It's okay, I didn't want to sleep in too late anyway. Did you sleep well?"

"Well enough. It's mostly because I have you here next to me."

"And if I hadn't been here?"

"It's very likely I'd have spent a good portion of my night worrying about you," he confessed.

I grew concerned at his admission. I knew Levi was worried about what was going on, but he always seemed so in control and levelheaded. Admitting he'd have been lying awake at night worrying about me told me that I might not have realized the severity of the situation. The problem with this is that I already thought it was incredibly serious but not so much that it'd keep Levi awake at night.

"Will you talk to me about why that is?" I asked, hoping I sounded encouraging.

He looked me in the eyes and shared, "A couple of reasons. Any time I have a case, I expect there are unknowns. That's part of the business. But cases like yours have unknowns that I don't like. When my firm is hired by someone who wants to confirm their spouse's fidelity, there's a clear-cut answer to how the case will end. Either someone is being faithful or they aren't. Generally, there isn't some mysterious outcome by which we could be blindsided. In your case, someone is threatening you. We don't know the extent of their obsession with you, and we certainly don't know how far they'll go. Any case like this would make me worry, but it's my second reason that would keep me from sleeping well if you weren't next to me."

He paused.

I waited for him to continue, but when a few seconds had passed and he didn't I asked, "And what's that reason?"

He held my eyes with an intensity I'd never experienced before now.

Finally, he confessed, "The more time I spend with you the more I'm finding that I am no longer just beginning to care about you. I simply do. I care about you, Elle... a whole lot more than I know what to do with."

Holy smokes.

I was so caught off guard that I stared at him in silence. For a long time.

He cared about me a whole lot more than he knew what to do with.

"Levi?" I murmured.

"Yeah?" he whispered back.

"Will you tell me what had you upset on the phone just a few minutes ago?"

He took in a deep breath and let it out before he answered, "You're a very popular woman, Elle."

"What?"

I looked up at him, puzzled at his statement.

He went on to explain, "That was Trent on the phone. He's one of the guys on my team. The guy is a genius on the computer. Anyway, he checked into your social media accounts. There are more than a handful of people with the initials B.B. that follow you."

"I thought you said Michael when you were on the phone," I pointed out.

"Michaels," Levi clarified. "Trent's last name is Michaels. When we are speaking with him, we typically call him by his last name and you'll probably hear the guys call him that when they're talking among each other."

"That makes sense. Okay, so how many followers is more than a handful?"

"Two hundred and fifty-seven not including the ones that could be made into B.B.," he replied. "What I mean by that is, someone who is named William or Robert could easily be called Bill or Bob, but they don't use the nickname on their social media account. Trent has to go through all of those as well, which adds another couple hundred to the list."

I took in a deep breath and began to panic. "Do you think it's one of them? How will Trent know who it is? What's he going to look for? I mean, I can't imagine that there's going to be a big sign on their personal page that says how much they hate me."

Levi's arms tightened around me as he said, "Relax, sunshine. Trent's been doing this a while now. He knows what to look for and he'll do it quickly. I expect he'll get through them all before the end of the weekend."

I relaxed slightly and wondered, "He's going to work over the weekend on this?"

Levi laughed at my question and explained, "Stalkers, criminals, and other bad guys don't just work on their craft during the week. If we don't work on the weekend, that gives them two extra days to do more harm. Regardless, while we give Trent the time he needs to look into this, I'm going to make sure nothing happens to you."

"Okay," I murmured.

"You okay?" he asked.

I cuddled further into him and admitted, "I think I lucked out."

"What does that mean?"

"A few minutes ago, you said that you cared about me a whole lot more than you know what to do with. I think I lucked out because I'm finding that as time goes on, I'm realizing just how much I really, really like you."

He gave me the biggest smile I'd ever seen before he teased, "No kidding?"

I shook my head.

"Well, I'd love the opportunity to show you just how pleased I am to hear you say that."

"What did you have in mind, my superhero?"

"Your superhero?" he asked.

"Are you someone else's?" I retorted.

Levi rolled me to my back and came to hover over me. "Not at all. I'm only yours, sweetness."

As I wrapped my arms around his neck and parted my thighs to allow him to settle between them, I replied, "Good answer."

At that, he dropped his head to mine and pressed a kiss to my lips. I opened my mouth and allowed him to slip his tongue inside. My hands moved along his bare back while his hands slipped up along my sides, my nightie going along for the ride.

Levi's mouth disconnected from mine as he pulled the nightie over my head.

His mouth was inches from my lips when he whispered, "Have I ever told you how much I love that you don't sleep with any panties on?"

I gave him a devious grin and replied, "I don't think you've ever said the words, but you've showed me several times already. That said, I'm loving the fact that you've decided I shouldn't be alone in this and kept your undergarments off last night."

He grinned against my lips while he simultaneously slid his hardened length inside.

"Levi," I moaned.

He thrust slowly in and out of me and growled, "Love that, too."

Levi continued at this slow pace for some time before he pulled out of me.

I whimpered at the loss of him.

"Turn, sweetness," he encouraged, his voice gentle. "I want to take you from behind."

I shuddered at the thought. I turned over and went up on my hands and knees. I arched my back and wiggled my ass in front of him. When I looked back at him, I saw the intense heat in his eyes.

Levi brought his hands to my hips, squeezed, and ordered, "I still want to see your eyes when you come, Elle. Okay?"

"Yes."

My voice was filled with need and lust. I rocked back a bit and pushed my ass into him.

He understood my intent and filled me instantly. My back arched as my head dropped back, exposing my throat. Levi's grip on my hips tightened.

"Fuck." His voice was a deep, throaty growl.

He was no longer interested in taking his time. Levi powered into me from behind. His strokes were long, hard, and incredibly satisfying.

"Oh, God. You feel so good, Levi."

He kept at it. I did my part, though. I dropped to my forearms, keeping my ass in his hands with my back arched, and I squeezed him from the inside.

"Every part of you, Elle," he panted. "It's like honey everywhere. So fucking sweet."

I loved hearing him talk like that. He knew what to do to get me to where I wanted to be, where we both wanted to be, but when he said things like that I climbed to the top so fast. He had me on the edge of soaring.

Levi knew I was close because he ordered, "Give them to me, Elle."

I looked back over my shoulder at him.

He thrust harder, never letting my eyes go.

"Let go and fly, sunshine."

And so I did.

He did, too.

Levi made that happen and I knew that no matter how high he took me, especially with the way he looked in my eyes, he'd always be there to catch me when I came down. That realization flooded through me as I fought to keep my eyes on him.

That was precisely when it happened.

I fell.

I fell so hard for him.

We talked this morning and I told him how much I really, really liked him. It wasn't a lie, but it wasn't the full truth.

I didn't just like Levi.

I was beginning to love him.

A lot.

My orgasm tore through me as Levi slowed his strokes, spilling his hot release inside me, until he eventually stopped moving.

We stayed like that for a bit, the fingers on his hands biting into the flesh on my hips while we stared silently at each other. Something flashed in his eyes before he looked away and pulled out of me.

Whatever just happened was big.

So big, it was beyond words.

After what I had just experienced and the fact that Levi no longer had my hips in his hands, my arms buckled and I collapsed to my belly on the bed.

Levi maneuvered himself around me and fell to his back beside me. He stared up at the ceiling with his forearm draped across his forehead for a long time. His mind was working hard. I left him to it since I was attempting to process my own overwhelming thoughts.

I didn't get very far when Levi turned his head to the side and looked at me.

"Something's changed," he announced.

What?

I lifted my head from the pillow and wondered, "Pardon?"

"You know what I'm talking about, Elle. I know you know exactly the moment I'm referring to. There's no way to deny what just happened."

Fuck.

I wasn't prepared for this conversation.

"Levi, I don't know what you are talking about."

He rolled toward me, pressed a kiss to my temple, and maintained, "Yes, you do. It's okay. I'll wait until you are ready to discuss it."

That made me fall even harder. He wasn't going to push me in this.

I stayed silent and dropped my head back to the pillow.

After some time had passed, Levi changed subjects. "So, I'm not sure what's on your agenda for today before you perform, but I need to get to the venue at some point before this evening. I spoke with the owner of the place earlier this week and explained the situation. He was more than accommodating of my request to check out the venue ahead of time so that I can have a game plan should anything arise."

"Sure," I agreed. "Can we do breakfast first?"

"Of course," he answered. "Go get cleaned up and get ready. I'll take you out for breakfast."

"You don't have to take me out, Levi," I shared as I rolled to my back and sat up in the bed.

"I know," he began as he sat up and kissed my cheek. "But I want to. Now go get ready."

I knew it would be useless to argue about this so, considering I was feeling famished, I scooted out of the bed and walked to the bathroom to clean up and get ready.

Thirty minutes later, Levi and I were on our way to breakfast. We went to a local breakfast joint and ordered. While Levi ordered, I used the opportunity wisely and pulled my phone out of my purse. The moment the waitress walked away, Levi turned his head back to me and smiled. I took a picture.

"Am I going to end up on the internet again?" he teased.

I smiled big at him and nodded.

His lip twitched as he shook his head.

Then, I went about posting the picture of him with the caption: **If touring results in having breakfast across from this guy, I might have to seriously consider more tours.**

After blasting Levi's picture all over the internet, I tossed my phone back in my purse. We spent nearly the next two hours talking and eating. A large majority of my time at breakfast was filled with laughter. It was then that I realized just how true my photo caption was.

There was something about what was happening between the two of us that was so effortless. Levi and I just clicked. It had been that way since the day I met him. The physical attraction was always there, undoubtedly, but it was now so much more than that. Something I couldn't begin to quantify.

The circumstances surrounding us getting together were less than desirable, but it threw us together in a way that made it impossible for us to avoid developing a deeper connection. I found that since I had now experienced life with him, I wasn't sure how I ever lived without him in my life.

It was the little things.

The fact that he accepted me with all my obsessions and never made me feel like a crazy person because of them made me want to hold on to him for a long time. A very long time.

Of course, it was an obsession that led us to this point. Someone else's obsession with me. At least, that's what we were assuming it was for the time being. This was the one thing I wished we didn't have between us now.

Levi is the best at what he does, but it doesn't change the fact that I don't like that we have this to deal with instead of just enjoying getting to know each other better and working on what we have with one another. Even though he does his best to keep himself levelheaded and mostly unaffected, I see how he is when we walk out in public now. His eyes are constantly scanning, looking for any possible threat that may come my way. I hate that for him. For us.

"Are you ready to get out of here, sunshine?" he asked, interrupting my negative thoughts and bringing my attention back to the present moment.

"Yeah."

With that, Levi paid the bill and we left to head over to

the location at which I was going to be performing. Not quite two hours later, we finished at the venue and were on our way back to our hotel. Even though there were still a couple hours left before I was set to head back to the venue, I needed to account for the time it would take me to get ready.

If I was being completely honest, though, I wanted time alone with Levi. When we were at the place I was set to perform, I allowed him to do his thing as I watched. That, coupled with the eye-opening realization I had earlier that morning of where my heart was, made me want to cuddle up in his arms where I felt safe, protected, and dare I say it, loved. Of course, it also brought me a bit of inspiration and had me itching to write some music.

After parking the car outside of the hotel, Levi came around to open my door. As we walked to the door of the hotel, I looked up at him and worried, "I hope you don't mind that I don't have any big plans for the day. Considering I'm performing for the next three nights and there is a flight in the middle of all that, I'd prefer to just take it easy."

Levi opened the door and ushered me inside when we reached the front of the hotel. Once we made it to the elevator, he confirmed, "I'm completely fine with it, Elle. In fact, I'm content to do whatever it is you need me to do to help you relax."

"I'm sorry. I know you are not used to sitting around and doing nothing. I promise I won't make it like this every day. You know, the hotel has a gym if you need to get a workout in."

We stepped inside the empty elevator when the doors opened. Levi hit the button for our floor and pulled me to him as the doors closed.

"I'm not leaving you alone," he informed me. "Besides, I can think of other ways to get a workout in our room."

A knowing smile spread across my face, but I wanted to tease him.

"I said I wanted to take it easy, Levi."

He gave me a sexy grin in return and promised, "You can. I'll do all the work."

I melted into him and he held me tighter. The elevator chimed, indicating we had reached our floor. We stepped off the elevator, walked to our room, and went in.

Then, we spent a good part of the afternoon making sure Levi got a workout in. I didn't let him do all the work, but he was no slouch either. When all was said and done, we were both covered in sweat and breathing heavy. It was then I decided that not all workouts were bad.

CHAPTER 11

Elle

"**I** KNEW IT WAS GOING TO WORK."

I said this to Levi as we packed up our things to head to the airport. We were leaving this morning to go to Phoenix for my show this evening.

Last night, I performed at the Denver venue. There was an amazing turn out. Back in Rising Sun, I had grown used to the crowds. I was a hometown favorite; I expected the reception I received there. Denver proved to me that I didn't need to be a local for fans to come out in droves to see me, and that blew me away.

So, the night was a success.

On all fronts.

Levi was on this trip with me because I was dealing with the stalker situation, but it was as though it didn't exist last night. This was precisely what I was referring to when I made my statement to Levi just now.

"You knew what was going to work?" he asked.

"My post. Before we left your place on Thursday. The one of you, Cruz, Pierce, and Dom. Last night was smooth sailing. I think my stalker has gone running scared."

"As much as I wish that were true and hope that would be the case, I'm afraid that one night of no activity does not equal your stalker running scared," he advised.

"Sure it does," I insisted.

"Sunshine, I don't want to burst your bubble or dim this glow of happiness you have right now, but I'm telling you that I've been doing this long enough to know that it's not over yet. People who become obsessed like this might go quiet for a few days, but they don't just stop."

I dropped my shoulders and head in defeat.

Levi walked over and placed my chin between his thumb and forefinger. He lifted my head to his and reassured me, "It's going to take time, Elle. I'm frustrated, too. Do your best to focus on the things that make you happy, like singing, and I'll worry about this situation."

"You really don't think it's over?" I asked.

His head tilted to the side and his face warmed. "I'm sorry, but I know it's not."

The look on his face told me that he wished he could have given me a different answer. Seeing it made me realize that as much as I hated hearing what he said, he was even more disappointed that he had to admit it. Not wanting to make him feel even worse about the whole debacle, I decided to move on.

"So, Phoenix is next. Are you ready?"

He nodded and added, "I love watching you sing, El. There's nothing quite like it. Though, I'll be happier when I can enjoy it without having to worry that someone has it out for you."

"Me too," I agreed.

Levi kissed my head and motioned toward the door, "Come on. Let's get you on your plane and to your next group of fans. Pierce should be there when we arrive. His plane is set to land about twenty minutes before ours."

With that, we were out the door and on the way to the airport.

A couple hours later we had gone from the beautiful

mountains of Colorado to the stifling heat of the Arizona desert.

Just as Levi said he would be, Pierce was there waiting for us when we arrived.

We walked out to the rental car and I listened as Levi and Pierce talked.

"Michaels was halfway through the list when I left today. Nothing obvious yet, but he has two that he is having Tyson do a little digging on. While he's pretty sure they're clear, those two accounts didn't sit well with him. He just wants to be certain there isn't anything he overlooked," Pierce informed him.

"Right. And the Phoenix venue?" Levi pressed.

"I contacted them when your flight landed. Told them we arrived and needed to check it out. They are waiting for us now. I figured we could head there before checking in at the hotel."

"Agreed."

We arrived at the rental and I interrupted the conversation.

"Hey guys?" I called.

They both turned their attention toward me.

"I'm cool with whatever you need to do to continue being the superheroes that you are and if checking out the venue now is needed, that's fine. However, I've been to Phoenix a few times in my life and when I'm here I always get lunch at least once at my favorite place, which is in Tempe. Would we be able to make a stop for lunch between the venue and the hotel?"

Pierce agreed with a shrug of his shoulders, a nod. "That's cool with me," he said.

Levi's eyes cut to Pierce and he informed him, "Her eating habits are shit. You could have just agreed to the worst meal you'll ever have in your life."

Pierce's gaze came back to mine and he looked worried.

Apparently, Levi wasn't the only health nut in the bunch.

"Relax," I began. "We're going to The Chuckbox."

"The what?" Levi asked.

"The Chuckbox," I answered nonchalantly. "And we are going there so I can get *The Big One*."

Pierce chuckled, "Sounds promising already."

"Dear God, I hope we don't die," Levi announced.

I was slightly ticked off when I warned, "You're going to regret you said that. You have no idea on all the goodness you are about to experience. In fact, I'm going to promise you now that I won't even rub it in your face when you're eating your words."

Levi just laughed at me and opened the door of the rental to let me in.

For the next hour, I fantasized about my upcoming meal while Levi and Pierce scoped out the venue. When they finally finished and were ready to leave, I had to stop myself from jumping for joy.

Lunchtime.

I've never been good with remembering details of how to get to places if I've only ever visited them a couple of times, but when it came to places like The Chuckbox, I always remembered. I gave Levi directions and before I knew it, we were pulling off University Drive into the parking lot.

"Are you sure this is the right place, Elle? I don't see a restaurant," Levi questioned.

"Turn around," I said from beside him in the car.

He turned his head and looked at the building behind us. Pierce, who was sitting in the backseat, had turned to look as well. They sat, staring at the not so large building on the corner. There were misters hung above the covered outdoor seating spraying water to help with the dry, desert heat. The outdoor seating consisted of tables with tree stumps used for seats.

My belly growled at the thought of mouthwatering delights that awaited me.

"You're kidding, right?"

I turned to look at Levi. He was practically scowling.

"What does this place even serve?"

"Oh. Only the *best* burger you will ever eat in your entire life. They have a few other items on the menu, but I highly suggest you get a burger."

Levi stared at me.

"Come on," I began. "Just trust me."

I turned in my seat and didn't wait for Levi to come open my door. I hopped out of the rental and walked away as Pierce and Levi followed behind me. I was practically jumping out of my shoes, I was so excited.

We walked inside and I was shocked to see that we had entered at just the right time. The lunch crowd had not yet arrived. With only one small group of four ahead of us, I took the time to tell my superheroes about the menu.

"So, there are different sizes for the burgers. You both could easily handle The Great Big One, probably even the Double Great Big One. Regardless, you order the size you want, tell them which cheese you prefer, and whether you want it on a wheat or white bun. After it's made, you can put any condiments you want on it from the condiment bar over there."

I pointed to the condiment bar in the middle of the room.

The people in front of us had ordered and it was my turn. Since they hadn't moved out of the way yet while they waited for their food, I did what the locals did and shouted my order.

"A big one with cheddar cheese on a white bun," I shouted.

"Fries?" he yelled back.

"Yes!"

"Next!"

He looked to Levi. I looked up to see him looking a little nervous at the thought of shouting his order out.

"Levi, you have to tell him what you want."

"A great big one with cheddar on wheat!"

A grin spread across my face.

"Fries?"

"No!"

I laughed. Levi needed to learn to live a little. I'd be sure to pass off some of my fries to him.

Before I had the chance to do anything else I heard Pierce shout, "A great big one with American on wheat."

"Fries?"

"Ah, what the hell," he mumbled under his breath. "Sure," he shouted back.

Yes! Hearing that gave me hope for Levi down the road. Maybe with a little work, I could get him to chill out every now and then for a special occasion.

Not long after we gave our orders, our food was ready. We picked up our trays with the food and grabbed drinks. We all settled on water. Pierce and I stopped at the condiment bar. Then, we moved to the table where Levi was sitting, waiting for us.

"No ketchup?" I asked as I sat on a log next to him.

"You said it's the best burger I'm ever going to have. I don't think it'll be good to ruin it with ketchup."

"Fair enough."

Pierce joined us and I couldn't wait any longer. I dove in and took the biggest bite. I closed my eyes, dropped my head back, and moaned. I had so missed this. I chewed, swallowed, and opened my eyes. I took another bite and looked to the side to find Levi holding his burger in front of his face, but his face turned toward me.

"What?" I asked, my mouth full of food.

"It's so good you're moaning?"

I slowly nodded my head.

A few seconds passed before Levi turned his head back to his burger and took a bite. As I watched, waiting for his reaction, I popped a fry in my mouth. He chewed, swallowed, and took another bite.

Yep.

He knew it was good.

I smiled inwardly and went back to my burger. After a few more bites, I looked back to Levi and found he was looking at me again.

"I'm sorry," he sighed.

"For what?"

"You were right. This place might not seem like much, but it's incredible. I think it was the best burger I've ever had," he shared.

I held a fry up between us and asked, "Care to try a fry?"

He lowered his head to my hand and used his mouth to take the fry from my fingers.

I pulled my lower lip in between my teeth and kept my eyes on his mouth as Levi ate the fry.

"Jesus Christ," Pierce mumbled from the other side of the table. Our eyes went to him and he continued, "I might have just had the best burger I've ever eaten as well, but if this little show is any indication of what I'm in for through the LA performance I might have to reconsider going anywhere but the venues with you two."

"Sorry, Pierce," I murmured. I had completely forgotten he was there. "That wasn't nice of us. I promise we will behave from here on out."

"Don't make promises you can't keep, Elle," Levi warned, clearly not in agreement with my sentiments.

"I can keep that promise," I retorted. "You think I can't resist your charm?"

"Shit," Pierce hissed.

I think he sensed a bit of danger in the air at my challenge to Levi.

"I know you can't," Levi began. "But it'll be adorable to watch you try, sunshine."

I narrowed my eyes at him and went back to my burger. To be quite honest, I wasn't sure if I could resist him. I mean nobody could tell me that this man wasn't impeccably beautiful.

Thirty minutes later, with a happy belly, I was back in the car with Levi and Pierce on the way to our hotel. This was, of course, not before I documented my lunch escapades with them. I didn't simply snap a photo this time, though. I took a short video clip and posted that instead with the caption: **Lunch with superheroes.**

Not long after I was back in the rental car, I checked my phone and saw that I had already received an overwhelming response to the video I had posted. If I had to guess, I'd say at least ninety percent of them were women who were drooling over Levi and Pierce wanting more details on them.

I turned in the seat and looked back to Pierce.

"Are you single?" I asked.

"I'm sorry?" he responded, obviously taken aback by my question.

I held up my phone and explained, "I put up a video clip of you and Levi at lunch with me. The women are drooling over both of you."

Pierce rolled his eyes.

I continued to wait for an answer.

"You're serious?"

I lifted my eyebrows and nodded.

"Yeah, I'm single."

"Great," I beamed as I turned back in my seat to face the front. "I'll let all the ladies know you are on the market."

I typed out a reply on my post letting everyone know that Levi was spoken for but that Pierce was a free agent.

Replies immediately poured in. Everything ranging from women leaving their phone numbers and asking if he had his own social media accounts to some giving detailed replies of what they wanted to do to him.

I laughed out loud.

"Do you have any social media accounts, Pierce?"

"No," he answered immediately.

Damn it.

"Okay, then do you mind taking off your shirt for a photo?"

"Elle?" Levi called from beside me in the driver's seat. His tone indicated he was growing short on patience.

"Yeah?"

"Pierce isn't taking off his shirt so you can take a picture of him," he growled.

"It's not for me, Levi. It's for the ladies."

"I don't give a shit who it's for—it's not happening."

I let out a huff and sat back in my seat.

"Fine, but when Pierce misses out on meeting the woman of his dreams, just remember that it was you who denied him that opportunity."

Levi laughed as he insisted, "Pierce, I'm sure, is not looking for the woman of his dreams on the internet, Elle. And if he were, I'm guessing he could manage that on his own."

"Hey, you can't rule it out. You never know where you'll find love. It could happen in the unlikeliest of places."

We had just pulled into a parking space at the hotel when Levi turned off the rental and looked at me, "You've got that right, sunshine."

My lips parted and my lungs stopped functioning. Levi winked at me and got out of the vehicle to come around to open my door. I continued to stare at the space where Levi once was.

"Looks like someone just got the shock of a lifetime," Pierce's voice filtered into my ears from the backseat.

I slowly turned my head to him and whispered as I trailed off, "Did he just…"

A beautiful smile spread across Pierce's face.

"Yep," he started before his eyes went to my door. "Pull it together, rock star. Incoming."

He moved to get out of the car as I heard my door open. I twisted my body and shifted in the seat. Levi's eyes were burning into mine. He held his hand out to me. I placed my hand in his and stepped out.

Levi and Pierce grabbed the bags and we all went to check in. At Levi's insistence, his receptionist at Cunningham Security, Deb, managed to secure a separate room for Pierce on the same floor as us. The three of us rode the elevator together to the top floor.

We stepped off and found that Pierce's room was two doors down from ours. Levi waved the key card in front of the sensor on the door and the lock clicked. He pushed the door opened and allowed me to step inside. As I walked in I heard him speak to Pierce.

"Don't care if you step out for a bit; you've got the spare key for the rental. I just need you ready to head out in about four and a half hours."

"I'm staying in," I heard Pierce reply.

I continued to walk into our suite and straight for the bathroom. Exhaustion.

Mostly mental at this point.

Since I had the time, I figured I'd take a quick shower and then nap for an hour before I had to start making an effort to make myself look decent. I didn't want to admit that I was also doing this to avoid what had just happened out in the car.

I walked into the bathroom and immediately turned on the shower before walking back out into the bedroom to take off my shoes. Levi stepped into the room moments later with the bags. He had a puzzled look on his face, but remained silent. I grabbed my bag with the toiletries in it and took it with me into the bathroom.

Levi didn't follow.

After I spent longer than usual in the shower, attempting to delay the start of a conversation I wasn't sure I was prepared to have, I finished my business in the bathroom and emerged in one of my nighties.

Levi was sitting on the edge of the bed, his elbows on his thighs, his hands clasped together, and his head down. He looked up when I walked into the room.

His face was littered with concern.

It made me feel horrible to see him like that.

"Elle, are you okay?" he asked gently.

Now I felt even worse.

I shrugged and responded, "I'm just tired from all the traveling. I was hoping to take a quick nap before I have to get ready for the show."

He stood up from the bed and walked to me. Levi's strong, protective arms wrapped around me and I melted right into him, pressing my cheek to his chest.

"You can talk to me, sunshine. I know it's more than that."

I took in a deep breath and blew it out.

"I don't know what to say, Levi," I admitted. "There's a lot happening in my head at the moment with everything that's going on right now between the tour, the stalker, and us. I'm having a hard time sorting it all out. I just need a little time."

His arms tightened around me as he pressed a kiss to the top of my head.

"Take the time you need. I'm not going anywhere. One thing

I'm going to ask is that you don't shut down on me. If you need time, take it. If it becomes too much to handle on your own, please come and talk to me. Okay?"

I inhaled his scent before I let out a breath and whispered, "Thank you."

"No problem. You need some sleep?"

I nodded into his shirt.

"Alright. Do you want me with you or do you need time alone?"

God. He was so incredibly good to me.

"You can stay if you want, but I'll be alright by myself."

"I'll give you time on your own. If you are okay with it, I'm thinking I'll call Pierce and have him come here. I'd really like to get a workout in, but I don't want to leave you alone. Pierce can stay out in the other room while you sleep. Does that work for you?"

"Sure," I answered quietly.

"I'll set the hotel phone to 'Do Not Disturb' so it doesn't wake you. You set the alarm for whatever time you want to get up. I'll get in a workout and come back in plenty of time to shower and be ready to go."

"That works."

"Get in bed," he urged me.

I walked to the bed, pulled back the blanket, and climbed in. My head hit the pillow and Levi stood there looking at me, pure adoration present in his features.

"You are so beautiful," he started as he moved toward me. After pressing a soft kiss to my lips, he stated, "I'll be back soon. I won't leave until Pierce is here. Get some rest, sweetness."

He turned and walked out of the room.

Within minutes, and even though my head was a mess of thoughts, I fell asleep.

CHAPTER 12

Elle

FELT LIKE I HAD JUST CLOSED MY EYES WHEN THE ALARM WENT off, indicating I needed to get up and get ready for my show. I reached over to the bedside table and turned off the alarm.

Keeping my eyes closed, I tried to process where my head was. I found that all my nap did for me for the last hour was take me away from the thoughts that consumed me. I was no closer to sorting my feelings on any of it. Unfortunately, needing to get ready for the show took priority, so I couldn't spend any time now trying to figure it out either.

I sat up in the bed and twisted my body to get out. When I did, I saw the red light lit up on the hotel phone, indicating there was a message left. I picked up the phone and pushed the button to listen to the message.

I was horrified the second the voice piped through the phone. Barely three words had been said before I threw the phone and screamed.

The bedroom door flew open a second later and Pierce took in the scene. The phone was no longer on the bedside table and I was sitting on the edge of the bed, shaking and out of breath.

"What happened?" he asked.

I couldn't stop shaking. Not only was it physically

noticeable, but I could feel my insides trembling. My stomach was clenching and I felt sick.

Pierce must have realized I was about to completely lose it. He came over, sat next to me on the bed, and wrapped his arms around me.

"Relax, honey. Tell me what happened."

My arms bent and my hands rested on his forearms. I was so terrified I felt my fingernails dig into the skin on his arms. I felt bad, but I couldn't control it.

I took in two deep breaths, trying to settle myself. It was useless.

"There was a message," I managed to get out. "On the hotel phone."

"Okay," he replied.

I was still shaking so bad, but I felt Pierce run his hand up and down my back trying to settle me.

"Can you tell me what it said?"

I shook my head furiously, felt the tears welling up in my eyes, and rasped, "The voice. It was so scary. I couldn't listen to it."

"Alright. It's okay, rock star. Just breathe and try to relax," he said softly.

I took in two more breaths and proclaimed, "I need a new name, Pierce. Rock stars are badasses. You and Levi are rock stars. I'm not. I'm fucking terrified."

My body began to tremble uncontrollably again as the tears rolled down my face.

"Elle, honey, calm down."

Seconds passed and I heard the door to the room open and close. Pierce's body went solid, which made me tense. Despite the rigidity in his body, he continued to move his hand along my back trying to comfort me.

"What the fuck?" Levi roared.

My eyes shot to his and the second he saw mine he moved quickly to me.

As he came around the other side of me and pulled me out of Pierce's arms and into his lap, he ordered, "Reynolds, update me."

"I don't know much," Pierce explained. "I was out in the other room when I heard the crash and her scream. I came in to find the phone over there on the floor and Elle shaking and terrified on the edge of the bed. She said there was a message, but the voice was too scary. She didn't listen to it."

"Listen to it," Levi seethed.

As Pierce moved to pick up the phone, Levi's hold on me grew tighter. One hand went to the hair at the back of my head while his lips touched my temple. He kissed me lightly there and brought his mouth to my ear.

"I've got you, sunshine," he whispered.

I shifted my body in his lap, trying to get closer to him.

There were several moments of silence that passed before I heard Pierce place the phone back on the receiver.

"What is it?" Levi asked.

I lifted my head from Levi's chest to look at Pierce. His expression was a mix of anger and caution.

He gave Levi a slight shake of his head and stated, "A voice changer was used to leave the message. That's why she was terrified listening to it."

"What was said?" I asked.

Pierce's eyes came to mine and his expression went from angry to calm when he answered, "I'm going to let Levi make that call. I'm not going to be the one to deliver this to you."

"Give me the phone," Levi asserted, holding his hand out.

When he had the phone up to his ear, he nodded at Pierce indicating he should play the message.

Levi's grip on the back of my neck tightened as he listened.

"Play it again," he ordered.

After listening a second time, he pulled the phone away from his ear and handed it back to Pierce.

"Start looking into this for me. See if we can track down where the call came from."

Pierce nodded and took off.

Then, Levi's eyes came to mine. "Do you trust me to take care of this for you?" he asked.

I nodded, "Of course, I trust you. What did the message say?"

He held my eyes and remained quiet.

"Tell me," I pleaded.

"Elle, I really don't want to do that."

"Please," I continued to beg.

A look of defeat washed over his face as he took in a breath. He then shared the chilling message with me.

"What makes you think you deserve to have it all? I'm watching, you greedy…" he trailed off, struggling to tell me the rest.

"Bitch?" I guessed.

He shook his head.

"What?"

"It's not worth repeating and is certainly something I'm not going to say to you. Regardless, it wasn't nice."

"Was that all?"

"No," he answered. "You can't have it all anymore. Somebody has to stop you."

"Oh my God. Levi, what do you think they're going to do?"

"If I have anything to say about it, nothing. But if you're asking what I think they have planned, I honestly don't know. I'm sorry I left you here."

I dropped my head to his shoulder and gave myself a few

minutes to come to terms with what had just happened. It took some time, but sitting there being held by Levi brought me comfort. When I felt significantly calmer, I spoke.

"It's not your fault," I tried to reassure him. "It would have happened whether you were here or not. You made sure I was physically safe by having Pierce here. I'm okay now, but I'm behind schedule. We have to leave soon and I need to make myself look decent."

"You look beautiful, Elle."

My arms tightened around him, giving him a hug.

"Are you okay?"

I pulled my face from his neck, kissed him on the lips, and answered, "I am now, thanks to my superhero."

"Alright, I need to shower," he declared. "Hopefully by the time I'm finished, Pierce will have some news for me. I need to see what I can get handled before it's time to leave."

"Okay."

Levi kissed me before standing with me and making sure I was steady on my feet. Then, he walked to the door of the hotel room where he set the latch and the lock on the door. After, he moved to the bathroom to shower.

I needed to get started on my hair and makeup, so after picking out my clothes I moved to the bathroom where my makeup and other toiletries were. Levi was still in the shower and as I stepped into the room, his head turned in my direction.

His body.

If this stalker situation hadn't taken up so much of my time just a little bit ago, I would have climbed in there with him. Unfortunately, I was running behind so getting in the shower with him was not an option.

"Sorry," I yelled out so he could hear me over the water. "I need to get to work on my hair and makeup."

"I don't mind. Do whatever you need to do, sweetness."

I loved when he called me that.

I started on my hair and got about halfway through it when it hit me. There was something about this moment that was so intimate, so wonderful. Sure, we were in a hotel, but this felt natural. I was doing my hair in front of the bathroom mirror while Levi took a shower.

I loved it.

Not more than two hours ago my head was a mess of confused thoughts and now it couldn't be any clearer. I didn't know if it was the fact that he gave me what I needed by giving me time to myself earlier to nap and collect my thoughts, the comfort he gave me the second I was in his arms after that voicemail, or this very moment standing in the bathroom with him while we got ready together, but the steam from the shower was doing little to hide what was now so evident.

Levi was mine.

I was his.

And I loved him.

The feeling was overwhelming and I tried my best to re-main focused on finishing my hair. Somehow, I got through it and finished the last section as Levi turned off the water in the shower. I set my curling iron down, unplugged it, and watched him in the mirror.

He dried himself off and wrapped the towel around his waist.

My mouth watered at the sight of him.

I needed to distract myself, so I pulled out my toothbrush and began brushing. Oddly enough, Levi walked over next to me and pulled out his as well. Then it was the two of us standing there brushing our teeth together. I couldn't stand it anymore. I quickly finished, rinsed out my mouth, and lifted my head up to look at him in the mirror again.

I stared.

He noticed, finished brushing, and held my eyes.

When I said nothing, he spoke.

"Elle, what's wrong?"

My eyes searched his face, but I couldn't manage to find my words there.

"I can see it," he started. "Please say whatever it is because I know with that look in your eyes it can't be bad."

"I think…" I trailed off, unsure of myself.

He waited.

My throat was tight, but I finally managed to get out, "I think I'm in love with you, Levi."

A grin slowly spread across his face before he teased, "It's about fuckin' time."

Shocked, I asked, "What?"

"Sunshine, I fell in love with you the first time I heard you sing. After that, I knew there was no way out when you looked at me with those eyes."

"Levi," I whispered.

I watched in the mirror as he moved closer to me. He stood behind me as his hands went to the hem of my nightie. He slid the satin up my sides and over my head.

"I have to get ready," I said softly.

"You just told me you love me, Elle. I need to show you what that means to me. You've got to give me this," he pleaded as his fingertips began tracing slowly over the skin at my hips.

"You could show me when we get back tonight," I suggested.

"I'll do it then, too," he promised. "I'm begging you. Please don't make me wait until tonight to make love to you."

I couldn't say no to that, so I said nothing.

Levi's hands moved from my hips to my belly. One hand traveled up to cup one of my breasts, while the other moved down my abdomen and stopped right between my legs.

I leaned back into him.

As his fingers slid through the wetness, I tilted my head back into his chest and looked up at him.

When his gaze came to mine and one of his fingers had entered my body, I acquiesced, "Okay, Levi. Make love to me."

He lowered his head to mine and claimed my mouth. This kiss was different. It was passionate but possessive. His finger continued to slowly move in and out of my body while his other hand slid up over my breasts, past the skin at my throat, and around the back of my head into my hair.

I moaned into his mouth and reached my hand back behind me to run over the length of him. Finding the edge of the towel, I opened it and put my hand back on him, where I began stroking him. Now, it was Levi's turn to groan into my mouth.

After a few minutes of the two of us doing a lot of touching, Levi picked me up and carried me out of the bathroom and back into the bedroom. He put me down on my back in the bed and settled himself between my parted thighs.

"I wanted to take you in my mouth," I confessed.

"Later, sunshine," he said, his voice husky. "Right now, I want to love you."

When he put it like that I couldn't help but give him what he wanted, so I agreed, "Okay, whatever you want."

That was it.

The next thing I knew, Levi was inside me.

Filling me.

Loving me.

He took his time with me, moving slowly and building me up.

My hands moved along the solid muscle of his arms and shoulders while I moved my hips against his. The soles of my feet were planted in the bed, helping me get the leverage I needed to move with him.

"Levi," I whispered, as my head fell to the side.

"Give me your eyes."

It took me a few seconds, but I managed to bring my eyes back to him. Knowing how I felt in this moment, about him and the connection between our bodies, I was certain he was getting the sexiest, liquid honey eyes he had ever seen.

"Such sweetness," he rasped.

Yep. I knew it.

"I'm going to come, Levi," I told him.

"Wait for me, Elle."

Oh God.

No.

I couldn't.

It was too much.

He felt too good.

"Levi, please. Hurry."

He picked up his pace, ever so slightly. This only served to increase the need I had to give in to the pleasure and let go.

"Say it, sunshine."

"What?"

"Tell me. I want to hear you say it."

It took me a few seconds, but I realized what he wanted.

"I love you."

"I love you, too."

Oh my. Hearing the words sent me over the edge.

"Levi," I called out as my orgasm tore through me.

"Oh fuck, Elle," he growled as he came with me, our eyes never leaving each other.

Levi pumped his hips against mine a few more times before he collapsed against me and quickly rolled to his back. He wrapped an arm around my back and took me with him.

After giving ourselves several minutes to come down from the high, Levi spoke. "Feels so good."

With my cheek to his chest and my fingertips tracing lazy patterns over the skin there, I asked, "What does?"

"To know that I can finally tell you how I feel about you whenever I want and not have to worry about you running scared."

"Did you really fall in love with me the first time you heard me sing?"

"I can't sit here and say I am so sure of myself," he confessed. "I knew there was something about you that I hadn't ever felt before. I couldn't explain it at the time to be anything more than just a serious attraction. As I began spending time with you, that feeling grew deeper. The day before we left for Denver and I heard you on the phone with your girl, I knew. You were about to get off the phone with her and you told her you loved her."

I lifted my head to look at him and wondered out loud, "What does me talking to Leah and telling her I love her have to do with how you feel about me?"

"When I heard you say that to her, all I could think was that I wished I was on the receiving end of that sentiment."

I tilted my head to the side and took in his contented face.

"I'm sorry you had to wait to hear it."

"It only matters now that I've heard it. Twice. And it feels so good, Elle."

I agreed, "Yeah, it does."

My head went back to Levi's chest where I stayed for a few minutes wrapped up in his arms. Then, even though I really wanted to stay right where I was, I knew I needed to get ready for my show.

"I have to finish getting ready. I have zero makeup on and I'm convinced I now have sex hair. I can't go out there to perform looking like this."

Levi rolled me to my back and said, "You look sexy as fuck

right now, sunshine. But, you're right, you better go get ready because I don't want anyone else seeing you looking like this. This look is just for me."

I cocked an eyebrow at him.

He ignored it and kissed me on the lips. "I'm going to throw some clothes on and call Pierce. Finish getting ready. We'll be ready to go whenever you are."

"Okay."

"Love you, Elle."

As the warmth spread through my body hearing him say those words to me, I beamed, "I love you, too."

The joy in his expression was undeniable.

I loved seeing it.

He gave me one more peck on the lips before he got up out of the bed and reached out a hand to help me up. I took off to the bathroom to finish getting ready while he got dressed and walked out into the living space to handle business.

A few minutes later, I heard the hotel door open when Pierce arrived but did my best to block out the reason he was there. The simple fact was that I was in a situation that I couldn't control. Sure, I guess there were plenty of things that I could do to help myself in this situation, but the reality is that it's not what I do.

I sing.

I read.

I write music.

I play my guitar.

I hang out with my friends.

I spend time with my family.

I buy copious amounts of lip balm.

I do not investigate.

I do not fight bad guys.

I wouldn't lie. When I thought about the situation too

much, it scared me. I experienced anxiety over it, but I had someone I believed I could depend on to keep me safe.

And the best thing about all of it now was that I was in love. I just told Levi how I felt, found out that he felt the same about me, and I wanted to live in that moment now. I could allow what happened today to consume my thoughts and prevent me from doing what I loved, but I refused.

I was in love.

Nobody was going to do anything to put a damper on that. At least, not today.

On that thought, I put on my pomegranate flavored lip balm, gave myself a once-over, and walked out to meet Levi and Pierce. I walked up to Levi, gave him a quick kiss on the lips, watched his eyes heat, and left for my show.

Levi, I'm certain, decided he liked pomegranates.

CHAPTER 13

Levi

"**D**O I LOOK OKAY?"

Elle.

Fuck, but did I love her.

We were currently in Tucson. We spent the night in Phoenix last night and got up this morning to make the two-hour drive to Tucson, where she was performing for the third time in as many nights. Elle performed last night and, thankfully, there was no additional contact from her stalker.

That situation had been pissing me off since day number one when Elle showed up at my office terrified out of her mind, but now I was beyond pissed. My girl was being targeted by someone for reasons unknown to all of us and every time I turned around my team and I were hitting dead ends.

I've had previous cases where the person of interest was elusive and very difficult to locate. We worked our asses off and would eventually find our target. It required a great deal of patience and levelheadedness, which was something I always had the luxury of having, the ability to persevere and remain rational when things were getting difficult.

Unfortunately, now that Elle was involved, I was finding that I didn't have so much tolerance and I was afraid that it'd eventually make me do something illogical. I wasn't prepared to see harm come her way and what I told her brother the day we filled him in on the situation was the truth. I'd lay down my life to protect her if it ever came to pass.

My little ray of sunshine.

There was no better way to describe her.

She lit up my world just being in it. It was evident her friends adored her. When she got onstage, I knew her fans felt the same way. Elle was the kind of person that made everyone happy. When she walked into the room, she didn't need to be loud or obnoxious to get noticed. She was the kind of person that most people couldn't help but be drawn to.

Of course, I also received admission from her yesterday that she had fallen in love with me. Now that I had that, I wasn't liking the fact that I may need to die to keep her safe. Obviously, I wouldn't think twice about it, but I was finding that I very much enjoyed being with her.

As I looked at her now, standing in front of me all dolled up ready for her show tonight, I couldn't help but let that feeling of contentment spread through me. And she wanted to know if she looked okay.

"No," I answered honestly.

Her eyes rounded and she took a step back as she looked down at what she was wearing. I had to laugh. She couldn't seriously think she looked bad.

"Sunshine, you don't just look okay. You look magnificent," I quickly explained.

"I was getting ready to go change my whole outfit," she retorted. "That wasn't nice!"

"Sorry, Elle, but it's just too easy to get you. Give it some time; you'll soon learn that no matter what you're wearing or what your hair and makeup look like, I always think you look beautiful."

"Levi…" She trailed off as she stepped back into me and

wrapped her arms around my waist. She pressed her cheek to my chest and held on tight.

I put one hand in her hair at her neck and kissed the top of her head.

"Are you ready for your performance tonight?" I asked.

"Yeah, but I'm exhausted. I'm so happy I have the day off tomorrow and don't have to perform again until Tuesday night. Of course, having to get on a plane tomorrow is not my idea of fun either. I hate flying."

"So, let's drive," I suggested.

Elle pulled back and looked up at me. "What?"

"If you don't want to fly, we can drive. You don't have to perform until Tuesday night in LA. From here to LA is what? Seven hours? I'll drive you."

"You'll road trip with me?"

"To be honest, I'd prefer to do that instead of flying as well."

"I think I really, really like you," she joked.

I brought my lips to within inches of hers and corrected her, "I think what you meant to say is that you really, really love me."

"That, too," she approved just before she kissed me.

She tasted like watermelon.

This woman and the flavored lip balms. I used to think it was innocent, but now I had a feeling she purposely put it on before she'd kiss me. I knew flavored lip moisturizers were a thing, but not in the variety that Elle had exposed me to. I didn't know any flavors existed beyond cherry and strawberry. Oddly enough, I wasn't sure I had tasted either of these flavors on her lips yet even though I'd spent quite a bit of time kissing her lately. To top it off, I had yet to taste the same flavor on her more than once.

Last night, it was pomegranate.

Pomegranate.

Who the fuck makes pomegranate lip balm?

Now, watermelon.

If she kept this shit up, I'd be happy to spend the rest of my life kissing this woman and doing nothing else.

I tore my mouth from hers, kissed her on the forehead, and said, "Come on. Let's get you to the venue so I can get started on spending more than a few hours with you alone and uninterrupted."

Her body visibly reacted with a shiver before she nodded at me.

She turned to walk toward the door when she stopped and inquired, "Wait. You won't have me alone. What about Pierce?"

"Pierce has a plane ticket, Elle. Not only do I want you to myself for the drive, but I'm willing to bet Pierce wants nothing to do with a seven-hour road trip in the car with us. He'll fly and meet us in LA."

"Oh, okay," she sang, approving of this arrangement.

She turned back on her heel and made her way to the door of the hotel room. I followed directly behind her.

Pierce was waiting for us just outside the elevator, so the three of us made our way to the venue for Elle's performance.

A few hours later, I was relieved that we had gotten through another night on this tour without any incidents. I walked Elle backstage to her dressing room, so she could grab her things. When we got back there, she asked, "Do you mind staying for a drink or two? I figure since we don't need to worry about being on someone else's schedule tomorrow and can go whenever we're ready, it's okay if we sleep in a little. And this place reminds me a little bit of Lou's. I'm feeling a bit homesick and would love to just take some time to enjoy the fact that I'm almost halfway through this tour."

I could give her that. As much as I wanted to take her back to the hotel and keep her to myself, I also wanted to make sure she could let loose a little. Besides, if she had a couple of drinks in her before I took her back to the hotel, I figured that wouldn't hurt in the least.

"Sure," I agreed.

We walked back out to the front. I told Pierce we were going to stay so Elle could have a drink and then we'd be heading out. He didn't mind.

After ordering Elle a drink from the bar, we found a booth and sat down.

"You guys are going to make me drink alone?" she asked.

"I'm driving, El," I answered. "And I don't drink."

Pierce replied, "I'm on the job. Drinking is not an option."

"Well, if I had known that we could have just gone back to the hotel. I feel bad now."

I was about to respond, but Pierce attempted to convince her it was fine before I could. "It's been three days of performing, Elle. You can take a minute to breathe if that's what you need. I don't mind and I'm willing to bet Levi doesn't either. It's okay. Just relax and enjoy yourself for a minute, honey."

"Thanks, Pierce. I appreciate that."

The three of us spent the next hour or so in that booth giving Elle the break she had been craving. She did a lot of talking and asked Pierce and me all about the work we do. She wanted to know the kinds of cases we worked, which were our favorite, which we despised, and how dangerous things got sometimes. We answered what we could and I did my best to make sure she knew that no matter what the danger was that we faced, my entire team was highly skilled. We knew what to do in a high-pressure situation and had the training to handle ourselves well. The last thing I wanted was her worrying about what could potentially happen.

After finishing her third drink, Elle announced, "Okay, I'm going to head to the ladies' room and then we can get out of here. Thanks again for giving me this."

As I stood to let her out of the booth, I responded, "Anytime, sunshine. Whatever you need, just ask." I squeezed her hand before I continued, "I'm watching you all the way there and back. Got it?"

She looked toward the bathroom. It was only about twenty-five feet away from where we were seated and, after realizing I had a clear line of sight to the door of the ladies' room, Elle nodded her head at me.

She took off toward the bathroom, and I watched her all the way there. Once she pushed through the door and stepped inside, I sat watching the door like a hawk. I didn't have to look at Pierce to know he was doing the same.

A waitress came up and asked if we needed refills. I never took my eyes off the bathroom door. I heard Pierce tell her we were all good. A few minutes had passed at this point, and that's when the door opened and Elle stepped out. Her eyes locked with mine and I knew immediately something wasn't right.

Not taking my eyes off her, I stood and ordered the waitress to call the police.

"What? Why?"

"Just do it," I demanded.

"Reynolds," I bit out.

He was moving right behind me. As we made our way across the room toward her, I saw it happen. A man in a hooded sweatshirt grabbed her around the waist and pulled her down the hall in the opposite direction. A woman, who I hadn't seen before, had been standing directly behind Elle and followed them down the hall.

Pierce and I struggled to make our way through the crowd

of people and all I could think about was getting to my girl.

We made it to the hallway, where the crowd had significantly thinned out, and took off running. Sure enough, there was an exit door that led out to the parking lot in the rear of the building. We stepped outside and I scanned the dimly lit lot searching for signs of her.

"There," Pierce said from beside me as he pointed in the direction of where Elle was being held up against a car with this man hovering over her pressing his body into hers.

She was on the other side of the parking lot.

Fuck.

We ran.

I could tell she was struggling against him.

Fight, sunshine.

We were maybe fifty feet away when Elle yelled out to me.

"Levi!"

She was terrified.

His hand was around her throat, so she struggled to get out that single word.

The man turned, saw us, and threw Elle to the ground. He moved to get in the passenger side of the SUV.

"I've got her," I shouted to Pierce. "Do not let him get away."

Pierce made it to the side of the SUV before the man could even close the door. He ripped him out of the seat and took him down to the ground. I went to Elle.

"Elle, are you hurt?" I asked as I picked her up and carried her away from the side of the vehicle.

"Oh my God," she cried in my arms.

"Shh, it's okay. I've got you," I said softly.

Burying her face in my chest, she burst into tears. I did what I thought she needed in that moment, which was to hold on tight to her. I heard the sirens in the distance. They were muffled by Elle's crying and the grunts coming from the guy Pierce was currently apprehending.

"You're safe, sunshine. Please tell me if you are hurt."

She was so wound up and just pressed her body closer to mine.

Minutes later, the police arrived.

The waitress I told to call them had apparently followed behind Pierce and me and saw what was happening. When the police pulled into the lot, she directed them around the back to where we were.

Clutching Elle tight to my body, I moved closer to where the SUV had been parked so that I could hear the interrogation and what was being said. In the midst of me taking care of the only thing that mattered in the last few minutes and Pierce handling the animal that put his hands on my woman, the woman who had followed behind Elle out of the bathroom took off in the vehicle.

Pierce was giving a description of the vehicle to the officer along with the partial plate number he managed to catch before the woman drove off. My guys were fucking fantastic. Pierce not only took down the guy who grabbed Elle, but while doing that he also got a partial plate number for the vehicle the second suspect was driving.

Pierce then went on to explain what happened from the moment Elle performed until the moment they arrived.

A second officer walked over to where Elle and I were standing and explained, "I need to ask her some questions."

I looked down at her and asked, "Elle, can you do that now?"

She took a minute to gather her bearings and pulled out of my arms. She stayed close to my side while I kept an arm wrapped around her shoulders.

"Can you tell me what happened, darlin'?"

Elle's voice was trembling and scared when she murmured, "We should have just gone back to the hotel after the performance."

"What happened is not your fault," I assured her.

I looked to the officer and shared more of the backstory.

"I'm Levi Cunningham, owner of Cunningham Security in Windsor, Wyoming. Elle is currently under the protection of my firm as we investigate a case for her. She's being stalked—someone entered her apartment a few weeks ago and has been contacting her ever since. We're doing everything we can to locate the individual but have been unsuccessful so far. She's a well-known singer and has a pretty sizable fan base. We've narrowed the list down to possible suspects, but it spans several hundred people so it's taking time to go through."

I paused a second and Elle started speaking again. "I've had performances for the past three nights. I merely wanted to relax for a bit, so we stayed so I could have a couple of drinks. We should have just gone back."

Her fingers dug into the skin at my side as she tried to fight back her emotions.

I spoke to the officer to continue the story, "We were about to leave, but Elle needed to use the restroom first. As soon as she opened the door to walk out of the bathroom, I knew something wasn't right. My partner and I started moving across the bar toward her and thankfully got out here before they could get away with her."

The officer interrupted, "We know there was another individual involved who took off in the SUV. Did I hear someone say it was a woman?"

"Yes," I answered.

"She had a knife," Elle added.

I froze.

"Pardon?" the officer asked.

"I was just washing my hands and noticed her standing there staring at me in the mirror. I was creeped out. When I turned to walk toward the door to leave, she held out a knife and stopped me."

She stopped speaking and took in a deep breath as she leaned her weight into me. I took it and squeezed her shoulder to give her the support she needed.

"If I didn't do what she said, she told me I'd know what it felt like to have the cold metal blade penetrate through the skin of my back."

She couldn't fight it anymore. Elle began to cry. I couldn't say I wasn't a mess of emotions as well. My Elle. Scared. With a knife at her back.

"I remember seeing Levi when she opened the bath-room door," she got out through her sobs. "I remember being grabbed, but nothing else until his face was in mine delivering a message."

My body locked even tighter.

"What was the message?" the officer asked.

Her body began trembling as she, I'm assuming, mentally recalled what he said to her. It took her a bit to speak, but she managed to relay the message. Elle rasped, "You think you can have it all? You better watch your back, you greedy, selfish cunt."

Pierce was standing nearby, heard what Elle said, and when I looked him in the eyes he turned to walk back to where the fuckwad who delivered that message to Elle was standing.

My attention came back to the officer when he spoke again.

"Was that all?"

She took in a deep breath, shook her head, and ended, "Looking forward to seeing you soon."

"Were you hurt, Ms. Blackman?"

She held up her hands and answered, "Just some cuts and scrapes from when he threw me to the ground."

"I can call a paramedic to come and have you checked out," he offered.

"No, it's okay. I'd really like to just leave and go back to my hotel now."

He nodded and brought his eyes to mine. "Do you have a card?"

I pulled one out of my pocket and handed it over to him.

"I'll reach out to you with any updates. We'll get our men searching for the second suspect and deliver any information we find that can be helpful to you and your team."

"Appreciate it, Officer."

"No problem," he returned. His eyes went back to Elle and he continued, "We'll need you to come down to the station to make an official statement. I hate to have to make this any worse than it already is, but it's protocol. If you want to get this over with, I'll call over and let them know you're coming now."

"Sure," she squeaked out as she wrapped her arm around my waist and squeezed.

The officer walked away to notify one of the several other officers that had arrived on the scene while I held on to Elle.

I looked over to find Pierce in the face of the man he'd taken down mere minutes ago. Pierce was attempting to find out who the bastard was that hired this guy so we could put an end to Elle's misery. From what I could tell based on the guy's reaction to Pierce's inquisition, he had no idea who hired him. My guess is that he was somehow contacted anonymously and he likely did it for money, not really caring about or considering the consequences of what he was being hired to do. Pierce could tear someone down with the best of them, but Elle was scared and had already dealt with enough, so I decided we needed to waste no more time in getting her back to the hotel.

"Reynolds," I called out.

He looked to me and I jerked my head, indicating he could leave it alone. Pierce took one last look at the asshole, said something menacing, and walked over to us.

"You okay, rock star?" he said to Elle as soon as he was standing in front of her.

She nodded and stated, "Yeah."

"Were you hurt?"

"Just a few scrapes and cuts on my hands," she replied. "Other than that, it's just the emotional wounds."

Pierce's eyes came to mine. "I'll drive," he started. "Keep her in the back with you."

We walked to the rental, got in, and Pierce drove us to the station so Elle could make her statement. After, Pierce drove us back to the hotel.

The three of us walked in and got on the elevator. Finally being in a place that was well lit with mirrors surrounding us, I saw just the barest hint of something I was not happy to see. I pulled Elle's hair away from her neck and confirmed it. I clenched my jaw, doing my best to tamp down the anger I felt. Pierce saw my face, looked to Elle's neck, saw what I did, and had the same reaction.

Marks along the skin of her neck where that vile piece of shit put his hands on her.

Pierce announced, "I'm calling Cruz and updating him. Assuming he doesn't need me on anything back there, I'm staying for the remainder of the tour. On my own dime."

I lifted my chin at him, knowing if I spoke about what I just saw I'd lose my shit.

Elle lifted her head to Pierce.

His face softened when he looked at her, but since she still hadn't seen her own neck, she didn't understand it.

She looked to me in confusion.

"Elle…" I trailed off. "He marked you."

"What?" she asked.

"Your neck, sunshine."

Her head snapped to the side, allowing her to look in the mirror. Instinctively, her hand went to her throat, where her fingertips traced over the spots that his hands had left a physical reminder of her ordeal.

Elle's eyes welled with tears. She tried to stay strong, but the tears rolled down her cheeks.

The elevator arrived at our floor and the doors opened. I ushered her out and down the hall toward our room. As I pulled the room key out of my pocket, Pierce offered, "I'm down the hall if you need anything."

"Thanks, Reynolds."

"Pierce?" Elle called.

"Yeah?"

"Thank you," she said softly.

He jerked his chin up before he turned and walked toward his room.

I pushed open the door to our room and let Elle in ahead of me. She walked through the suite to the bedroom and finally into the bathroom. I followed behind her and, standing in the doorway to the bathroom, watched as she pulled her hair up and tied it up on top of her head before removing her jewelry. After all of her necklaces, bracelets, and earrings were off, she began removing her clothes and boots. She stepped out of the boots, pulled her top over her head, and dropped her shorts to the floor.

Elle turned to face the mirror and my heart broke for her as her hands balled up into tiny fists.

"I don't fight bad guys," she whispered.

What?

She continued to stare at her reflection in the mirror.

"Elle?" I called gently.

She looked at me and repeated, "I don't fight bad guys, Levi. You do. I sing. I eat chips. I read books. I spend too much money on lip balm. I do not fight bad guys."

"I know."

"I didn't like how it felt. I was helpless tonight. And terrified. And I didn't know what to do to help myself. I hope I am never in a situation like that again, but I know I don't ever want to feel powerless again. As much as it's not what I do, Levi, I'm begging you to teach me how to fight the bad guys."

"Anything, Elle. Whatever you need to make you feel safe, I'll give it to you. Dom can train you in self-defense. He's in California with us tomorrow. If you want to start tomorrow, we'll make it happen. If you want to wait until we are back in Wyoming, know that we will have you covered either way."

She visibly relaxed. Her shoulders dropped and her fists were no longer clenched.

"I'm sorry," I lamented as I walked toward her. "I should have walked you over to the bathroom. It was a rookie mistake and you paid the price."

"It's not your fault, Levi. I don't blame you and I don't want you blaming yourself for this. The only one to blame is the person who's after me. And when you catch him, I want the chance to tell him what I think of him. And I want to know why he did this."

"If it's in my power to give you that, sweetness, I will. But know that I will not do anything that will jeopardize your safety again."

"I know you never would," she said softly. She waited a

moment before continuing, "Will you shower with me and then hold me tight the rest of the night?"

Of course, I would. I wasn't sure I was prepared to let her more than an arm's length away from me at this point.

"Yeah. But in between the shower and the bed, I want to take care of your hands. I'll call down to the front desk and get a first aid kit up here."

"Okay," she agreed.

"I love you, Elle."

She smiled, the first I'd seen since before tonight's ordeal, and returned, "I love you, too."

At that, I turned on the shower and stripped out of my clothes. Elle removed her bra and panties. Then, we proceeded with a shower, first aid, and Elle being wrapped up in my arms the rest of the night.

CHAPTER 14

Elle

THE INCESSANT CHIMES FROM MY CELL PHONE WOKE ME.

I was cuddled up in Levi's arms and someone was disturbing that. Considering the frequency of the chimes, I knew something was up. I rolled over in the bed and sought out my phone on the nightstand.

I looked at the screen and watched as the texts poured in.

They were from two different people.

Both were expected, but one had me slightly concerned. That person was Charley. She was texting me because, apparently, she found out about what happened last night. The other person was Leah. She, too, learned of the events following my performance last night and, obviously, wanted to check in on me.

Charley's texts started off as her showing concern for me and wanting to make sure I was alright. Then, the tone of the texts changed because Wes found out. He was currently losing his shit about the situation and Charley's texts were serving as a warning.

Did I mention I loved my sister-in-law?

She had the forethought to at least warn me that a call from Wes was imminent so I could prepare myself.

"What is it?" Levi asked.

Levi was beside me in bed and, unfortunately, my phone had woken him up as well.

"Leah and Charley. Somehow, they know about last night. They wanted to check in on me," I answered.

"Fuck. It's got to be on some news media outlet," he hissed. "Let them know you're okay so they can stop texting."

"There's a problem, Levi."

He lifted his head and asked, "Which is?"

"Charley said Wes just found out and is losing his marbles. A call is going to be coming from him any minute now. I can pretty much guarantee you that."

He acknowledged this with a nod of his head and asked, "How are your hands today?"

"They don't hurt. Whatever that ointment was you put on last night had some pretty serious pain relief stuff in it. The burning stopped almost immediately."

"Let me look at them," he said, obviously still concerned about the well-being of my hands.

I held them out to him and allowed him to remove the bandages. The redness surrounding the scrapes last night was nonexistent this morning. He kissed both palms and I felt my belly flip at the sweet gesture.

Unfortunately, I didn't get to bask in that too long because my phone rang.

Wes.

Shit.

I stared at it knowing he was not going to be happy and wondering if I should avoid picking up the phone until later when he had some time to cool off.

"Answer it, sunshine. Don't make him worry any more than he already is," Levi urged.

Good point.

I answered the call and put the phone to my ear.

"Hi, Wes," I greeted as I sat up in the bed and rested my back against the headboard.

"Please tell me you weren't hurt," he pleaded.

"I'm okay. I just have a few scrapes on my hands and bruising on my neck."

"Everything I've read says that you were abducted after your show last night in Tucson," he began. He went on to recount all the details of last night's catastrophe. I was surprised at how accurate it all was.

"That's the basic gist of it. Where did you read this?"

"The fucking internet, Elizabeth Blackman," he roared. "And I'd like to know why that is? Why did my baby sister not call me last night the second she was safe to tell me what happened so I wouldn't have woken up to this terrifying news that someone held a knife to her back and tried to kidnap her?"

Damn.

He was using my full name.

This was a pretty good clue, as if I didn't already have one, that he was pissed.

"Wes, please calm down."

"Maybe I could do that, Elle, if I had any indication that when shit happened you'd call me and let me know. I read that shit this morning and I wanted to fucking vomit thinking something had happened to you. Where the fuck was Levi? I thought he was with you."

Trying to keep my voice neutral, I answered, "Levi was there. After performing for the last three nights I just wanted a few minutes to relax and have a drink. In fact, Levi and Pierce were both there."

I continued to fill in the holes in the story for him so he knew what happened from start to finish, including the stop at the station to give my statement. I ended, "By the time it was all done, I was exhausted, scared, and no longer running on adrenaline. I should have called you, but I didn't. I'm sorry."

"Jesus Christ, Elle," he clipped. "Are you sure you're alright?"

"Physically, it really is just some scrapes on my hands. Levi actually got a first aid kit from the hotel last night and bandaged them up. I have bruising on my neck where the guy gripped me and held me against the car, but that's all. I'm not going to lie to you, though. I'm scared. I don't know why someone is doing this to me. Last night, I felt scared and helpless."

"I wish you'd cancel the tour and come home until this situation gets resolved," he confessed.

"I appreciate where you are coming from, Wes, but I can't do that. It's not fair to me, and it's not fair to my true fans. On the bright side, I don't have to perform again until Tuesday night so I have some time to relax. Levi is actually going to drive me out to LA instead of flying. I don't really want to fly and he told me he'd have no problem driving me if that's what I preferred. Dom is going to be meeting up with us out in California after the LA show. Pierce was supposed to fly back to Wyoming, but after what happened last night, he decided to stay for the remainder of the tour."

"Please be careful, Elle. And if anything else happens, please don't make me read about it on the internet, okay?"

"I promise to call next time," I assured him.

"Appreciate it. Charley misses you and wants to talk with you. Can you spare a few minutes for her?" he asked.

"Of course. I have things to share with her anyway."

"You can share them with me," he offered.

"No. No, I cannot. This is girl talk territory. I absolutely will not share it with you. Trust me, you'll thank me for not sharing it with you."

"I should have known better," he muttered. "What you just said is more than I care to know about. Hang on, I'll put Charley on. Love you, Elle."

"Love you, big bro."

While I waited for Charley to get on the phone, I looked over at Levi. He had a look of adoration on his face.

"Do I need to make myself scarce during girl talk?" he inquired.

"It's up to you. I don't mind if you stay, though."

He gave me a grin and shifted his body closer to mine. Draping an arm over my thighs, Levi rested his head in my lap.

"Elle, honey, I was so worried about you," Charley's voice filtered into my ear.

"I'm okay, love. Levi's with me and has taken such great care of me. I promise, I'm good now," I told her as I stroked my fingers through Levi's hair.

"I assume you gave Wes the details of your whole incident last night?"

"Yeah."

"I'll get the details of that from him then. What I really want to know is how things are going with you and Levi?"

I looked down at Levi's head resting in my lap, his eyes closed as he held on to me.

"They're perfect," I sighed.

"Is it getting serious?"

"It is for me..." I trailed off. I thought a moment and continued, "I'm in love, Charley."

The hand on Levi's arm that was draped over my thighs squeezed my leg. It was gentle and sweet. I put my free hand to the top of his head and lazily ran my fingers through his hair.

"Oh, Elle. I'm so happy for you. I knew it. I knew that day you first met him here when he was covering Emme that you two were going to end up together."

"Well, I'm happy you were right about that," I admitted.

"So," she started. "Is the sex good?"

"That's the best part. I'll spare you the details right now since Levi's here and I don't want his ego inflating, but trust me when I say that it's absolutely fabulous. He's great at finding and fighting bad guys, but sex easily tops the list of his talents."

I felt Levi's body vibrate with laughter.

When he settled down, his fingertips began traveling up my thigh. He lifted his head and brought both hands to the hem of my nightie. The next thing I knew, my nightie was up around my waist, Levi's hand was at my knees separating them, and he was moving to settle his body between my now parted thighs.

Charley was talking, mentioning something about telling Emme and Zane the good news. I was agreeing with her up until Levi put his face between my legs and put his mouth on me.

"Oh God," I moaned.

His head shot up and he gave me a wickedly sexy grin. A moment later, his mouth was back on me.

"Elle? Are you okay?" Charley said into my ear.

"Perfect," I squeaked out. "Listen, love…" I trailed off because Levi was distracting me with his tongue.

I fought to remain silent, but it was useless. I moaned again into Charley's ear.

"Oh my," she said. "Go get some love from your man, honey. Stay safe and call me later."

"Okay," I panted. "Later."

I tossed the phone back onto the nightstand.

Levi did not stop. He continued to kiss, suck, and lick my clit. I kept my hand in his hair, not wanting to let him move from me. This only motivated him further. He grew hungrier, his tongue working me faster, deeper.

"Levi," I gasped.

He kept at me, taking me higher and higher.

It was like magic.

One hand began traveling up my body to my breast. His thumb circled my nipple over the satin fabric of my nightie as his mouth continued to feast on me. The sensation was divine and it took mere moments for me to feel the familiar feeling deep in my belly.

I had one hand at the opposite breast, the other at the back of his head. I moved my hips against his mouth.

He growled and relentlessly ate.

Seconds later, I was calling out his name, clutching his hair in my fingers as my legs trembled.

Levi pulled back slightly and pressed a soft kiss on the sensitive spot before trailing more soft kisses up my body.

He eventually made his way to my mouth and kissed me there. I tasted myself on him and grew more turned on, not even understanding how it was possible.

I pressed my hand to his shoulder and pushed him to his back. Straddling him, I allowed my mouth to make the same journey on his body, only I was headed south. He slept naked next to me last night, which meant I didn't need to fuss with the removal of any clothing. I crawled down his body and curled my fingers around his length. Wanting to waste no time in bringing him pleasure, I immediately wrapped my mouth around him.

"Fuck," Levi groaned.

I pulled back, looked up at him, gave him a coy smile, and put him back in my mouth. My hand fisted the root of his cock while my mouth and tongue slid along the rest of his length. I worked him just as hard as he did me. The hunger I had for him surpassed anything I'd ever experienced before. My free hand came up and massaged his balls before I slid my thumb down to the skin just beneath them. I lightly brushed my thumb back and forth across the skin there before applying a bit of pressure.

"Jesus Christ, sunshine."

His voice was thick with emotion.

I loved that I did that to him.

Levi allowed me to continue playing with him for a bit, until finally he pulled himself from my mouth, grabbed me under my arms, and hauled me up his body.

"Don't want to come in your mouth," he informed me before using one hand to position himself.

With my lips next to his, I whispered, "Then you better do it between my legs, love."

He growled again and slammed me down on him.

"Ride me, sweetness."

I did as he wished and rode him.

Levi lifted my nightie over my head and tossed it to the side before bringing his hands to my thighs. I moved my hips, rolling over his length slowly. He gave me time to work and build myself up, but soon took over. He gripped my hips and thrust mercilessly into me.

It took about point two seconds of him doing that for me to be on the verge of an orgasm. I think he knew because he slowed his pace.

"Levi," I called out, begging him to bring me there.

"You want to come?" he asked, thrusting slow and hard into me.

"Please," I pleaded.

He picked up his pace. "Tell me, Elle."

I threw my head back.

He stopped.

"Give me your eyes and say it, sunshine."

My head fell forward. I tried to lift my hips, seeking out the friction I was so desperate for, but Levi held me still.

I whimpered as I brought my eyes back to him. He held firm in his position, saying nothing and not allowing me to move.

"If you don't finish fucking me, Levi, I may have to reconsider how much I love you."

A devious grin spread across his face. "That's my girl," he beamed as he began moving inside me again.

It didn't take long, and before I knew it, he had me there.

"Come with me, Elle, but give me your eyes when you do."

So I did.

I came with Levi.

And I gave him my eyes.

When I finally collapsed on top of him I realized that, like last night, life might not always be all rainbows and sunshine, but with Levi by my side there wasn't anything that I couldn't endure and move beyond.

"I love you, Levi."

"I love you, Elle. But for the record, you will not reconsider how much you love me. That shit can grow as much as you want, but it never dies. You got me?"

"I've got you."

Levi's hands traced gently up and down the skin of my back for a bit. I basked in the feeling of having him like this.

"Do you want to get on the road early this morning?" he asked.

I lifted my head to look at him and answered, "Yeah. I was hoping we could stop and sightsee a little on the way out to LA."

"If that's what you want, I'll make sure you get it."

"Thanks, love."

"You keep calling me that, there isn't much I won't do for you."

I cocked an eyebrow and teased, "Good to know."

Levi and I stayed in the bed for a bit longer before we got up to get dressed and pack up our things. He called Pierce in that time and let him know that we'd take him to the airport before we got on the road. I needed to call Leah, but figured it'd be best to wait until we were driving. I knew she'd want the scoop on everything that had happened in my life over the course of the last three days and, because she was my bestie, I wanted to share it with her without feeling rushed.

An hour and a half later, we had dropped Pierce off at the airport and were on the road to LA. This is what I loved. Being carefree with a relatively loose schedule. I had to perform on Tuesday night, but it was still early on Monday and there was plenty of time to go at my own pace.

The best part of it all was Levi. He was with me and didn't mind a roughly seven-hour drive in the car with me to take me where I needed to go. Him making a sacrifice like that made me fall just a little bit deeper in love.

"We're stopping for gas at the next exit," he informed me after we had been driving for a while.

"I need to use the bathroom, so that's perfect."

"I figure we'll fill up and see if we can find a decent place to grab lunch. Then, we'll get back on the road."

"Works for me."

Levi pulled off at the next exit and filled up the rental. While he did that, I searched my phone for restaurants that had good ratings. I found a place that was only twenty miles away. We had to get back on the freeway, but it was on the way to our destination.

Perfect.

Levi filled the tank and then walked me to the bathroom. He was still not real keen on letting me out of arm's reach, and considering what happened last night, I had no issues waiting for him to walk me.

When we got back in the car, I gave him the address to put in the GPS and we were off again. I figured I'd use the drive to the restaurant to call Leah and fill her in on everything.

The phone rang once.

"I have texted and called you several times since this morning," she offered in the way of a greeting.

"I know, LP. I'm sorry. I wanted to wait until we were on the road and I'd have uninterrupted time to talk to you."

"On the road?" she repeated. "Wait. What time is it? Did you miss your flight, E?"

I laughed.

"No, Leah. Relax," I started. "I was talking to Levi earlier in the day yesterday and told him how much I hated flying and deadlines and he told me that since I didn't need to be in LA to perform until Tuesday night that he'd be more than happy to make the drive with me. So... we're road tripping it from Tucson to LA."

I was sure she could hear the excitement in my voice. I loved exploring new places like this.

"What a colossal waste of time," she retorted, quickly diminishing my cheerful mood. "Why would you ever want to spend that many hours in a car when you could fly to your destination and spend more time there?"

"There might be wonderful things to see and do at the destination, Leah, but do you realize how many places I get to see by road tripping? Think of how much beauty I'd be missing out on by flying over all of this. Besides, you know me. I like to go with the flow. I don't like having every single minute of my life planned and scheduled. It's good to be spontaneous. You should try it sometime."

"No thanks. I like being in control, knowing what's going to happen and when. How do you function like that, Elle?"

I took in a deep breath. This was a never-ending battle with her. It was one of those things that she always had to make comments about. Leah believed in order and timelines. She would plan a vacation and account for every single second of her trip. I couldn't ever do that. Vacation, to me, is a time to relax and enjoy myself. Sure, I'd select a few things I'd want to do while on vacation, but I wouldn't plan my days out from the minute I woke up until the minute I went to bed. Leah was that extreme. Sometimes I wondered how we ever became such close friends because in so many ways we were so very different. Somehow it worked, so I tended not to dwell on those differences.

I let out the breath and said, "Moving on. I wanted to update you on the situation last night. I'm guessing that you must have read about it online as well?"

"I was horrified when I read it, E. I can't even imagine how you must have felt. Was the story online true? They said a knife was held to your back."

I closed my eyes and recalled feeling the point of the sharp metal pressing into the middle of my back last night.

"Yeah," I whispered. "It was terrifying."

"So, what was it about? Was it just some obsessed fan?" she wondered.

I went on to tell Leah the story and all the events as they happened last night. I hated reliving it, but she was my best friend. I knew if something like this ever happened to her, I'd want to know. She was alarmed at what she learned and was concerned for me. I told her she didn't need to worry because thanks to our spontaneity at least my stalker didn't know I wasn't on a plane right now. To add to that, I went on to tell her that not only was Dom meeting us in California on Wednesday, but also that Pierce decided he would be staying with us for the remainder of the tour.

"There's going to be three of them and one of you?" she asked.

"Yep," I answered. "And I told Levi I want to learn self-defense. He said Dom can start training me as early as Wednesday."

"Self-defense?"

"I was petrified last night, LP," I started. "I don't ever want to feel that way again. Maybe I won't be able to fight off all the bad guys always, but at least I'll have some skill to try to defend myself. I know that Levi and his team are going to do everything necessary to keep me safe, but it won't hurt for me to be able to at least put up a good fight in case something like that ever happens again."

"I can understand that. It's just that you're not the self-defense type."

"You might be right about that, but I'm also not the type to sit down and let someone torture me either. It's bad enough this jerk is tormenting me with notes and flower deliveries. Last night, it went to another level. I refuse to feel like that ever again."

"Well, I'm meeting up with you in California on Wednesday. We need to do some serious catching up. I'm pretty sure there's more to the story that I haven't yet been told. I'm also certain that it involves Levi."

"You would be correct," I responded. "But you're right. It will be better if I fill you in in person in a few days. In fact, I've got to go because Levi is pulling off the exit now and we're headed for lunch. I'll see you when you get in on Wednesday and give you the full rundown then."

"I'm looking forward to it. See you soon!" she shouted before she disconnected the call.

I pulled the phone from my ear and tossed it into my purse while I fished out my lip balm. I looked toward the driver's side of the car and found Levi had come to a stop in the parking lot of the restaurant that was just off the exit and was looking at me.

"What?" I asked as I applied the strawberry flavored mois-turizer to my lips.

"I love you," he confessed.

I smiled back at him and replied, "I love you, too."

"Hungry?"

I nodded.

"Then how about you let me taste your lips real quick so I can get you inside and feed you?" he suggested as he brought a hand up to cup my cheek.

I nodded my agreement.

Ten minutes later, Levi made good on his promise to get me fed.

CHAPTER 15

Elle

I T WAS TWELVE HOURS FROM THE TIME WE LEFT TUCSON UNTIL WE arrived in Los Angeles. The reason for the five-hour delay was because Levi and I made several stops on our road trip from Tucson. Our stops weren't just to fill up the car with gas either.

Nope.

We made the most of our journey and thoroughly enjoyed it. We made stops in multiple towns along the way and did some sightseeing, shopping, and even some light hiking. Well, I did the shopping. Levi? Not so much. The hiking was more his idea and I decided that a compromise was in order considering he did this for me. My time alone with Levi brought me a bit of inspiration, so I pulled out my notebook several times along the way and jotted a few words down.

Being such an active person, I thought the ride in the car would have made him crazy, but if it did, he never allowed it to show. When it came down to it, I noticed he was the most relaxed I'd seen him throughout the entire tour. Initially, I couldn't figure out why, but then it dawned on me that he wasn't worried about me the way he had been from the minute he saw me sitting in his office that day a couple weeks ago. With the last-minute decision to drive out to California instead of flying, he knew that if someone was stalking me to the level they had been, the road trip to LA wasn't something they'd know about. I think that it brought him a bit of comfort to know that he could relax and just enjoy spending the time with me.

Now, we were in California and had just checked in to our hotel suite. I made a beeline for the shower while Levi made calls to Pierce, to let him know we were in town, and Cruz, to check in on things back home at the firm.

I had finished in the shower and was standing in my nightie drying my hair when Levi stepped inside the bathroom. He was just staring at me, so I turned off the hairdryer and asked, "What's wrong?"

He shook his head. "Nothing at all, sunshine. Just trying to let it sink in that you're mine."

"Everything okay at home? The firm?" I questioned, wondering if there was something he wasn't telling me.

He took three steps toward me and settled my mounting anxiety when he explained, "Yes. I talked to Cruz about what happened last night. The whole team was worried about you. Dom had Deb rearrange his flight. He's flying out on the red-eye flight tonight and will be here first thing in the morning. With the heightened attempts to contact you and approach you, we figure it's better to have an extra person covering you."

I guess that made sense. "Okay."

"I'm going to take a quick shower. I'm wiped after today. When I get out, will you be ready for bed?"

"Yeah," I answered.

Levi gave me a quick kiss on the lips before he moved to get in the shower. I went back to drying my hair. When I finished, I applied my lotion and walked out of the bathroom back into the bedroom. While I waited for Levi to finish in the shower, I grabbed my phone and tapped out a quick text to Wes. I didn't like that I had unnecessarily worried him last night and thought it would go a long way if I checked in with him tonight.

Me: Hey, bro! Just wanted to let you know that Levi and I made it to LA. I didn't want you worrying.

Wes responded almost immediately.

Wes: I always worry about you, Elle. Thanks for checking in, though.

Me: Well you can worry a little less. Dom is taking the red-eye flight out tonight, so I'll have an extra set of eyes on me for the remainder of the trip.

Wes: Good. Dom's a crazy motherfucker. I'm glad he'll be there. Stay safe.

*Me: I will. ☺

I hadn't posted on social media in a while, so I decided to check my accounts and give updates.

Holy cow.

As soon as I opened my Facebook account I was inundated with notifications. Apparently, word of my debacle last night had spread like wild fire and my fans were concerned. I wanted to set their minds at ease, but responding individually would have taken an eternity. On that thought, I went live. Within seconds, I had several thousand fans 'tuning in' to my live feed.

I spoke into the camera.

"Hi guys! First, I wanted to say thank you to everyone who reached out and expressed their concern for me over the incident that occurred last night. I'm sorry I didn't check in with all of you sooner, but I wanted to let you know that I'm okay. You can see that I've got a couple of scrapes on my hands here and a bit of bruising on my neck, but otherwise, I'm physically fine. I also wanted to let you all know that I'm currently in LA and I'm so excited to be performing here tomorrow evening."

I watched as hundreds of my fans asked questions or expressed their love for me. So many of them had been so worried about me and it made my heart feel so full that people who didn't even know me personally felt so deeply for me.

Levi stepped out of the bathroom in nothing but a pair of sweats that rested low on his hips, just as I began answering a question that kept popping up from multiple fans, concerned about my security for the remainder of the tour.

"I appreciate all of the well wishes, love, and support from each and every one of you. There is no need to be worried about me. I have an amazing security team, led by my boyfriend, Levi. They'll have extra eyes on me for the remainder of the tour and I feel completely safe under their protection."

More questions filtered across the screen. The focus shifted from my well-being to my mention of a boyfriend. My fans wanted details.

I looked to Levi and gave him eyes that pleaded with him. I kept him out of view of the camera and explained to him, "My fans want to know all about my boyfriend. I don't think they should know all about you, but would you mind saying hello?"

He shook his head and gave me a smirk before walking over to sit next to me on the bed. My heart exploded when he came into view of the camera and said, "Hello."

The comments went crazy.

Holy shit! He's hot!

Girl, you are so lucky.

Can we see the rest of him?

Comment after comment came through. Levi watched and his eyes rounded. I whispered, "They think you're perfect, love."

He looked to me, his eyes sparkling and intense, and whispered back, "I don't hold a candle to you, sunshine."

I nearly forgot I was streaming live. I turned back to the camera and saw more comments.

Sunshine? Did he just call her sunshine? That's the perfect name for her.

I'm swooning over here.

These two are #relationshipgoals.

Too turned on by Levi and not wanting to share him any longer, I spoke.

"Okay, friends, it's time to go. You now know Levi's off the market, but maybe tomorrow I'll get the two other guys on my security team to say hello. They are both single. Thank you again for all of your love and support. I love you all to pieces."

I ended my live session and set my phone on the bedside table. My eyes came back to Levi and he announced, "We're relationship goals, Elle."

I laughed hearing him use the modern-day slang. "That's because you're hot and said nice things to me in front of them."

"Whether they're watching or not, I'm inclined to agree with what they said."

My voice was quiet when I admitted, "Me too."

"I know it's been a long day, but I'm in the mood for some honey from you, sweetness. Are you going to let me love you before we call it a night?"

"I thought you'd never ask."

With that, Levi snaked an arm around my waist, pulled me down in the bed, and came to hover over me. Then, I gave him his favorite look with my eyes and let him love me before we went to sleep.

Levi's phone rang early the next morning. I didn't know what time it was, but we were still cuddled up in bed. I was utterly exhausted and it was still dark in the room. Of course, we had the room darkening shades pulled, so it could have been much later than I thought. It was so deceiving.

Levi was on his back; I was curled into his side. His arm was wrapped around me.

He reached over to swipe his phone off the nightstand and answered, "Yeah?"

Within seconds, I felt his body tense. He pulled his arm from around me and sat up in the bed.

"Where did you get the lead?" he asked.

Silence as he waited for an answer.

"You've got to be kidding me."

More silence.

"How sure are you?"

The silence stretched on for a long while this time.

"I'll talk to her. Dom and Pierce, too. We'll come up with something and I'll let you know before we do anything."

Levi waited for the caller on the other end of the line to finish speaking.

"Right. I'll be in touch later this morning. Good work, Michaels."

I watched as Levi dropped the phone from his ear and set the phone back on the nightstand. He settled on his back again in the bed.

"What is it, Levi? What did Trent find?" I asked quietly.

"It's a woman."

My brows pulled together at this statement. Puzzled and looking for clarification, I pressed him for more information, "A woman? What are you talking about?"

"Your stalker, Elle. I think we all just naturally assumed to some degree that it was a man. We were wrong because

Trent is pretty convinced he's found our target. Turns out, it's a woman."

"Who is it?"

"Do you know anyone named Becky?"

I took a few moments to think. I knew a lot of people. Nobody close to me was named Becky, but it was possible that I had met a fan with that name.

"I can't recall anyone specifically. What's the last name?"

"Blunt."

"Becky Blunt?" I scoffed. I couldn't help it. That was the most ridiculous name I had ever heard of for a psychopath.

"It's not funny, sunshine."

"I'm sorry, Levi. It's just…" I paused to regain my composure.

When I got myself under control, I sat up, turned on the light next to the bed, and looked at Levi.

"You think someone named Becky Blunt is stalking me? That name doesn't sound very menacing."

"I'm passing along the information I was given. Trent is good; I have no reason to doubt him."

"So, what makes Trent think that this woman is stalking me?"

"The livestreaming video session you did last night," he started. "Apparently, he went through and saw the names of all the people who watched it. Becky stuck out to him because it wasn't a name that came up when he went through the list of your followers. Evidently, she watched you last night, but she doesn't even follow or like your page."

"Okay. I don't understand how that translates into her being a stalker. I mean, maybe she doesn't want to actually follow the page for some other reason. I highly doubt this means anything."

"Elle?"

"What?"

"Trent went to her social media page."

"And?"

"She's your stalker."

The tone of his voice and the way he said it sent a shiver through my body. Suddenly, I didn't think it was so funny.

"Tell me," I urged him through a whisper, feeling my throat get tight.

"Every time you post something, she posts something nearly identical. She never shows her face in her posts, but Trent says there is no denying that everything she posts is related to what you've posted. He said that sometimes, you'll post something and it's not even an hour later when she does something remarkably similar. There have been several instances of her copying verbatim what you've said. Once or twice might lead us to believe it's coincidental. When it's nearly every post, that tells us something else."

"Which is?"

"She's obsessed."

Fuck.

Holy fuck.

Why?

Who was this?

"What are we going to do now?" I wondered.

Levi sat up in the bed and explained, "You need to get out of the nightie and put some clothes on. I'm going to call Pierce and Dom. When they get here, I'll clarify what Trent needs us to do."

"Okay," I agreed.

With that, I got up and put some clothes on while Levi called the boys. I moved to the bathroom, did my business, brushed my teeth, and made myself look half decent. Levi threw on some clothes and I grabbed my phone off the nightstand.

A few minutes later, there was a knock at the door. I sat on the couch in the living room of the suite and opened Facebook while Levi opened the door. I searched for Becky Blunt and went to her page. As I scrolled through her feed, it was like I was reliving my own life. I heard the guys walk back into the room, but I was too shocked at what I was seeing to look up from my phone.

Silence settled over the room as I'm sure they took me in and realized I was about to lose my shit.

"Elle?" Levi called.

I looked up and saw them all looking at me with worried and concerned looks on their faces. My breathing came quick, my teeth clenched together, and my leg was tapping ferociously on the floor.

I stood.

"This is the most ridiculous shit I've ever seen in my life!" I shouted.

Dom turned his head to Levi and asked, "What's going on?"

"I'll tell you what's going on," I seethed. "Trent managed to figure out who the bitch is that's obsessed with me and it seems she has absolutely *nothing* better to do with herself than to stalk my entire fucking life."

"Elle, sunshine, calm down," Levi pled.

"Calm down? How can I calm down, Levi? I just scrolled through a few days' worth of posts on her Facebook page and it was like reliving my own life. I didn't think it was that bad when you told me about it this morning. Seeing it? That's something completely different. There are instances where entire sentences or questions I've asked in my posts are copied in hers, only hours after I've posted them. Who is this psycho? And why? Why would someone spend their time doing this?"

"Levi?" Pierce called.

Figuring that speaking to me was likely not a good option at this moment in time, Levi brought Pierce and Dom up to speed.

"So, what's the plan?" Dom asked.

"Yeah," I started. "That's an excellent question. I'd love to know what the plan is."

"Trent is digging, trying to figure out who this is and where they are from. From there, we'll have a better idea on how to proceed. In the meantime, he needs Elle to be as active as possible on her social media accounts. We need to build up evidence of the obsession. We'll have, at a minimum, the police report from Tucson. In addition, we have all the notes Elle's received. If we can show just how deep Becky's fixation on Elle is, it'll only strengthen the case against her."

Pierce piped up. "I realize we want to get as much evidence against this Becky character as we can, but wouldn't it also speed up the process if Elle just made the accounts private and blocked the bitch? Someone who is this neurotic isn't going to be able to handle not knowing what's happening in Elle's world. She'd have to find another way and it could bring her out quicker."

"Elle can't," Dom explained. "At least, not on all social media platforms."

My head shifted and I looked at him.

"Certain platforms will allow you to block specific people from seeing what you post. Others don't give that option when it's a business page. So on Facebook, for example, if Elle wants to continue having a page that promotes what she does, she's unable to prevent an individual from seeing it. The only way she'd be able to block her would be if this Becky chick actually interacted on the page. Even then, I don't believe it would prevent Becky from seeing it; I'm pretty sure she just wouldn't be able to interact on the page anymore. From what Levi just told us, Trent said she's not even someone who has liked or followed the Facebook page. She just likely consistently watches it to keep tabs on Elle."

"This is outrageous," I ranted. "I don't even understand

why someone would do this. I mean, you'd have to have no mind of your own for you to try and live vicariously through another person. When you find her, don't forget what you promised me, Levi. I want five minutes with her and I want to know why."

He nodded his head and reassured me, "I already told you if I could make that happen for you, I would."

I closed my eyes and took in a deep breath. I had been awake for not even a full hour yet and I was already exhausted.

When I opened my eyes again, I looked at the three concerned men in front of me and quietly said, "This is my life."

"I'm not following you, Elle," Dom informed me.

"Social media is what it is. I wasn't very thrilled with the idea of it initially, but I've seen how much my fans appreciate that communication from me. It's their way to have that connection to me. Doing this tour has confirmed what I already knew would be the case, which is that I prefer the small, hometown feel. I'm not planning to do this touring stuff on a regular basis. It's just not what I'm into, nor is it what I want as a regular thing in my life. That said, my fans have come to these sold-out shows just to watch me perform. These people are so supportive of me and they are very important to me. What she's doing is simply attempting to make a mockery of my chosen career path. I didn't even have enough time to go through everything on her page and, to be honest, I don't really care to do that. However, to do what she's doing in the way she's doing it by copying every single thing I do and trying to spin it as something significant in her own life is distasteful, fake, and arrogant all wrapped up into one."

"I get the distasteful and fake," Pierce chimed in. "But why do you get arrogance out of this?"

I explained, "As I said, I've only scrolled through and seen a few posts, but if she isn't copying exactly what I say she's attempting to diminish what I've posted. It's like she believes, for whatever reason, that she's better than me. For example, the first stop on the tour was in Denver. Levi and I did some sightseeing and I snapped a few photos. I ended up posting one to my Facebook account. In the text of that post, I spoke about the beauty of Denver and a specific location we visited. She ended up posting something about an hour after I made that post with a picture of some place she's been. She went on to not only talk about how great the place she visited was, but she also goes so far as to mention Denver in the post and attempts to diminish the beauty of Denver. I mean, seriously? The only way you can feel good about where you've been is to talk badly about the places I've been? It's like an 'anything you can do I can do better' mentality. What a narcissist. I can't wait to meet this egotistical, conceited, and shameless piece of work."

"Got it," Pierce admitted nervously. "Didn't mean to get you any more riled up."

I gave him an apologetic look and sighed. "I'm sorry. I think I need food. Can we go have breakfast?"

Pierce and Dom chuckled.

Levi visibly relaxed and said, "Yeah, Elle. We'll go have breakfast. After, I'm taking you for the biggest bag of potato chips I can find."

I smiled at him before walking over and wrapping my arms around him. He hugged me and pressed a kiss to my head.

Then, the four of us made our way out to have breakfast.

CHAPTER 16

Elle

THE NEXT TWO DAYS PASSED IN A WHIRLWIND OF EVENTS, BOTH spontaneous and calculated.

Levi took me out to breakfast on Monday morning with Pierce and Dom. They drove separately in the rental Dom picked up when his flight arrived early that morning. I attributed their need to go in a separate vehicle to the outburst I had in the hotel room that morning and, to be honest, couldn't blame them for their choice.

On an empty stomach, I was feeling livid about everything I had learned that morning. There was little that would calm me down and alleviate the rage coursing through me knowing someone was likely having fun doing what they were doing. Once I had food in my stomach, I came to my senses and went from being angry to being smart. I'd let this witch be stupid enough to bury herself with the evidence. Trent said he wanted me to be more active on my social media accounts, so that is what I was going to do.

As the four of us sat together at breakfast, we came up with a plan. This was, again, after I had put a significant amount of food in my body.

Trent was going to be collecting the evidence. He was taking screen shots of her public posts in case she attempted to alter or delete them at any point in the future. When it came to keeping me safe, the guys collectively concluded that it was best to remain on high alert since we were unsure of just how far Becky would take things.

I didn't disagree with this assessment. Clearly, the bitch was overly obsessed and extremely unstable.

Next on our list of things to cover was strategy.

I wanted proof.

Concrete evidence of this sick and twisted obsession.

"I continue what I'm doing," I stated. "But I kick it up a notch."

"How so?" Levi wondered out loud.

"I give her more of me. More posts. More information. It's only going to get her working overtime to follow what I'm doing, which is eventually going to result in her making a mistake in the end."

"What is your plan to accomplish this?" Dom asked.

"Ok, so I don't know what this woman's motivation is. I can't understand the intensity of the fixation this woman clearly has with me, but if any of you had to guess, what would you think her reason for it is?"

"With women?" Dom started. "Jealousy. It's always about jealousy with bitches."

I cocked an eyebrow at him and explained, "We aren't all bitches. That said, that's precisely what I believe is the issue. Or, at least, that's what I'm rocking with right now. For whatever reason, this Becky character is jealous about something. What? I have no idea. But, if she can see that I'm still blissfully happy, doing well, and enjoying my life it's only going to infuriate her more. She knows what she's doing to me, so she knows what I'm dealing with right now. I'm going to let her see that she's not affecting me. And the reality is, I am all those things I just said. Sure, this is like a thorn in my side right now, but when it comes down to it, what she's doing doesn't matter in the grand scheme of things. She'll eventually be exposed for the person that she is and I'll still be blissfully happy doing what I love with my life."

I paused a moment letting that sink in. It was the truth. I could spend my time worried about what this woman was doing or I could continue going about my business, focusing on myself and my life. Yeah, I'd always wonder why, but I wasn't going to allow it to put a damper on my happiness and all of the good that I had in my life.

"I'll need your help, though. All three of you, for the remainder of the tour, starting now."

"What do you want us to do, sunshine?" Levi asked from beside me.

I gave him a huge grin before I described my next move. "She can copy the words of my post all she wants. She can attempt to put down the places I've been or the things I've experienced. No matter how hard she tries she's not going to be able to take away what those places and experiences mean to me. She also will *never* take away what the people in my life who truly love and care for me mean to me. So, you're all going to need to be okay with your faces on my social media. Last night, I did that live session. Trent found her. As you know, after my fans went crazy over you, I promised them a peek at Dom and Pierce. Today, we're going to give them that."

"Fucking hell," Dom swore.

"Not again," Pierce added.

I turned to the two of them, practically batted my eyelashes, and begged, "Please?"

They both looked to Levi before they turned their attention back to me.

Pierce took in a deep breath and blew it out before he asked, "What specifically do you want us to do?"

I grinned at him.

They were going to cave.

"I'll ease you into this. We'll start with just pictures, but soon enough I want you guys on a live session with me. If it's jealousy that's fueling Becky's obsession, seeing me surrounded by three hot guys whose mission it is to keep me safe will have her beyond envious. I'm just going to keep throwing all the goodness I've got in my life at her and see how she responds. Hopefully Trent is monitoring her account like a hawk."

The looks on their faces told me they weren't thrilled with this idea, but they knew that Trent had asked for me to be active on my accounts. If this was going to help the case, they were willing to do what was necessary, despite how much they did not want to do it.

The rest of breakfast was spent with Levi and the guys discussing the game plan for my performance that night. A trip to the venue was in order, but unfortunately, we wouldn't be able to get into the place until after two o'clock.

As we walked out of the restaurant, I stopped a woman and asked her if she'd mind taking my picture with Levi, Dom, and Pierce. I huddled up next to them and she snapped the photo. I thanked her and walked with Levi to our rental.

Dom and Pierce followed us to a local convenience store so Levi could do as he promised and buy me some chips. I took the time on the drive there to post the photo of me with my bodyguards. Levi called Trent to let him know what our plan was thus far and that he should follow up with any further updates.

LA had the opposite vibe of what I was craving at that moment, so I spent most of the day at the hotel relaxing before my show. I called and talked to Charley. I felt so bad about the last time I spoke with her and how the call ended that I needed to redeem myself. Levi kept himself busy with Cunningham Security stuff, so I didn't need to worry about him attempting to have his way with me while I was on the phone with her.

Leah called not long after I hung up with Charley. She was supposed to be meeting me out in California in time for the San Francisco show, but ended up needing to cancel her flight. Unfortunately, there was an emergency at the clinic and she needed to stay. She was so disappointed, but I did my best to reassure her and let her know that I wasn't upset. On that note, we planned to get together when I was back in town. She said she'd definitely be at my show at Lou's when I returned to Wyoming. I chose not to fill her in on the stalker situation update. With her not being able to come out for the second leg of the tour, if I dropped that news on her she'd have gotten all worked up. I figured I'd wait until I returned home and things settled before I upset her even more. I knew if the roles were reversed I'd have worried myself sick thinking someone was doing to her what they were doing to me.

That night, I was thankful for a reprieve from Ms. Blunt. Obviously, we had no idea when she'd strike next, but I couldn't help sitting there wondering what she was doing during those times she wasn't actively scheming. It frightened me to think that she was always thinking of ways to get to me and how she could kick it up a notch. If I wasn't being given flowers with notes, having notes hidden in my car, or having the edge of a knife pressed into my back, I worried that she was spending her free time planning her next move. Considering the severity of contact was escalating, I often wondered what would happen next. Regardless, I tried my best to be grateful when there wasn't any scary stuff happening.

Immediately following my performance Monday night, we went back to the hotel. This was not before Dom texted a few photos he took with his phone for me during the event.

He thought it would be good to show Becky that not only was I continuing to do what I loved, but also that tons of people were coming out to watch me perform. I thanked Dom for the photos, posted a few, and the four of us took off for the night.

I was going to be performing in San Francisco the following night and wanted to get a good night's sleep. Making love to Levi was part of my plan that evening, so it was even more reason to not waste time hanging around.

The next morning, Levi and I packed up our things and checked out. Once again, he offered to drive me to my next destination so that I could avoid the flight. Honestly, I think he secretly craved the time alone with me without the threat surrounding us. Given my disdain for flying, I immediately agreed. Dom and Pierce also decided to drive. They figured the drive wasn't that bad and a couple hours on the road was no big deal.

The drive was only a bit over five hours, so we knew we'd have plenty of time to get there and get settled before I needed to start getting myself ready. We didn't have the same amount of time on the second road trip that we did on the first, but I still enjoyed having that time alone with Levi. I learned a lot more about his family, his childhood, and his decision to start his own private investigation firm. The conversation then shifted to me. Levi knew about as much about my family as I did his. In fact, I felt like I knew his brother, Zane, better because he and Wes were always together. I gave Levi my story, which really wasn't anything crazy. My childhood was typical, much like his. We were both fortunate to come from very loving families. I mostly talked to him about my music career and how I always knew that singing is what I wanted to do with my life.

Aside from spending most of my time learning about Levi and jotting down a few more words in my song inspiration notebook, the only other thing I did on the drive was catch up with Emme. Apparently, she had watched the live feed with Levi the previous night. She ended up sending me a private message through my social media account and told me how happy she was for us. Seeing how we were with each other for those brief moments had solidified for her and Zane that Levi and I were meant to be together. She wanted the four of us to get together when Levi and I got back to town for a double date. I told Levi and he agreed, so Emme and I planned a get together later in the week after I returned from the tour.

Emme also went on to tell me that Zane told her he hoped things continued to go well for the two of us. He wanted to see both of his brothers get what he got when he found Emme. He was convinced Levi had found that with me. I told her I thought he was being a little presumptuous and rushing things a bit. Zane didn't think so and was now only hoping his younger brother, Cruz, wasn't far behind.

We were having such a good time on our drive that the next thing I knew we had arrived in San Francisco. As soon as we got to town, we checked in at the hotel and, unfortunately, ended up ordering room service. I knew it wasn't Levi's idea of a great meal, but we didn't have the time we'd need to go out to a restaurant.

When the food arrived, I apologized.

"I'm sorry about the food situation. This tour has made you go so far outside of the normal diet you'd eat. At least, it's almost over."

"It's fine, Elle. You don't need to apologize," he insisted.

"I feel bad, though. You're doing this for me and you aren't even able to maintain your strict diet."

"Really, sunshine. I'm fine. Besides, every hotel we've stayed at has been in a suite with a full kitchen. I could have very easily made runs to the grocery store and picked up food if I wanted to do that. Considering we're spending so much time on the road or with you getting ready for your shows, I'd much rather spend the little time I do get alone with you not cooking food. When we get home, it'll settle down and I'll get back to my normal routine. Until then, though, I'm good spending my time with you."

I stayed silent a moment letting his words sink in and warm me to my core. He was making all of these little sacrifices for me along the way.

"I'm thinking that I'm going to need you to finish your dinner and then join me in the shower for some fun before I have to get myself ready for the show tonight. Then, after we get back here tonight, I'm going to see to it that you get rewarded handsomely for the wonderfully sweet things you've said and done for me lately."

Levi set his hand on my thigh, squeezed, and whispered softly, "Kiss me, sweetness."

I swallowed a bite of my food, leaned over, and kissed him. He didn't allow the kiss to be just a simple peck on the lips. This was full-fledged, open-mouth kissing. I let out a delicate moan, which led Levi to squeeze my thigh again and pull away.

"Finish eating, Elle. If you take too long to do that, you should know now that you'll be late to your show tonight."

My body visibly reacted to his words. Levi couldn't miss it. His eyes traveled the length of my body, but ultimately came back up and settled on my eyes. I'm certain they were his favorite shade of honey.

With that, I got back to my food and finished eating. When I popped the last bite in my mouth, Levi bent over, picked me up, and carried me into the bathroom, where he made sweet love to me up against the wall of the shower.

In the end, I was a little late for my show.

It didn't bother me in the slightest because sex against the wall of the shower with Levi was just that good.

I began to wonder if I was on a lucky streak because the San Francisco show went off without a hitch. There was no contact from the stalker and my fans seemed to really enjoy the show. I stayed for another hour following the conclusion of the performance to sign some autographs. We were catching a flight to Las Vegas in the morning, so I really did not want to stay out late. Knowing that I wasn't fond of the idea of doing another tour, I wanted to give my fans, who might not ever be able to see me perform again, the opportunity to meet me in person and get an autograph.

Later, Levi took me back to the hotel and, as promised, I rewarded him handsomely. Levi learned that he liked being rewarded. I learned that I loved how he held me afterward.

As I soaked up the warmth and happiness there in his arms I realized that what I had said earlier was the truth. I was blissfully happy. The stalker situation sucked, but we were making headway on figuring it all out. I had faith in Levi and his guys to do what they do and bring an end to the green-eyed monster that was trying to trample on my happiness. Aside from that, being held in Levi's arms I realized that I was feeling full of joy at what this situation brought to my life.

Levi.

Love.

Clarity.

It was funny. On our drive to San Francisco, I told Levi how I always knew that I wanted to be a singer. Beyond that, I had no specific thoughts of what else I wanted in my life. Now that I had him, I finally knew. I knew what I wanted to experience, feel, and live every single day from that point forward.

I wanted peace. I wanted the freedom to not be bound

by schedules and deadlines. I wanted to sing. I wanted to be obsessive about lip balm and coffee mugs and potato chips. I wanted my family and friends. I wanted all of that and I knew, more than anything else, I wanted to have it all with him by my side.

It was on those thoughts that I pressed my body closer to Levi's. As his arms tightened around me protectively, I took in a deep breath and drifted off to sleep.

CHAPTER 17

Elle

"**I**T'S ENDING."

That was me talking to Levi as I walked out of the bathroom into the bedroom where he was lying on his back in the bed with the blanket slung low across his abdomen.

Two more shows and I was on my way home.

I could not wait.

I arrived in Las Vegas earlier this afternoon and came to the realization that my mini-tour was coming to a close.

When our flight landed, Levi, Pierce, Dom, and I got our rental vehicles and checked in at our hotel. After, the four of us went out on the Las Vegas Strip. I'm not sure if they were all about it or not, but they didn't complain when I asked if they'd mind. Certainly, I didn't believe they felt the same way that I did, which was that it would have been a crime to be in Las Vegas and not walked the Strip.

We saw the fountains at the Bellagio, rode on the High Roller, and walked through several hotels, some for the décor and others for the casinos. The guys didn't gamble, but I figured if I was in Vegas I had to do it. Needless to say, I didn't win.

With all of the excitement throughout the day, it didn't leave much time for me to think about the tour ending. Now that Levi and I were back in our hotel suite, getting ready for bed, it was hitting me full force.

"What is?" Levi asked as he pulled back the blankets so I could climb into the bed next to him.

"The tour. Only two more shows before we head home for the final performance at Lou's," I answered, melancholy in my tone.

"You're going to miss it," he stated, matter-of-fact, pulling me against his body, my front to his.

"Not the air travel," I began. "I think I've made it pretty clear that I don't like being bound by timelines and travel schedules associated with flying, but I'll miss the performing. I'll miss meeting my fans in different parts of the country. I'm afraid I'll forget what it feels like to be onstage and see people, who aren't from my hometown, coming to watch me perform."

I paused a minute, letting that reality sink in, before I continued.

"Most of all, I'll miss not being able to see the sights of all the beautiful places we got to see on our road trips throughout the tour. I'll miss having that time alone with you in the car driving from one state to the next and making impromptu stops along the way to see what beauty some quaint little town holds. That was, by far, my favorite part of this tour."

Levi's arms tightened around me as he said, "You can always plan another tour."

"I know, but I'm not sure I want to do another one. This was exhausting. It felt rushed. I didn't have time to relax and enjoy the places I went to the way I would have liked."

"Do you have a record label?"

I jerked my head back and looked up at him. "What?"

"A record label. Do you have one?"

"No."

"So, then who is telling you that you need to tour like this where you give yourself very little down time? You are your own boss, Elle. You can make up the rules. If you want to tour for the reasons that made you happy this time around, then plan it so you can enjoy those things a little more. You don't have to answer to anyone about it. If you'd prefer not to fly, make sure there is enough time for you to get from one location to the next without needing to rush."

I took in his words. It was true. I was my own boss and could set the touring schedule as I saw fit. Why drive myself crazy having to jump from one location to the next? I knew if I kept up with something like that on a regular basis, I'd end up getting to a point where music would no longer bring me the same joy it has for so many years.

"You're a smart man, Mr. Cunningham," I teased.

Levi rolled me to my back and settled over me, framing my face in his hands. "You didn't think I was just all looks, did you?" he joked back.

I shook my head and retorted, "There's only one small problem with your plan."

"Which is?"

"You."

"What about me?"

"It won't be the same without you…" I trailed off as I looked away from him.

I felt Levi's fingertips press into the sides of my head. "Look at me, sunshine."

I looked at him.

"I'd never let you go alone," he whispered softly. "If this continues between us the way it's going now, you'll never go on a tour without me."

My lips parted as I struggled to find words.

Levi saved me from my silence.

"The time I've spent with you over the last week has meant a lot to me, Elle. Watching you perform in sold-out shows across several states fills me with such a sense of pride. I see you onstage, doing what you love, and all I can do is think how lucky I am that you're mine. More than that, though, just like you I've loved the time alone with you. On the road. In bed at night. All the moments that I get to have learning more about you. Whether it's discovering that you really do own every flavor of lip balm ever invented or just how spontaneous and laid-back you are, I've fallen deeply in love with all of it. All of you. I love how you love life and what blows my mind about it is that it's the opposite of what I thought I'd ever want or need in mine."

I was now having an even more difficult time trying to speak because he said so much sweet stuff. As he held my eyes, I eventually squeaked out, "How so?"

"You know what I do for a living. It requires a level of preciseness and strategy. I'm constantly planning what's next, especially when I'm on a case. When I'm with you, I find that I don't care to do that. It doesn't matter what's happening next because I know it's going to be fucking magnificent regardless."

"Levi," I whispered.

"No joke, sunshine. I've been working nonstop for years now, not ever taking time to stop and really enjoy life. I wasn't unhappy, not by any means, but I also never felt this good. My days were packed from morning to night, sometimes longer. And yet, they never felt as full as they do now that I'm with you."

I felt all warm inside at his beautiful words. My eyes got sexy.

Levi watched as it happened.

"Kiss me, love," I begged. "Kiss me so good."

"You want to give me my honey?" he asked.

My eyes, so heated, told him everything he wanted to know.

"Yeah," he began, his voice deep and husky. "She wants to give it to me."

He brought his mouth to within inches of mine.

He inhaled.

"Berries," he stated.

"Mixed," I added.

A sexy grin spread across his face before he took my mouth and tasted mixed berries on my lips.

My thighs were pressed against his sides and my hands were at his shoulders as we kissed. After everything he had just said to me, I couldn't help the moan that escaped from the back of my throat.

Things rapidly went from slow and languid to quick and energetic. I used my feet and slid them under the waistband of his boxer briefs before I pushed them down his legs. After using his hands to slide my nightie up around my waist, Levi slid two fingers through my wetness and groaned, "Slick as honey."

He pulled his fingers from me and stuck them in his mouth, while simultaneously pushing himself inside me. My hips lifted from the bed to meet his as he filled me.

"Oh, Levi," I moaned again.

We moved like that for a bit, our pace steady, but it wasn't long before Levi was rolling to his back and taking me with him. I rode him hard, my body moving effortlessly over his. He gave me time to do my thing, going at my own speed, which was close to matching his when he had been on top. Levi held on to my thighs as I continued to ride him, until suddenly his fingers dug in deeper and he said, "Stop."

I froze on top of him and was about to ask what was

wrong when one of his hands slid around to my ass and he explained, "I want you to ride me, Elle, but I want to see this ass bouncing as you do it."

Reverse cowgirl. Levi was feeling adventurous.

I lifted off him and turned my body around so I was looking away from him. After settling my legs on either side of him, I put one hand to his thigh, curled my fingers around him, and lowered myself down onto him. Then I slid my hands down and cupped his balls.

"Fuck."

I smiled to myself. I loved making him like this.

Putting both hands to his legs, I leaned forward and began to lift and lower myself on his shaft. This position put him at just the right angle, and I was mere minutes into it when I felt myself getting close.

"I want your eyes, sunshine. When you get there, you've got to give me that sweetness."

I kept moving.

"It feels so good," I whimpered, knowing this was going to hit hard and fast.

"Give me your eyes and take it, El."

I wasn't sure how I managed it, but somehow, I glanced back over my shoulder as I continued to move and gave Levi my eyes. The second my eyes connected with his, it happened. Pure pleasure shot through my entire body, my muscles quaking with the effects of my orgasm. I couldn't begin to describe the sounds that came from me.

I kept my eyes on Levi and watched as he found his release. One hand gripped my ass as the other dug into my calf.

My movements began to slow until, finally, I stopped. I had no energy left and fell forward as my arms could no longer hold me up.

"Oh, that was incredible," I gushed.

Levi's body vibrated with laughter while his hand gently stroked along the skin on my ass cheek.

"You're quite the cowgirl. I should have known from that first day I saw you in those boots at my place."

"What can I say other than to be totally cliché and admit that you've got the world's best saddle?"

"Feel free to go for a ride any time you'd like."

"I'll be sure to keep that in mind." My voice was a mix of lazy and sated.

Levi gave me a minute to catch my breath and come to my senses before he moved, pulled himself from my body, and helped me up.

"I'm going to go clean up and then I want to fall asleep in your arms."

He squeezed my shoulder and softly stated, "Okay, hurry up."

After I cleaned up, I crawled back into the bed and over Levi. As soon as I reached the opposite side of him, he hooked an arm around my waist, hauled me up against his body, and kissed me. When he pulled away, he stared intently at my eyes before whispering, "I love you so much, sunshine."

"I love you more," I replied.

His hold around me tightened and he pressed a soft kiss to my forehead. A few minutes later, when I was nearly asleep, I heard him whisper, "Not possible."

Warmth spread through my body.

Just before I fell asleep, those two words were repeating over and over in my head and I knew in that moment that I hadn't ever felt so content before in my entire life.

The next day, Levi and I slept in. We had a lazy morning, filled with some slow lovemaking, followed by breakfast in the form of room service. Levi asked me how I wanted to spend the day.

"At the pool, doing nothing but sunbathing," I answered.

He stared at me.

"Is that okay?"

"Yeah, Elle, it's okay. You just surprised me with that. I thought you'd be taking me all over the city today."

"I like to keep you on your toes," I teased. "Besides, I have a show tonight and tomorrow night. Yesterday was enough Vegas excitement for me; I want to just spend the next two days relaxing."

He mumbled under his breath, "All of it."

"What?"

Levi shook his head and answered, "Nothing, sweetness. I'll let the guys know they are off the hook today. You and I can spend the day at the pool before your show tonight."

I gave him a big, bright smile and said, "Thanks, love."

Several hours later, my body was glistening under the hot, desert sun. It was late afternoon and I had successfully spent nearly my entire day soaking up the sun's rays. I did take a dip or two in the pool to cool off throughout, just to keep from overheating. The day couldn't have been more perfect.

I was in the lounge chair, decked out in my yellow bikini, a pair of shades, and a hat when I saw Dom and Pierce walking our way. They both were wearing a pair of board shorts and nothing else.

Holy crap.

They were both in phenomenal shape. They were both one hundred percent solid muscle, but where Pierce was lean and trim, Dom was jacked. Sure, I had seen lots of fit people throughout the day at the pool and, of course, I had Levi beside me all day long, but there was something different about Dom and Pierce.

They weren't like everyone else at the pool.

They carried themselves differently.

They were like Levi.

They exuded confidence.

It was like they knew not only what their bodies looked like, but also what they were capable of. The people they passed on their walk toward us couldn't take their eyes off them. Those people were mostly women. The few guys that noticed them were mostly feeling intimidated. I couldn't say I blamed either group.

"Elle?" I heard Levi growl from beside me.

"Yeah?" I asked, nonchalantly, not taking my eyes off the sight in front of me.

"You can stop drooling anytime now."

I turned to look at Levi and exclaimed, "I am *not* drooling!"

"I'm sitting right next to you, and I can see behind your shades. You haven't blinked once in the last two minutes. Not to mention, your mouth opened the minute you saw them and it still hasn't closed."

I snapped my lips together and narrowed my eyes at him. Of course, he couldn't see that I was doing that since I was wearing sunglasses, but it made me feel better.

Dom and Pierce made their approach, so I didn't continue the conversation with Levi any further.

"You've been out here all day?" Pierce asked, clearly shocked.

"Yeah," I responded. "That's the whole point of making it a lazy day of sunbathing."

He shook his head in disbelief.

"Where were you guys all day?" Levi chimed in.

"Shooting range," Dom started. "We spent a couple hours there after we checked out the venue for tonight, grabbed some lunch, came back and got a workout in, but this fuckin' heat is ridiculous. Figured we'd take advantage of the pool. I'll take the snow any day of the week over this shit."

"The shooting range?" I repeated in a questioning tone.
They nodded at me.

"You mean, shooting guns?"

They nodded again, only this time they laughed, too.

My head jerked to Levi and I asked excitedly, "Oh, please, can we do that tomorrow?"

"I thought you wanted to relax and sunbathe?"

I waved my hand in the air and affirmed, "Yeah, but we did that all day today. And I said that before I knew that a shooting range was an option."

"Have you ever shot a gun?"

I shook my head.

He just stared at me.

I pulled down my shades, gave him sexy, bedroom eyes, and begged, "Please?"

"Fuck," Levi hissed under his breath.

"Boss, I do not envy you. Pierce, bro, make sure I never end up in a position where a woman looks at me like that and I just cave," Dom joked.

I bit the inside of my cheek trying not to laugh. The eyes worked.

Levi stood from the lounge chair next to mine and held his hand out to me. "Ready to go up to our room and get ready for your show tonight?"

He was removing me from this situation. I was ready to go up, but I wasn't going to just leave.

"Not yet," I began, digging through my bag at the foot of my chair. I pulled out my phone, opened a social media app, and looked to the three men in front of me. "We need to go live now."

"Now?" Levi asked.

I sighed and stood up. "Levi, love, it would be incredibly selfish of me to not go live right now."

"Selfish?" Pierce questioned.

"Seriously? I can't deny the ladies the perfection that stands before me. So, put your happy faces on, boys, and get ready to say hello."

I switched the setting to 'live' on my phone and pressed the button to start recording. Within a few seconds, I had several hundred followers tuning in and the number was steadily increasing. I spoke to them.

"Hey everyone. As many of you already know from posts I made yesterday, I am here in Vegas. Today, I have spent my entire day lounging poolside. I am about to head up to my room to start getting ready for my show tonight, but knowing how many of you feel about my security team I couldn't possibly keep this from you."

I flipped the camera around and Levi, Pierce, and Dom came into view on the screen. None of them looked happy.

Comments poured in; I could barely keep up reading them.

I glanced back up at the guys and, noting they were still not amused, I flipped the camera back to front-facing. When my face took up the screen I explained, "I'm sorry they aren't looking very happy. I think the heat has gotten to them."

My eyes peeked over the top of the phone at them. I could see that it was not, in fact, the heat that was bothering them. I didn't want them irritated with me, so I knew I needed to smooth things over. I turned my back to them and scooted closer so they were now on the screen standing behind me.

Pierce was first. I thought back to the time in the hotel room where I received the voicemail message from my stalker. Pierce was so calm and took control of the situation, immediately reassuring me that everything was okay. He also single-handedly took down that guy in the parking lot back in Tucson while getting a read on a partial plate for the getaway car.

"This is Pierce. He might be all kinds of good-looking on the outside, but that's not all there is to him. He is very smart and anticipates things before they happen. This guy has a huge heart and I'm incredibly lucky he's been there on at least two occasions to help me in situations where I might have otherwise fallen apart. Out of the goodness of his heart, he chose to stay on this tour with me to make sure I remain safe, even though he was scheduled to return home after the LA show."

Dom was next.

"This is Dom. Yes, he's huge and built like a Mack truck. Anyone would be crazy not to feel safe around him. And yes, ladies, I know... the beautiful smile and the dimples. I get it. But again, just like Pierce, he's so much more than what he looks like. He's funny and knows how to have a great time. I'm told that when it comes to the work he does, he's a badass, crazy motherfucker. I don't exactly know what that means in his line of work, but it makes me feel safe. Dom is the life of the party kind of guy, but he also knows when to be serious. When we get back to Wyoming, he is going to be giving me lessons in self-defense."

I moved to Levi and tilted my head up to look at him. I beamed a smile at him. He looked down at my smiling face and his softened.

"This is Levi," I started. "A real, live superhero. He's my boyfriend and, not taking anything away from Dom and Pierce, he's the hottest of the bunch. What you see on the outside pales in comparison to the person he is on the inside. He is the owner of a well-respected, highly sought security firm and is smart, talented, and very protective. Beyond that, he's incredibly loving and sweet. He makes me feel like I'm the most beautiful woman in the world and I'm proud to admit that I never thought I could ever feel as happy as I do when I'm with him. He's changed my life and he loves me like I never thought possible."

I paused a moment and glanced back up at him. The corners of his eyes had crinkled with adoration. When I turned to look at Dom and Pierce, I was happy to see that they were no longer moody.

Mission accomplished.

"So, there you have it. Now you know there is more to these guys than them just being a bunch of gorgeous bodies and handsome faces. Levi is spoken for, but I hope whoever ends up with Dom or Pierce will consider themselves extremely fortunate to have found such a great guy. I've got to get going now, but I hope you all have a wonderful weekend. If you're in Vegas, I'll see you at my show tonight. Later, loves."

I ended the live session and turned around to face the guys. They were all smiling at me. I smiled back.

"Ready, sunshine?"

I nodded.

With that, Dom and Pierce stayed behind and used the pool to get a reprieve from the desert sun. I'm convinced a few women were more than happy about this fact.

Levi escorted me up to our suite where he insisted on showing me what my words to my fans meant to him.

CHAPTER 18

Levi

"**M**ICHAELS."

"Hey Trent. I got your message from earlier, but Elle insisted on spending the entire day sunbathing. You said it could wait, so I figured I'd wait until we came back to the suite for her to get ready so I could talk. What's happening?"

"Hey, Levi. Yeah, as it turns out, our stalker is only slightly more than a bit jealous of your woman."

Fucking wonderful.

"How so?"

Trent laughed. "Considering you've been in ninety percent of the posts Elle has made lately, I'm surprised you didn't just expect this. On the bright side, Becky is playing right into our hand."

I was growing frustrated. "What is she doing now?" I asked, my patience gone.

"Elle's been doing a great job with showing just how great life has been lately. Between the road trips and the live session with you to the fun and games last night on the Las Vegas Strip and even the live session with you, Dom, and Reynolds roughly an hour ago, Becky is livid that Elle is happy. The posts on all of Becky's social media accounts are her taking shots at Elle."

I found this surprising. Putting herself out there directly like that didn't make sense to me. "Wait, she's calling out Elle directly?"

Trent went on to explain, "No. Unless someone managed to make the connection between Becky Blunt and Elle Blackman, it wouldn't seem obvious to the average person. Knowing what we know, it couldn't be more obvious. She never uses Elle's name, but I'd like to think she's expecting Elle will see this at some point. Essentially, after the road trip to San Francisco and all the festivities that Elle posted about from your night on the town last night, Becky ended up posting something today about people who lived life disorganized and chaotic. She also made statements about people who thought they deserved to have it all and how they'll trample over everyone else to get it."

I took a minute to process what Trent was saying. Elle wouldn't take this lightly. She was successful, but she worked hard for that success. Trampling on people was not something Elle could or would do. She was kind and generous. She cared about people and she adored her fans. Despite how much she loved singing, she would never purposely set out to hurt someone to accomplish her goals and realize her dreams. I also didn't like what hearing this meant from an investigative standpoint, but I wouldn't make any assumptions or bring that part of it on Elle until I was certain.

"Elle's going to be hurt hearing this," I told Trent.

"That's not even the worst of it, boss."

Damn it.

"What do you mean?"

"Well, had I spoken to you earlier it would have been the worst. Now that it's been roughly an hour since Elle went live with you and the guys, Becky's jealousy is skyrocketing. It probably would have been enough for Elle to show she was hanging with the three of you, but then she went on to talk about what each of you has done for her and how there's something to all of you beyond just your looks. Becky just posted a direct response to Elle's live session."

Trent paused a moment. He knew he had to tell me what was said, but I'm sure knowing whatever it was made it not such an easy task.

I gave him some time, but when he didn't say anything I lost my patience. "Just say it, Michaels. I get it, but whatever it is I'm sure I'll need as much time as I can get to figure out how to give this all to my woman."

"Be alert the next two nights, Levi. This psychopath is calling Elle's character into question. She's making mention of people who act like whores. I'm convinced she's jealous that Elle's surrounded by a bunch of men who would lay down their lives to protect her. The fact that those men are good-looking, according to Elle and ninety-nine percent of her followers, is adding fuel to Becky's fire. She actually said, and I quote, hopefully promiscuous acts won't lead to devastating consequences that someone's asking for."

"Are you fuckin' telling me that this bitch is hinting at Elle being sexually assaulted or raped?"

Trent let out a sigh.

"I wouldn't put it past her. To be safe, don't let Elle outside of arm's length of you or any of the guys at any point in time."

"Jesus Christ," I bit out. "Can you give Dom and Pierce a briefing? I don't want to have to repeat this shit a second time. It'll be bad enough having to tell Elle, let alone needing to have her listen in while I tell them about it."

"You've got it. Anything else?"

"Is Cruz around?"

"Yeah," he started. "Want me to transfer you?"

"Please," I responded. "Thanks, Michaels. Keep watching those accounts."

"Will do. Hang tight."

I waited while Trent transferred me through to Cruz.

"Levi?" Cruz's voice filtered through the phone.

"Yeah," I responded. "Just got the update on our stalker from Trent and figured I'd check in with you on everything else."

Cruz laughed.

"Considering you already know we've got shit under control here, I'm guessing you aren't really looking to check in on anything else. You need perspective right now, don't you?"

That was the truth. And I was grateful Cruz knew it.

"I'm trying to keep my shit together right now while my girl is in the bathroom getting all dolled up for her show tonight. She's going to walk out any minute now, looking beautiful, and I've got to break this news to her. How the fuck do I tell her that this bitch is making threats about sexual assault and rape? Who thinks like that? And a woman no less…" I trailed off.

"Jealousy and obsession, bro. Jealousy is something we can all understand, but when the jealousy leads you to obsess over someone, that's where it crosses lines. You aren't going to be able to understand it because it's fucked-up logic."

"Elle doesn't take well to this stuff," I explained. "She completely loses her mind and goes off on a tirade. I don't want her worked up before the show. Maybe I should wait to talk to her about it until after the show."

"That's not a good idea," my brother started. "I know you will be on high alert now with this news, but shit happens sometimes. If tonight happens to be one of those nights, you need to make sure Elle understands there is a much more serious threat than someone simply stalking her and copying her every move. Don't let her be blindsided by it. And if she finds out after something happens that you knew and didn't tell her, how's that going to be for you?"

"Damn it."

I heard the bathroom door open and knew my conversation with Cruz was over now. I needed to tell Elle what Trent found and make sure she knew I'd do everything in my power to keep her safe.

"Alright, Cruz. Elle just walked out of the bathroom. I've got to go."

"Okay. Do what you've got to do and protect her. I'm looking forward to having another sister-in-law."

Damn.

My gut tightened.

Elle.

As my wife.

An image of her dressed as a bride flashed in my mind and I instantly felt the tension leave my body. I had to laugh. The words I said to her a couple weeks ago were ringing true. When we went to tell her brother about what was happening with her and the fact that Elle and I were looking to pursue something between the two of us, I told her to make sure Charley was there. I explained how there's nothing like having a good woman there for you when you're dealing with something that makes you feel frustrated or angry. Unfortunately, I thought it'd be particularly selfish of me to expect she could help me deal with the anger and frustration I felt with this situation when she was the one who would likely need someone there to talk her down.

"A bit early for that, don't you think?" I retorted, not wanting to admit the truth to Cruz about what I felt for Elle.

"She's it for you. I can see it. The rest of the team sees it. Why would you waste time?"

"The rest of the team hasn't even met her. What are you talking about?"

Cruz burst out laughing now.

"Bro, she's done how many live sessions on social media. Trent's tracking that shit. You don't think we've all watched it?"

Fuck.

I kept quiet.

"Not only does your silence tell me everything I need to know," my brother began. "But I'm also not blind. You're gone for her, Levi."

"Yeah," I admitted.

"She's good for you," he assured me. "Perfect, in fact. It's quick, yeah, but don't waste too much time and make sure you lock it down with her."

"Let me worry about this situation first."

"Yeah. Okay. Go talk to your woman. We'll see you Sunday."

"Later," I said as I disconnected the call.

I dropped the phone to the table in front of me and stared at it.

The door from the bedroom into the living room opened and, without looking, I knew Elle walked in. She immediately sensed something wasn't right. Instead of getting my attention by simply asking about it, Elle walked over and stood in front of me.

She didn't say anything.

My eyes left the table, traveled from her boots up her tanned, sexy legs to her cut-off shorts. They continued their ascent up her torso, to her slender and exposed neck until, finally, they found her face and those beautiful fucking eyes. At the moment, those eyes were worried.

I leaned back on the couch and held my hand out to her. She placed her hand in mine and climbed into my lap.

Elle sat there silently, letting me hold her. I kept one hand resting on her bare thigh while the other ran up her back, into her hair, and stopped at the back of her head.

"You look beautiful," I shared.

She gave me a small smile before she spoke. "Thank you."

I searched her face, looking for something. To be honest, I wasn't sure if I was looking for indication from her that it was okay to give her the news now or if I was simply searching her face to make sure I committed to memory the way she looked.

Elle's hand wrapped around the back of my neck and into my hair. Her eyes went from worrying to silently pleading.

"I talked to Trent, sunshine," I began, not wanting to keep it from her any longer. "I need to talk to you about something."

"Okay," she said softly.

"It's not good and I need you to know that I will do whatever I've got to do to make sure you stay safe and this doesn't touch you."

"Tell me, love."

"She doesn't like you, Elle," I started, my voice strained. "Her jealousy has gone to another level. There's no doubt this is a sick obsession. Unfortunately, the fixation is now at a point where it's no longer just online."

She grew tense in my lap.

"Is everyone okay? Are Wes and Charley alright? What about my parents? Leah?"

Trample people? Elle wasn't even concerned about her safety in this moment. She was worried that something had happened to the people she loved.

"They are all safe," I reassured her. "It's you."

Her brows furrowed.

"What do you mean?"

I took in a deep breath and let it out. Then, I told her. I

explained that someone had taken this thing to a level that was beyond unacceptable. She learned that Becky wanted to see physical, sexual, and emotional trauma come her way.

At first, Elle looked terrified. As I continued to talk and enlighten her on everything Trent found, she no longer looked terrified. She looked angry. Fuming, in fact.

"Are you kidding me?" she screeched.

"I wish I were."

"So, this bitch is the one that's obsessed with me to the point I need to fear for my safety and hire a security team. I realize I didn't actually hire you, but that's not the point right now. All I'm saying is that she is the reason I even have not only you but also Dom and Pierce around right now. Knowing that, she has the audacity to call me a whore and basically say that I deserve to be sexually violated?!"

"Elle, it's fucked. I know," I agreed, keeping my voice neutral, hoping it would help calm her. "I debated on whether to even tell you this now because I didn't want you upset before your show. Of course, I'd never hide anything from you but thought it might be better to wait. I talked to Cruz and he thought I should tell you now. He was right; I don't want you blindsided with this should anyone attempt to get to you tonight."

Elle's body went rigid.

"They aren't going to touch you, sweetness," I assured her. "I'm with you the entire night. Even when you are on-stage, you won't be more than a few feet away from me. We've got Dom and Pierce with us, too. Trust me, Elle. We will keep you safe."

"I trust you, Levi," she insisted. "I know you won't let anything happen to me. I'm just over this whole situation. I don't understand what someone could possibly be getting out of it. I didn't understand it when it was just the social media stuff. Now? Being held at knifepoint and nearly kidnapped to realizing that someone wants to see me sexually assaulted is a whole other level of crazy. I don't care how much I dislike someone; I could never wish harm like that on anyone. Friend or foe."

"That's because you are who you are, El. It's like Cruz just said to me a few minutes ago. This isn't likely to be something we'll ever be able to fully understand because we don't work like this. We will find her, but locating someone's whereabouts is completely different than understanding their logic, particularly when it's crazy logic. You need to be prepared for that. I know I've said it a few times now, but you might not get an answer as to why she's doing this."

Elle let out a frustrated sigh.

"I love you," I shared as I squeezed her thigh.

She leaned into me and pressed her body into my chest, her face nuzzled in my neck.

"I want this to end, Levi," she sighed, her frustration evident.

I'd give anything to take this away from her.

"I know, sunshine. I do, too. We're working on it. I promise you, we'll put an end to this. It's just going to take some time."

Elle stayed silent a bit before she spoke again. "I love you, too."

Just then, there was a knock at the door.

"Dom and Pierce," I informed her. "Are you ready to go?"

She nodded.

"Okay, wait here while I get the door."

I shifted Elle out of my lap and stood. Before walking to the door, I used my thumb and tipped up her chin.

I pressed a soft kiss to her lips and instantly regretted it. My regret had nothing to do with not enjoying the kiss and everything to do with the fact that Elle's lips tasted of coconut and I had Dom and Pierce waiting outside the door.

Shit.

Reluctantly, I pulled away and walked to the door. I opened the door, took one look at their faces, and knew they had spoken to Trent.

"Is she alright?" Pierce asked.

I shook my head as I let them in. "Not really, but she's managing as well as you could expect considering the circumstances," I answered.

They acknowledged my response with chin lifts and walked into the suite. When they entered the living room area, they saw Elle sitting on the couch.

I hated seeing her like this.

Frustrated and unhappy.

She looked up from her lap as we entered the room and moved to get up from the couch.

"I'm just going to grab my bag and we can leave."

Elle walked into the bedroom. Pierce and Dom gave me concerned looks.

When Elle came back into the room a minute later, she had a look of determination on her face.

"Okay, boys. Ready?"

We nodded at her.

"Don't let me get violated tonight."

"Elle," Dom called.

When her eyes went to him, he continued, "That's not fuckin' happening. Not tonight, not ever. Do not joke about that shit."

She held his eyes and deadpanned, "I wasn't joking."

"We've got you covered, rock star," Pierce chimed in. "You'll go there tonight, do your thing, and be back here in a couple hours safe and sound."

"I know. I trust you three to keep me safe. That said, when we get back to Wyoming, Dom, I want to start training with you immediately."

"Sure," he agreed.

"I mean it," she persisted. "I'm not going to be a victim."

"You won't be. We'll train when we get back, babe."

Elle nodded at him. "Thanks."

Pierce turned to me and explained, "We'll go ahead of you. We met with the owner of the venue earlier today. Cool guy. He understands a bit of what we're dealing with and is willing to accommodate us in any way we need. As soon as we get there, I'll make sure he knows the threat is heightened. He'll give us what we need to be certain Elle stays safe."

"Thanks, Pierce," I responded. "We're coming right behind you. See you in a few."

With that, the guys let themselves out and I walked to Elle. I put my arms around her and held her a minute.

"I can't wait to get home, Levi," she sighed.

"I know."

"I feel like I could deal with this so much better if I was home. The constant traveling, not having any of my family or friends around, and having to live in constant fear of whether she's going to do something is starting to take its toll on me. Right now, you are the only thing I've got that's keeping me from completely breaking down."

Fuck, I wanted to find this bitch and stop this shit. My girl was strong, but she was beginning to crumble.

"Sunshine," I started. "For the next two nights, I'll be what you need me to be and then some if I can help make this easier for you to deal with."

"I feel like I'm suffocating, Levi. I'm genuinely trying to act like it doesn't bother me and just go about my business, but the reality is that it does bother me. I can't just shut that feeling off. It's so consuming, it's like I can't breathe right now. I want to be able to breathe again."

"I'm with you, Elle. Just keep breathing," I urged her.

"I'm trying."

I pressed a kiss to the top of her head. Elle pulled her face back to look up at me.

"It's easier to breathe when you love me," she admitted.

My gut twisted as I gave her a warm look.

"Then let's get you to your show so I can get you back here and give you all the love you need to breathe easy for at least the next day."

"I think I need lots of love, Levi."

"I'll make sure you get it, sweetness."

"Thank you for being so good to me."

"It's easy, Elle. You're so easy to love...especially when you taste like coconut."

She beamed up at me.

That smile with those sparkling bedroom eyes.

"You like it?"

"Number three," I admitted.

Confusion washed over her face.

"Grape is still in the lead, watermelon is a very close second. Coconut is number three," I explained.

I could see her mind working a minute, so I left her to it.

"Okay," she finally piped up. "Take me to my show, keep me safe, and bring me back here as quickly as possible so you can give me lots of love."

With that request, I took my woman to her show.

I kept her safe.

Then, I brought her back and gave her a lot of love.

CHAPTER 19

Elle

"**T**HAT BITCH!!"

"Elle, what's wrong?"

Levi's words just barely broke through my rage. I was seething mad.

The posts made on social media that were either verbatim of mine or attempts to diminish what mine meant were already enough to deal with. I was slowly getting to a point where I realized that Becky could do that all she wanted; it was creepy, but it didn't have any real effect on my life. The threats of sexual assault were not okay and I knew I'd never be alright with that; however, this new development was where I drew the line.

"I need more security!" I shrieked. "This woman is possessed."

"What is going on?" Levi pressed.

"You said Trent is a genius with computers, right?"

Levi's brows pulled together, but he answered, "Yes."

"She's invaded my privacy, Levi."

"What?"

There was a knock at the hotel suite door. Dom and Pierce. The four of us were set to go to the shooting range today before my final show in Vegas later tonight. Levi moved to open the door.

After opening the door, Levi announced, "Perfect timing, boys. Elle's losing her shit, and she was just about to tell me why."

"We can come back or just meet you there if you'd prefer," Dom offered, clearly not liking what he was hearing.

Part of me wanted to laugh. Dom thought I was losing my shit with Levi and not over the crazy psychopath in my life right now.

"Stay, Dom," I started. "It's about Becky."

"Fucking hell. What now?"

I took in a deep breath and repeated the words I said to Levi just minutes before, "She's invaded my privacy."

The three men stood before me and waited for me to continue.

"She accessed my private messages on Facebook."

"How do you know this?" Pierce asked.

"While Levi and I were waiting here for you, I decided to pull out my phone and check in to my social media accounts," I began. "When I went to Facebook, I thought I'd look and see if there was anything new. I mean, I prefer not to look at her stuff at all, but this whole situation has gone to another level. I figure it's better to be proactive at this point."

I paused a moment before I continued, "So, I get to her page and see that she's made a post talking about family meetings. She attempts to make it appear as though she's talking about people in new relationships and how it must be nerve-wracking. There are too many little things throughout the post that tells me she's gone this far."

"I don't understand," Levi confessed. "How does her talking about family meetings have anything to do with invading your privacy, El?"

"We're getting together with Emme and Zane when we get back. Emme and I sent a few messages back and forth with each other when we were on the drive from LA to San Francisco.

She was telling me how happy Zane was for the two of us and how he knew, just from seeing the live session you and I did, that we were meant to be together. Emme said Zane knew you found something good and was hoping Cruz would soon find something just like it. If you look at what she's posted, you'll see what I'm saying."

I held my phone out to them. Dom took it out of my hand and read it before passing it to Levi who, after reading it himself, passed it to Pierce. After all of them read what she wrote, Levi cautioned, "It's a far stretch."

My head jerked back.

He didn't believe me?

"Excuse me?" I whispered in shock.

"I don't know, Elle. I mean, you don't think it could be the slightest bit coincidental. Look, she knows you are with me, obviously. Zane's one of the top snowboarders in the world. It's possible she's just trying to find something to talk about and, on the surface, it looks like this was methodical."

"You think I'm crazy?" I retorted.

"I'm not saying that."

"Well, it sure sounds like it," I shot back.

"She's been doing a lot that would be difficult for anyone to deny was intentional. This is just a little more far-fetched. I'm not saying it's not possible, but it's just a bit unlikely."

Dom and Pierce looked like they were standing in a mine field.

"Whatever. You don't believe me, that's fine. I know. Deep down in the pit of my stomach, Levi, I know. I am certain she got into my account and read my messages. This post she made tells me what I need to know."

My eyes welled with tears at the thought that he didn't trust my instinct. Levi held my eyes and I could see the guilt. I decided to let him off the hook.

"Can we go?" I asked.

"What?"

"The shooting range. I'd like to go. Can we leave now?"

"Sunshine…" he got out before I cut him off.

"Please, Levi," I begged.

I was already on the verge of tears. We had just experienced a fight in front of two of his employees, who were also his friends, and it was awkward.

Thankfully, Levi gave in and nodded his head.

With that, we left.

The ride to the shooting range was mostly silent. Dom tried to lighten the mood and I did my best to shake off what happened, but it hurt. Levi loved me, and he didn't believe in me.

I took some time on the drive to reach out to Wes. I didn't plan to tell him what happened with Levi and me, but I wanted to tell him about the situation with Becky. Maybe an outsider's perspective would help.

I tapped out a text to him explaining briefly about Becky and her most recent post. I also told him about my conversation via private messages with Emme. He replied almost instantly.

Wes: Hang tight. Let me look at her page.

Me: Okay.

Several minutes had passed before he finally gave me his thoughts.

Wes: It's evident that she's the stalker. Seeing your stuff and then everything she posts, you'd have to be blind not to see that. The most recent post, though? I'm not so sure. Is it even remotely possible she's making statements based on what she might be assuming would happen? I don't know every detail of your conversation with Emme, but there isn't anything I can see in what she posted that's indication she viewed those private messages.

Me: You too? Why does nobody believe me? Am I crazy?

Wes: What are you talking about?

Me: Nothing. Never mind. I'll be home tomorrow.

I looked up and realized Levi had just pulled in to the parking lot at the range. I felt my phone vibrate in my hands.

Wes was calling.

I wasn't going to do this now. I turned the phone off.

Levi parked and we all got out. As the four of us were walking in, Levi's phone rang. I knew it was Wes.

"Hey guys, go ahead in and stay with her. Let me take this call," Levi requested of Dom and Pierce.

I gave him a glance and I'm certain he saw the hurt in my eyes. I quickly turned away and continued walking into the range with the guys. Levi stayed outside.

Once inside, I tried to shake off the thoughts I had about the Becky situation and decided to use the frustration over the whole debacle with Levi to my advantage.

"Okay, boys," I called out to get Dom and Pierce's attention. "What do I have to do?"

Pierce explained, "We're going to go up to the front counter and choose a gun for you to rent. They have a few books you can look through of the firearms that are available."

"Sweet."

Pierce grinned.

"We'll help you pick one that makes sense," Dom added.

We walked up to the counter and Joe, the clerk, asked how he could help.

"Looking for lane and gun rental," Pierce shared. "With ammo."

"Sure," Joe said. "How many lanes?"

"Three."

"Handguns or rifles?" Joe asked as he pulled out a couple of binders and set them on the counter.

"Handguns," Pierce answered.

"Wait," I called. "Rifles? Like assault rifles?"

"You're not shooting an AR, rock star," Pierce announced. "At least, I'm not going to be the one to make that call."

"As should be the case, Pierce. I'm a grown woman and can make the call myself," I declared.

I turned my attention to Joe.

"Excuse me, Joe, but I'd like to look at the rifle catalog as well," I stated sweetly. "Will you help me choose something good?"

"Elle," Pierce warned.

Joe looked worried.

Dom chimed in. "I'll help you."

"Dom, it's not a good idea."

"It's fine, Reynolds. Here's what's going to happen, Elle. We rent a couple of handguns and an AR. You shoot the handguns first, learn what to do, how to hold them, and get comfortable with the recoil. If you can handle that, we'll move on to the AR."

I grinned up at Dom.

He winked at me and we went about the business of selecting some handguns and rifles to shoot. The guys got a bunch of ammo to go with it all and, after we grabbed ear and eye protection, the three of us went into the range.

The range officer brought the guns we chose over to our lanes and Dom immediately went about showing me what I needed to do. If I was being honest, I had to admit I was a little nervous. I listened to Dom's instructions and watched as he loaded the bullets into the magazine. After he inserted the magazine, he set the gun back down in front of me.

We used the switch on the wall of my lane to move the target back. Dom took the time to explain what the best shooting distance was based on the type of gun being used. He set the target at an appropriate range and offered his encouragement.

"Alright, rock star, let's see what you can do."

With the gun in my hand, I swallowed hard, looked up at him, and admitted, "I'm a little scared."

"Okay, put the gun down," he ordered.

"What?"

"Put the gun down," he repeated.

I set the gun back down and looked back to him for an explanation.

"Be sure about what you're doing, Elle," he instructed. "You're putting yourself behind something that can do some serious damage. The last thing you need to do is be scared behind it. I understand being nervous since you've never done it before; that's okay. Scared is not. If you are scared, you can't be prepared."

That made sense.

"When you're feeling confident, pick up the gun and hold it like I showed you."

I gave myself a minute to get my head sorted. Dom was right. While I hoped I never needed to be in a situation where I'd have to use a gun, I knew it was imperative that I had the confidence to use it appropriately and without fear.

I picked up the gun, held it in my hands as Dom showed me, and pointed it at the target.

"Now remember, keep your arms strong and use your sights to line up the target," Dom repeated a portion of his earlier lesson.

I did as I was told.

"Whenever you're ready, go for it."

A few seconds later, I went for it. I shot off a round and my body jerked back slightly, but Dom was positioned right behind me so I didn't move too much.

"Again," he instructed.

I shot off another round.

"Good. Now do it again and keep trying to hit the same spot on the target."

I went through several more rounds until I had emptied the magazine. I set the gun down and the target began moving toward me.

"Reynolds, check this shit out," Dom said from behind me.

Pierce popped his head around the wall and looked at my handiwork. His eyes dropped to mine and he asked, "You sure you never shot anything before?"

I nodded.

He grinned at me and praised, "Badass, rock star."

I took this to mean I did a good job, so I looked up at Dom and practically begged, "Can I try the assault rifle now?"

He chuckled and suggested, "How about we get a few more rounds through the handgun before we do that?"

My shoulders slumped in disappointment, but I agreed, "Alright."

Dom helped me load another magazine and I prepared to find a new spot on my target. Once I was ready, I started again. According to the guys, I had done really well with my first try. Halfway through the second magazine, I realized I was much more confident. I held my body well and I was no longer rocking back into Dom after each shot was fired.

The slide shot back indicating I had fired through all the rounds, so I carefully set the gun back down. That's when I realized the two lanes beside me that we had rented were both being used. I turned around and saw that Dom was no longer standing behind me.

Levi was standing there, watching me. I'm not sure how it was possible, but there was a mix of heat and remorse in his expression.

I didn't know what to say.

"Killer shot," he praised.

"Thanks," I said quietly. I wasn't sure if he could hear me considering he had on ear protection.

Levi took the remaining two steps toward me and closed the distance between our bodies. When he was inches from me, he lowered his head to me and said loud enough so I could hear, but not so loud that anyone else would, "I'm sorry if I hurt you this morning, Elle. When we get back to the hotel, we can talk about it."

"Okay," I agreed.

He pressed a gentle kiss to my cheek and I melted on the spot. It was so tender and sweet; and though I was still upset by what happened earlier in the day, I couldn't deny that the kiss made me feel just a tad bit better.

"Can I try the assault rifle now?" I asked.

Levi's eyes rounded and he pulled back.

"The assault rifle?" he began questioning me. "Was one rented with the intention that you'd be using it?"

I nodded.

"Who thought that was a good idea?"

"Me."

I could tell he was struggling with this, which was exacerbated by the fact that he was likely trying to avoid another argument.

"Fuck," he muttered.

He turned and moved out of my lane. A minute later he was back with Pierce.

"Let's go," he instructed as he held his hand out to me. "We're switching lanes. The rifle is over two lanes."

I placed my hand in Levi's and we walked over to the lane on the end. He took the time to instruct me, much like Dom had with the handgun, on everything I needed to know about using the assault rifle properly. After giving me a quick but thorough lesson, Levi stepped aside so I could try it out.

I picked up the rifle and held it as Levi had shown me.

"Hang on," he requested. "Let's adjust the stock so it's in a good position for you to hold and shoot it."

Levi adjusted the stock, confirming that I felt comfortable with the position it was in. Once we had that all sorted, he leaned down and reminded me, "Remember this is different than a handgun. Your whole body is going to feel this. The stock is pressed into your shoulder, which is part of the reason the recoil is easier to control and hitting your target is generally much easier. Even still, you'll feel this in a much different way than you did the handgun. The sound is going to be much deeper, too."

I nodded my head in acknowledgment of everything he just said to me.

"I'm right behind you whenever you are ready."

I took a minute to focus in on the target and pulled the trigger.

Holy shit.

That was incredible.

I did it again.

It was even more amazing the second time.

I continued through the entire magazine. When I had emptied it, I set down the rifle, flipped the switch on the side to pull my target in, and turned back to Levi with the biggest smile on my face.

His lustful eyes went back and forth between me and the target I had blasted to smithereens.

"That was so much fun," I beamed up at him.

"I can see you enjoyed yourself," he replied. "You did a hell of a job, sunshine."

I took the target down and stepped away from the rifle.

"Do you want to try?" I asked him. "You should. Everyone should experience doing that. Wow, what a rush."

"I've already shot rifles before, Elle. I hadn't planned on shooting one today, but since you're so amped about it, I'll do a few rounds."

It was then Dom snuck his head around the corner and peeked over into our lane. I held my target up and showed it to him. He grinned at me, gave me a fist bump, and praised me, "Solid work!"

"Thanks! Levi's going to shoot a couple rounds. Will you take my picture with my targets? I can't wait to share this. If nothing else, Becky will know not to mess with me."

Dom laughed at me, but took pictures for me anyway.

The four of us spent the next hour swapping lanes and shooting different guns. I had such a great time that I asked Levi if he'd take me to the shooting range again when we got home. He agreed.

We stopped for a late lunch before we made our way back to the hotel. When we arrived back at our suite, I walked in ahead of Levi and went straight through to the bedroom. I kicked off my sneakers, closed my eyes, and dropped to my back on the bed. Seconds later, I felt Levi's body come over mine.

My eyes slowly opened as my hands instinctively went to his shoulders.

"It was Wes that called when we got to the range," he shared.

I dipped my head and confirmed, "I figured as much. I turned off my phone when he called me not two minutes prior."

"Why did you do that?" he asked, his voice soft.

I took in a deep breath and blew it out.

"I don't like the way it feels when the people I love most in the world, people I've put my faith in, don't trust my judgment. It hurts to know I have one hundred percent confidence in you and you don't trust my instincts."

"Elle, I'm sorry for making you feel like I don't believe in you," he apologized. "That's not the case at all. This isn't about me not trusting you. I know it's possible that Becky got into your account, but I think there's part of me that doesn't want to believe we're dealing with someone who is not only crazy but also has the capability to pull that off. She's got to have some serious skills to hack into your account. She's making such calculated moves and I don't like it. For me, it'd be easier to believe that there was one thing that she did that was simply coincidence."

When he explained his reasoning behind what he said this morning, I understood it. Of course, that did little to change what happened earlier… and the fact that it happened in front of Dom and Pierce.

"I appreciate you offering me an explanation of your line of thinking, but it was embarrassing, Levi. You made me feel like a fool in front of Dom and Pierce and, more than that, you broke my heart by not standing by me in something I felt so strongly about. It makes me question whether I should give you my thoughts on anything moving forward. From where I'm standing, if you can't support and believe in what I'm saying when I give you the bad news, why would I ever want to share the good with you?" I asked.

Defeat washed over his face and he dropped his head down.

When he lifted it, he insisted, "I never meant to disappoint you, sunshine. You've got to believe me when I say that. It kills me to hear you say you feel like you need to reconsider what you share with me. I'm with you, Elle. One hundred percent. Please don't doubt that. I want you to give me all of it—every thought running through your mind, every instinct in your gut, and every single emotion in your heart. Don't take that away from me."

"I believe you, Levi. I felt your apology in the kiss you gave me at the range. I just needed to tell you how this made me feel because as much as you don't want me to take those things away from you, I don't want to do it that much more. I want you to have them and I want to know I can trust you with them."

His face softened and he promised, "You can, sweetness. I swear you can."

"That's good because right now I'm feeling lots of emotions in my heart that I'd like to share with you, the first of which is that we should kiss and make up."

Levi grinned and challenged, "Oh yeah? What other emotions do you have for me after I kiss you?"

A seductive grin slid into place and I teased, "I guess you'll have to wait and find out."

"Is that so?" he wondered with his lips inches from mine.

I didn't answer him.

I lifted my head and gave him my mouth. He took it before taking the rest of what I was offering.

It was then that I realized that having a spat here and there wasn't so bad because Levi went above and beyond when he wanted to make things up to me.

CHAPTER 20

Levi

THERE WAS A KNOCK ON ELLE'S DRESSING ROOM DOOR.

We were at the venue for the final show of the road portion of the tour and were scheduled to head out early tomorrow morning to go back to Rising Sun, where she'd close out the tour with a performance at Lou's.

I couldn't remember ever feeling more grateful in my life.

I loved watching Elle perform. Her voice, the emotion she put into each song, and the happiness I knew she felt in doing what she loved made viewing her performances magnificent. All that said, I was more than ready to get back home, where I would be able to be far more productive on her case. I wanted to bring this whole situation to an end. A big part of my reason was obviously because I wanted Elle safe; however, the bigger part of my reasoning was about something she said to me.

The first night we arrived in Las Vegas she told me she felt like she was suffocating. This whole ordeal was taking its toll on her and I didn't like seeing her distressed. She wanted to be home where her family and friends were and I couldn't say I blamed her. I made a promise to her that I'd be whatever she needed me to be for her over the next two days until we returned home to Wyoming. Telling her that seemed to help only marginally, but at least it was something.

I was determined now. The minute she finished with her final performance, I planned to personally find who was doing this to her. I knew my team was already busting their asses to locate this nuisance, Becky, but my patience was wearing thin. I wanted my girl breathing easy again. I wanted her biggest worry to be about what flavor lip balm she was going to wear that day.

Now, I turned to move to the door while Elle ate a handful of potato chips.

I loved her.

Never in my life did I think I'd ever grow to love someone who could plow through nearly a half a bag of potato chips in no time flat, but here I was. Not only was I in deep with her, but I found myself checking to make sure she had those chips at the ready.

I opened the dressing room door and saw one of the employees from the venue standing there with a bouquet of flowers.

Not again.

Please not again.

"These were just delivered for Elle," the girl informed me.

"Was it an individual or a floral company that brought them?" I asked.

"A woman brought them. She wasn't with a floral company."

A woman brought them. Perhaps Becky was here. Fuck.

"Any idea what she looked like?"

"Yeah, she was a little taller than me by maybe two to three inches. She had long, platinum blonde hair and a beautiful set of hazel-colored eyes."

Fuck. Fuck. Fuck.

"Do you recall what she was wearing?"

The girl shook her head and lamented, "Not all of it. I

just know she had on a pair of cowgirl boots and cut-off jean shorts. I remember this because she had such beautiful tanned legs and I really loved her boots."

"Thank you," I offered as I took the flowers from her hand.

I turned around and saw Elle staring at the flowers. She was frightened.

I set the flowers down on the table and pulled the envelope from them. After tearing open the sealed envelope, I pulled out the card, flipped it over, and read the note.

It's almost over. This will end soon for you. -B.B.

I immediately pulled my phone from my pocket, found the number I was looking for, and tapped on it. I kept my eyes on Elle, who was growing more and more concerned by the second.

"Boss," Pierce called.

"I need you and Dom in Elle's dressing room now," I demanded.

"On it."

I disconnected the call, slid my phone back in my pocket, and walked to her.

Elle stood and wasted no time in asking about the card.

"What does it say?"

I hesitated. I knew I wasn't going to be able to keep this from her, but that didn't change the fact that I'd prefer to not tell her.

Elle knew I was struggling to say it to her. She placed her hand over mine, the one clutching the card. She turned my hand over and peeled back my fingers to show the card.

The door to the dressing room opened as Elle pulled the card out of my hand. I shifted my body to the side so that I could confirm it was Pierce and Dom, but immediately brought my gaze back to my woman.

She was set to go onstage in roughly fifteen minutes and

she was about to break down. Her eyes filled with tears before she slowly closed them and tears spilled down her cheeks.

"Why won't she stop?" Elle rasped quietly.

I wrapped my arm around her shoulders, took the card out of her hand, and pulled her into my chest. That only served to intensify her reaction. She completely lost it and her body was wracked by sobs.

Dom walked over and took the card from me. His face grew hard as he passed it off to Pierce, who had nearly the identical reaction.

"Got anything on the delivery?" Dom asked a few minutes later, after Elle began to settle a bit.

"One of the employees brought them up. Gave me a thorough description of the individual who delivered them. It wasn't the floral company."

"Well, at least we can work with that," Pierce chimed in. "What are we looking for?"

I clenched my jaw and delayed responding knowing it would send Elle over the edge again. She must have realized, based on the silence in the room, that there was more than just this card to be upset about because she pulled her tear-stained cheeks back from my chest and looked up at me.

As I looked down at her, I said, "Elle."

"What?" she responded.

I shook my head and explained, "No. Elle is what we're looking for. The employee described the woman who delivered the flowers to be about Elle's height with long, platinum-blonde hair and hazel-colored eyes. She also said the woman was wearing cut-off jean shorts and a pair of cowgirl boots."

Elle sucked in a sharp breath.

"Do we think that Becky is here? Is she impersonating Elle?"

"It sure fuckin' seems like it," I told Pierce. "What the fuck?!"

I took a second to sort the shit out in my head. I was normally very levelheaded and systematic. I didn't usually lose my cool and could sort through most situations relatively easily just by clearing my mind and taking it a step at a time. Unfortunately, with Elle involved, I found it wasn't so easy.

I looked down at my girl. Instantly, my nerves calmed.

"If you don't want to perform tonight, you don't have to," I assured her. "If you do, we have you covered."

She took a moment to think.

"I don't want to risk anyone's safety here, but I really don't want to disappoint my fans, either. I'm not sure what to do."

"Dom, Pierce, and I will be fine. We can handle whatever comes at us tonight, if anything. I'm a few feet away from you the entire time you're onstage. Dom and Pierce have eyes on the crowd and will be constantly scanning. We'll be fine."

"Don't let her take this away from you, rock star," Pierce added. "If you don't perform, she wins. And while your safety may not be something we want to talk about winning or losing, you don't let anyone steal what brings you happiness. Like Levi said, we've got you covered."

We watched as Elle took in our words and thought on it a moment. It wasn't long before she decided.

"She's not going to keep me from doing what I love. She might try, but she's going to fail. I love what I do and I have a lot of people who love and support me in what I'm doing. I won't let her ruin that."

That was my girl. She might feel herself starting to crumble, but somehow, she always manages to pick herself back up and push through.

"Alright," I started turning my attention to the guys. "It's almost time for her to be onstage, so I need you guys to go out and begin scanning the crowd. Let their security team here know our threat has increased and we're going to need them to be checking in with you both throughout the night. Anything that doesn't seem right, don't take any chances. You see anyone who looks like Elle, don't waste time."

They both gave me chin lifts in acknowledgment and turned to leave. Once they disappeared through the door and it closed behind them, I turned my attention to Elle.

"Are you okay?" I asked her.

She sighed. "I'm not going to lie, Levi, I'm so over this. The same question keeps running through my mind. I want to know why she's doing this. The fact that we've identified that she looks like me takes this to a whole other level. That, coupled with her inability to think for herself in all of the on-line posts she makes, is a clear indication of just how crazy this woman is. It's scary to think someone could be this obsessed. I just want to know why. I get that it's jealousy, but I don't understand what the jealousy stems from. It's extraordinarily frustrating and very upsetting."

I hated this for her. I couldn't say I disagreed with any of her sentiments, either. When this was all said and done, I just hoped that not only would Elle be safe, but also that she'd get the answers she was looking for. I wanted her to know why. As much as I believed she deserved to know the truth, I also knew that there was a very real possibility she'd never get that truth.

"I understand what you're feeling, sunshine. We're going to do whatever we can to get this sorted as quickly as possible and get your life back to normal. In the process, I'm hoping I can get you some answers."

The corners of her mouth tipped up as she let the genuine concern I felt for her seep in.

"Thank you for being my hero, Levi."

I pulled her against me again and kissed the top of her

head. "I'll feel like more of a hero when I put this situation to bed for you."

"I know," she sighed. "But in the meantime, at least you're doing a good job of taking me to bed."

I tried hard to suppress a laugh, but it was useless. I squeezed her neck gently and blurted, "Love you, Elle."

As her arms wrapped around my waist and she pressed her cheek to my chest, she proclaimed, "I love you, too."

Ten minutes later, which happened to be five minutes past the time Elle was set to take the stage, she was finally ready to step out there. My nerves were on edge. Dom and Pierce, I knew, were doing their job thoroughly and would catch anyone that stood out in the crowd. I just hoped they'd find this woman and we'd be able to put an end to this nightmare.

Elle was introduced and walked out onto the stage. The crowd was roaring.

Damn.

My girl was sensational.

People loved her and she deserved every bit of that love.

I stood offstage, but Elle was never out of my sight and was not ever more than a few running strides away from me. If something went down, she was my only priority. Get her. Get out.

Nearly an hour and a half later, I knew Elle's show was coming to a close. To say that I was starting to feel a bit relieved was an understatement. I knew we weren't out of the woods yet, but we were close. Of course, Dom and Pierce hadn't found anything yet, so I knew there was still the potential for anything to happen. Just another two songs and then I could get her back to the hotel, where her safety wasn't at such high risk.

Just then, my phone rang. Without taking my eyes off Elle, I pulled it out of my pocket.

"Yeah?" I shouted into the phone hoping I could hear over the noise.

"You've got to get her off the stage and back to the dressing room for cover," Dom yelled back.

I looked to where Dom had been standing and saw he was no longer there.

Fuck.

"What's happening?"

"Just get her out now, Levi!"

He disconnected the call.

Fuck.

I did what I had to do. It took me about ten strides to get to her. Halfway through those strides, Elle turned her head toward me. She did this because the crowd began cheering when they noticed I had stepped out onto the stage with her. Unfortunately, I wasn't there for any good reason. It happened quickly. I made it to Elle and scooped her up in my arms. The microphone fell from her hand and onto the floor. I hauled her offstage, keeping my body toward the audience to shield her from whatever was happening out there.

"What's going on, Levi?" she asked, scared out of her mind.

I ignored her question, mostly because my focus was getting her to a safe place. I weaved through the halls and made it to her dressing room. The door was open, so I quickly carried her in, scanned the room, and then locked it behind us.

It wasn't until we were safe inside the dressing room that I set her down on her feet. I took in her face and noted the fear in her features, silently begging me to tell her what was happening.

"I don't know, Elle," I started. "I don't know what's happening yet. Dom called me and said I needed to get you off the stage immediately. I asked what was going on, but I don't have any answers yet. They know we are here; we wait until they return."

"Do you think she was here?" Elle asked, her eyes rounding.

I shrugged my shoulders. "Can't say. I know they wouldn't have had me walk out on that stage in the middle of your performance if they didn't think there was a valid reason for it."

Elle didn't get a chance to respond because her phone started ringing. She walked over to her purse and pulled her phone out.

"It's Leah," she informed me before she answered. "Hey, Leah."

Calm.

Elle was calm.

She pulled her shit together so she wouldn't frighten her friend.

My girl was definitely not crumbling.

That is, she was not crumbling until she listened to whatever Leah was saying to her on the phone. Elle's face went neutral to horrified in a matter of seconds.

"Oh my God. Are you serious?" she shrieked.

There was a knock at the door. Elle went rigid.

"Levi," Dom's voice called. "It's us."

I opened the door and they stepped inside.

Frustration on their faces.

"I'm okay, LP. I'm back in my dressing room now. Dom and Pierce just walked in. Let me go and see what they've found. I'll try to call you back in a little, but if not, I'll see you tomorrow when I get home."

She paused a moment.

How did Leah know something was wrong? There was no way news traveled that fast.

"I promise. I'm okay. Let me see what's going on."

Silence.

"Okay. Thanks for checking in. Love you, too."

Elle hung up the phone and wasted no time.

"I knew it," she exploded. "She was in my account. I knew she was. Now, we have proof."

What?

"Somebody better fill me in," I ordered, no patience left.

Pierce piped up. "Dom got a text from Michaels saying that he should be paying attention to the potential threats in the crowd, not live streaming. Dom shot back a text telling him he wasn't live streaming and had no idea what he was talking about. That's when Trent called and explained that Elle was live streaming her own show. He just assumed since Elle was performing that it must have been one of us that was doing it for her. As he was on the phone with Dom, trying to give a location of where in the venue the stream was being shot from, the feed took a turn. Thousands of people who aren't here were watching, thinking this was innocent and that someone from Elle's team was streaming the show live for her fans. Minutes before I called you, Becky or, we're assuming it was Becky, started interacting with the audience. She never spoke; she used the message feature. I don't know everything that she typed, but Trent said she was making threatening statements about Elle no longer being able to sing, that Elle needed to be stopped before she stole even more of the spotlight. It was bad enough that Michaels insisted we get Elle out of there. I didn't know it was happening until I saw Dom signal to me to follow him. We took off in the direction of where Trent said the stream was coming from and that's when he said the session ended. Dom disconnected with Michaels, called you, and we tried to find Becky. Nobody came close to matching the description you gave us earlier."

"Motherfucker," I swore. "This bitch is right under our noses."

"Leah said she watched the whole stream. She said people were enjoying being able to watch it until it turned scary. Nobody understood what was going on because obviously, it made no sense that we'd be saying things like that from my own personal live stream session."

Elle's phone rang again.

She looked down at it, saw who was calling, and answered quickly. "I'm okay, Wes."

Damn. He was probably going out of his mind.

"Clearly, it wasn't us streaming. It was her or, at least, we believe it was her. Flowers were delivered to me right before the show and I probably shouldn't have gone on to perform tonight, but I didn't want to disappoint my fans. You know how important they are to me."

Silence while he spoke.

"Yes, there was a card and it was signed by her again. The only difference is that we believe she was the one who delivered the flowers to the venue today. The employee brought them to my dressing room and gave Levi a description of the woman who brought them... she pretty much described me. This woman is psychotic, Wes. I'm so glad I'm coming home tomorrow. I just want to be around my family and friends again."

Elle waited while Wes talked to her.

A minute later she responded, "She's right. Tell Charley I said thanks and that I'll give an update when we get back to the hotel."

Wes spoke again. Elle's face softened.

"I know, Wes. I'm sorry to have worried you. I'll see you both tomorrow. Love you, too."

She disconnected with her brother and began to fret,

"Wes and Charley were panicked. Leah was panicked. They all can call and check on me. None of my fans have that option. Charley thinks it might be a good idea to let everyone know that I'm alright. If you think it's okay to do, I'd like to do that for my fans when we get back to the hotel tonight. I'm guessing you aren't going to allow me to go back out there and finish my set, even though I've only got two songs left."

"You wouldn't be wrong to make that assumption. I'm sorry, El, I know what your fans mean to you, but I can't let you go back out there. If you want to give an update online tonight when I have you back at the hotel, I'm good with that."

Her shoulders slumped and she nodded.

I was grateful she wasn't going to try to fight me on this.

"I'll let the owner of the venue know what's going on," Pierce offered.

"Thanks, Pierce. We'll head out to the car. Meet you outside?"

He gave a chin lift and walked out of the room.

At that, Elle got her things together before Dom and I covered her and got her safely to the car. A few minutes later, Pierce met us at the car and we took off. Then, I made sure we got my beautiful girl back to the hotel safely. It wasn't until we walked through the doors of the suite that I was finally able to relax.

CHAPTER 21

Elle

"That's the last of it," I murmured.

I zipped up my suitcase and moved to the bed.

Levi and I arrived back at the hotel not long ago. We showered together as soon as we got back. Shower was all that we did, though. I think we were both lost in our own thoughts over what happened at my show tonight. After we showered, the two of us took to packing up our suitcases since we had an early morning flight out of Vegas back to Wyoming. This was only after I blasted out an update on my social media accounts, letting my fans know what happened and that I was okay. Of course, I also apologized to the fans who attended the final show in Vegas that it got cut short. As much as I hated certain aspects of touring, I knew I was going to come back to Vegas at some point in the future to deliver another show for these fans. They deserved that from me, and I was sure to tell them that.

I couldn't wait to get home. This was, without a doubt, the only time throughout the entire tour that had me looking forward to getting on a plane.

Climbing into the bed, I pulled back the covers and settled myself underneath them. Levi, who had finished packing his suitcase quite a bit before me, crawled into bed beside me and turned off the bedside light. He wrapped an arm around me and pulled my body toward him; my front was pressed to his.

My body was tense. I knew he could feel it. I knew because his was only slightly more relaxed than it had been when we were at the venue tonight and I knew that my tension and anxiety were not helping him find any peace.

Quite some time later, we were still there in the dark, our bodies pressed together, and neither of us was any closer to finding sleep.

He broke the silence when he whispered into the top of my head, "I'm sorry, sunshine."

The sentiment was a pained one.

"Sorry?" I questioned, confused at the apology.

"You were right in your assumption that she got into your account and I didn't act appropriately based on your instincts."

I didn't want him punishing himself over this. He explained his reasoning behind the reaction he had and I wasn't going to hold it against him.

"It's okay, Levi. I understand why you responded to it the way you did. You can't dwell on it now."

"No, Elle, it's not okay. I put you at risk tonight. If something had happened to you…" he trailed off.

I pressed a kiss to the upper part of his chest.

"Nothing happened to me. You made sure of that," I reassured him, my lips still just barely touching his skin.

His body was still rock solid.

"I should have had Trent look deeper into it when you said something about it this morning. I'm so sorry," he repeated.

I sighed. "Let it go, Levi. Please, let it go for me. I'm here in your arms, and it's the place I feel the safest."

He relaxed only slightly.

"Just hold me tight and keep me close to you tonight. In the morning, take me home."

Levi's arms tightened around me and he pressed a kiss to the top of my head.

"Love you, sweetness. I love you so much."

"More, my hero. I love you more."

Levi's hand slid up my back and into my hair before he gently tugged and pulled my face away from his chest. It was too dark in the room to see the expression on his face, but I didn't need to see him. I could feel his emotion.

"I already told you, Elle… that's not fucking possible."

My insides warmed at hearing him say this to me again. I stayed quiet and settled into that warmth. Levi wrote off my gut feeling and hours later there was a serious threat to my safety. After he considered the devastatingly harsh reality of that, I believed he needed this win.

I let him fall asleep that night believing that he loved me more than I loved him. Deep down, I knew that wasn't possible.

No sooner did I fall asleep when I was being woken by the incessant chime from Levi's alarm. We needed to get up.

Home.

I was finally going home and I could not wait.

I missed my family. I missed my friends. I missed being carefree, not having to worry about the pressures of a scheduled life. Today, Levi was taking me home and giving all that back to me.

"Morning, Levi," I practically sang as I watched his eyes flutter open.

"Sunshine," he returned as he fell to his back and pulled me on top of him.

My excitement was too much to contain. "We need to get up and get moving. We've got a plane to catch."

"Never thought I'd see you so excited about flying," he shot back.

"I'm not excited about flying. I just can't wait to get home and see my family and friends. I miss my hometown fans. I miss Lou's. I miss sleeping with you in your bed. I miss being able to spend my days as I wish, whether heading out shopping for lip balm or lounging by a pool. I miss feeling like I'm in control."

A gorgeous grin spread across his face before he teased, "You miss my bed?"

"No. I miss my bed. I miss sleeping with you in yours," I clarified.

"Right," he started. "Once this situation with Becky gets sorted, I'll want to try out your bed."

I shrugged my shoulders nonchalantly and agreed, "Works for me."

A feeling of sadness swept through me. While I was beyond thrilled to finally be going home to Wyoming today, I hadn't been to my own place in weeks. I missed it.

Levi, noting the shift in my mood, assured me, "I'm going to be trying out your bed very soon, Elle. I know you haven't been in your own space for quite some time, but now that we're heading home I'm going to make certain we get this case wrapped up as quickly as possible. We are getting close. I just need you to hang in there with me a little bit longer."

"I know. I'm hanging."

"If it helps, I have to admit that I like having you in my bed. If it weren't for the creepiness and safety factor, I'd be inclined to let this situation go so you wouldn't leave me to go back to your place."

I loved him.

And I loved him even more when he said things like that.

"I'm not leaving you," I told him. "I'm just going home."

"I'm looking forward to the time when home for you is with me."

"Levi..." I trailed off softly.

He held my eyes a moment before he did an ab curl and sat up in the bed, taking me with him. Levi pressed a sweet kiss to my lips and affirmed, "Love you, sweetness."

"I love you, too."

"Let's get you home."

I nodded and moved with Levi to get ready so he could take me home.

It was a couple hours later when our plane landed.

It felt so good to be back home. I let out a sigh of relief, turned to Levi, and gave him a huge grin. I got back as good as I gave.

After we got our luggage and got in the truck, Levi turned to me and stated, "I know you probably want to get back to the house right away since you have your performance tonight, but I wanted to make a quick stop at the office to go over a few things with the team before tonight."

"Sure," I conceded.

I did want to get back to the house, but I also looked at this as an opportunity to meet some of the other members of the team. Aside from Levi, Cruz, Pierce, and Dom, I hadn't met any of the others.

Twenty minutes later, we pulled into the lot at Cunningham Security. Levi parked, came around to open my door, and walked me inside. Upon entering, we were greeted by a woman with auburn hair in a stylish pixie cut sitting at the front desk.

"You're back," she exclaimed from behind her desk. "And you've decided to share her with the rest of us."

Levi's arm, which had been wrapped around my shoulders as we walked through the lot, dropped to my waist as he said, "Elle, this is my receptionist, Deb. Deb, this is my girl-friend, Elle."

Deb stood, rounded the desk, and pulled me into her arms. She was an older woman, maybe in her late forties, and she was definitely one of those people that aged well.

With her mouth at my ear, she whispered, "It's so good to finally meet the girl that's put a smile on his face. He wasn't ever unhappy, but he never smiled like he does now."

Deb's words filled me with such joy. Because she gave me that, I hugged her back and shared, "He's done the same for me."

When she pulled back, she gave me a genuine smile and looked to Levi. "I'm so happy for you, Levi."

"Thanks, Deb."

She nodded before she surmised, "I assume you want to talk with the boys?"

"Quickly... before Elle's performance tonight."

Deb turned her attention back to me. "They can't wait."

When my brows pulled together in confusion, she went on to explain, "Just about all of them are planning to be there tonight. Most had already planned on it, but after last night... well, the rest of them refused to sit back when they knew someone was terrorizing you more aggressively."

I felt myself grow tense.

I had tried to put last night out of my mind. I knew it wouldn't stay there forever, but any reprieve I could get would be welcome. Coming home, I should have expected that it was going to be brought up in discussions and that would likely continue until Becky was found. I sure hoped that happened soon.

"You've got nothing to worry about, sweet pea. These boys will keep you safe. I've seen it happen on more than one occasion. You can trust them," she assured me.

I relaxed a bit, looked up at Levi, smiled, and whispered, "I already do."

A few moments of silence had passed before Deb's voice filled the reception area again. "Oooh, that look," she started as she began rounding the desk again to move back to her seat. "Boy, do I hope this is the start of something good around this place. Too many men here not settling down. I could get used to seeing these gazes."

Levi's head turned toward Deb and he gave her a look.

"Don't give me that face, boy. You know I'm just telling the truth." She brought her gaze to me and continued, "This many beautiful men in one building and I've got nothing. Not a single scrumptious detail about what happens when they aren't here. I might be old enough to be their mother in some cases, but that doesn't mean I can't appreciate a good thing when I see it."

I started to laugh.

Levi did not.

"Alright, Deb. Nice chat. We're walking away now."

With that, he brought his hand to the small of my back and gently nudged me forward, out of the reception area and down the hall. He stopped in the doorway of one of the offices and the guy who had been sitting behind the desk with three computer screens on it stood and was staring down at his phone as he walked toward us.

He must have realized we were there because he finally looked up at us.

"Didn't realize you were stopping in," he informed us. "Good to see you back, boss."

He looked to me and offered his hand. I placed my hand in his and shook when he said, "Nice to finally meet you, Elle. Trent Michaels."

I froze.

This was the guy. He was the one who found Becky. Or, at least, he found her social media accounts that indicated she was the one who was stalking me.

I dropped his hand and threw my arms around his neck.

"Thank you," I rushed to express the minute I had my arms around him. "For finding her and for everything you've been doing since then."

I pulled back, grasped his hands with mine, and continued with tears in my eyes, "Thank you for looking out for me last night. If you hadn't been watching... who knows what could have happened?"

"What's going on?" I heard someone call from behind me.

Before I could turn to see, I heard the same voice say, "Bro, why is Michaels holding hands with your woman?"

Cruz.

I was still looking at Trent. He squeezed my hands and smirked at me. My eyes rounded, and I immediately dropped his hands.

My head snapped to Levi to find him looking less than impressed at what he just witnessed.

"Hey, Elle. Welcome back," Cruz broke through the silence.

"Thanks, Cruz. I'm happy to be back," I offered in return.

Cruz turned back to Levi and reported, "Got an update last night from Dom and Reynolds."

I walked back to Levi and slid my arms around his waist. He instinctively pulled me close to him by wrapping an arm around my shoulders.

Cruz went on, "I'm happy to see that Elle wasn't hurt. We're all planning on being at the show tonight. With this bitch continuing to target Elle, none of the guys are willing to sit this one out."

"Oh no," I blurted. "I'm the reason everyone is going to be working tonight. I guess it's safe to assume I'm not going to be anyone's favorite."

"You're my favorite," Levi reminded me with a gentle squeeze of my shoulder.

I leaned further into him and rested my head on his chest.

"The entire team isn't far behind," Michaels added.

Shocked, I asked, "What?"

"I might have been the one keeping tabs on everything online, but once the guys found out that you were doing live sessions, they've all been watching. It's been a great source of entertainment."

I felt my face flush.

Cruz tried to help ease my embarrassment by mentioning, "It's cool, Elle. I think once we watched the pool scene in Vegas and the guys here saw that you appreciated what not only Levi but also Pierce and Dom had done for you... well, that sat well with them. Besides, when it comes down to it, you aren't the reason we're working tonight. Becky is."

Levi piped up, "Speaking of which, I'd like to discuss the game plan for tonight. Everyone around?"

Trent answered, "Other than Dom and Pierce, everyone is here."

"Great. Let's round everyone up and meet in the conference room in five."

Trent and Cruz gave Levi a chin lift. Levi ushered me out of Trent's office and down the hall to his own.

Once we stepped inside, I waited for him to close the door and I burst out with a rapid-fire apology, "I'm sorry, Levi. I hope I didn't upset you back there. I didn't even think anything of it. It was a bit of a shock to my system meeting Trent. I mean, I knew I was going to eventually meet him, but it caught me off guard. I had tried to put last night's events out of my head for the day, but then Deb was talking about it and I couldn't help it. Meeting Trent... all I could think about was that if he hadn't been watching that feed last night, something really bad could have happened to me. I swear, Levi—"

"Calm down, Elle," he cut me off. "I didn't like watching you hold hands with Trent, but I already knew and understood where your head was. It's okay. Don't get all worked up over something that isn't necessary."

I let out a sigh of relief. "I thought you were upset with me and that's why you told the guys you wanted to meet in the conference room in five minutes and not right away. I figured you wanted to talk to me about what happened in there."

Levi's face softened.

"Sunshine, I love that you appreciate the work my guys are putting in for you. Again, that doesn't mean I'm happy about the hand-holding, but that's not why I wanted you to come in here. I wanted five minutes so I could bring you in here and taste those lips."

"Oh."

My belly began to tingle at the prospect of being naughty in his office. I took the two steps toward him to close the distance between us and slid my hands up over his solid chest and shoulders until my fingers ran up along the back of his neck and into his hair. Then, I let Levi taste my lips.

He groaned into my mouth almost immediately.

I concluded he liked the way I tasted.

With an arm around my waist and the other at my ass, Levi lifted me. I quickly wrapped my legs around him while he began to walk, not ever breaking the seal of our mouths against one another. The next thing I knew, my back was against his desk and he was hovering over me.

His lips were still against mine, his tongue still in my mouth. He was hard between us; my hips were moving against the solid length of him.

I moaned as I continued to search for a way to get closer

to him, my fingers itching to remove the clothing from his body. My guess was Levi's hands were itching to do the same because one hand remained at my ass while the other slid up my side to my breast and squeezed.

Lately, I'd been feeling as though I was suffocating with everything happening around me. I hated it. Now, I felt completely breathless and didn't care if I ever took another breath of oxygen.

Unfortunately, Levi pulled his mouth from mine and rested his forehead against mine.

"Damn," he started. "Birthday cake."

In my head, I gave myself a pat on the back. I knew he liked how I tasted.

"This was a bad idea," he continued.

"What?" I whispered.

He pulled his head back from mine so he could look me in the eyes.

"I need to go down the hall and have a meeting with my team so everyone is on the same page for tonight. The problem is that I need to be focused on that meeting and not on the fact that you taste like a celebration. You really do own every flavor ever made, don't you?"

I shrugged my shoulders and feigned innocence.

"Not now," he went on. "But you should prepare yourself. We will be finding time in the very near future to make love on this desk. I think I like the idea of knowing I'm going to come in here to work and your delicious ass was sitting on it."

I nodded in agreement to this because I really kind of wanted him to make love to me on his desk. I would have preferred this precise moment, but with the meeting he needed to have and the fact that I needed to get back to his place to get ready for a performance tonight at Lou's, I could settle for knowing it was on the menu.

"How long is your meeting going to take?" I asked, my throat tight.

Levi cocked an eyebrow and answered with a question, "Who wants to know?"

"Your honey maker," I rasped with a roll of my hips against him.

He growled.

"I'll make it as quick as possible," he promised. "We're going straight to my place afterward."

I lifted my head to his and gave him one last taste of birthday cake. After getting his fill or, at least, as much as he could have without someone coming to look for him, Levi stood and helped me off the desk. We made our way to the conference room, where Levi and his team discussed the details of my case up to this point and their strategy moving forward.

I sat back and looked around the room. My stalker situation sucked, but on the bright side, I was in the company of some incredibly beautiful men, who were doing everything in their power to keep me safe.

Best of all was my man. I hated what Becky was doing and how her actions were negatively impacting my life, but I had to admit that what she did only seemed to make my life better. The reality was that Levi and the members of his team would find Becky and put a stop to her harassment and threatening actions. Once that stopped, she will have been nothing more than a blip on the radar and I'll be happier than I can ever remember. Part of me wanted to know why Becky was doing this and I was certain that curiosity would never leave me, but another part of me was beginning to think that if I got the opportunity I should thank her. There had been an attraction between Levi and I for quite some time now, but it wasn't until Becky that we acted on that pull to each other. That attraction turned into love.

A love that resulted in Levi finishing his meeting quickly because I tasted like a celebration.

A love that allowed me to give Levi that look with my eyes.

A love the likes of which I'm unsure how I ever lived without it.

CHAPTER 22

Elle

"**A**REN'T YOU WORRIED THAT IT'LL ESCALATE TONIGHT?"
My dear sister-in-law's worried voice came through the phone.

Levi and I had arrived back at his place about an hour ago. He made good work of demonstrating just how much he loved my birthday cake flavored lip balm. I still had a couple hours left before my performance tonight at Lou's and knew that Levi was nowhere near finished with me. If I was being honest, this made me extremely happy since I was in the mood for some serious affection from him.

I was currently lying on the couch in the family room with Levi's arm under my waist, his head resting on my belly. When we returned from his office, he was intent on making sure we wasted no time dealing with climbing stairs to get to the bedroom. So, we ended up here in the living room on the couch. The fact was I didn't care where he had his way with me, I just knew I'd been burning up for him since he came to settle over me when my back was pressed against his desk.

When we were pulling into the driveway earlier, my phone rang. I saw that it was Charley and Levi explained, "You want to answer it, go ahead. But let it be known that

I'm not waiting any longer, Elle. I'm getting you out of this truck and I'm going to have you immediately."

I decided it was wise to wait and call Charley back.

Now that I'd given Levi what he wanted, what we both wanted, and we were settling in for a brief rest before we went at it again, I decided to return Charley's call. She was concerned about me performing again tonight given the events of last night's show.

"I can't say for sure that it'll be tonight, but I suspect that it's going to escalate at some point," I replied. "The way I see it, the quicker it escalates, the faster she's caught."

"I'm so afraid for you, honey," Charley continued to fret.

"I know, love. I understand what you're feeling, but to be honest, there's a part of me that hopes she tries something tonight."

"WHAT?!" she shrieked. "Are you crazy?"

I had to laugh, but I did so only briefly so that I could fill Charley in on why I'd made such a ludicrous statement.

"The entire team will be there tonight. Becky's not aware of that. Quite frankly, tonight would be the perfect time for her to make a move."

Charley stayed silent a minute before she finally repeated in a questioning tone, "The entire team?"

"Every single one of them," I reassured her.

"Wow," she whispered. "Levi's not messing around, is he?"

My heart squeezed. I loved that Charley saw how much Levi cared about me. "He's got a thing for my lip balm flavors."

Charley laughed. "I'm frightened for you, but I'm also so very happy that this has helped you and Levi to stop avoiding what I saw happening between the two of you back when Emme was going through her stuff."

As I ran my fingers through his hair, I admitted, "I was just thinking the same exact thing earlier today."

"I've got to go get ready since we're meeting up at Emme and Zane's before heading over to Lou's tonight. Can't wait to see you tonight, honey. Love you."

"Same here. Love you, too."

I disconnected the call and tossed my phone to the end table behind my head. When Levi heard it drop to the table, he stated, "She's worried."

It wasn't a question. He already knew how Charley felt, but I responded anyway. "Yeah."

"So, what is it that the two of you were on the same page about?"

"What?"

"You just said to her that you were just thinking the same exact thing earlier today. What were you thinking about earlier today?"

"Part of me is a mix of scared and angry about what Becky's doing, but there is the part of me that feels thankful she's done this."

Levi lifted his head from my belly and pressed me further. "And what exactly are you thankful for?"

I knew my eyes went liquid the second his bored into them. After giving myself a moment to settle into that feeling, I answered quietly, "You."

A devilish grin spread across his face. "You're finally feeling the way I did about a day into this."

"I despise what she's doing," I declared. "I hate it. It's creepy and it makes absolutely no sense. I won't lie and say I'm not scared at times, but she gave us the push we needed to pursue this thing between us. Charley said she knew back when Emme was going through her ordeal that you and I had sparks flying. Becky is seriously irritating me, but I have you now. People go through all sorts of obstacles to find love. If this is what I need to go through to deserve love, then I'm willing to endure it."

Levi's voice was husky when he spoke. "You deserve love, sunshine. And you don't deserve to go through this just to have it. I made a bad decision back then to not pursue you. I hate that you think this was needed for you to get what you should have gotten from me a long time ago."

"Don't do that," I started. "You saw the bright side in this at the beginning. It took me until now to really see that bright side. Don't start questioning what didn't happen between us before this situation arose. All that matters to me now is the fact that you've done nothing but prove to me that I'm the luckiest woman alive. I feel beautiful, loved, and cherished because of you."

"Elle..." he trailed off.

"Kiss me, Levi."

I thought he would move and slide his body up mine to kiss me, but he didn't. Instead, Levi's mouth touched the skin just below my bellybutton. He pressed a kiss there. Then, he began moving his mouth up my body. He kissed the spot just below the center of my ribcage. His hands slid up my sides and came to cup the sides of my breasts. He kissed the skin between them before he peppered kisses across each one, ultimately landing on my nipples.

Yes, I felt beautiful.

I felt loved.

His mouth moved along my collarbone to the skin at the side of my throat. I hooked a leg around his hip and he slid inside me.

"Love you, sweetness. Love you so much," he whispered when his mouth reached my ear.

I turned my head slightly toward his so my mouth was at his ear. "I know," I whispered back. "I feel it every day."

Levi took my mouth and moved inside me. He did this for quite some time before he tore his mouth from mine, lifted himself up, gripped my hip in one hand, and my thigh in the other. One of his legs dropped off the side of the couch, where his foot went to the floor and he hiked my leg up higher. His eyes looked to where he was moving in and out of me.

His expression changed.

He picked up his pace.

"Oh, Levi," I whimpered.

The sound of our bodies colliding mixed with the scent of sex in the air was satisfyingly stimulating. I grew more and more aroused with each thrust of Levi's cock into me.

"Faster," I panted. "Please, harder."

My ankle was now up on Levi's shoulder, one of his hands wrapped around that thigh as he continued to power into me, harder and faster.

"Slick and sweet as honey," he growled.

"More, Levi."

He gave me more.

He gave it hard.

He gave it deep.

It was so good.

"Are you going to come with me, Elle?"

My eyes closed and I nodded.

"Give them to me, sunshine. Give me those eyes and take what's yours."

My orgasm ripped through me. It started between my legs and seized my limbs. My eyes were focused on Levi's. I was torn between trying to keep my focus on his reaction to finding his release and thoroughly enjoying what he just did to me. It didn't take long for me to realize that I could easily do both.

Levi slowed his thrusts until they eventually stopped. He stayed there inside me, looking at me. I had just had my third orgasm in a very short period of time and was completely spent. When Levi's hand left my thigh, I didn't have the energy to keep it up on his shoulder. It began to fall; his hand caught it and guided it safely down.

"It's still early, right?" I asked.

"Just after lunchtime. Why?"

My eyes began to drift shut. "I think I need a nap before getting ready to go to Lou's. I'm exhausted."

"You need to eat," he said softly.

I shook my head. My eyes were still closed as I proposed, "How about food after a nap? I'm too tired."

"Okay," Levi conceded as he pulled himself from my tired body.

Not even seconds later, I felt his arms slide between the couch and my upper back as well as under my knees. He was going to carry me upstairs.

More proof of how much he loved me.

Minutes later, Levi settled me into his bed, slid in next to me, and pulled the covers up over our bodies. With his body pressed close to mine and the warmth I felt, it was a matter of seconds before I drifted off to sleep.

"Elle?"

Levi's voice filtered into my ears in the darkness.

I was still in his bed.

I rolled to my back and opened my eyes. Levi was hovering over me.

"Hey." My voice came out sleepy.

Levi smiled at me and cautioned, "Can't keep sleeping if you're going to make it to your show on time tonight. It's getting late and I know you'll need time to get ready."

"Thanks for waking me."

"I want to make you something to eat. Most everything

substantial is frozen. Figured I'd could make some tuna sandwiches since that'll be quick and easy. This way, you can have a pile of potato chips with it."

I knew he had been on tour with me and got used to my pre-show rituals, but it still made my belly flutter when he did sweet things like plan food to include my pre-show chip consumption.

"I love you, Levi."

His face softened as he tilted his head to the side. Then, he held my phone out to me and noted, "When I was downstairs, I heard this going off with text message alerts. Your girl has been trying to contact you."

"Leah?" I wondered.

He nodded and added, "Yeah. Figured I'd bring it up so you could reach out to her. I'll go make some food in the meantime."

I grinned up at him, sat up in the bed, and took the phone from him. "My hero."

He gave me the phone, leaned over and pressed a kiss to my lips before he walked out of the room.

Looking down at my phone the screen showed that Leah was, in fact, trying to reach me. I read her text.

Leah: How was the flight? Are you back in town?

That unanswered text was followed up with a missed call and another text shortly thereafter.

Leah: Did you get in yet? Worried about you after last night—and I never heard back from you.

There was another missed call after that.

I quickly tapped out a text to let her know I was back.

Me: Sorry, LP. I was napping. I'm back and everything is good.

She responded immediately.

Leah: Napping?!?! I've been worried out of my mind that something bad happened again.

Me: I'm sorry. We came back, went to Levi's office, and then here. I was exhausted and needed to get a couple hours of rest in before tonight. You're coming, right?

Leah: Yes, I'll be there. Wouldn't miss it! Can't wait to see you.

Me: You too. Going to get ready. See you tonight! So much to fill you in on.

Leah: Later, E!

I set my phone on the bedside table and decided to go meet Levi downstairs to eat. A large majority of my clothing was still in my suitcases, which were still in Levi's truck. On that thought, I found one of Levi's T-shirts and threw it over my head before I walked out of the room and down the stairs.

As I descended the stairs, I heard Levi talking. I made my way into the kitchen and found that he was on the phone. He must have seen me out of the corner of his eye because he turned, did a full body scan, and gave me a grin and a wink.

"As we discussed earlier, the original plan was to arrive an hour ahead of her performance. Let's do an extra thirty minutes to account for this new information," he said into the phone.

Damn it.

What now?

I was half tempted to run back upstairs to grab my phone and see if there had been any new postings from Becky, but Levi disconnected the call, set his phone down, and walked toward me.

His hands came around my waist while he buried his face in my neck.

"I love this look on you, sunshine."

"A T-shirt?"

He pulled his face from my neck and shook his head while smirking at me. "No. You in my T-shirt. Hungry?"

I gave him a quick nod.

At that, we moved to the stools at the island, where Levi had already set the food. I felt a smile tugging at my lips as I looked at the plates. A tuna sandwich, lots of carrots, and a handful of chips on his plate. A tuna sandwich, lots of chips, and a handful of carrots on mine. I loved his heart for trying to offset the unhealthy chips in my diet by adding a few carrots.

I picked up my sandwich and took a bite. Levi took that opportunity to start the conversation.

"You talk to Leah?"

I answered with a nod.

"All good?"

"Yeah. She was just worried since the last she spoke to me was after what happened last night in Vegas. I didn't reach out to her after that and never said anything after we got back in town. She just wanted to check in, but I let her know that everything was good and confirmed that she'd be at Lou's tonight."

He acknowledged everything I said with a downward jerk of his chin since his mouth was full of food. I took the opportunity to shift the conversation at this juncture.

"We're leaving to arrive at Lou's thirty minutes earlier now?"

Levi set his sandwich down and stated, "That was Cruz. As it turns out, Becky went live today."

"Really?" I began, shocked. "That's great. So, was he able to confirm that she looks like the woman that delivered the flowers in Vegas?"

He shook his head. "No, she never spoke or showed her face."

I stayed silent, waiting for him to give me more information.

"She went live outside of Lou's late this morning."

I gasped.

Then, I quickly pulled myself together.

"This is perfect, Levi. Everyone is going to be there. This madness is finally going to end tonight."

"Don't get ahead of yourself," he advised. "We can't guarantee anything. She may or may not try something. Regardless, I wouldn't say it's worth getting excited about. I get you want this to end, but I'm not exactly thrilled about any of this having to happen at all."

I popped a chip in my mouth and admitted, "Well, I'm hopeful that we're getting close and I'll be able to get back to actually enjoying my life without this constant annoyance."

He shook his head at me.

"What?" I asked defensively.

"The change in you from when this started until now," he started. "It's amazing to me. You went from being terrified about this to now practically wishing Becky shows up at Lou's tonight. I'm proud of you and how courageous you've become."

His words made my heart swell. Still, I needed to be honest. "It's all thanks to you. What you and your team have done for me, making me feel safe and protected, that's given me the confidence to face this head on. And I wasn't joking—starting this week, I want Dom to start training me in self-defense even if this situation gets dealt with tonight."

"Not going to say no to giving you the tools you need to protect yourself," he began. "I hope you never need to use them, but I'll make sure you have them."

At that, we both turned our attention back to the food and finished eating. After, I took off upstairs so that I could get ready for the last performance of my tour. As I did that, I took the time to reflect on what Levi said while we ate sandwiches and potato chips.

He was right. It had only been a couple of weeks, but I was finding that my mindset surrounding the stalker situation had changed drastically. I didn't think I'd ever forget the fear, anxiety, and pure terror I felt that day I walked into my apartment and found the photo on my bed. Even still, from the moment I ran into Levi's office and he held me as we sat on the couch in his reception area, I began to feed off his confidence. It took time, but the more we learned about the stalker, the more I tried to stop being fearful and start being smart. I didn't want someone else controlling any part of my life; though, I guess it was actually the opposite. The obsession Becky had with me was really controlling her life. She couldn't seem to survive without watching my every move.

These thoughts took me back to the why of it all. I hoped I'd have the opportunity to ask why Becky had this obsession and was doing what she was doing. Knowing how much I hated things like scheduled days and flying, I found it difficult to understand why someone would want to live their life controlled by a fixation with someone else's life. It frustrated me to know that I might not ever get the answer to these questions.

While thoughts of unhealthy obsessions and control filtered through my brain, I sat on the edge of Levi's bed and slid my foot into my boots. He had perfect timing because he walked in the room at that very moment.

I stood.

He took me in, from top to toe.

"You're so beautiful," he marveled.

I walked to him, pressed up on my toes, and placed a firm, closed mouth kiss on his lips. "You're not so bad yourself."

Levi kissed me back. His was not closed mouth. When he pulled away, he asked, "Ready?"

"Yep. Let's get out of here so you can continue to be my hero, keep me safe, and find this bitch," I ordered as I started to walk out of the room.

I heard him laughing as he followed behind.

CHAPTER 23

Elle

HAD BEEN AT LOU'S FOR NEARLY FORTY-FIVE MINUTES WHEN MY people finally started showing up. I loved Levi and his team, but that didn't change the fact that I missed my family and friends. Considering I hadn't seen them in a couple of weeks, I was so excited when they arrived early.

I was standing next to the table I reserved for my friends as Charley and Wes walked across the saloon. I felt the happiness and warmth at what being home meant.

My family.

Charley wasted no time in getting to me and pulling me into a hug.

"Oh, Elle. I missed you so much, honey."

Family. I couldn't have been more grateful that Wes found her and brought her into my life. "I missed you too, love. How's married life treating you now that the honeymoon is over and you've been back to reality for a few weeks?"

She pulled away and I realized I already knew the answer. Of course, she answered me anyway. "It's fantastic. I swear, I'm the luckiest woman in the world. How are things going with you and Levi?"

I pretended to think on it a moment before I answered, "We're going to have to call you the luckiest married woman in the world because I'm certain I'm the luckiest woman in the world, too."

Charley laughed. "That works for me. I don't mind sharing the title with you. I am overjoyed to hear that he's making you happy, Elle."

I didn't get an opportunity to respond because Wes interrupted us. He wrapped an arm around my shoulders and pulled me tight to his chest. "Missed you, El, and I've been worried sick about you."

I looked up at him. "I know you have. I'm sorry this has taken its toll on you."

"He's not the only one," I heard someone shout from beside me.

I turned my head to my right and saw Leah standing there. I gave her a sad face before giving her a hug.

"Okay, it's safe to say that everyone missed me. I missed you all, too, and I'm sorry that you were worried about me. It's been stressful all the way around."

"You never called me back last night after what happened and we didn't get to talk about it earlier today when we were texting," Leah started. "What ended up happening? Did you ever find the person who was doing the live feed on your account?"

I took in a deep breath.

"Unfortunately, they never caught her. I think by the time they got through the crowds, she had enough time to get away."

"She?" Leah repeated.

"I told you I had a lot to fill you in on," I began. "Yes, she. We know who's doing this, but we haven't actually found her yet."

Her head jerked back. "Who is it?"

"I don't know her, but her name is Becky Blunt."

"I still think that's the most ridiculous name ever for someone who is supposed to sound ominous," Charley chimed in.

I laughed and turned my attention to her. "I know. I had the same reaction when Levi told me. After I burst out laughing, I asked him if he really thought it was possible that someone with that name was really a threat."

"Ridiculous name or not, there's nothing funny about this situation," Wes pointed out.

I rolled my eyes at him and shared, "You sound just like Levi."

"Speaking of Levi, where is he? If he knows who this is, why isn't he here making sure you're safe?"

I scanned the saloon for Levi and found him standing in a huddle with Gunner, Tyson, Lorenzo, and Holden. They were all members of his team that I met earlier that day.

"Over there," I answered, as I kept my eyes on him and allowed a smile to spread across my face.

"Why do I feel like I'm missing something? I can't understand why he's over there and you're standing here when all of this is going on," Leah pressed.

I brought my gaze back to my best friend and my face softened even further. She was so panicked and worried about me.

"He's over there speaking to members of his team. They're all here tonight. They've been tracking Becky since the first half of my tour. Let me tell you, LP, the bitch is crazy. It'd take me hours to tell you everything that's happened with her. The bottom line is that they're close to finding her."

Leah's eyes searched back and forth and she looked worried.

"What's wrong?" I asked, noticing the significant change in her.

Her eyes filled with tears as she cried, "I didn't know about any of this. Why didn't you tell me?"

"It's been so crazy with the tour, getting from one venue to the next, all the stuff that she has been doing, the planning we've been doing on our end to build a case against her, and I just didn't want to tell you everything over the phone because I knew you'd worry. I wanted to wait and tell you when I got back."

"Well you're back now," she shot back.

Wow, she was really taking this hard. "Tonight. After the show, I'll fill you in on everything."

"Promise?" she asked, her voice small as the tears slid down her cheeks.

I nodded and attempted to comfort her, "I promise."

"I'm going to run to the ladies' room and get myself cleaned up. I'll be right back," she murmured.

As Leah walked away, I looked back to Charley and Wes. They took in my face and immediately noticed my melancholy and worried mood.

"I feel horrible," I admitted.

"She's hurt, but she'll be alright," Charley offered.

Wes added, "I understand your logic, Elle, but think about it from our perspective for a minute. If I just now found out that you knew everything that was going on and you never filled me in on it for weeks, I'd be upset, too."

"Now I feel even worse," I confessed.

"What's wrong, sunshine?" I heard Levi ask from beside me.

I didn't get to answer because Wes continued talking.

"Charley's right, though. Leah will be fine because she's your best friend. She's hurt, but once you explain it all and give her some time, she'll move past it."

"I hope you're right. I didn't mean to hurt her."

"You give her the time, she'll know you didn't," he reassured me.

"Elle?" Levi called.

I looked up at him and asked, "Are you finished with the team?"

He nodded.

I took him by the hand and directed him toward my dressing room. His face was littered with concern. A tear fell from my eye before I simply blurted, "I hurt my best friend."

"What?"

I went on to explain to him what had just happened out in the saloon with Leah. He listened to me, never interrupting once. When I finished, he decided, "It'll be fine, Elle."

"How do you know? She is one of the sweetest people I've ever met and she's been there for me since we were back in college, supporting me every step of the way in my pursuit of becoming a singer. Something bad started happening to me and I kept the good news we got about it from her. I didn't see it that way at the time; I merely wanted to tell her in person, where I knew she'd at least be a little less worried seeing that I was physically ok."

"You said she's your best friend and she's a sweet person. She's not going to hate you, sweetness. She is probably a little hurt, which is understandable. She'll forgive you."

"I promised her I'd tell her everything tonight after the show."

"Do you want to do that at my place?" he offered.

I dipped my head and confirmed, "As long as that's okay with you."

He brought his hand up to cup my cheek. "Of course. Anything you need, sunshine. If it's in my power to give it to you, I will."

My eyes closed at the gesture and the sentiment. He was so good to me. "Thank you," I whispered.

"Looks like you've got a few minutes left before you head out to the stage. You need some time to warm up your voice?"

"That'd probably be a wise idea."

"I was hoping you'd say that. Listening to you back here, I can enjoy your voice completely. Once we're out there, I can't. My focus is on keeping you safe. Besides, I like having a bit of this all to myself."

"Well then, love, you should have a seat and enjoy the next ten minutes while I warm up my pipes."

At that, Levi sat and listened while I did some vocal exercises. Throughout it all, the look of adoration never left his face.

After I finished, Levi walked me back out to the saloon. We stood off the side of the stage until Lou introduced me. While we waited, Cruz walked over, looked to Levi, and confirmed, "Everyone is in position, blending in. If Becky tries anything tonight, we've got men everywhere."

That made me feel better.

Cruz brought his attention to me and maintained, "We've got you covered tonight, rock star."

"Thanks, Cruz. I appreciate what you all are doing for me. I need to figure out a way to pay you back."

My gaze went to Levi, who was clearly not okay with me bringing up paying anyone for anything. To avoid a total meltdown, I quickly added, "Not with money, Levi. I'm just saying that what you all are doing for me means a lot and I want everyone to know how much I appreciate it. That's all."

"Elle?" Cruz cut in.

I looked to him.

"You've already paid us."

My head dropped to the side as I tried to understand what he meant. "How so?"

Cruz jerked his head to Levi and explained, "First, you got this guy out of the office for an extended period when you went on tour. It was a welcome reprieve for all the guys. Levi's not an asshole, but he's serious about work. Trust me, we should be thanking you. And for me, knowing you've made my brother happier than I've ever seen him is more than enough for me."

My eyes got wet and my throat got tight at Cruz's words. He essentially made all the vocal exercises I did a waste of time. I was certain I would completely lose it if I tried to speak, so I stayed silent.

Cruz decided that he hadn't gotten me worked up enough because he continued laying it on thick, "Emme's going to officially be my sister-in-law in a couple more months. If you follow behind her not too long after, I'll be good with that."

My eyes rounded, but before I could even react Lou had introduced me to the crowd. Somehow, I shook Cruz's words from my mind and turned to walk onstage. Before I could walk away, Levi grabbed my hand. When I looked back at him, he didn't say anything. He merely held my eyes, silently reassuring me with his own. I took in a deep breath, gave him a warm smile, and walked away.

I made it to center stage and scanned the crowd as they cheered for me. Front and center, I noticed more of my people had arrived. Joining Wes, Charley, Leah, Zane, and Emme were Monroe, Stone, Nikki, and Luke. My parents were also in attendance. They hadn't seen me since before the whole stalker situation began. Of course, I talked to my mom very soon after Levi moved me into his house, but I hadn't had an opportunity to visit with them.

Aside from them, I managed to spot most of Levi's team scattered throughout the saloon. As Cruz said, they were all blending in. That is to say, they were blending in as much as guys who looked the way they did could blend in. I tried to push aside the reality behind why they were there and put my effort into focusing on all the incredible people who were there because they loved me.

Then, I started singing.

Once I started, I no longer had to try to push away those horrible thoughts about what was really happening in my life because I was lost doing what I loved.

Many songs and quite some time later, I was thankful to have finished my set without incident. Despite the amount of times where I said I hoped Becky would try something tonight, there was a small part of me that wanted my final show of the tour to go off without a hitch. At least I had gotten that.

I walked off stage, right into Levi's arms. He held me tight and pressed a kiss to the top of my head.

"Are we hanging tonight or heading home?"

I tilted my head back and reasoned, "I think we should head out so I can talk with Leah."

"Sounds good."

"But I have one favor I need to ask of you first," I went on.

"Sure. What do you need?"

I took a deep swallow and bit my lip before I explained, "My parents are here. I haven't seen them in a couple weeks now and I'd like to introduce them to the person that's not only been keeping me safe but has also made me the happiest woman alive."

Levi's expression changed. The change was good. "Of course, sunshine. I'd love to meet them."

With that, Levi walked me out to where my parents were sitting with the rest of the gang. James and Linda Blackman were not the type to spend their evenings at a saloon, but they would occasionally come out to my shows. Having not seen me in a while, I'm certain, was the reason for tonight's appearance. On those occasions where they would show up, they'd typically hang around long enough after my shows to chat a few minutes with me before they took off.

Don't get me wrong. My parents absolutely loved and

adored me. They supported me one hundred percent in my chosen career path. It was the same for Wes. Lou's just wasn't their scene; so, when I finished performing, they usually called it a night.

I walked up to the table, holding Levi's hand, and stopped just behind my parents. I put my free hand on my mom's shoulder. She turned and looked up at me. The second her eyes were on me, she practically jumped out of her seat and pulled me into her arms.

"Oh, Elle," she cried. "I've been so worried about you."

I had to drop Levi's hand to fully embrace my mother. I tried my best to soothe her. "I know, mom. I'm sorry to have put you through all of this. We are close to getting this all figured out."

She pulled back and put both hands on the sides of my upper arms, where she gently squeezed. "When?" she asked.

I didn't have an answer for that, so I stayed silent.

Thankfully, my dad chimed in. "Are you okay, Elle?"

A huge smile spread across my face before I answered, "I'm amazing. This stalker situation is just a minor inconvenience."

It was more than a minor inconvenience, but I didn't want to alarm them any further.

I continued with what I really wanted them to hear. I reached back to grab Levi's hand and made introductions. "Mom and Dad, I want you both to meet Levi. Levi, these are my parents, James and Linda."

Levi used his free hand and offered it to each of my parents as they all exchanged pleasantries.

My mom was first to speak afterward. "Thank you for looking out for her."

"She's my precious little girl," my father chimed in. "Kills me to know what someone is doing to her."

"I completely understand your concerns, Mr. and Mrs.

Blackman, but I want you to know she's in good hands. Elle's case is my top priority right now."

My father's eyes dropped to where my hand connected with Levi's. "Seems to me that it's more than just her case that's going on here."

Before I had the chance to respond, Levi spoke firmly. "Yes, sir. I'm in love with your daughter. And I want you to understand that the way I feel about her does not distract me from doing my job properly. It only makes my need to protect her run that much deeper."

"Always liked your brother," my dad started, referring to Wes' best friend and Levi's brother, Zane. "I'm thinking I might be able to like you just as much."

I blew out a sigh of relief. They liked him. My parents seemed more than confident in the unspoken promise Levi just delivered; he'd do whatever he had to do just to keep me safe. I loved them so much for taking him at his word and I loved him so much for giving them that peace.

My mom caught my attention when she spoke again. "We're going to head out of here now because we have our flight leaving in the morning, but please, Elle, check in more frequently. At least until this situation has been resolved."

"I will, mom. Thanks for coming out to support me tonight."

"We love you! Of course, we'd be here."

My father added, "Stay safe, Elle. We'll see you when we are back from vacation in a week."

I gave him a warm smile before giving them both goodbye hugs.

After my parents left, I turned toward the rest of the group, all of whom gave me praise for my performance. I told them all that I was calling it a night, partly because I was exhausted from the tour, but mostly because I needed to set things right with my best friend.

"Do you want to just follow us back to Levi's place?" I asked Leah.

"It's getting late. If you want, we can just meet up tomorrow. I know you've got to be worn out from the tour. I can wait another day, E."

To say that she no longer seemed angry with me was an understatement. More than anything, she seemed to be very hurt. I didn't want to allow that to go on for another minute.

"I'm good to do this tonight," I declared. "It's important, and as it is, I shouldn't have waited this long."

"Leah's right, Elle," Levi cut in. "It's late."

He turned his attention to Leah. "I've got a couple of spare bedrooms. Why don't you stay at my place? You and Elle can talk for as long as you both need, but then you won't need to worry about driving home even later."

My heart swelled and my feelings for this man grew at that very moment. He was not only looking out for me and what I needed, but he'd do it while keeping my friend's safety in mind.

"Well, I mean, if you don't mind," Leah stammered.

"Not at all."

Leah's eyes cut to mine and she divulged, "I'd prefer to run home real quick and grab a few things. Can you text me the address and I'll meet you there?"

"Sure."

At that, she took off while Levi let Cruz and the rest of the team know we were heading out. I thanked them for coming and they all gave me praise on my performance.

Once Levi and I were in his truck, I knew I had to tell him how I was feeling.

"I love you, Levi," I started as I looked over at him.

He took his eyes off the road only briefly to glance over at me. "I love you, too."

"Thank you so much for doing this for me and Leah tonight. It means a lot to me."

He shrugged his shoulders and kept his eyes on the road. "She means a lot to you and she's upset. It doesn't take much for me to see that when your friend is hurting, it affects you. I don't like seeing you upset, so I'm going to do what I can to make it better for you."

"You're so good to me."

A grin spread across his face and he responded, "Well, your lips tasted like pancake syrup tonight. I love all of your different flavors, so I figure I've got to do what I've got to do to keep you around."

Warmth spread through my body.

"I'm right where I want to be, love."

Levi didn't say anything. He reached over and wrapped his hand around mine. Then, he held it the rest of the way back to his place.

CHAPTER 24

Elle

"**S**HE SHOULD BE PULLING IN TO THE DRIVEWAY ANY MINUTE now."

Levi and I had arrived back at his place just over thirty minutes ago and about twenty minutes after we returned, I received a text message from Leah telling me that she was leaving her place.

"Thank you again for allowing her to stay the night here in your home," I stated for the second time that night.

"You don't need to keep thanking me, sunshine. I just want you to be happy."

I leaned into him and squeezed my arms around his waist attempting to let him know just how happy he made me. Levi held me tight, silently reminding me just how much he cared about me.

"I couldn't wait to get back from the tour to be around the people that make this place a perfect place to call home. Thank you for going on tour with me, but more importantly, thank you for bringing me back safely."

A few minutes later, there was a knock at the door. Levi moved to open it and I followed along beside him. Leah walked in with a weekender bag carrying some things for her overnight stay.

"Did you find the place alright, LP?" I asked.

"Yep. No problems at all," she answered me before turning her attention to Levi. "Thanks for allowing me to spend the night tonight. I've really missed spending time with Elle and I appreciate you giving us this time together."

"It's not a problem at all," Levi declared.

He then turned his attention to me and explained, "I'm going to lock up everything and head up to bed so you two can catch up."

"Oh, now I feel bad," Leah broke in. "We're making you go to bed early and alone."

"I've got to get up and head into the office early tomorrow morning, so it's not a big deal," Levi started. He didn't take his eyes off me when he wrapped a hand around the back of my head and continued, "I won't be alone all night, right?"

"No," I whispered.

With that, Levi leaned in and kissed me softly on the lips. "Wake me when you come to bed, sweetness."

I dipped my head in acknowledgment of his request.

"Goodnight, Leah," he expressed as he started walking away.

"Night."

Levi took off to lock up and head to bed, while I ushered Leah into the family room. Before she arrived, I got out a few snacks and a bottle of wine. I figured a bit of alcohol might help in this situation. I poured each of us a glass and we made ourselves comfortable on the couch.

"So, tell me everything."

I took in a deep breath. "Oh, where do I begin? Ok, so you know what happened in the beginning. I was receiving the flowers with cards that had creepy messages and there was the whole knife in the back and attempted kidnapping situation. We initially all assumed that the person responsible for everything was a man. Trent, who is part of Levi's team and a computer genius, has been monitoring everything on my accounts. When I did a live session while I was on tour, he ended up finding out that this Becky Blunt woman watched it."

"Yeah, but E, you've got thousands of followers. What made him pick her out of the crowd?"

"The day I left to go on tour, Trent started going through all of my followers on social media that had those initials from the notes I'd been receiving before I even left to go on tour. By the time I did the live session, he had gotten through everyone and there wasn't anyone who stood out as a possible suspect. Trent went through the people who watched the live session and saw her name. He realized she wasn't one of my followers and decided to do some digging. As it turns out, the bitch is crazy."

Leah's face changed. She looked panicked and worried for me. I quickly tried to quell any fear she had and explained, "On the surface, if you looked at her social media accounts, you wouldn't think anything of it. Now, if you set hers next to mine, you'd see the similarities, which are overwhelmingly alarming. She is obsessed with me. Beyond obsessed. When you look at each of our profiles you'd see the connection, it's just irritating. But when you add in the fact that she's sending the notes, having me held at knifepoint, and more, it's downright frightening."

"Why would someone do this?" Leah wondered.

I let out a sigh and declared, "That's the million-dollar question. I wish I knew. It's the one thing I keep asking every time something else happens. I've gotten a scary phone call where a voice changer was used and she's even managed to invade my privacy by accessing the private messages on my social media accounts. To top it off, she's hinted at me being deserving of sexual assault. I just don't understand why anyone would ever want to spend their lives constantly focusing on someone else. Wouldn't life be so much more enjoyable by actually concentrating on yourself? It's exhausting, LP. I've had thousands of questions and scenarios run through my head trying to figure it out and none of it makes sense."

I paused, dropping my head back on the couch to stare up at the ceiling and giving her a moment to process everything I had said before I continued, "Of course, there's the obvious explanation."

"Which is?"

I brought the glass of wine up to my lips and took a sip before I turned my head toward her and concluded, "Jealousy."

Leah stared at me for quite some time before she admitted, "Gosh, E, this is making my head spin. I can't imagine having to deal with this; yet somehow, you're managing to keep it all together surprisingly well."

A small laugh escaped the back of my throat. "Talk to me after you've witnessed me finding out a new piece of information on this case."

She gave me a knowing smile and countered, "I can only guess how that goes down."

"You'd probably be right in your assumptions," I began. "But in all seriousness, it's Levi that's helping me stay sane. Throughout the entire tour, he was so good about making sure I didn't become overwhelmed with the stress of not just touring, but also this whole situation."

"Sounds like you've finally found Prince Charming."

I closed my eyes briefly and took in my best friend's words. She was right.

"Yeah, I have. And I've got Becky to thank for that. If this hadn't happened, I'm not sure Levi and I would have ever gotten together. I guess that's the silver lining in all of this."

"I'm happy you're finally getting what you deserve," Leah added gently.

"Okay, enough about me. What about you? How is everything at the clinic?"

She rolled her eyes at me. "That's the only thing in my life that I understand. Animals. Everything they do is based on instinct. On the bright side, animals do not provide the drama that people do."

"Still no luck figuring out how to break the news that you don't really want to be a vet?" I pressed.

Her eyes filled with tears. "I don't want to disappoint my family. I'm afraid they'll see me in a negative light if I don't do what's been expected of me for so many years. Sure, I care about the animals, but I don't feel fulfilled doing this every single day. Something is missing."

I hated this for her. I couldn't imagine living my life doing what made someone else happy or feeling like I couldn't do what would truly make me happy because the people in my life who are supposed to love and support me would judge me instead.

"I know we've had this discussion about a billion times, but do you have any idea on what you'd want to do?"

"Not really," she mumbled, shrugging her shoulders. "It's not like it'd matter anyway."

I shook my head in disbelief. "You ask how I'm managing to deal with what I'm going through, but I sit here and wonder how you do it. How do you put on a happy face every day knowing that you're essentially dying inside? They're your family. They should support you no matter what you choose to do, and they should do it without passing any judgment."

"I know. And there's the rational part of my brain that tells me that, but there's the other part that believes they'll think anything else I might do with myself is beneath me."

There wasn't much I could say to change her mind. We'd done this for years. She'd tell me how she really felt, but she'd never tell the people who needed to hear it. Seeing her mood grow somber, I decided to change topics.

"How are things on the dating front?"

She scoffed, "I told you the only thing I seem to understand in life right now are animals. Don't even get me started on men."

"No luck?"

She shook her head. "I went out on a date that first night you were on tour. I thought it went well and the guy said he'd call, but I never heard from him again."

"I'm sorry, LP. You'll find your Prince Charming soon."

"I won't hold my breath," she retorted.

A crazy thought flashed through my mind and my eyes rounded.

"I'm not sure if I like that look," Leah worried.

A devilish grin spread across my face and I explained, "I just had the greatest idea. Levi's entire team is single. We should set you up on a date with one of them."

"Really? That guy Dom is so hot," she shared, her face lighting up.

"He's a crazy motherfucker, too. At least, that's what I'm told. But beyond that, he's a really nice guy that's super laid-back. I'm thinking he'd be perfect for you."

My best friend was back in good spirits.

Mission accomplished.

Leah and I spent the next hour catching up on everything, filling up on wine. I gave her more of the specific details of Becky's shenanigans and the fun from the tour. She listened, particularly when I spoke about Dom, and then brought me up to speed on all the gossip that I missed out on while I was away.

After we consumed the entire bottle, I finally showed her to the guest bedroom at the opposite end of the hall from where Levi's bedroom was. Since Levi had a couple of spare rooms, I thought this was better than sticking her in the room I had stayed in my first night here. Once I got Leah settled, I made my way down the hall to Levi's room. He was sleeping, but had asked me to wake him when I came to bed. I felt bad doing it, but I knew he'd probably be pissed in the morning if I didn't.

After stripping out of all my clothes and pulling a nightie over my head, I climbed under the covers and scooted across the bed toward him. He was on his side with his back to me. I pressed my front to his back and wrapped my arm around him. I slid my hand from his chest, down his abdomen. I only made it a few inches before he seized my wrist and rolled in the bed so that he was facing me.

"Everything good between you and your girl?" he whispered.

"Yeah," I whispered back. "Thank you for giving me that time with her tonight."

Levi's hand slid up my back into my hair. "Anything, Elle. I'll always give you anything I can."

We were in the dark, but I managed to make out the features on his face. I leaned in and kissed him on the lips while I slid my hand down his abdomen to his hardened length.

"Taking charge here, sunshine?"

"It's the half a bottle of wine I consumed," I answered, trying to relieve my sober self of any blame. "You said you'll give me anything you can. I want this and I want to give you some honey."

I felt him smile against my lips. "How do you want it?"

"On my side with you behind me," I replied, my voice a breathy whisper.

Levi slid his hand down to my hip and pushed me to my

back. He wrapped his arm around my waist and turned me so that my back was now against his front. Levi wasted no time in sliding my nightie up and out of his way. Then, he positioned himself at my slick center and entered me.

Once he began to move, I interlocked my fingers with his and closed my eyes.

"I love you, sweetness," he rasped in my ear.

I turned my head toward him and gave him my mouth, while he continued his delightful, languid thrusts into me.

"So good," I murmured. "You're so good to me."

He melted my heart when he said, "You give back just as good as you get."

Knowing I made him feel just as good as he made me feel, not just physically, filled me with such joy.

I couldn't focus too much on the emotional bliss I was feeling because it was being overpowered by the physical pleasure he was giving me.

I moaned as he pushed in and pulled out of me, all while squeezing my fingers in his and peppering kisses on my cheek, my jaw, my neck, my mouth, and my shoulders.

Arching my back, I pressed my ass into his lap. Now, it was his turn to moan.

"This is my home, Elle. Right here…" he bit out on an inward thrust. "With you is my home."

It was on those words my body took over and I climaxed. Tears leaked from my eyes, my soul touched by the words he spoke.

Feeling the reaction my body had to what he said, Levi found his release and buried himself to the root inside me.

The two of us stayed connected like that for a very long time, Levi's arms tight around me as my hands gripped his firmly. Levi eventually pulled himself from my body and fell to his back. He turned me and took me with him.

Minutes later, without any more words, our breathing evened out and we both fell asleep.

It was early the next morning when I felt the bed depress and heard Levi call, "Elle?"

I turned toward the sound of his voice and opened my eyes.

"I've got to get going, sunshine. I need to get into the office and take care of some things that I want to research on your case. I'll set the alarm before I leave. If you and Leah decide to go anywhere, please call me first."

"Okay," I agreed, my voice husky with sleep. "What time is it?"

"Just before eight."

"Will you kiss me before you leave?"

He leaned in and divulged, "Planned on it."

Levi touched his lips to mine as I wrapped my arms around his neck. He gave me a kiss that was intended to last until he returned later. When he pulled back, I questioned him. "Are you expecting a long day?"

"I wish I had an answer for you, but I'm not sure yet. There are quite a few things I want to look into, one in particular that's not sitting well with me. It'll just depend on how long it takes me to fully investigate those things and alleviate the concerns I have with them. I'll call you throughout the day just to touch base."

I didn't like this sudden shift in his mood. It seemed he had thoughts about what was going on that he hadn't filled me in on.

"What's going on?"

"Nothing I want you to be concerned with just yet. Give me the day to scrutinize some stuff and I'll fill you in when I get home."

"I get the feeling I should be worried," I admitted.

His face softened. "I'm sorry. Just trust me to research this properly so I can ease both of our minds."

"I do."

Levi bent over me and gave me a quick kiss. "Love you."

"Love you, too."

With that, he turned and walked out of the room.

I stayed in bed for quite some time thinking about the last few weeks of my life. Everything from the stalker and security team, to love and Levi. After all of those thoughts filtered through my head, I decided to get up and check in on Leah.

I walked down the hall to the guest bedroom and knocked on the door.

"Yeah?" she called from inside the room, but I was already walking in. As I stepped inside, I saw that she had just gotten out of the shower and was just about ready to start her day.

"Morning, LP. Sleep okay?"

"Yeah. I've got to get to the clinic, but I'm not heading in until around ten. I figured if Levi's got all the ingredients here I could whip you both up a batch of my waffles."

I grinned huge at her and reminded her, "Levi left a little while ago to head into the office, but I'm more than willing to have your waffles. I'll come downstairs with you to make sure he's got everything here and then, if you don't mind, I'll run back up here to shower quick while you make them."

"That works for me."

Leah and I made our way downstairs to the kitchen where we found that Levi did, in fact, have all the ingredients she'd need for making her waffles. After making sure she had everything she needed, I went back upstairs and hopped in the shower. I made quick work of my shower duties, so that I'd have a few minutes to dry my hair without having to let my breakfast get cold.

As I walked back out into the kitchen not much later, I

found that I had timed it all perfectly. Leah had just set the waffles on plates.

"Perfect timing," she started. "Breakfast is ready."

"I've been salivating since you said you wanted to make these. I think it's been easily six months since I've had your world-famous waffles."

She held out a mug with tea for me and said, "Enjoy!"

At that, we dug in.

As was not uncommon, I overate.

CHAPTER 25

Elle

"**G**O AHEAD AND GO," I REPEATED FOR THE THIRD TIME. "I can clean up."

"It's no problem, E. I don't need to arrive at work any earlier than they are expecting me. I still have some time."

Leah and I finished breakfast and were cleaning up the kitchen before she had to head out to get to work.

"Well, I feel bad. You cooked breakfast and you need to go to work today. I don't have much planned other than trying to get through the mounds of laundry I have stuffed in my suitcases."

"Alright," she acquiesced. "I'll run upstairs, brush my teeth, and grab my bag."

She took off up the stairs while I finished loading the dishwasher and wiping down the countertops.

After, I picked up my phone and checked in on social media. It dawned on me that Becky had indicated she was in town yesterday; yet, she didn't do anything last night. I decided to check her social media news feeds. I typed in her name and clicked on her profile.

My blood went cold.

After yesterday's post just outside of Lou's, there hadn't been anything. That is, until this morning.

A picture of a syringe against a plain background. The caption stated: *Change of plans. This ends today.*

Suddenly, I didn't feel so well. This was no longer a simple stalker. This was deadly obsession.

I began to feel dizzy and disoriented. My free hand instinctively reached out to the counter of the island.

I needed Levi.

Leah's footsteps were coming down the stairs. Thank God.

As she walked out into the kitchen with her bag, she noticed something wasn't right. "Are you okay, Elle?"

I shook my head and gripped the countertop tighter. "She wants to kill me."

"What?"

"Becky wants me dead," I struggled to get out. "I don't feel good."

Leah came over to me and acknowledged, "You don't look very good either. Why don't you go sit down?"

She took the phone out of my hand and set it on the island before she wrapped her arm around my waist and attempted to help me to the living room so I could get to the couch. I took three or four steps before my legs buckled. Leah was so tiny she came down to the floor with me.

"Something's wrong," I pointed out. "Please call Levi."

"Okay, hang on."

Leah was no longer at my side. I closed my eyes briefly trying to dispel the dizziness I was feeling. I felt like I was drunk.

My eyes opened a few seconds later when I heard my phone ringing right next to me. Leah had it in her hand and announced, "It's Levi."

"Answer it," I begged. "Tell him to come home."

I watched as she declined the call and set the phone down on the floor too far for me to reach.

I spoke again, but my speech was very slow. "Leah...What are you doing?"

She just looked down at me.

My phone rang again. My eyes shifted to where it was on the floor. It was close, but too far considering my limbs felt like they weighed several hundred pounds each. The phone stopped ringing.

I continued trying to breathe, but everything felt like it was in slow motion. My body felt tired.

I nearly closed my eyes when the phone started again. This time, Leah answered.

"Hello?"

Silence as she listened.

"She's not able to talk right now, Levi."

That's when I saw it.

The syringe.

In Leah's hand.

"Levi?" I called out, but my voice wasn't very loud.

My eyelids were heavy, but I knew I couldn't close them.

"Well, right now she's got a sedative running through her body. You see, I know that physically she'd probably best me in a brawl, but if her faculties aren't there, then I can do what needs to be done."

Silence again.

I couldn't believe it; Leah was Becky.

My best friend, who I loved and adored, wanted to kill me. The pain that tore through my heart at this realization was like nothing I had ever experienced before.

I felt the tears fall from my eyes and drip down toward my hairline.

Leah laughed into the phone. It was evil and cold-blooded. "You can certainly try, but it won't work. All I need to do is inject her with this syringe I've got in my hand and her heart will stop. When you arrive ten minutes from now, you'll find her lifeless body on the floor of your kitchen and I'll be long gone."

Levi

From the moment I spoke with Trent while I was with Elle on her tour and he told me that someone indicated she trampled all over others to get what she wanted, I knew something about that didn't sit well with me. Those words indicated to me that Elle's stalker was someone who had a personal grudge with her. There was no doubt in my mind that Elle knew Becky. Since Elle didn't recall knowing anyone with that name, I had a feeling Becky was just a pseudonym.

I never wanted to mention it to Elle because she'd take it hard. My goal was to locate the individual and put an end to what was happening before Elle had to face the reality that someone she knew was out to get her.

I walked into my office this morning, leaving my beautiful girl home in my bed. Truth be told, I hated leaving her there, but more than that, I disliked the idea of someone else being out free to continue to terrorize her. I wanted to put this situation to bed and if that meant I needed to forego some additional time in bed with Elle right now to make that happen, then I needed to suck it up and get it done.

Yesterday evening, before Elle's performance, I told Trent, Cruz, and Holden that I wanted them in early so we could discuss some of the concerns I had and see if we could put our heads together and figure this out.

We spent the next hour discussing the case, going over all the details. I gave them my concerns and they had agreed that this person was definitely someone that Elle knew personally.

"Let's look at the social media feeds again," I told Trent.

He pulled up Becky's account on the projector screen and set it alongside of Elle's. We went through each post, the most recent of Becky's being from last night outside of Lou's, working our way backward trying to find anything that made a connection. It was beginning to feel like we were grasping at straws. I was losing patience with the whole situation when something in one of the pictures caught my eye.

"Stop," I ordered Trent as he was scrolling.

I stared at the picture. I knew my eyes weren't deceiving me, but it seemed so improbable that what this picture was showing and, ultimately, telling me was the truth. I knew if it were the truth, not only was Elle going to be crushed, but she was currently in very real danger. My stomach twisted.

"Scroll up, Michaels. Go back to the post about traveling."

He scrolled up to it, and I knew I had figured it out. The post was all about disorganization and living spontaneously instead of having routine and order. I had listened to and then discussed with Elle how her friend felt about organization and the fact that Elle seemed to live life off the cuff.

"Bro?" Cruz called from beside me.

"It's Leah," I seethed.

"Her best friend?" Cruz questioned.

I nodded.

"Wait," Holden interrupted. "Are we talking about the little redhead from last night?"

"Yes," I answered, pulling my phone out of my pocket.

"How do you know?" Trent asked.

"The bag in the other picture. Leah stayed at my place last night so she and Elle could catch up on everything. The girl found out last night that Elle knew a whole lot more about the case than she told her about and she pretended to be hurt by it. I'm guessing she realized we were on to her and it wouldn't be long before we figured out who Becky was. She's at the house with Elle now. I've got to get home."

I tapped on the screen of my phone and called Elle. The phone rang several times before it went to voicemail.

"Fuck," I yelled. "Cruz, I need you to drive."

"Boss!" Trent yelled.

I turned and saw him staring at the projector screen. A picture of a syringe with the caption underneath it: *Change of plans. This ends today.*

I dialed Elle's number again.

Leah's voice came through the line, "Hello?"

I put the phone on speaker and tried to keep my voice neutral. "Hi, Leah. I forgot something at the house that I need to have Elle look at for me. Can you put her on the phone?"

"She's not able to talk right now, Levi."

Fuck.

We just barely heard Elle's strained voice call my name.

"What's wrong with her?"

"Well, right now she's got a sedative running through her body. You see, I know that physically she'd probably best me in a brawl, but if her faculties aren't there, then I can do what needs to be done."

I pointed to Trent and Holden. They offered chin lifts, indicating they knew what I needed them to do. Cruz and I took off.

"Stop whatever it is that you are planning to do and listen to me. You aren't going to get away with this, Leah. I'm already on my way there now and even though I'd never lay a hand on a woman, trust me, I'll show you no mercy if you hurt her."

"You can certainly try, but it won't work. All I need to do

is inject her with this syringe I've got in my hand and her heart will stop. When you arrive ten minutes from now, you'll find her lifeless body on the floor of your kitchen and I'll be long gone."

"Leah…" I yelled out, but she disconnected the phone.

"FUCK!"

"Dom's already on the way," Cruz informed me. "Michaels texted. He disabled the security system from the office. Leah won't expect him and isn't going to know when he gets there. Holden has an ambulance already on the way."

"Christ, Cruz, she doesn't have any time left."

"She's going to be fine. Dom's going to get there in time," he attempted to reassure me. I'm not certain that he believed what he was saying.

Dom

It was a nice day out, so I decided to ride the motorcycle to work. I was just about to turn it on when my phone rang. I pulled it out of my pocket and saw it was Trent.

"Yeah?"

"You're home?"

"Just got on the bike and was about to head in."

"Go to Levi's. Elle's there alone with her stalker. It's the best friend."

"The quiet, little redhead?" I confirmed.

"Yeah. She's already administered a sedative. Levi and Cruz just left, but they're ten minutes out. You're two minutes away."

"A minute and a half on the bike. Completely disable the alarm."

I dropped my phone in my pocket, turned on the bike, and broke a couple of laws speeding over to Levi's place.

I made it there in record time and parked the bike halfway down the driveway so I had the element of surprise on my side. I made it to the door and picked the lock. I moved quietly in the house toward the direction of voices.

"Why?" I heard Elle whimper.

Elle's speech was slow, clearly indicating that she had been given a strong sedative.

I made it to just outside the kitchen without being noticed and found that Leah's back was to me and she was leaning over Elle, the syringe in her hand.

"It doesn't matter anymore now, anyway. You've ruined this for both of us," Leah exploded. "I just need to finish this before your precious Levi shows up. It's such a shame that you had to be so greedy. The perfect career, the perfect man, the perfect family and friends. What about the rest of us?"

Leah bent down closer to Elle and I made my move. She pierced through Elle's skin with the syringe and I pulled her away.

She yelled out as I wrapped my arms around her attempting to control her flailing arms and legs.

"Elle!" I called out.

She was unresponsive.

I scanned the kitchen looking for something to use to neutralize the bitch, so I could check on Elle. I moved out into the garage and found zip ties. I carried Leah back in the house, zip-tied her wrists together to the handle of the refrigerator door. There was no way Leah was moving that. Then, I moved to Elle.

"You're okay, rock star. Can you hear me?" I asked gently as I pulled the syringe from her body. It looked full, but I had no clue if any of its contents entered her bloodstream.

She wasn't responding.

I pressed my fingers to her neck and found a pulse. It was weak, but it was there. "Elle, baby, talk to me," I urged her as I ran my hand through her hair, attempting to comfort her. I figured if she had a pulse she might still be aware of what was happening, even if she couldn't respond to it.

Still, I got nothing.

I kept one hand on the top of her head and reached the other one down to hold one of her hands. "Are you with me, El?"

She squeezed my hand.

Thank fuck.

I continued to talk to her.

"Levi's almost here. There's an ambulance on the way. We're going to get you help. You're doing great, rock star."

Tears leaked from her eyes.

The door opened; Levi and Cruz rushed in and froze on the spot, seeing Elle's motionless body on the floor.

I wasted no time in filling them in.

"She's got a weak pulse. The syringe pierced her skin, but it's still pretty full. Not sure if anything entered her system from that. She squeezed my hand when I was talking to her."

Levi knelt down on the other side of her. He took her other hand in his and brought his face close to hers.

"I'm so fucking sorry, Elle. Can you give me your eyes, sunshine?"

She didn't.

I removed my hand from the top of her head, but the second I did that Elle's hand tightened again in mine.

"You want me to stay, rock star?"

She squeezed again.

Levi kept talking.

"Dom's staying. I'm staying. We've got you, sweetness."

More tears fell from her closed eyes.

Thankfully, we heard the sirens in the distance.

I glanced up to see Cruz boring daggers from his eyes into Leah.

"Cruz?" I called.

He didn't take his eyes off her. "What the fuck is wrong with you?" he bit out.

Leah didn't answer. She sat there staring off into space. Clearly, she was fucked-up in the head. Not only did she stalk her best friend for weeks, but she had just attempted to kill her and sat there as if nothing happened.

"Cruz!" I shouted.

This time he looked at me.

"Let the medics in."

His eyes dropped to Elle on the floor and pain sliced through his face before he turned on his boot to let the paramedics in.

A minute later, they barreled through the door with a stretcher and a bunch of equipment. It was tough knowing she didn't want to let go of my hand, but also knowing I needed to let them help her. I figured it was more important that Levi stay with her.

"Do we know what she was given?" one of the paramedics asked.

"A sedative for sure," Levi answered. "There's something in that syringe that will stop her heart, but I don't know what it is."

"Was she given any of that?"

"The needle pierced her skin, but I don't know if any of that got into her system. I pulled it out as soon as I could."

The police arrived minutes later as Elle was being loaded onto the stretcher. She still hadn't opened her eyes. We'd had plenty of interaction with the Windsor Police Department, so they knew the instant they walked into Levi's place who the suspect was. One officer began interrogating Cruz and me, while another removed Leah from the zip ties and handcuffed her.

As Cruz and I answered questions, Levi walked past right alongside Elle's stretcher. He still had her hand in his. He looked at me and pleaded, "Call Zane, let him know. Make sure someone calls Wes. When you finish here, come to the hospital. Rising Sun Medical Center."

I gave him a chin lift and watched as they wheeled Elle out of the house.

Cruz and I spent the next thirty minutes answering questions and seeing to it that the officers knew exactly what Leah said to Elle when I entered the house. Cruz filled them in on what she said to Levi over the phone. The two of us explained the stalker situation, the Becky Blunt social media accounts, and all of the attempts to harm Elle.

After we gave them all the information, Cruz called Zane and Wes to let them know they needed to get to the hospital, but didn't provide them with any specifics. After the officers left, I waited back to make sure Cruz was alright.

"You good, man?" I asked.

"Fucking hell, Dom. Both of my brothers have had some bullshit happen to their women. Men as strong as the two of them are and they've been reduced to messes in these situations. I hated seeing what happened to Emme a couple months ago and what just happened to Elle, but watching my brothers go through that is more torturous because they never fall apart like that."

I laid my hand on his shoulder and gave him a squeeze. "They've got you to keep it together for them."

He let out a laugh and maintained, "I might seem like I've got it together and I'll certainly joke with them about it after everyone is safe, but in the moment, that shit guts me."

"And if the roles are ever reversed, it'll be the same for them watching you."

"Fuck me if that ever happens. This is enough to make me not want to find a serious relationship."

I had no response to that because it was the truth. If you could avoid the heartache and terror that you'd feel if someone you loved was in danger, I can't imagine why you wouldn't.

"You want to get over to the hospital?" I asked. "I'll take care of locking up here and then meet you guys there."

Just then, Holden and Pierce showed up.

"Is she okay?" Pierce asked.

"Unconscious, but she had a pulse and was breathing. She squeezed my hand a couple times."

"Fuck," Pierce hissed. "Her best fucking friend."

"Clearly, she wasn't," Holden pointed out.

We let that truth settle between us a minute before Pierce spoke again. "Michaels is waiting for a call from us. He'll get the security system set up again as soon as we give him the word. Then, we'll all head over to the hospital. If you guys want to leave now, we'll get everything squared away here."

"Thanks, man," Cruz sighed.

"We'll catch you over there. They took her to Rising Sun Medical Center," I added. "When you talk to Michaels, let him know the WPD is going to need the evidence he's been gathering online. And we're going to need to get the security footage from here over to them as well."

"Got it," Holden acknowledged.

At that, Cruz and I left. He got in his truck while I hopped on my bike. Then, we took off to check on our rock star.

CHAPTER 26

Levi

THOSE BEAUTIFUL EYES.

I was certain I was going out of my mind because I hadn't seen those eyes.

My girl.

My little ray of sunshine.

Seeing her lying there on the floor of the kitchen, unmoving, is something I'll never forget for as long as I live. Crouching down next to her, feeling her squeeze my hand, and watching the tears fall from her eyes, I wanted to take it away from her.

The pain.

Not physical pain.

No.

I knew Elle, and I knew that deep down she was hurting. Her best friend tried to kill her. Once we got Elle past the physical trauma she suffered, I knew it'd take a lot of time and effort to help her get past the emotional wounds she just received. This was bound to cut her deep.

I was pacing the waiting room of the hospital, daydreaming about her eyes, when Cruz and Dom walked in.

"Have you heard anything?" he asked.

"Nothing yet, Cruz. I'm going out of my mind."

A minute later, Wes, Charley, Zane, and Emme rushed into the hospital.

Despair.

Nothing but despair in their faces.

"What happened?" Zane asked the minute they were standing in front of me.

"I shouldn't have left her there with that bitch," I declared. "She didn't move. She couldn't move her body. She couldn't even open her eyes."

I was getting worked up and they all knew it. Every second that passed that I didn't get to look in those eyes was absolute torture.

Emme was immediately wrapping her arms around me. I held on tight to her.

"She's going to be okay, Levi," Emme attempted to reassure me. "She's a strong woman and she is in love. That's what will get her through this. Your love will get her through this, but you've got to keep it together for her. Be strong for her. I know you can do it because your brother did it for me."

My throat was so tight, it was a wonder I could say anything. "Emme, I just want to look in her eyes again."

"You will. I promise."

"Cruz, what happened?" Zane pressed.

"Leah. Leah was Becky. Leah was the one stalking her. She was obsessed with her," Cruz explained. He then went on to explain everything from Leah staying at my place last night to our meeting at the office this morning. Cruz described the most recent social media post and phone conversation I had with Leah. "Leah explained that she had given Elle a sedative and that even though we were already on our way, she knew she had ten minutes before we'd be back there. She said it would be plenty of time for her to administer something that would stop her heart," Cruz told them.

He paused a moment giving everyone some time to take in what he just said. Wes was gutted. Charley stayed pressed to his side, the two of them trying to support each other.

Cruz continued the story. He let them know about everything including Dom getting to my place first and the horrific scene we encountered when we finally arrived back at my place and saw Elle on the floor.

"Fuck," Wes choked.

Seconds later, the doors opened and the doctor came out into the waiting room.

"Family of Elizabeth Blackman," he called out.

All of us walked toward him.

A little taken aback, he asked, "You're all her family?"

Wes stepped forward, "I'm her brother and, yes, we are all her family. How is she?"

"We're still waiting to get a few tests back, but as of now it appears as though she was only given a very strong sedative. It's going to take some time for it to fully wear off, but I expect, pending the results of the remaining tests, that she'll be fine.

"Has she woken up yet?" I asked.

"I'm afraid not. It's just going to take time. She could wake up in the next five minutes or it could take her a few hours."

"Can we see her?" Wes questioned.

"Sure," the doctor started. "They just transferred her from the emergency room up to the fourth floor. She's in room four seventeen, and she'll be spending the night. If all her tests come back negative and there aren't any further complications, she should be able to go home tomorrow. Follow me and I'll show you to the elevators."

The doctor turned and we followed behind him through the doors and down the hall to the elevators. We piled on and made our way up to the fourth floor. We made it to Elle's room, where Charley, Wes, Emme, and Zane entered ahead of Dom, Cruz, and me.

Then, I saw her.

My beautiful girl.

Hooked to an IV, her eyes were still closed. I never felt such tightness in my throat.

I moved by everyone and walked up next to Elle's bedside. I took her hand that didn't have the IV in it and kissed the back of it.

Wes walked over to her on the other side of the bed as Charley followed behind him. He put his hand to her forehead and brushed her hair back before he pressed a kiss to the top of her head.

"Elle, we're all here for you," Charley said softly. "Wes, Levi, Emme, Zane, Cruz, and Dom. We're all here."

Emme came and stood next to me. She rested her hand on the blanket covering Elle's leg. Her voice was quiet when she spoke. "We all love you, Elle."

I felt a twitch in Elle's hand and looked at her face. Her head fell to the side toward me and she slowly opened her eyes.

Those eyes.

I'd never seen anything more exquisite in my entire life. As beautiful as it was to see her eyes, I hated seeing the sadness. It hadn't even been a full minute that her eyes were open when tears fell from them.

"Sunshine," I rasped.

My heart broke for her. Not only had she just gone through some physical trauma with what the sedative did to her body, but worse was the fact that today she realized she lost her best friend. I despised Leah for what she did, but it didn't change the fact that for years she was someone very important in Elle's life. There was a long road ahead for her.

She held my eyes a few more moments before she moved them to everyone else in the room. She started at Emme, went to Zane, then to Cruz, followed by Dom, Charley, and finally, Wes. I watched as her chest rose and fell rapidly as she looked at her brother.

Wes' face softened when she first brought her eyes to him, but once she started to break down, he struggled to remain unaffected.

He brought his hand to her forehead again and reassured her, "You're okay. Just relax, Elle."

Her eyes left Wes and went back to Dom. That's when she spoke her first words since waking up.

"Thank you," she croaked.

"It's nothing."

What else could he say? This hadn't been easy on anyone.

Her head fell back to the side and she looked at me.

"I'm tired," she whispered.

I dipped my head at her statement.

"We'll head out and let you rest, darling," Zane offered. "You need anything at all, we are here for you."

"Thank you, Zane."

"We'll call later and check in with Levi," Cruz explained. "In the meantime, Dom and I will update the rest of the team. They're all worried about you."

"Thanks, Cruz."

Just as they were about to walk out of the room, Elle called out, "Dom, wait."

They stopped and looked at her.

"I'm sorry," she lamented.

"Sorry? For what, rock star?" Dom asked, clearly just as confused as the rest of us were as to why Elle was apologizing to him.

"Last night, when I sat with her to catch up, our

conversation drifted to her nonexistent love life. I might have mentioned that everybody on Levi's team was single. She thought you were hot. I had planned on trying to set you up with her today..." Elle trailed off. She took in a deep breath and finished, "You're too good for her."

Dom gave her a look that told her he understood she was struggling with what her friend did to her. He knew that saying anything negative about Leah now wouldn't help the situation.

At that, Dom, Cruz, Zane, and Emme walked out of the room.

"I'll call Mom and Dad," Wes stated.

Elle shook her head and begged, "Don't ruin their vacation."

"I'm not keeping this from them," he started. "I'll make sure they know you are going to be fine and that you insist they enjoy their vacation. Don't worry about them. I'll take care of it."

Wes and Charley each gave Elle a hug before they left.

As the door closed behind Wes and Charley, I brought my eyes back to Elle. She looked tired, but she was devastated.

"What can I do for you, sunshine?"

"Will you climb in this bed and hold me while I sleep?" she asked.

I gave her a small smile and explained, "I think it'd be frowned upon by the staff for me to do that."

She closed her eyes and insisted, "I don't care. I'll deal with that when the time comes. Right now, I want you to be next to me, holding me and keeping me safe while I sleep."

I kicked off my shoes and slid in the bed beside her. Her body was still very weak and she struggled to turn toward me. I helped her to turn, being careful not to disrupt her IV, and wrapped my arms around her.

It felt so good to have her in my arms again knowing that she was going to be okay, at least, physically. The emotional trauma was going to be another story.

I kissed the top of her head and did my best to offer her comfort when I knew that, more than anything else, her heart was hurting.

"I love you, Elle. And I'll do whatever it takes to help you get through this."

She burrowed her face into my chest. Within minutes, her breathing evened out and she was asleep.

It was late the next morning when we received Elle's discharge paperwork. She could go home.

Yesterday, she fell asleep in my arms and I held her until she woke again just over an hour later. We spent the better part of the day in her bed, watching television, though Elle drifted in and out of sleep throughout the day. Emme and Zane stopped by again just before dinnertime. Emme loved to cook and figured we'd prefer a home-cooked meal over hospital food. She wasn't wrong. Zane took Emme by my place and got Elle some of her own clothing so she'd be more comfortable.

While this helped Elle's mood a bit and she was thankful for the thought, she wasn't her usual bubbly self. It killed me to see her so downtrodden. Part of me wished I could see inside her head and know what she was thinking.

Zane and Emme had dinner with us and left. Charley and Wes called to check in on her as did Cruz on behalf of the entire Cunningham Security team. My parents, David and Trisha, found out about what had happened and called me to make sure I was doing alright. Of course, my mother insisted that as soon as Elle was back to feeling like herself, she wanted to meet her.

We also received the results of the final tests the doctors were waiting on yesterday. Everything came back negative and it seemed that nothing other than the sedative had made its way into Elle's system.

Now, she was ready to go home.

Elle was very quiet throughout the day yesterday, but she seemed to be in slightly better spirits this morning.

"I can't wait to get out of here and get a shower," she sighed as we walked out to my truck. Thankfully, the other thing Emme and Zane brought yesterday was my truck.

"Can't say I disagree with you on that one," I noted.

We got in the truck and I drove us back to my place. I pulled into the garage, turned off the truck, and came around to help Elle out.

As we walked in through the man door into the house, I tensed. I wasn't sure what kind of reaction she'd have to being back for the first time after her whole ordeal. Sure enough, the second Elle entered the kitchen, she stopped and stared at the floor.

I put my hand on her back at her shoulder blade and stood with her. I stayed quiet and let her process whatever it was she needed to process in her head. After a few minutes passed, she turned to me and stressed, "I'd *really* like to take a shower now."

I nodded and expressed, "Whatever you want, Elle."

She walked out of the kitchen, her pace much faster, and went up the stairs. After she entered the bedroom, she moved through it to the bathroom, where she immediately turned on the water in the shower.

"Elle?" I called.

She turned and looked at me. There was anger in her

eyes. I knew it wasn't directed at me, but I hated the look. This wasn't her.

"What can I do for you?"

She shook her head and replied, "Nothing."

I heard her say the word, but I could tell deep down it wasn't how she really felt. She was standing right in front of me; yet, she was so far away. Still, not wanting to upset her further I motioned with my head toward the bedroom. "I'll be right out here if you change your mind."

She nodded in response.

I turned, walked out of the bathroom, and sat on the edge of the bed. My elbows were resting on my thighs and my hands were clasped over my knees. As I sat there staring at the floor, all I could do was agonize over how to best help her.

Had this situation played out the way it did with a total stranger, I knew Elle would not be so far removed from everyone from an emotional standpoint. It would have been easier for her to accept what happened and move on from it. The fact that it was her best friend was weighing on her mind.

Other than what she said to Dom yesterday in the hospital, she never brought Leah's name up again.

I must have been sitting there for a good ten minutes when it dawned on me that the water in the shower didn't sound right. It sounded like it was on, but nobody was in there. Worried, I walked over and gently pushed the door open. When I looked at the reflection of the shower in the mirror, my stomach sank.

My poor girl was sitting on the floor of the shower with her knees up to her chest, her head resting on her knees, crying her eyes out.

I stepped inside the bathroom, stripped out of my clothes quickly, and went to her. Sitting down beside her, I wrapped one arm around her back and the other under her knees.

Then, I settled her in my lap, where I let her cry it out as I stroked her back.

Elle cried for a long time. I didn't try to stop her. I couldn't imagine the pain she was feeling at what she had just been through. Not only had she faced the fear of being so close to death, but also coming to terms with the fact that it was the person she thought was her best friend that put her in that position.

It was a long while later when she finally quieted herself and began to calm down. I waited for her to give the signal and indicate what she needed from me next. Eventually, Elle pulled her face from my chest and looked up at me.

"I'm sorry."

My eyes searched her face as I brought a hand up to brush a wet strand of hair from her forehead and cheek.

"Sweetness, you've got nothing to be sorry for," I said gently. "I don't know how you kept it together this long."

"I have a feeling I'm not done crying about this."

My face warmed, giving her what I hoped was a bit of sympathy, and I remarked, "I didn't think that you would be yet. If you need to cry, I'll be here to hold you through it."

She closed her eyes and took in a deep breath. When she opened them again, she suggested, "We should probably finish in here before you run out of hot water."

"Yeah," I agreed. "You sure you're alright?"

She was honest when she replied, "For now."

At that, we got up off the floor, finished in the shower, and got out. Thankfully, we were out before we were out of hot water.

CHAPTER 27

Elle

SHOCK.

That's all I was feeling.

I woke up yesterday morning determined to get life back to normal after having been traveling and performing at eight different locations over the course of a little over a week. My best friend offered to make me breakfast before she had to go to work. While I showered, she made a breakfast for me that had a sedative in it.

She set the meal in front of me, watched me eat it, and then did nothing to help me when I grew dizzy and eventually collapsed on the floor. She waited, allowing the sedative to work its magic. She watched as I lost control over my body. And then she allowed me to listen while she told my boyfriend over the phone that she was going to inject me with a syringe that contained medication that would stop my heart.

It's a miracle that the shock of realizing the truth about my best friend didn't make my heart stop instead.

She was sweet and shy. She was a tiny, redheaded girl with freckles that showed up when she spent too much time in the sun. She showed the world an innocent, caring, loving individual; however, the reality is that she was someone completely different.

She was a fraud.

She was a liar.

She was a manipulative, calculating bitch.

She was anything but a best friend.

It had been a couple hours over the twenty-four-hour mark since I had breakfast with her. I found myself flopping back and forth between extraordinarily angry to devastatingly sad. There was no in between.

When Levi brought me home earlier today and I walked into the kitchen, I stood there staring at the floor where I knew she had hovered over my body with that syringe. All I could feel was anger and rage. Once I got in the shower and the warm water hit my body, the anger slowly melted away and was replaced by sadness. I had never felt such devastation before in my life.

Levi came in and held me while I cried. He didn't ask me to talk about it; he only offered me the support I needed when I needed it. On one hand I was licking my wounds over losing my best friend and, on the other, I was thanking my lucky stars that Levi had come into my life. Unfortunately, the feelings I had surrounding the situation with Leah were currently overshadowing those I had for Levi.

This didn't mean that I didn't love Levi. That couldn't be further from the truth. It was just that I was having a hard time focusing on anything other than the fact that someone I loved and trusted tried to kill me.

I finished in the shower, threw on fresh clothes, and made my way over to my unpacked bags from the tour. I rummaged through them and found one of the books I picked up from the bookstore in Denver. I took the book and went downstairs.

I found a comfortable spot in the living room and sat. I'm certain Levi was lost at what to do for me, but unfortunately, I couldn't help him figure that out. The truth was, I wasn't sure what I needed when it came to the whole situation. I opened the book I held in my lap because the only thing I was certain of was that I needed an escape from reality for a little while.

Levi left me to it for a bit until, finally, he interrupted my reading. Normally, I'd be angry that someone interrupted me while I was reading, but if I was being honest, I'd read through two chapters and had no idea what was going on since my mind was so preoccupied.

"Elle?" he called to get my attention.

I looked up at him from the book.

"It's been a while since you've eaten. I was going to make some lunch for the both of us. Did you want anything special?"

I closed my eyes, shook my head, and shrugged my shoulders before I answered, "As long as it doesn't have any added sedatives or heart-stopping medication, it'll be fine."

"Elle..." He trailed off.

Immediately, I regretted saying that to him. "I'm sorry," I lamented. "I shouldn't have said that."

Levi walked over to me, put his finger under my chin, and comforted me. "You don't have to be sorry, sunshine. I just don't want you to ever think that because you trusted one person who did you wrong that anyone else you trust will do the same. I'd never hurt you, El."

A single tear fell from my eye.

"I know," I whispered. Then, for some reason I couldn't understand, I continued, "Why did she do it? Why did she hate me so much?"

"I wish I could give you that answer, but I don't know. I can certainly speculate and give you my opinion."

More tears fell and I felt another ugly-cry session coming on. Unfortunately, this time I was unable to leave it at just the crying.

I shook my head in disbelief as I cried, "How could I have

not known that it was my best friend this whole time? I never suspected her."

"None of us did, Elle," he explained as he swiped at my tears using the pad of his thumbs. "I do this for a living. I didn't know. My entire team is trained and they didn't suspect her. There's no way you could have known. Many people who are wired this way are very good at putting on a show. They can make others believe that they're somebody they aren't."

"I should have known," I insisted.

"Don't do this to yourself. You didn't know and you shouldn't have known. You shouldn't have suspected her because she never should have done it. You were a loving and trusting friend, and she didn't honor that friendship. I know with it being so fresh in your mind it's tough to see, but there was nothing you could or should have done differently. Quite honestly, I think after you give this some time you'll realize that you're so much better off without her. I never liked the way she spoke to you."

My brows pulled together. "What do you mean?"

"She was condescending to you all the time. When we decided to drive instead of fly while on your tour, she had something negative to say about it. All the posts she made online when she wasn't trying to be just like you were of her trying to drag you down. Remember the post you made about Denver? Why did she need to try to outshine you when she posted several hours later about a place she had been? She needed to compare that place to Denver to make herself feel better. You did nothing wrong, sunshine. You've got to believe that. This was all a competition in her head."

I took in a deep breath and blew it out, trying to make sense of it all.

"What's going to happen to her?" I asked. Part of it was curiosity but, if I was being honest, it was mostly worry. It made no sense that I was worried about the person who had done what she did to me, but I was.

"I don't know all of the details yet; however, my best guess would be based on what the police found, the video footage from here yesterday, and the evidence Trent has been collecting online that she's in a load of serious trouble. Had yesterday not happened, it would have probably been limited to cyberstalking at worst. Considering what she did yesterday, cyberstalking is likely the least of her concerns. I'm guessing she's looking at attempted murder charges."

"Oh my God," I whispered.

"Don't worry about it now, sunshine. Tomorrow, I'll make some calls and see what I can find out. Try not to think too much about what's going to happen to her. I'm sure she had to know that there'd be consequences for her actions."

"Levi, I wish I knew why."

He sighed as he pulled me into his chest and held me tight to his body. He let me cry a bit. When I began to settle, he added, "I talked to Dom a little while ago. He told me a bit more about what happened yesterday. When he walked in, he heard you ask her why she was doing what she was doing. Elle, based on her answer, I'm inclined to believe this was all jealousy. She couldn't handle you being happy. You're living your life feeling fulfilled, waking up every day doing something you love. You said it yourself—she wasn't happy doing the job she's been doing since she started going to school for it."

"I knew she wasn't happy. I tried to make her see that it wasn't worth continuing to live a lie. I supported her one hundred percent. Why couldn't she do the same for me?"

"You're in the spotlight, Elle. You're out there. People see you and they immediately fall in love with you."

I shook my head in confusion.

"My guess is that she didn't like the fact that people adore you the way they do. I can't say how it is for her because I really don't know her all that well, but is it like that for her? Do people automatically gravitate toward her?"

"All the time," I explained. "We've always had people around us, no matter where we are."

"That's both of you, Elle," Levi pointed out. "I'm talking about her. By herself. When you aren't there."

I dropped my eyes to my lap to take a minute and think about it.

He was right.

When I brought my eyes to his again, he knew that I had figured it out.

"It was you the entire time," he started again. "She couldn't handle you being the center of attention. The big difference between the two of you is that you're in the limelight because your chosen career path puts you there. You aren't seeking anyone's approval in doing it, either. She's not getting any attention, craves being the center of it, and was working her ass off on social media to find it."

"But she didn't get it, Levi. It makes no sense," I offered, not wanting to accept his explanation.

He shrugged his shoulders and reasoned, "Maybe not, but that's what she was hoping would happen. Perhaps she didn't think she'd ever be caught."

"I feel like an idiot," I confessed.

"You're not an idiot. You gave one hundred percent of yourself to your friendship with her and she destroyed that. Don't let her bring you down, Elle. You are an incredible human being and loving friend, who was treated horribly. I understand how hurt you are, sunshine. Take the time you need to mourn the loss of the friendship and what it meant to you, but try to get yourself to realize, sooner rather than later, that it didn't mean the same thing to her. I know you're crushed over this, but she doesn't deserve your tears. It's like you said to Dom... you're too good for her."

Disbelief still coursing through me, I instructed him, "I may need to hear that a few more times before it starts to sink in."

Levi kissed my forehead and promised, "I'll see to it that you get that."

I leaned into him and wrapped my arms around him.

"Thanks, love," I whispered.

"So, can I make you some food?"

I dipped my chin and wondered, "What are you planning to make?"

"Haven't quite figured it out yet," he replied. "Do you have something in mind?"

"Grilled cheese."

Levi rolled his eyes at me, shook his head, and smirked. "I should have known it wasn't going to be something with protein and vegetables."

"Sorry. I hate to say it, but it'll probably never be that," I vowed. "Is that a deal breaker?"

He leaned in to kiss my lips. When he pulled away, he answered, "Nope."

At that, he stood and walked out of the family room toward the kitchen where he made me a grilled cheese sandwich. Of course, he put some cucumber slices on the side.

After lunch, Wes and Charley stopped over to visit with me. Cruz came by to check in with me, as did Pierce, Dom, and Trent. They all came at different times throughout the evening and it was nice having something to occupy my mind. I also decided to reach out to my parents. I knew that it would ease their minds a bit if they heard my voice. Relief didn't begin to describe what they felt when they finally had the chance to talk to me. They insisted on leaving from their vacation early, but I managed to talk them out of it.

By the time all my visitors left, it was late and I was exhausted. Levi and I called it a night. It was when I was wrapped in his arms in his bed, my back to his front, that my thoughts drifted and I, once again, felt the utter devastation of losing my best friend. Unfortunately, as tired as I was, it wasn't enough for me to find sleep when my mind and my heart were consumed with pain.

I didn't want to be a burden to Levi anymore, so I tried my hardest to control my breathing. I quietly cried as I reminisced about times I had with Leah.

Good times.

Times that I'd never experience with her again.

Logically, I now knew the friendship was toxic, but matters of the heart rarely followed reason.

I felt Levi pull me closer to his body and knew it was just a subconscious movement as he slept because he never said anything. There wasn't much else he could have done in that moment anyway, so I was thankful for the comfort he unknowingly provided me.

That was when thoughts of Levi took over and my mind could settle into some peace. Not long after, I drifted off to sleep.

Levi

I woke up this morning feeling helpless after not being able to sleep well all night because I was so worried about Elle.

After we got into bed last night, I told her I loved her. She repeated the sentiment and I held her. It wasn't long before I heard her crying quietly in the pillow. I knew immediately she was trying to muffle the sounds, the evidence of her broken heart.

Uncertainty coursed through me. It was such an odd feeling. Typically, whenever I was presented with a situation, I knew what to do. Maybe I didn't always have the right answer or the best solution on the first try, but I was rarely tentative about what to do. I always did something.

That is, until now.

When Elle came to me weeks ago terrified about learning that someone had been in her apartment and was stalking her, I knew what to do. When she told me she was going on tour, I knew what to do. And when she showed me how distressed she became having to fly to the next stop on the tour, I knew what to do.

But now that she had been seconds away from death and deceived by her best friend, I didn't know what to do. Her heart was broken and I didn't know how to fix it.

Hearing her struggle to cry quietly last night, I thought it was best to leave her to it. Even still, I didn't want her to feel alone. I tightened my arms around her and held her a little closer. She continued to cry for a bit after that and, throughout it all, I felt like such a failure.

Elle and I finished up breakfast about an hour ago. I didn't want to leave her home alone just yet, but didn't want to make her feel like I was suffocating her either. I tried to give her the comfort and security of knowing I was there if she needed me, while also making sure she had her own space. After breakfast, she said she wanted to go up, change out of her nightie, and get ready for the day.

I took this as a good sign. She wanted to do her normal things. Of course, I didn't want to be naïve and assume she'd magically gotten over it all, but trying to get back to her routine might help give her some peace and comfort.

While Elle was upstairs doing her thing, I took the time to call in to the office and get updates. Cruz filled me in on Elle's case.

"Michaels sent all of the proof he's been collecting online as well as the footage from your place over to the WPD yesterday afternoon. I followed up first thing this morning with Detective Baines. She confessed to it, bro. Everything. Not that there were any doubts considering the mounting pile of evidence, but at least Elle won't have to go through any more bullshit with all of this."

"Thank Christ," I started. "I'm not sure how well she would have handled any more stress."

"How is she managing since I saw her yesterday?" Cruz asked.

"Torn up. She cries a lot; she cried herself to sleep last night. I feel useless, Cruz. I don't know how to help her. She seems to be a little better today. Honestly, I think she's putting on a brave face when the reality is that she's bleeding inside at losing her friend."

Cruz sighed. "It can't be easy, that's for sure. Maybe the two of you should both talk with Zane and Emme. You know what they've been through. It might help to get more perspective."

This wasn't a bad idea.

"While Elle was on tour, she and Emme had planned on having the four of us get together for dinner," I told him. "I'll see how she manages today and bring it up to her."

I spent a few more minutes talking with Cruz about the other cases the firm was managing. Everything was running smoothly and I was beyond grateful for the team I had working for me. They stepped up when I needed them to and I was convinced that I wouldn't be nearly as successful as I am without every single one of them.

After I got off the phone with Cruz, I figured I'd run up and check on Elle. She went upstairs well over an hour ago to get ready and never came back down. I reached the top of the stairs and walked toward our bedroom when I realized she was in the guest room she stayed in the first night she spent there. She was emptying her clothing from all of the drawers.

"Elle?" I called to get her attention.

She jumped and spun around, clutching her chest. "Oh my God, you scared me."

"I'm sorry," I offered an apology. "I didn't mean to scare you. What are you doing?"

"Packing."

"Packing?"

She nodded.

Confusion washed over me. "Is there another tour you didn't tell me about?"

"No," she replied.

"Care to enlighten me as to why you are packing?"

A look of confusion washed over her face before she answered, "So I can go home."

"Home?"

"To my apartment," she explained. "I don't have to worry about anyone stalking me anymore, so now I can go home."

Fuck.

The second she said those words, I realized how much I didn't want her to leave.

"You want to go back to your apartment?" I questioned, my throat tight.

She held my eyes a minute, something flickering in them, before she responded, "Well, yeah. I mean, all of my things are there. My bed, the rest of my clothes, my books that I really want to read, and my lip balms to name a few."

I stayed silent. I didn't want this. I wanted her here.

She set the clothing in her arms down on the bed and walked toward me. "Levi, what's wrong?"

My heart was in my throat. I wanted to be selfish and tell her to stay, but after what she had been through, I needed to give her the freedom she'd been robbed of for the past few weeks.

I brought my hand up to the skin at the side of her throat. "I'm going to miss having you here, sunshine."

Her hand came up and wrapped around the back of mine before she reassured me, "I'll miss being here, but life has to get back to normal. You need to get back to work. I know you're staying here because you're worried about me. I appreciate that more than I could ever tell you, but I don't want Leah to have any more control over our lives. The one good thing she did was bring us together, but I want us to make the choices in what happens with our relationship moving forward. I'd like for us to have a bit of a normal relationship for a while. I want to spend my days hanging out at my place giving myself a manicure, or cuddling up on my favorite chair to read a great love story. Then, when the evening rolls around, I want to be able to call you or have you call me so you can tell me all about your day. I want us to talk on the phone for hours. I want to be able to invite you over for dinner and a sleepover and I'm hoping I'll get an invite to your place in return."

"Okay, then I'd like to invite you for dinner and a sleepover here tonight."

She laughed.

I knew she thought I was teasing her, but I was serious. Fuck, I didn't want this. I loved her. And because of that I'd give her what she wanted, no matter how much I hated it.

"I want to be home tonight, love," she said softly as she looked up at me innocently with those beautiful honey-colored eyes.

"Any idea on when you'll be inviting me for an overnight visit?"

"This weekend," she answered immediately.

It was only Wednesday.

"The weekend starts on Friday after work, right?"

She gave me a nod.

I dropped my head to the ground, feeling defeated.

Elle's hand came up and she allowed her knuckles to brush along the skin of my cheek. "This is going to be great for us, Levi. Trust me."

When I lifted my head, I insisted, "Friday is so far away."

Her eyes went liquid and she dared, "Then you better make good use of the time you have left with me now."

"Elle..." I trailed off. "Are you sure? After everything you've been through—" I managed to get out before she cut me off.

"I'm sure, Levi. In fact, I know that a little bit of love from you is exactly what I need after what I've been through. You've been showing me love from the minute this thing started between us. After what happened Monday morning, you've not wavered once in giving me all of the emotional love and support I need. Now, though, I really want your physical love. Will you give that to me?"

I stared at her briefly before I captured her mouth with mine. She tasted like brown sugar and cinnamon. With my mouth still connected to hers, I bent slightly to pick her up and carry her to our bedroom.

Then, I made good use of the time we had and gave her what she needed.

EPILOGUE

Elle

MORE THAN A MONTH HAD PASSED SINCE I WAS NEARLY KILLED by a person I loved and trusted. I had lived more than a month of my new life without the person I had considered to be my best friend by my side and I still wasn't sure how I felt about it all.

There were good days.

There were bad days.

Then, there were very bad days.

There were also very good days.

Thankfully, I had more good than bad.

It wasn't easy to get to the point that I'm at now. In fact, it's really only been in the last two weeks or so that I've started to really accept the reality of the situation and what my role in all of it was.

Nothing.

It took time to get to a place where I realized that I did absolutely nothing wrong in this situation.

Over the course of the last few weeks, I've talked a lot with Levi's soon-to-be sister-in-law, Emme. She's been through a bit of her own hell, having dealt with sexual assault and physical abuse at the hand of her ex-boyfriend. He kidnapped her a couple months ago and, thankfully, Levi and his team found her only a few hours later. I'm amazed by how strong she's become over the last few months and talking with her has helped me gain fresh perspective from someone who's been there.

I've also spent a lot of time writing new music. I pulled out my song inspiration notebook and my guitar and went to work. It was cathartic and I found I felt much better after a music session.

My focus has slowly shifted over time and I'm no longer spending as much of my day thinking about Leah and what she did. I'm sure my heart will hurt for a long time whenever I think of our friendship and the perception I had of it for so many years.

When it comes to Leah, she dealt her own hand. She decided her fate. The evidence Trent delivered to the Windsor Police Department coupled with Leah's guilty plea meant there would be no trial. She simply received a sentence. I debated for quite some time about whether I wanted to be there for her sentencing, but I ultimately decided against it. I already knew what the outcome would be based on the discussions I had with Levi. She would be spending life in prison for attempted first-degree murder.

There was an odd dichotomy happening inside my head when I learned this. Logic told me that this is what she deserved. Leah was a smart girl; she knew there would be consequences for her actions. She, I'm certain, knew the punishment would be severe and still chose to go ahead with her sick, evil plan. On the other side of it all, though, I had to swallow the fact that my best friend since college was going to be spending the rest of her life in prison. Regardless of what she did to me, it didn't change the fact that I had grown so close to her over the years. As a result, the reality of her fate hit me hard.

This is where Levi was my saving grace. He made it very

clear that he wasn't fond of Leah in the beginning, but particularly loathed her now. Regardless of his personal feelings toward her, he made a valiant effort to understand the pain I was going through and was there for me every step of the way. He laughed with me on my good days and held me tight on the bad ones.

I moved back into my apartment and while we spent many nights at either of our places, we still spent many nights apart. On those nights, I knew Levi would be there to lend an ear if I needed him. I could call him at any point during the day or night and he'd drop what he was doing to listen.

Our relationship had grown so much in the weeks following my near-death experience. I found that while I adored every second I was around him, I absolutely loved our late-night phone calls. They weren't always about Leah and that whole situation. Sometimes, we just talked about random things. He'd tell me about his day at work and I'd tell him about the newest love story I was immersed in. Often, our calls would be quick, lasting only twenty minutes, but most of the time he'd call me after his evening workout and shower and talk with me until I fell asleep. Of course, there were the nights that his work had him occupied and he'd be working a case, but even in those situations he always reached out just to connect with me. On those nights, I found I had the most inspiration and motivation to create more music.

What I loved most in all of it was Levi's willingness to sacrifice. I knew from the moment I told Levi that I wanted to move back home that he wasn't thrilled with the idea. It was something I needed at the time, though. He could have fought me on it and made it difficult, but he didn't. Every sacrifice he made only served to make my love for him grow. It filled me with such warmth to know he'd move mountains to not only keep me safe physically but also to give me the things I needed emotionally. He would give up the things he wanted to give me what I needed. And now, weeks later I knew there wasn't anyone else with whom I'd rather be.

Levi was the love of my life.

As I steered my car into his driveway, this was precisely the thought running through my mind. That, and the fact that I was finding I hated not seeing him every day.

It was Friday evening. Levi planned to come home from the office early so he could shower and pick me up at my apartment before taking me to Lou's. I was going to be performing for the first time since everything happened with Leah and was excited to finally be getting back to what I loved.

Feeling overwhelmed by my love for Levi when I woke up this morning, I decided on a change of plans and wanted to surprise him. I got ready for my show earlier than necessary, hopped in my car, and made my way to his place. I still had my key, but didn't want to use it. I rang the doorbell and waited. Not even a minute later, the door opened and there stood my handsome man.

He looked shocked and a little confused at seeing me there.

"Hey, love," I greeted him.

He stepped back and allowed me to come inside.

"What's going on, Elle? I was just about to leave to come and pick you up."

I shrugged my shoulders and replied, "I didn't want to wait to see you and felt like surprising you."

His face softened and he asked, "Is there a reason?"

I gave him sexy eyes and answered, "I love you."

He grinned and stepped in closer to me while he wrapped an arm around my waist. Just as Levi bent his head down so he could kiss me, I held my hand up in front of my face. He pulled back and gave me a questioning look.

"You need to prepare yourself, Levi."

"For what?"

I gave him a coy smile and explained, "For the flavor you are about to taste on my lips. I'm thinking this might be your new favorite."

"I don't know," he doubted me. "You've not been able to knock my number one choice out of that spot for a while now. And I've tasted a lot of flavors since then."

"This one is different. Trust me."

He thought on it a moment and examined my lips. "Are you going to let me try them now?" he finally questioned.

My head gave a subtle movement indicating he could try.

He wasted no time and brought one hand up into my hair, while the arm around my waist dropped lower so his hand was at my ass. Then, he pressed his lips to mine. Once he tasted me, I knew I was right. He groaned and his fingertips dug into the cheek of my ass as his grip on my hair tightened. He used every part of his mouth to taste mine. His tongue, his lips, and finally his teeth all took turns devouring me.

I loved it.

It was a long time of heavy kissing before he finally pulled his mouth from mine.

"Fuck me, sunshine. Honey? You found honey flavored lip balm?"

"What's the verdict?" I asked, already knowing the answer.

"Do we have time for me to properly show you what I think of it?" he countered.

I shook my head.

He thought a moment as he searched my face before he spoke again. "Okay, I need to show you something. Then, I've got a question to ask you."

I asked him what he thought of my lip balm flavor, certain I knew what his answer would be, and now I wasn't feeling so sure. In fact, I was downright nervous.

"What is it?" I wondered, the nerves in my voice undeniable.

He took me by the hand and led me through the house. We walked down to an area of the house I never really spent any time in. Usually, I was always in Levi's bedroom, the bathroom, the kitchen, or the family room. The only time I ever went to this part of the house was the day he first brought me here and gave me a tour. I didn't remember much except that a few of the additional rooms were large and empty.

We stopped outside the closed door to one of the rooms, where he turned and looked at me. "I miss having you here with me, sunshine," he started, his voice gentle. "This house never felt big to me until after you moved back to your apartment. I know that going back there is what you needed at the time, but it's so empty here without you that I'm beginning to hate it."

He turned the knob on the door and pushed it open before he put his hand to the small of my back to guide me in ahead of him. It was like I was in slow motion. My eyes scanned the room. The entire space had been remodeled. My eyes filled with tears when I realized exactly what Levi had done.

I turned to him and whispered, "You built me a library?"

"I want you here with me, Elle. I love you. That's not changing. I know you need your own space and I remembered you talking about one day having a library in your home to fill with all the books you currently keep in boxes. I want you to move back in with me, sweetness. This time, I want it to be permanent."

I turned back to the room and stared in awe at it. I couldn't believe Levi had done this for me. While I stared at it, he started speaking again.

"I want it to be your space, so I didn't have it painted or any furniture added. I want you to fill the shelves with your favorite love stories and have the space to sit and read if that's what you want to do. If you're feeling like you want to write new music, I want you to do that here. I want to be able to walk in this room any time of any day and see you sitting there doing the things you love. Whatever you want to do to decorate it and make it yours, just tell me and I'll make it happen. I want to give this to you, Elle."

"I'm going to cry, Levi," I admitted.

"Come here," he murmured softly as he pulled me into his arms.

I buried my face in his chest and took slow, deep breaths. I really didn't want to cry before my show since I had already taken care of my makeup. A few minutes later, I managed to rein it in and pull back to look up at Levi.

"You okay?"

"Yeah."

"It's alright if the answer is no, sunshine. If you aren't ready for it, I understand. I won't like it, but I'll accept it."

I tilted my head to the side and shared, "I was just thinking about this today on the way here."

"A library?"

"No. I was thinking about how much I appreciate everything you've done for me since the day I ran into your office months ago. But beyond that, I was thinking about how much I'm starting to dislike being away from you and not being able to see you every day. I love talking to you on the phone at night, but I'd rather talk to you in person, make love to you, and fall asleep with your arms around me instead."

His face lit up.

"Is that a yes? Are you going to move back in with me?"

"Yeah," I started. "It's a yes."

His hand came up and gripped the side of my neck. He squeezed gently before he remarked, "Welcome home, Elle."

"Stop," I ordered. "I don't want to cry."

"Alright, then let me have another taste of this honey before we go."

I couldn't help myself. He built me a library. So, I leaned in and gave him another taste of honey.

It was roughly an hour later at Lou's when my people started arriving. My brother always came to my shows. He always brought his friends with him to support me. This included Zane, Stone, and Luke. Now that all of them were in relationships or, as far as I knew in Luke's case, hooking up with a woman, those women now all came to support me as well. In the weeks following my overnight stay at the hospital, all of those women checked in on me. It felt good to have genuine friends around me. Cruz, Dom, and Pierce all came out to Lou's tonight as well. I guess my first time performing since the tragic event was enough to get them to come out. The whole group of us was huddled at the front of the saloon right by the stage talking with each other until it was time for Lou to announce me.

The girls and guys all pulled me in for a round of hugs.

"How does it feel to be back here ready to perform?" Charley asked.

"I'm ready. I've had enough time off and I'm so excited to be back here doing what I love. I just wish I knew what I was going to do about all of my marketing moving forward since Leah used to handle all of that."

"Lexi," Monroe stated.

"What?" I asked.

I heard Cruz make a sound beside me.

"Luke's sister, Lexi," Monroe clarified. "Back when I got my studio opened, she was about to graduate from college. She hadn't found a job yet, so she came and worked as my receptionist. Her work at the studio was so much more than her just being a girl who answered the phones. She is young being fresh out of college, but she's got a bright future in public relations. She still does all of my marketing campaigns for the studio, and she's done such a phenomenal job that I needed to hire a couple more instructors and two new receptionists. She's looking to make a full-time gig out of a PR career, and I think she'd be perfect for you."

I was so happy to hear this. "I'd love to meet her. Can you arrange it for me?"

"Sure. I'll have her reach out to you this weekend. You're going to love her. She's great. Right, Cruz?" Monroe asked teasingly.

My eyes went to Cruz.

Uh oh.

I had a feeling there was a story I didn't know. I made a mental note to figure out what that story was and I planned to do it sooner rather than later.

The whole group spent the next few minutes catching up with each other. I was feeling fantastic.

Levi was by my side the entire time and eventually squeezed my hip. When I turned to look up at him, he stated, "Lou's announcing you soon. Can I have a minute alone with you before you go out?"

"Of course," I said to him. I turned back to my friends and motioned to the stage with my hand. "I'm set to go out soon, so I'm going to head back and get ready. I'll catch up with you all afterward. Thanks for coming."

They all wished me luck before I took off with Levi backstage.

"What's wrong?" I asked when we were alone.

He shook his head. "Nothing. I just wanted a few minutes alone with you before you go out there."

"Oh," I started as I slid my arms around his waist and stepped toward his body. "Well, guess what I did before when I was in my dressing room."

He narrowed his eyes. "I don't know. What did you do?"

"I reapplied my lip balm."

His eyes grew intense. "Two hours, right?" he asked.

"For what?"

"Your show."

He wanted to leave when it was finished.

I pressed up on my toes and brought my mouth to his ear. I whispered, "An hour and forty-five minutes."

He turned his head slightly toward me and kissed my cheek before he spoke. "I really hope you're alright with leaving right afterward. I'd like to taste more than just this mouth today." He pulled my body tight to his. I felt his arousal between us and moaned. Levi went on, "I want to devour every inch of you, Elle."

I was breathless when I replied, "We can leave as soon as I'm finished, love."

He smiled against my lips and ordered, "Give me some honey now, sunshine, and make it good. It needs to last until I can take you back to our place and get more sweetness from you."

Our place.

On that thought, I gave Levi a good dose of honey. When Lou announced me and I needed to go onstage, I tore my mouth from Levi's and noted he looked more than satisfied with what I gave him.

He winked at me before I walked out and sang for my fans.

Two hours later, he took me to our place. I was with Levi and I was home. That's where he made good on his promise to devour me while I delivered what I thought were my sexiest eyes he'd ever been given.

Please turn the page to read the Author's Note about this book.

Did you love this story? If so, I'd be so appreciative if you would share your thoughts in a review on Amazon or Goodreads. Also, be sure to flip a few more pages to find all the ways to connect with me on social media. Happy reading!!

LOVE GIVEAWAYS? Be sure to sign up for my monthly newsletter. There's something given away every month!!!

Author's Note

In order to not spoil this story, I've added this Author's Note at the end of the book. If you have not yet read *Obsessed* and don't want to ruin the suspense/surprise, don't read this yet!

Levi and Elle's story is a very personal one for me. I wrote this book to help myself cope with something happening in my own life. Even after writing and publishing it, I'm still dealing with this issue.

I have my very own stalker. One who married into my family and destroyed relationships. One who continues to do what she's doing.

And while there's a very long story that goes along with it, complete with emails and screenshots and all sorts of evidence, it's far more than I'm prepared to share right now.

That said, I wanted my readers to know that the story comes from a real place and that the actions of Elle's stalker are very much the same to what I experienced. Not all, but most. And there are also things I've faced that Elle did not.

One day I do expect I'll share the full story, but for now, I'm doing my best to deal with it in a way that is both professional and legal.

For a sneak peek at Lexi & Cruz's story, *Overcome*, turn the page.

PROLOGUE

Lexi

THIS HAD TO BE A MISTAKE.

Everything I had learned told me that this wasn't how it was supposed to be. It was supposed to look different. Sound different.

I had it wrong. If I ever told anyone, they'd tell me I was mistaken. But something was gnawing away at me inside telling me this wasn't right. It didn't feel good and it wasn't what I wanted.

But where was the struggle? The blood? The bruises? The cries for help?

This is supposed to happen in an alley behind a dumpster. I'm supposed to be kicking and screaming and fighting.

But I'm not.

This doesn't happen in a dorm room. This doesn't happen in a bed. This doesn't happen with the guy you like.

But it is.

This must be a misunderstanding.

I wore a short skirt. I went on a few dates with him. I agreed to come back to his dorm room tonight. I cuddled up next to him. I leaned in to kiss him. I even enjoyed kissing him.

And in a matter of minutes, it all changed.

When the soft caresses and tender kisses turned into

rough and forceful restraint, the butterflies I felt in my belly disappeared and were replaced by paralyzing fear.

When he rolled me to my back and pinned me to the bed, I froze. I didn't fight. I didn't scream. I didn't try to get away. I only said no and asked him to stop.

The weight of his body hovered over mine.

I said no.

I sank deeper and deeper into the sheets.

But I liked him.

He gripped my wrists above my head.

I said no.

He forced my skirt up around my hips.

Maybe I had been asking for it dressed like this.

He pushed my panties to the side.

I said no.

He smiled through my growing opposition.

But I had flirted with him.

Then he raped me.

And I only said no.

I withdrew. I went somewhere else. Physically, I was still there, but my mind took me to a different place. Finals were coming up next week and I had a paper due in two days. I needed to get back to my dorm so I could finish proofreading that paper. I was always a good student and I focused on that as I lay there silenced and still in the bed of his dorm room.

Suddenly, my mind was back in the room with my body and he was still on top of me.

I wanted to scream. It was there, at the back of my throat, but it wouldn't come out. The fear seeped into every part of me, but most especially, it silenced my voice. If I screamed, this might end up looking like an actual sexual assault.

It could be violent and bloody.

It could be worse.

My breath was caught in my throat. Perhaps it got stuck there simply to protect me.

But what about what my parents had told me?

Always stand up for yourself.

Before my parents dropped me off at college, my father gave me a lecture. "Don't go out alone at night. Make sure someone you trust always knows where you are and who you're with. Stay safe. And if someone ever tries to hurt you, you fight back."

I didn't heed his advice. I didn't fight back.

I didn't know for sure, but guessed that it couldn't have been more than twenty minutes later when my attacker finished. He rolled off me and fixed his clothes.

Feeling ashamed and embarrassed, I quickly got up off the bed without making eye contact and pulled my skirt back down.

It was over.

I needed to get out, so I moved toward the door.

But his voice stopped me as I wrapped my hand around the doorknob.

"Don't act like that isn't exactly what you wanted tonight."

That's when I knew.

Maybe I didn't run. Maybe I didn't fight. But just because I didn't fight, didn't mean that I gave my consent.

And just because I liked him doesn't mean it wasn't rape.

Want the rest?? Available now.

ACKNOWLEDGEMENTS

To my husband, Jeff—Thank you for making me laugh, even when I had every reason to cry. I'm obsessed with the way you protected me through this. I love the way you love me and my crazy mind. And I love your one-liners…

To my boys, J&J—Thank you for snuggles and the smiles. I'll love you forever.

To my readers—Thank you doesn't seem like enough. I appreciate your support, words of encouragement, and excitement over my stories. I love you all so much!

To B.G.—Thank you for being one of the few who completely understands. Our personalities couldn't be more similar. It's fabulous being surrounded by like-minded individuals. And remember, resist the urge to enable…as if you ever would.

To K.C.—Thank you for knowing a lot of people! You're responsible for forging a long-lasting, genuine friendship. I hope you know how much that means to me. I promise cookies when I see you again.

To M.B.—Thank you for what seemed like endless hours of time working on this project with me. The inspiration for this story is something that caused a lot of strife in my life and I didn't think I'd ever get to a place where I could laugh so much about it. Thank you for your hard work and your honesty. I'm looking forward to many more laughs.

OTHER BOOKS BY A.K. EVANS

The Everything Series
Everything I Need
Everything I Have
Everything I Want
Everything I Love
Everything I Give

The Cunningham Security Series
Obsessed
Overcome
Desperate
Solitude
Burned
Unworthy
Surrender
Betrayed
Revived

Road Trip Romance
Tip the Scales
Play the Part
One Wrong Turn
Just a Fling
Meant to Be
Take the Plunge
Miss the Shot
In the Cards (Coming April 6, 2021)

CONNECT WITH A.K. EVANS

To stay connected with A.K. Evans and receive all the first looks at upcoming releases, latest news, or to simply follow along on her journey, be sure to add or follow her on social media. You can also get the scoop by signing up for the website newsletter.

The newsletter is delivered once a month, sometimes twice, and includes a monthly giveaway. Be sure to sign up:on my website.

Website: www.authorakevans.com

Facebook: www.facebook.com/authorAKEvans

Facebook Reader Group: www.facebook.com/groups/1285069088272037

Instagram: www.instagram.com/authorakevans

Twitter: twitter.com/AuthorAKEvans

Goodreads Author Page: www.goodreads.com/user/show/64525877-a-k-evans

Subscribe on YouTube: bit.ly2w01yb7

ABOUT A.K. EVANS

A.K. Evans is a married mother of two boys residing in a small town in northeastern Pennsylvania. After graduating from Lafayette College in 2004 with two degrees (one in English and one in Economics & Business), she pursued a career in the insurance and financial services industry. Not long after, Evans realized the career was not for her. She went on to manage her husband's performance automotive business and drive the shop race cars for the next thirteen years. While the business afforded her freedoms she wouldn't necessarily have had in a typical 9-5 job, after eleven years she was no longer receiving personal fulfillment from her chosen career path. Following many discussions, lots of thought, and tons of encouragement, Andrea decided to pursue her dream of becoming a writer.

Between her day job, writing, and homeschooling her two boys, Evans is left with very little free time. When she finds scraps of spare time, Evans enjoys reading, doing yoga, watching NY Rangers hockey, dancing, and vacationing with her family. Andrea, her husband, and her children are currently working on taking road trips to visit all 50 states (though, Alaska and Hawaii might require flights).

9 781732 885806